Project StrikeForce

Kevin Lee Swaim

PUBLISHED BY: PICADILLO PUBLISHING
COVER DESIGN BY: THE COVER COLLECTION
ISBN: 978-0692201855

10 9 8 7 6 5 4 3 2 1
FIRST EDITION
PRINTED IN THE UNITED STATES OF AMERICA

DEDICATION

To Dave Wallace, who always told me I could.

ACKNOWLEDGMENTS

Thanks to all the active and retired military members who helped with this endeavor. Any mistakes contained herein are entirely mine. Special thanks to my beta readers. Your feedback was invaluable.

CHAPTER ONE

January
Fairfax, VA

John Frist stood on the rooftop, watching people enter the Red Cross building a hundred yards across an open asphalt parking lot, the traffic noise from Arlington Boulevard blaring in the background. As the brisk January wind knifed through him, he pulled at his jacket and clutched his binoculars tighter. The cold sharpened the smell of the city, the car exhaust and asphalt mixed with the barest hint of rot from the mulch around the damp shrubs below. He scanned the building across the parking lot, but nobody noticed the Ryder truck parked at the entrance. The lax security was rare in the DC area.

Who would bomb the Red Cross?

He had parked the Ryder truck just minutes before, quickly making his way to his rooftop perch. It had taken just seconds to disable the alarm on the rooftop door. He had reconnoitered the path the week before, looking for cameras, but the route through the side stairwell was clean. Even so, he kept his head down and the jacket pulled tight.

What would anyone remember, anyway? Just a man in his late twenties, dressed in slacks and a tan polo like the other office drones, his brown crew-cut grown shaggy and the hint of a five-o'clock shadow.

The civilians inside the Red Cross building went about their jobs, unaware of how they had failed. He could picture them in his mind, asking each other about the game while getting their overpriced coffee or flirting with the pretty girl down the hall.

They were ignorant of the real threat to the United States; ignorant of what real Americans had sacrificed so they could remain fat, stupid, and happy. His parents were killed by a drunk driver during his second year in Iraq. He followed procedure, informed his CO, but when he'd called the Red Cross, the record was lost. They'd blamed it on the Army, but he knew better. Without the Red Cross verification, his CO had denied his emergency leave. He had missed his own parents' funeral thanks to their stupidity.

The country was going to hell. He would never begrudge a man providing for his family, but the flow of illegals never ended. Before his deployment he'd thought illegals should be allowed to serve in the military as a path to citizenship, but now he understood it was a pipe dream. Illegals filled the cheap jobs companies needed to keep the economy humming. The politicians were fat and happy from all that money, a river of cash they rafted through on their way home to their nice houses and fancy cars.

That was about to change.

He worked the toe of his shoe against the roof ballast rock, his knuckles white as he gripped the binoculars. A school bus was pulling up to the front of the Red Cross, next to the Ryder truck. Were there kids inside? He stared through the binoculars. Yeah, kids. Maybe twenty. Maybe thirty. School trip, perhaps, coming to see the Red Cross regional headquarters.

Could he make it back down and across the parking lot?

The guards would soon notice the truck. Try and flee and he might get caught. Abandon the truck and they would raise security. No, the kids were simply in the wrong place at the wrong time. Casualties of war.

He swung the binoculars around. His escape route was clear. The explosion would trigger car alarms for blocks, the bleating noise echoing among the buildings, the dust thick in the air, choking, making it hard to breathe. People would flood out of the building. They would gasp and cry—a few might rush to help. He would go with the flow of people down the stairs and escalators, gaping at the destruction. Some would head to their cars, shocked, and he would go with them, an innocent bystander among the sheep.

A stolen car waited in the north parking lot. A quick wipe clean and he'd ditch it soon after in a wooded lot a few miles away. A bus ride to his truck and he would be back at his apartment before lunch.

He bent and placed the binoculars on the roof, grabbed his cell phone, and hit the speed dial. The call connected.

There was a deafening roar as the shock wave slammed against him, knocking him back. He peeked over the edge and smiled in awe at the destruction.

* * *

April
Washington, DC

The President of the United States of America sighed heavily, the sound echoing against the hardened concrete walls of his underground bunker, thirty meters below the White House. "I can't believe it's come to this."

The other occupant sat perfectly straight in his chair, his thinning snow-white hair neatly combed, his large and weathered hands resting on the table. "This is our best chance. The decision won't get easier."

Fulton Smith, the Director of the Office of Threat Management, waited for the President to make his decision. He had been a confidant to many presidents over the years, from his first meeting with the hardened and vulgar president from Missouri to this young man from Texas. His job was to ensure the safety of the Union, a promise he'd made to Harry Truman as a young man and reaffirmed to every chief executive since.

"How much will this cost?"

He handed the President papers from his metal briefcase.

The President scanned the document, his face pale. "Good Lord, we could build a stealth bomber for this."

"You never said my budget was limited. This is the cost. Besides, we've already started."

"Why do you even need my approval?"

"Because no matter how much power I wield, *you* are the President."

"How did you manage to move that kind of money around? And all those people?"

Smith shrugged. "You know better than to ask. We don't have to do this, Mr. President. Just say the word and we kill Project StrikeForce."

The President stared off, lost in thought, and then shook his head. "What if it doesn't work? What if he dies during the process?" The President stood and paced the small room, his feet shuffling against the blue carpet. "If this ever went public, it wouldn't just hurt me. This would devastate the country. The people would never trust their government again. You're sure you can keep this quiet?"

Smith raised an eyebrow.

"Of course," the President said, "I forgot who I was talking to." He paused. "It sounds like science fiction."

"Not science fiction," Smith said calmly, "an extrapolation of current technology, backed by a large amount of money and a very creative way of putting it together. We *need* this. I warned you. I told you Afghanistan would be messy and that Iraq would be a meat grinder. We had a plan to eliminate Hussein."

The President glared. "What message would that send? We can't just assassinate a sitting head of state whenever we please. No, sir. I wanted the sonofabitch dead, but I wasn't about to authorize that. Better that we went to war."

"Even with all that's happened?"

"We might have overstated the case, but Iraq was a threat and Hussein had to go. It had to be war, even a bloody one. Besides, you warned me about the consequences of assassinating Hussein. You argued against it as much as you argued for it."

"War is very complex. There is always the potential for blowback. I'd have preferred to assassinate him back in the eighties, but your predecessors wouldn't authorize it. Too many unknowns with the Iranians. That's why we need this program. We can stop problems before they become so unwieldy that the entire world gets sucked in."

The President sat down and stared at the folder as if expecting it to bite. "You really think this will work?"

Smith waited, the silence of the room broken only by the whispering of the air filtration system. "Mr. President, we need this. Bombs and missiles and planes are good when fighting a large military force, but to fight an idea? You need a targeted weapon. One man with superior technology. One man who can do what an army can't."

The President shuffled through the paperwork. "Who's your candidate? Someone from Delta?"

Smith shook his head and handed the President a dossier from his briefcase. "This is the best candidate."

The President opened the folder, then rocked back in his chair. "Are you out of your mind?"

"He's an excellent choice, actually. Young, no family, excellent military training, and he knows about complicated operations."

The President slammed his fist on the table. "He's a terrorist."

"The public doesn't know who he is or that you've captured him. With help from the Office, I might add," Smith said gently. "And you've finished interrogating him."

The President shook his head. "Anybody but him."

"His combat record was excellent," Smith countered. "He was an exemplary soldier until his accident. You read the reports."

"A lot of soldiers had it rough and they didn't blow up a building, for God's sake." The President paused. "So many fine young men and women have made the ultimate sacrifice on my orders."

"He made his choice. The concussion and PTSD might have twisted his mind. We can fix that. Physically he's almost perfect. He's bright, articulate, and driven. Moreover, no one knows you have him. There are very few loose ends to clean up if we fail." Smith put the papers back in his metal briefcase and sealed the locks. "Mr. President, we need a new type of warrior for a new type of fight."

The President fingered the papers, then slid them back across the table. "Do it."

Smith nodded, stood, and keyed open the steel door with his electronic token. He gave the President one last glance.

The President looked old and weary, hunched over the desk, recently emerged streaks of gray frosting his hair, his face starting to sag. Smith had seen the presidency wear men out, grinding them down, but none so fast as this one. "Mr. President. Sleep well."

The President nodded silently.

The steel door rumbled shut and sealed the President alone in his underground bunker.

* * *

Cincinnati, Ohio.

Eric Wise sat on his parents' couch, an ice-cold beer in one hand and a Colt M1911 in the other. The beer was courtesy of his retirement check, the pistol a gift from his grandfather, a souvenir from World War Two. He did not usually drink until after four, but he was commemorating. It was a warm spring day and he had been officially retired for one month.

The secondhand couch was soft but shabby. The particleboard coffee table appeared new, but the style was twenty years out of date. He vaguely remembered the green-and-brown shag carpet. It was stained and musty, even though he had shampooed it twice with a carpet cleaner rented from the Home Depot on Glenway.

He had been on a mission in a dusty little village in Afghanistan when he had gotten the news of his father's death, and leave time for his unit was exceptional, given their mission and the nature of their deployment. He had returned just long enough to bury his father but had been forced to stay longer so he could place his mother in a nursing home.

Her mental decline had been sudden. The doctor had told him the death of a spouse could trigger a sudden downward spiral in an Alzheimer's patient. He had been lucky to find a place that would take her on short notice. She had watched him go, leaving her in her sterile room, no emotion on her face, no sign of recognition.

It was on his way back to Afghanistan that he hit the wall and got sent back to Bragg for reasons never made fully clear. His commanding officer broke the news. His career was over. No further deployments. No further missions.

Instead, he was bounced out of Delta and back to the regular Army. His CO suggested a security job somewhere, maybe a consulting position with Blackwater.

When you're out, you're out. That's the Delta way.

He couldn't imagine life in the regular Army, not after Delta. Not after being an Operator. He was sure there was something outside the Army for a man with his skills and training, until the other shoe dropped. No consulting jobs. No private security gigs.

Blacklisted.

He had considered staying in the Army, but he had his twenty, so he retired.

He had been sitting around his parents' house for a month now, waiting for his pension. The Colt was the only thing real to him anymore. The checkered grips and the light smell of oil were old familiar friends. He sat with his beer and .45 and wondered if he would finally blow his brains out.

The doorbell chimed. He sat up, the gun moving of its own volition. He took a deep choking breath as it hit him. He was no longer at war. He was not being hunted, nor was he the one doing the hunting. He was a civilian, sitting in his parents' house, drinking a Miller High Life at 11:30 on a Tuesday morning.

He walked to the door and looked through the peephole. A black Ford Crown Victoria was parked at the curb, a driver at the wheel, military by his haircut and the way he watched the house.

An old man stood in front of the door, waiting. His hair was thinned and white and he had a powerful face, though age was taking a toll. He wore a dark navy suit, not stylish but not old and rumpled, a shiny metal briefcase in his hand.

His blue eyes, though.

Eric shivered. The eyes were alive, precise and sharp. The man was motionless, not even the slight swaying that people did without noticing. The old man had discipline, either a soldier or a spook, and access to a car and driver.

"Mister Wise, I know you are home. Probably watching me through the peephole. I would like to talk to you about a job."

Eric frowned. *A direct spook.* He wondered what the old spook would think of him, his hair unkempt, salt-and-pepper stubble on his face, beer on his breath.

He shrugged and unlatched the chain, opening the door. "A job, huh?" He dropped the Colt to his side and beckoned the man in.

The old man entered the house, glanced around, and took a seat at the kitchen table, motioning for Eric to join him. "My name is Fulton Smith, and I've come to offer you a job."

Eric considered his words carefully, then placed the Colt on the table. "Fuck you."

Smith's weathered face lit up with satisfaction. "Quite right. Tell me, if you would."

"You're the one who burned me. You stuck me here so when you came to offer a job, I'd jump at the chance."

Smith nodded. "Good, Mr. Wise. What else?"

"You have a lot of pull," Eric said thoughtfully, "because Delta is usually outside the sphere of influence of anything other than direct orders from the President. To screw with my deployment must have taken a lot of juice, and to keep it quiet so that I couldn't even find out more. Influencing Blackwater and every other contractor, though, that takes more than juice. That takes real power. Either you're really well connected, or you work for an agency which reports directly to the President. Of all the Delta Operators, you had to pick me. Why shouldn't I blow your brains out right now?"

"A meaningless threat?" Smith snorted. "Come, now, you were doing so well. From your point of view, it was probably torture. As far as why you were picked, it's because of your record, first in the Army, then in the Rangers, and finally in Delta. Even the one-off job you did in Europe a few years ago."

Eric's mouth dropped. "That came from you? That thing with the hijackers? You *do* work for the President."

"You would be surprised how many secret agencies have the President's ear," Smith said. "Mine is small but we perform a valuable service. I've sent several jobs Delta's way over the years, testing the Operators. Until I found you. I was sorry to hear about your father. No matter what you think of me, or will come to think of me, know that I truly *am* sorry. Your mother also. Mr. Wise, you are still young and strong, and your country needs you." He leaned forward. "Would you like the job?"

"Funny, you haven't even mentioned your agency or what it does. Plus, I'm still pissed about being blacklisted."

Smith regarded him with pale blue eyes. "I don't believe you are. Now that you know you are highly valued and there is something that requires your skillset, you want back in the game. Besides, once I offered the job, there was no going back."

"You're right," Eric sighed. He hated to admit it, but Smith had him. "I want back in."

Smith smiled. "Of course you do." He thumbed the briefcase open and withdrew a stack of folders. "I work for the Office of Threat Management."

* * *

Eric pondered the preprogrammed cell phone. He was stunned. If half of what Smith said was true, the Office of Threat Management had been responsible for shaping much of the past fifty years and Smith had been right there, leading it.

He glanced at the pictures on the fireplace mantel, pictures of him as a child, some with his parents and some of him alone. Never pictures of him with friends. The pictures moved from left to right: him as an infant, him in grade school, him and his dad at the target range, him with his mom after graduation, on the day he enlisted.

There were no pictures after that.

He sipped his beer, but it had gone flat. He set the can next to the Colt and picked up the gun. His father was dead now, and his grandfather, too. He wished he had asked them more about their time in the service.

On the day he had enlisted, he had begged his mother to drive him to the recruiting station. His father had been waiting when he got home that afternoon. His father never spoke a word, just shook his hand, then went to putter around the garage. His grandfather stopped by later, hugged him, then stood at attention, his back ramrod straight, and snapped off a salute. It was the last time he had seen his grandfather alive.

Physically his mother was now in Central West Community, a nursing home for Alzheimer's patients, but mentally? She had called him William at the funeral.

His father's name.

Then she had quit speaking, just staring when he tried to engage her in conversation. He picked up the phone to dial her number, then paused. What would he say? What would she understand?

He placed the phone on the table and walked through the empty house. Over the years, his parents had moved his childhood possessions from room to closet, to garage, to the corner trash. Only his bed remained, just big enough for a child but much too small for an adult. His growth spurt in high school had made sleeping on it sheer torture, but he found himself on it once again, even though his feet dangled over the end.

The offer from Smith gnawed at him. His retirement barely covered the bills and his meager savings account afforded him no luxuries. It wasn't as if he needed the money. He barely left the house and his love life was a distant memory. He hadn't had a date in two years, the last serious relationship five before that.

In the end, the choice was easy. He sat on his childhood bed, the musty yellowed sheets folded tight and crisp, and dialed the number. "I'm done here."

"I'm not surprised," Smith answered.

CHAPTER TWO

Kandahar Province, Afghanistan

His name was Abdullah walade Muhammad Younis, but the loyal Mujahideen in Afghanistan called him Abdullah the Bomber. He was one of the chosen few recruited during the eighties by the Maktab al-Khidamat, funneled from Saudi Arabia through Pakistan to the mountains of Afghanistan to fight the Soviets.

He stared through the binoculars at the base shimmering in the heat from the bare desert floor. Kandahar was dozens of miles away, and the base was the only thing breaking the monotony of the dusty valley.

A line of ancient pickup trucks and wooden carts entered through the south-side entrance. He could not blame the locals for cleaning the Americans' dishes and picking up their trash. They were poor. Centuries of fighting had ravaged the country, and even after they had worn down the Soviets, they had *still* been surprised when the Americans had attacked. The people of Afghanistan had seen so much of war; their children barely knew peace. The boys and girls rarely had the luxury of time to read and study the Quran.

His current student, Naseer, believed that women should not be taught to read, let alone read the Quran. He disagreed. It was every person's duty to read the Quran, including women. Not while they were menstruating, of course, even a fool knew that, but nonetheless they too had a sacred duty.

He also disagreed with Naseer's idea of using children to bomb the American base. Children should be protected from the cruelties of war. He would not sacrifice one American child in Jihad, let alone Afghan children.

Children were off limits. But soldiers? Soldiers were a legitimate target. The only way to fight the Americans, the most powerful army on earth, was a shadow war of bombs versus bullets. Naseer had found a local man named Fahad who worked in the American base, cleaning and doing menial labor, and Fahad had agreed to drive the truck full of explosives.

The dusty brown rocks poked him uncomfortably in the stomach but he dismissed the discomfort. It was a small price to pay to deliver the justice that Allah demanded, a small price for what the Americans had done.

He watched as soldiers committed a perfunctory inspection of the vehicles before waving them through. Yes, it was possible. The explosives would have to be powerful, hidden so they would pass the checkpoint.

He prayed silently to Allah for help in his quest.

* * *

Hebron, Kentucky

Eric took a cab to the Cincinnati/Northern Kentucky International Airport. Terminal One was shut down for construction, but he followed his instructions and a bored security guard took one look at his ID, nodded, and directed him toward a hallway. A windowless room and a pretty blonde lounging in a hard plastic chair were waiting at the end.

She looked up with cool blue eyes and nodded lazily. "I'm Nancy."

Eric smiled. Smith said he would have a liaison. "What time does the flight leave?" he asked.

"Now," she said as she stood. "I've been waiting for you. Follow me."

They walked through a set of doors, down a flight of stairs, and onto the hot tarmac. A Gulfstream G550 waited for them. He had flown in an older Gulfstream before, as part of joint CIA/Delta operation, but not the newer G550.

He stepped into the plane and was shocked again to find only a handful of chairs alongside a small table, and a large video screen against the facing bulkhead. A stack of folders sat neatly arranged on the table. "I'd start reading if I were you," Nancy said. "You should at least glance them over before we arrive in Gitmo."

"Guantanamo? Why?"

Nancy snorted. "That's what the files are for."

"Fair enough. What's with the layout?" he asked, pointing to the table and chairs.

"Cuts down on weight, gives us better range and more speed," Nancy said. "This is your personal plane now, no need for a lot of extras."

His own personal plane? A Gulfstream G550 started somewhere around forty million.

How big is the OTM's budget?

"I'll get started," he said.

"You do that. I have to get this bird in the air." She headed for the cockpit.

"You're not sitting back here?"

She glanced back over her shoulder. "Hard to sit back there and fly the plane."

The paperwork was so engrossing that he hardly noticed when the jet roared into the sky minutes later.

* * *

Guantanamo, Cuba

The plane nosed sharply down to the tarmac in Guantanamo, the thump of the landing gear breaking his concentration. He glanced out the window at the deep azure ocean only a stone-throw away and rubbed his eyes as the plane taxied to their hangar. When the plane came to a stop, Nancy exited the cockpit and handed him a package. "Did you get through the important parts?"

Eric sighed. "Yes. My cover is with the CIA."

"It's not a cover. At least, not *just* a cover. You are *actually* with the CIA. One of the benefits of working for the Office, we can place you anywhere. Just get the prisoner back on the plane so we can leave. I hate the humidity."

As they exited the plane, he noticed Nancy's feet. They were small and graceful, and she glided as she walked, always balanced, each step perfectly controlled. He knew that walk. It was the result of serious martial arts training.

The waiting Navy MPs drove him across the base to Camp Delta. After negotiating several rounds of security checks, he was taken by a different Humvee to a smaller set of concrete buildings away from the main camp. As an Operator, Eric had been to Camp Delta before, but he'd never been to Camp 7.

Camp 7 was different than Camp Delta. It was ringed with razor wire, but the guards were more alert. There were very few buildings, but some of the most valuable prisoners the US housed were located in Camp 7.

The damp heat wormed its way down his back as they entered the first building, and the high school locker room smell lodged in the back of his throat.

Three men greeted him, two white men with dark black hair and wire-rimmed glasses. They looked like former football stars turned investment bankers. The third man was black and muscular, with deep-set eyes and the beginnings of a smirk.

"Eric Wise?" the first man asked.

"Yes."

The black man never took his eyes from Eric. "You ready to see him, or you want to shoot the shit?"

"I'm on a tight schedule," Eric said. He opened the briefcase and handed a folder to the first agent. "Here's the paperwork."

"Kind of unusual," the first agent said. "No partner. That's a break in protocol. We don't like breaks in protocol."

"The paperwork's in order," Eric replied.

The second agent took the folder and studied it, then sat down at a desk against the far wall and typed on a computer.

The third agent continued to watch Eric, polite but alert, still smirking.

He wondered if he would have problems. The paperwork was valid, but he was violating all procedures for prisoner transfers. He could almost feel the suspicion from the three agents, but especially the third.

It was a standard part of Delta training for Operators to learn the basics of spy craft, and he had paired with CIA agents in the past. Still, the prisoner transfer was out of the ordinary, and he was missing the slick gloss that defined most CIA agents.

It had them spooked.

The third agent finally spoke. "You're not one of the usuals. You've never been to Camp 7, but I swear I've seen you before."

Agent number three suddenly seemed real familiar to him, too. A distant memory flitted through his brain. Afghanistan? Yeah, the village near Kandahar. Freeman, that was his name. Teon? No, Deion. Deion Freeman. It was Freeman's nose that he remembered, short and curved, the refined lines a study in contrast with his well-cut physique. It made him look delicate, but he knew better. Freeman had a sharp mind, a laconic attitude, and was known mostly for being a smart-ass. "I've spent some time near Baghdad," he offered. "I think we might have crossed paths there."

Freeman shook his head. "I don't think it was Iraq."

"Does it really matter?" He did not have time for lengthy explanations. He needed to get the prisoner and get back in the air.

"Nope, guess not," Freeman finally said. He turned to agent two. "Does it check out?"

Agent two rose and handed the folder back to Eric. "Yeah, it does. You're clear. You need an escort?"

"No, I'd like to talk to him alone. Give me fifteen minutes. Then, bring the gurney."

All three agents nodded. Agent two led him to a concrete building farther from the rest, unlocked the heavy metal door, and waved him inside.

The sole occupant was chained to the floor. He had committed the second mass bombing on United States soil by an American citizen.

Eric stopped, sizing up the big man. It was hard to tell with the man kneeling, but he looked close to six foot, late twenties, with dark brown hair and an angular face. His eyes were hazel, and at first appeared almost kind. Except, they never quite blinked enough.

Eric entered the room and signaled to agent two to shut the door behind him.

"You're John Frist?"

The prisoner raised his head. "Here to torture me?"

Eric shook his head. He had seen the signs before. Frist was definitely not okay. "You held up under some harsh interrogation," Eric offered. "It's not your fault you broke."

Frist glared at him, silent.

Eric continued. "We broke Khalid Sheikh Mohammed. He wasn't actually waterboarded. Just preparing him was enough. He sang like a canary."

"What do you want?"

"I'm here to offer you a way out."

The man finally blinked. "Out of what? I'm a terrorist."

Eric sighed. "Yeah, you are. You killed over five hundred innocent people. Children, even. The Red Cross? Really, how do you see yourself? As a hero?"

"I'm no hero," Frist said. "I just did what had to be done. No one in this country understands sacrifice anymore. If people knew what it really took to keep them safe, to protect the American way of life, the freedoms—"

"So you blew up the Red Cross?"

Frist's eyes widened. "It was the only way," he said.

"You're a little crazy, aren't you?"

"One man's crazy is another man's sanity."

Eric sighed. "That doesn't even make sense. Look, you were a good soldier, you had a rough time in Iraq. I get that. Then you came home and blew up a building full of people because you missed your parents' funeral. Something got jumbled up in your head and you blamed the Red Cross. I've read the reports. Now you have an opportunity to give back some of what you took when you killed those people. You should understand giving back to your country."

Frist rattled his cuffed hands, tick-ticking the shackles against the concrete floor. "Start the torture or shut up. Either way is fine with me."

"You never really leave the Army, John. You still belong to the US government." He removed the leather case from his pocket and withdrew a syringe. "Either way, you're going to volunteer. It's your choice."

Frist finally showed concern. "Drugs? You think you'll get more information with drugs?"

"Scared of needles?"

Frist shook his head. "I'm not scared of anything. Not anymore."

"Really? Because you look like you're about to jump out of your skin."

"Go ahead, drug me. It won't make a difference."

Eric grabbed Frist's arm and jabbed the needle in. "It will, actually."

Frist struggled against the drugs, his eyes rolling back. "Whu-zin-at?"

"Something that *will* make a difference. A difference in me having to listen to your mouth during the trip."

Frist collapsed on the floor, spittle dangling from his mouth. He moaned and tried to roll over, but the shackles prevented that. In moments, he was still.

Someone rapped on the door to the cell, and the meaty thunk echoed in the enclosed space. "You ready?" Freeman called out.

"Yes," Eric said. "Bring it in."

They rolled in the gurney. Freeman helped unlock the shackles and together they lifted the unconscious man from the floor. They dumped him on the gurney, tightening the leather restraints, then used a pair of handcuffs to secure the shackles to the metal frame. A sergeant helped wheel the gurney out and load it in the back of a truck for transport back to the hangar.

"Afghanistan," Freeman said suddenly. "That's where I know you from. You're Steeljaw. I remember now."

Eric shrugged.

"You were Delta," Freeman said. "How'd you wind up in the CIA?"

"The same way anybody does."

"The CIA is better than Delta. Nicer digs, hot coffee. Three squares."

"But you still wind up in some crummy shithole. Like Cuba…"

Freeman laughed. "Good luck with Frist. He deserves what he gets."

Eric thought about that, then nodded his agreement. "Yes, he does."

* * *

They were flying over the heartland when Nancy came back and plopped down in the chair across from him. Frist was motionless, the gurney chained to the floor at the back of the cabin.

"How'd the transfer go?"

Eric looked up from the paperwork. "Shouldn't you be flying the plane?"

"Autopilot," Nancy said. "With the updated avionics, the plane can actually land itself. Or, fly remotely like a UAV."

He nodded. "One of the agents recognized me from Afghanistan."

"Don't worry," Nancy said. "It's bound to happen. You're going to come across people you worked with. Your cover is airtight. I saw to it myself."

He grunted, then waved his hand at the files. "I can't believe we're doing this."

"He's a psycho and a traitor," she said, her voice rising. "We're going to recycle this piece of trash and make him useful."

He shook his head. "It's not that. I'm not saying he shouldn't pay for his crimes, but this is inhumane. It would be better to kill him."

"This is inhumane, but a bullet in the brain is better? Don't overthink it, just do your job."

He glared at her. "I understand my job."

She glared back. "You better."

He squinted, frowning. "What's your story, anyway? I haven't found a jacket for you."

"You won't, either," she said. "I don't have an official capacity. Unofficially, I speak for the Old Man when he's not around. You've got as much authority over me as you can make stick. Everybody else has to follow your orders. Me, I'll go along with it. Until I don't."

"That could be problematic."

Her icy blue eyes stared back. "Yeah, but it's not your problem. There's only one person I answer to and that's the Old Man. Because, unlike everybody else, he really *is* my old man."

His jaw dropped. "He's your father? Your name is Nancy Smith?"

"Yes. Now that you have some idea of who the Old Man is, you can imagine my childhood. He grew up in hard times, he'd seen a lot. He wanted me to be prepared."

"Everybody has stories about their childhood."

"Not like mine. Stay out of my way and we'll get along just fine."

"So, this is the speech?"

She raised an eyebrow. "What speech?"

"The yours-is-bigger-than-mine speech."

She laughed, and the smile made it to her eyes.

It finally hit him. She pinged his radar.

It had been eating away at him since they'd first met. She looked through him, not at him. The thousand-yard stare, they called it. The eyes stared off, not focusing, giving a better view of an opponent's hands and feet. She had the stare. He knew what it looked like because a lot of men in Delta had the stare.

He had it himself.

Her smiled faded. "I like you, Wise. Let's keep it that way. Don't get on my bad side and we'll get along fine." She stood and headed for the cockpit. "We'll be landing in an hour."

Eric watched her go, and this time noticed the bulge of the handgun in the side of her skirt. He turned to look at the unconscious form of John Frist. "Between you and me," he said to the unconscious man, "I really don't think I want to get on her bad side."

* * *

Groom Lake, Nevada

It was near dusk when they landed and taxied off the runway. A truck and Humvee waited for them. Eric stepped off the plane and gasped as the heat took his breath away. The dry air sapped the moisture from his lips and tongue, and he struggled to spit, the dust tickling the back of his throat. He knew that soon the desert would cool, quickly radiating its heat, but for now it was a furnace.

A pair of soldiers helped unload Frist and place him in the back of the truck. Nancy motioned for Eric to get in the passenger seat of the Humvee, and she drove while the soldiers followed in the truck.

From the files, Eric knew that much of the history of Area 51 was deliberately crafted misinformation. The real base was buried deep within the mountains. They roared west toward the mountain following a road invisible to the eye, but one that Nancy managed to negotiate. She glanced down at an LCD screen, then placed her thumb over a small square.

The thumb reader beeped and the ground began to rise in front of them. He watched, amazed, as the desert floor blossomed open, a long tunnel sloping downward underneath the false rock. They entered the cavernous tunnel and continued down the slope.

"It's not concrete," Nancy said.

He stared dumbly. "What?"

"I bet you were thinking the tunnel is concrete. It's not." The Humvee's headlights played across the slick tunnel walls. Eric turned to watch behind them as the false door shut, sealing them in. A long string of fluorescent lights in metal cages glowed above, stretching off into the distance.

"The original tunnel was hand cut," she continued, "but they enlarged it later with a nuclear tunneling device. They poured concrete to level the floor, but the walls are actually melted rock."

"Nuclear-powered tunneling machine?"

"Don't worry," Nancy said, grinning. "It isn't radioactive. Anymore."

He shook his head. "That really doesn't make me feel better."

They continued through the tunnel until they finally entered a large cavern. Eric had seen caves, large and small, and this was no cave. It was a long room, big enough for the Humvee and truck to swing completely around. A large blast door stood open, guarding another tunnel.

The soldiers lifted the gurney out of the truck and placed it on the flatbed of an electric cart, Frist still trussed up and motionless. Nancy slid behind the wheel and motioned for Eric to take the passenger seat. He was barely seated when she floored it.

The electric cart shot down the tunnel, the blast door closing behind them. She spoke to Eric as she drove. "A lot of people think we have aliens here, but trust me, it's just us. They'd probably be a lot more freaked if they knew the truth," she said wistfully.

They drove several hundred meters before coming to another door. It opened slowly and was as thick as it was wide. An armed guard stopped them and Nancy handed him identification. He nodded and they passed through the door and were greeted by several white-coated technicians.

The techs wore lanyards with their faces emblazoned on plastic cards. The first, a black man named Nathan Elliot, directed two others to take the gurney with Frist. Eric recognized Elliot as the lead scientist on Project StrikeForce, a burly man in his late forties who would look more at home in a barroom brawl than in a classroom. He knew the man's looks were deceiving; he held two doctorates and was considered the top in his field before being recruited into the OTM.

He saluted, but Elliot laughed and shook his hand with an iron grip.

"We're not big on formality," Dr. Elliot said. He motioned to Frist. "He's been asleep the entire trip?"

"Yes," Eric replied.

"Good. We'll get him to the lab and start immediately."

"That fast?"

Elliot grinned. "No need to wait, and I prefer him unconscious. We need to run tests before we insert the Implant."

Nancy led Eric through a labyrinth of hallways until they reached his living quarters.

"This is yours," she said, pointing to a door with his name embossed on a steel plate. "Inside you'll find a sitting area, a desk, and a kitchenette. Your bedroom, bathroom, and closet are in the back. We took the liberty of stocking everything you might need. There're a million channels to choose from, and we even have movies on demand." She shook her head. "It's a shame you won't have time to watch them. Read as much of the paperwork as you can, but get some sleep. You'll be observing tomorrow."

She left and he opened the door with his thumbprint. When he stepped inside, he let out a long whistle. It was big, five meters across and ten deep, and was decorated with dark wood furniture, not the barrack-style steel that he expected. It even had recessed lights.

The kitchenette had a full-size refrigerator. He found the bedroom in the back, with a simple bed and a plasma screen hanging on the wall. He was surprised to find a walk-in shower in the bathroom.

The toilet was functional, but he was most impressed by the completely stocked vanity with several types of soap, deodorant, toothpaste, and other sundries.

He opened the closet door and found it furnished with both military fatigues and street clothes, a rack of boots and shoes on the floor. He did not bother to check the fit. The Office did everything well, it seemed, and he knew they would be his size.

He turned out the lights and went back to the sitting room. "Might as well get to work," he said to himself. He sighed as he read the instructions for setting up his computer login.

It was going to be a long night.

* * *

Eric shook his head. The subterranean base was huge. According to his briefing papers, it originally housed America's secret aircraft program, especially their fascination with enemy technology. The US did a booming business in stolen Soviet aircraft during the Cold War, and as the engineers worked furiously to reverse-engineer and evaluate the jets, the hangars were soon bursting at the seams.

So, in the early seventies, CIA-designed boring machines had carved out the massive underground base. It was large enough to hold thousands of workers, with cavernous rooms for testing equipment, numerous machine shops, state-of-the-art manufacturing facilities, and underground aircraft hangars that opened to the desert floor.

Once Area 51 and the Groom Lake facility had entered the public lexicon, most of the operations had been shipped elsewhere and the underground base mothballed. The Groom Lake facility still warehoused stolen military aircraft, but the days of Russia or China making huge technological leaps in aircraft design were over. It was easier for them to steal American designs from outsourced vendors.

Smith realized that with the public interest in Area 51 dwindling, it was an excellent choice for the Office. Much of the traffic to and from Area 51 over the past decade had been to update and revitalize the underground base.

While the above-ground facility was starting to look shabby, the great rooms under the mountain had been cleaned and refurbished, with billions of dollars of high-tech equipment trucked in.

The base now housed over a thousand technicians. It boasted a well-stocked cafeteria, two coffee shops, and a small theater. There were lecture halls, large inviting rooms with stepped seating, plasma screens and projectors, and conference rooms with multimedia capabilities.

He knew the budget for the project was large, but when he finally read the report that gave the actual numbers, he was astounded. The Office had invested heavily in the base, and even more in Frist.

CHAPTER THREE

The next morning, Eric followed the map to a circular room full of lab technicians. Nathan Elliot was there, as was Nancy, sitting at the conference table at the front of the room. The big-screen monitor on the far wall was ablaze with charts and graphs, all of which could have been written in a different language, for all the sense they made to him.

Nancy glanced over. "Glad you made it. We've got a busy day ahead."

Nathan looked up from his laptop, his heavy brow furrowed. "We finished the diagnostics overnight. If we're lucky, we'll be ready for the Implant."

"How's the data so far?" Eric asked.

Dr. Elliot smiled. "The MRIs and CT scans show more brain damage than expected. We have concerns about that, of course; our procedures are highly experimental. We checked his leg, where a small piece of shrapnel was removed from the IED in Iraq. It healed nicely. Remarkable, given the IED killed everyone else in his Humvee."

Dr. Elliot paused. "He's quite healthy—physically, that is. Mentally? Given the trauma he experienced in Iraq, it's obvious that he suffered from post-traumatic stress disorder."

"A lot of soldiers suffer from PTSD. They don't all become terrorists," Eric said.

"That's correct. In his case, it appears the brain damage combined with the PTSD caused him to fixate on the Red Cross."

"That doesn't excuse what he did," Eric said.

Dr. Elliot shrugged. "I'm not saying it does. If the Wipe is successful, the mental trauma he experienced will disappear. He will be unmade. He won't remember anything from Iraq until now."

The Wipe was Eric's biggest concern. He listened as Elliot explained the groundbreaking studies that unlocked the mystery behind human memory, and with that came another discovery—how to wipe memories and replace them with false ones. The process was barely out of the theoretical studies but had been successfully tested on several death row convicts.

"For the Wipe to work," Dr. Elliot explained, "we need Frist to maintain a sense of self, a sense of his life until he went to Iraq. We need him to remember his training in the Army, to build on it. It would be a disaster if we accidentally erased much of what made him who he was."

"You're sure it will work?" Nancy asked.

"The tests have been encouraging," Dr. Elliot said. "First, we'll install the Implant. It will allow us to remotely administer drugs such as painkillers or stimulants."

"Continue the tests," Eric said. "I've got to check the training preparations."

* * *

Kandahar Province, Afghanistan

Abdullah sat cross-legged, waiting for Naseer. The cave was cold and the tin stove provided little heat. The chimney failed to vent all the smoke, and it settled on his worn clothes. His teapot steamed upon the stove top. A light, recharged through a solar cell, provided just enough illumination for him to read his journal.

He had written much of it as a young Mujahideen, when he had felt so lost and helpless, unsure if he would live to see the Soviets driven away. He had been barely older than a child during the war, blindly following orders in the name of Allah.

Now he was a grown man fighting another war.

There was a scrabbling outside, rock scraping against rock, soft voices whispering, and then a polite cough. Naseer entered the room, a short young man no more than twenty-two, with oily black hair plastered against his head. Abdullah had tried and failed to get him to stop smoking, and he stank of clove beedies. The dying man, Fahad, followed behind.

"Abdullah, are you there?" Naseer whispered, squinting in the dim light.

"Of course," he replied patiently, "I've been waiting for you. Is this Fahad?"

Fahad stumbled forward, and Naseer dragged him in farther. "Yes, this is Fahad. He is honored to meet you. You must forgive him, he is in much pain." Both Naseer and Fahad stooped to shake his hand, then sat cross-legged on the tattered rug.

Abdullah gazed thoughtfully at Fahad. The dying man looked thin and papery, as if he could blow away in a strong wind. His clothes were one step up from rags, and his sandals were so worn they offered little protection for his feet. His glassy eyes focused momentarily, then rolled away.

"Sit, please," he said to the dying man. "Would you like some tea?"

Fahad's eyes found him. "Sir, I would like that very much."

Abdullah nodded. "That is good. A sick man must drink tea. It helps the disposition." He took the worn teapot, held together with brass tacks, and poured three cups of black tea. He added a small spoon of brownish-white sugar to each, stirred, and handed Naseer and Fahad their tea, then gave them each a piece of dried apricot from a cloth sack. While they drank the tea and nibbled the fruit, Abdullah questioned Fahad. "Tell me, Fahad, what sickness consumes you?"

"It is cancer," Fahad said, warmth returning to his face. "I have been to many doctors. They say the cancer will kill me. Perhaps if I had money, they could give me medicine. I had to wait on a cot for two days to see the doctor in Kandahar. The cancer is in my stomach and now my lungs. He said that if I had money, there might be medicine that could help, but I don't have any money."

"Money *is* scarce these days," Abdullah agreed. He refilled the teacups, delicately pouring so as not to spill a drop. "Do you have children? A wife?"

"Yes, I have a wife and many children. I used to sell wares on the street, but I became sick. I heard the Americans were offering much money, and I begged them for a job. I am sorry, sir. I know I should not work for them—"

"Do not apologize, Fahad. Your family is important. How many children?"

"Five children, all boys."

"Five? That is good. You work for the Americans in the base?"

"I clean their kitchen," Fahad said. "I barely make enough to feed my children..."

Abdullah refilled the teacups yet again. "I'm sorry to hear that. I would like very much to help you with your sickness, but I'm afraid there is nothing I can do. I can provide money, but I must also prepare Jihad. You understand?"

Naseer nodded wisely, urging Fahad to nod as well.

"Yes, sir, I understand," Fahad said. "Naseer told me you could provide a small sum of money to my wife. To feed my boys." Tears streamed down his face, glistening against the pale skin.

"Fahad! Do not do this! You must not show such weakness in his presence," Naseer practically shouted.

"Please, Naseer," Abdullah said, gently taking Fahad's hand. "There is no reason to be upset. He is only worried about his family."

"Thank you, sir," Fahad said, gripping his hand tightly. "Yes, I only care about my family."

"Tell me, Fahad. You never made Hajj?"

Fahad shook his head. "No, and now I never will."

"It is all right. You are not able-bodied. Naseer tells me you are a good Muslim. I believe him. This thing I will ask you to do, this thing will be a great thing. Can you do it?"

"Naseer told me what you want. I can do it, Allah willing."

"I must ask you, Fahad. I want a truthful answer. Have you been smoking opium?"

Fahad's eyes darted to Naseer, who sat quietly, then back to Abdullah. "I have been, sir. I have been. Only to help dull the pain. I am so shameful." He sobbed, interrupted only by a racking cough.

Abdullah nodded his head. "I thought so. There is no reason to feel shame. You work hard for your family. The opium was to help the pain. I can see that. But I must ask you to stop. To complete this task for me, your mind must not be clouded with opium. Can you promise?"

Fahad nodded, the sobs trailing off. "Yes, sir, I promise. No matter how great the pain, I will never smoke opium."

"Very good. Naseer, please show Fahad where to wait."

Naseer rose and led Fahad away, returning soon after.

"Did you see the way I talked to him?" Abdullah asked.

Naseer nodded.

"It's not enough to learn to make bombs. You must learn to plan. You must learn to inspire."

Naseer frowned. "I must lie to people?"

Abdullah clucked his tongue. "I did not lie to him. I *comforted* him. I will ask him to lay down his life, and a few kind words will ensure that he does. He is a man. He has a wife and children that he loves. Every man should wish for that. Now he will perform his part, now that I have met him and talked to him. He will do it for Allah, and for the money to care for his family, and he will do it because I treated him with kindness and respect."

Realization dawned upon Naseer. "So, a kindness will motivate them?"

"Yes, a kindness will motivate them. Kindness motivates better than bullets, sometimes. And a bomb is no good unless someone is willing to deliver it."

* * *

Area 51

Eric watched Dr. Elliot and Dr. Oshensker through the observation window as they carefully sutured the incision on Frist's abdomen.

"The Implant was successfully inserted," Elliot's voice rattled from the overhead speakers. "The main feed is connected to the abdominal aorta. The Implant can now inject payloads directly into the bloodstream."

Eric pushed the talk button on the wall. "How does this help?"

Without looking up, Dr. Elliot answered, "The Implant is smaller than a deck of playing cards. It can be remotely triggered, and it carries several compounds that Dr. Oshensker and I have developed. What do you know of sea snails?"

Eric pushed the talk button again. "Not a thing, Doc."

Elliot stopped suturing and looked up through the window. "I'm not surprised. Sea snails are wonderful creatures, the cone snail in particular. They're found throughout the world. They have the largest pharmacopeia of any genus in nature. Their venom contains a chain of amino acids called conotoxins. They form the basis for a painkiller a thousand times more powerful than morphine. In an emergency, this will allow the subject to continue his mission rather than being incapacitated. Another compound will allow us to increase or decrease the subject's heart rate, attention span, and combat readiness. You can imagine how useful this will be."

"I can see that."

"Dr. Oshensker, if you will finish?" Dr. Elliot turned to face Eric, lifting the magnifying visor over his head. "Another series of compounds will interact with the subject's brain chemistry during the Wipe. They will alter the subject's short- and long-term memory. During the memory implant, we'll inject another compound that will alter the subject's emotional well-being." He smiled at Eric. "The effect will be to create a bond between the subject and his handler, a sense of trust and kinship. Also, we can alter the subject's aggressiveness."

"His aggressiveness? Do I need to remind you what he did?"

"I'm well aware. Dr. Barnwell has worked up a full psych evaluation, and between his research and our own, we've ensured the subject will perform within parameters. This is all in your briefing materials. Did you read them?"

Eric rolled his eyes. "I'm a little fuzzy on this memory and personality mumbo jumbo, and I don't remember reading anything about altering his aggression."

"You've been in a one-on-one, fight-for-your-life situation?"

Eric remembered Afghanistan, his NVGs on the fritz, the darkness lit with machine gun fire, a Taliban fighter dragging him to the ground, grappling, trying to choke him while he desperately reached for his knife. "Yeah," he said dryly, "I've been in a few."

"Imagine if you could have increased your aggression. Imagine being flooded with adrenaline, giving you hysterical strength."

Eric nodded slowly. "That would be useful."

"Of course it would." Dr. Elliot approached the window. "And, among other things, the Implant contains a chemical that will cause cardiac arrest. A kill switch, if you will."

Eric smiled. "Now *that* I understand."

Dr. Elliot turned back to the patient. "We'll run a diagnostic on the Implant and let you know when we are ready to proceed."

* * *

"You really need this guy?" Nancy asked.

"I do," Eric said. "I could use the help."

They were drinking coffee in the cafeteria. The Implant was still being tested, and he had spent much of the ensuing time preparing Frist's training plan. "I could use the help," he repeated. "I worked with him in Afghanistan."

Nancy sipped her coffee, her finger tapping the red folder on the table. "Deion Freeman, recruited right out of Harvard, a gift for languages. Spanish and German in high school. Pashto and Dari in college, plus a focus on Arabic. Worked in the Counterterrorism Center, handled some key reports to the OSA, highly recommended to be the OSA station chief, got his hands dirty in Afghanistan. That's where you crossed paths?"

Eric nodded, remembering the mission to exfiltrate the opium farmer for interrogation. Freeman had been key to arranging the mission. "He'd be a good fit."

"It's your call. You're the base CO as well as head of the project. You can request whatever you need."

He smiled. "I'll bet you have your own opinion."

She casually tucked wisps of straw-colored hair behind her ear. "He's good. He can help you with Frist. Plus, he'd be a boon to the Office. You have to understand, though, there's always a risk when we make the approach. If we give them too much info and they say no, we're in a bind. We might have to drop him in a hole."

Eric watched her eyes, waiting for the twinkle. There was none. "You're not kidding."

"You've been doing your homework, you should have an idea by now how this place works."

"Sorry, I'm used to things like due process."

She glanced away. "Due process doesn't exist here. Here we're trying to keep the world from destroying itself." She turned back to him, eyes empty. "I've briefed the Old Man and he's given the green light. I can have Freeman here in a few days. He might not be too happy about it. That's all I'm saying."

Eric smiled. "Since I'm recruiting, I have a few other men I think might be a good fit." He handed her a sheet of paper with a list of names.

She yanked the list from his hand, glanced at it, and rolled her eyes.

CHAPTER FOUR

The sun peeked over the mountains, the sky an indigo twilight caught between dawn and morning, when Fulton Smith's plane arrived. Eric braced himself against the morning chill as he watched the Gulfstream, a twin to his, taxi down the runway. The pungent smell of jet fuel washed over him, and his mind flashed back to other runways, other superior officers.

Smith stepped from the plane, his suit pressed, face bland.

"Good morning, sir," Eric said.

Smith smiled faintly. "No need for pleasantries. You're up to speed?"

"Getting there," Eric said.

"I'm sure you're doing well. Now, take me to the chamber."

Eric led Smith to his Humvee and they headed back to the base. He still wasn't used to the underground tunnel, but he had read the instructions and knew how to read the LCD screen in the dash. With the state of the Russian economy and the crumbling satellite infrastructure, there were hours between flyovers and the LCD screen gave the okay to raise the hidden door to the tunnel.

He glanced at the dash. The screen displayed the time of the next Russian satellite fly-by. By the time the satellite was overhead, Smith's plane would be parked in a hangar and they would be in the underground base.

He put his thumb on the reader and keyed the button to open the hidden door. They raced down the tunnel and he keyed the door closed behind them. They reached the main door and checked in through security, then switched from the Humvee to an electric cart.

He cleared his throat. "Sir, if you don't mind a question?"

Smith turned to look at him, the corridors whizzing by, the occasional lab technician or soldier stopping to let them pass. "Speak freely, Mr. Wise. Always with me, speak freely."

"How is this possible? I mean, we are far outside of what the Constitution permits. The Posse Comitatus Act states we are not to operate on domestic soil."

Smith nodded gravely. "I understand your concern, Mr. Wise. Let me explain. I was a young man when I met President Truman. He knew my grandfather, you see. I was ready to deploy to Korea when my brother was killed. I was summoned to the White House. I thought meeting the President was the most momentous thing that would happen in my life. I was wrong. I met the President and another man, a man named Barth. Barth never spoke during the meeting. The President recalled the times spent with my grandfather in Kansas City. He then asked what kind of man I would like to be. I said I hoped to survive the war, to marry, have children. I couldn't imagine anything else."

He paused, lost in thought. "The President had almost been assassinated. I think that above all else planted the seed in his mind. He asked if I'd accept a job. He felt that to maintain the United States, to continue the grand experiment, a more comprehensive solution was needed. He tasked me with creating the Office of Threat Management. An office that would work outside the laws, outside the Constitution. He tasked me with saving the world."

Eric took a right turn and continued up a long ramp, watching Smith out of the corner of his eye. "And you accepted."

"Of course. Suddenly, I wasn't going to war in Korea. I found myself at war here in the United States. Barth, as it turns out, was the President's man. A position long held and little known. He fixed things that needed fixing. One man who did the unthinkable. It wasn't enough. Over the next year, I built an organization, brought in soldiers and spies, scientists and researchers. There were threats everywhere. The Cold War raged. The country faced problems, internal and external. The outlook was grim. Nuclear war was a distinct possibility. We acted. We stopped riots, assassinations, bombings. We influenced, we spied, and we killed. We did this globally. We were not peaceful men. And we weren't always right. We became better at analyzing data, better at predicting the unpredictable. It was better to kill one man to stop a war. One life to save thousands. Or millions. A conflict in Africa that could spin out of control. Starvation in Turkey that could end with an occupation of the Middle East."

Eric nodded, steering the cart through the final hallway. "You still need someone to act."

"In most situations we funnel our data to existing agencies. But in extreme cases, yes, we need someone who can act. A weapon, to be unleashed only when necessary."

They arrived at the chamber. "We're here," Eric said.

Smith smiled. "Yes, Mr. Wise. We most certainly are."

* * *

The room was the size of a small gymnasium. A full-height glass window partitioned it in half, the back full of stadium seats, enough to hold hundreds of people. The seats were filled with white-coated technicians, and there were very few empty spots left.

Eric led Smith down to the front, a few meters from the ground. Their seats afforded them an excellent view and they watched as the techs behind the glass prepared for the experiment.

John Frist lay strapped to a plastic table in the center of the room, eyes closed. His chest rose and fell, his breathing slow and rhythmic.

Dr. Elliot stood in a yellow isolation suit, hovering over Frist. He shuffled nervously from foot to foot, trying to watch the different monitors that surrounded Frist. Dr. Oshensker sat at a nearby workstation, typing furiously.

Smith turned to Eric. "Do you understand the process?"

"I read the briefings."

"Then you know how dangerous and delicate this process is. We've had a measure of success, and Dr. Elliot assures me they have perfected the technology."

There was a flurry of activity as the technicians rolled two racks of equipment to the center of the room, placing them on either side of Frist.

"Dr. Elliot wasn't the first to create nanobots," Smith said, "but his breakthrough allowed us to offload the power and computing. He looked at it from another perspective. What did he really need to accomplish? He sends them the instructions, and a supercomputer will take care of the processing. The racks on either side of the subject will bathe him in an electric field, strong enough to power the nanobots, but not strong enough to cause cellular damage."

Eric gawked at the amount of equipment, and at Frist, unconscious on the table. "What if it doesn't work?"

"Then Mr. Frist died serving his country," Smith answered soberly.

Below, a nurse inserted a PIC line into Frist's chest. Eric watched for a moment. "Does it bother you what we're doing to him? The procedures? The enhancements?"

Smith turned his gaze to Eric. "Five hundred and twelve people died in the Red Cross bombing. Mothers and fathers, sisters and brothers. They loved and were loved. Many died instantly, but not all. Some died in the fire and some from smoke inhalation. Others died from puncture wounds or blunt-force trauma. One woman suffered a heart attack from stress. You know this. You've seen the reports." He turned his gaze back to the technicians working on Frist. "I've done terrible things in the name of freedom, ordered men and women to their deaths. I believe in the sanctity of life and I feel sorrow, even for Mr. Frist." He stopped and tapped Eric on the leg. "I also know that we do what *must* be done. We are the gatekeepers. Like as not, if I were asked to do it all again, I would." Smith paused. "This isn't about me, is it?"

"No," Eric said slowly, "I guess it isn't. I think I understand what you expect from me. No matter how I feel, I'll perform the job."

Smith nodded. "I have faith in you, Eric. Perhaps we aren't turning Frist into a monster. Perhaps we're helping him find redemption."

"Maybe," Eric admitted. "Or maybe we're going to kill him, right here and now, in front of all these people, with a completely untested medical procedure."

Smith nodded. "Perhaps. You've heard the expression, you can't make an omelet without breaking some eggs?"

"In this case, it's his skeletal system."

"The nanobots will do their job, or we wouldn't be at the human trial stage," Smith said.

The plasma screens showed a number of graphs, all green. Dr. Elliot directed a man to maneuver a steel-framed array with two glass tubes, each the size of two-liter soda bottles, directly behind Frist. One was filled with a clear liquid, the other with a liquid so dark it appeared to suck the light from the room. The nurse had finished inserting the PIC line and was busy hooking other IVs in Frist's arms and legs.

Dr. Elliot finished his last round of checks, whispered something to another tech, and stepped to the front of the room. "Test, test. Can you folks hear me?"

The people in the auditorium sat up and the talking abruptly ended. There were nods all around. Smith sat still, hardly blinking. The only noise in the room was the hum of the equipment and the faint whisper of the ventilation system.

The techs behind the glass took their seats at different workstations. The nurse finished hooking up the last IV and took a position behind Oshensker's workstation.

"Well," Dr. Elliot said, "it appears we are ready to begin. Dr. Oshensker is here, just as a precaution. Once the nanobots are inserted, we can't stop until the program completes. We must finish the process and extract the nanobots. If they are left in the subject's body, it could be disastrous."

The techs in the room nodded their heads. Eric knew they had worked on this for years, and not all the tests had ended well. When reading through the archives, he had stumbled across pictures of a rhesus monkey. The monkey was a bloody mess, as if it had been turned inside out.

Now we're risking a man, not a monkey.

Eric's eyes swept the room, wondering if they were nervous, and saw a twitch in Frist's right eyelid. He turned to see if anyone else had registered the twitch, but no one seemed to have noticed.

The door to the auditorium opened and Nancy joined them. Smith greeted her with a nod. "Nice of you to show up, dear."

"Wouldn't miss it. How are we?"

"Nathan is about to begin."

"Dr. Oshensker," Dr. Elliot called out. "What's the status of the test subject?"

"Well within parameters," Dr. Oshensker answered. "Monitoring program is in place and all vitals are normal. The telemetry is recording."

Eric was barely listening. He watched Frist, but there was no further twitch, no sign that Frist was conscious. He glanced up at the monitor showing Frist's blood pressure. The status was green, the blood pressure normal. According to the EEG readouts, Frist was unconscious.

Dr. Elliot turned to the nurse. "Kara, would you start the program?"

The nurse nodded and typed commands on her keyboard.

A large countdown clock appeared on the monitor. As it started to tick down, Dr. Elliot continued to lecture. "When we reach zero, the nanobots will be injected. There are billions in the cylinder. Once they are successfully inserted, we'll take a short break as they receive their positioning instructions. The next step is the nanocarbon material. Once that's injected, we'll start the Weave. The nanobots will use the buckyballs to form a mesh sheath over the skeletal framework, primarily the arms, legs, and ribs, rendering the skeleton much stronger than normal. Make no mistake, this will not render the subject bulletproof or invulnerable to harm. But, in combination with his battle armor, it will increase his chances of survival."

The timer reached zero and everyone took a deep breath. "We are injecting the nanobots now. This will take several moments. Please note that our test subject is completely unconscious. The migration of the nanobots would be excruciatingly painful if the test subject were awake," Dr. Elliot said.

The tube of clear liquid drained, quickly at first, then slowing to a trickle. In less than five minutes, the tube was empty.

"The nanobots have been injected and are en route to their destination along the skeletal axis. Keep in mind, they are incredibly small and are pumping through the bloodstream of a living organism. They must find their way to the skeletal structure and prepare for the nanocarbon material."

Eric was fascinated. They had just injected nanobots, which had cost millions of dollars to produce and a billion dollars to develop, into a living human being. He shuddered at the thought of billions of tiny ant-like robots plunging through his bloodstream and crawling along his bones.

On the screen, a number climbed until reaching eighty-five percent, and a gentle beeping started. "We've reached the threshold," Dr. Elliot said. "The nanobots that didn't make it to the skeleton will go inert when the process is complete. As the blood flows through the kidneys, they will eventually be filtered out and excreted through the urine. Kara, please begin the injection of the nanocarbon."

Kara nodded, and after a few mouse clicks, the black nanocarbon drained from the glass tube.

Eric was startled to see a triumphant smile on her face. It struck him as odd, her demeanor at odds with the other techs. He tried to remember details from her personnel file. He knew she was a registered nurse, recruited years before, cross-trained in the project's technology, but the rest of her file was a blur.

On the monitor, a graphical representation of Frist's body appeared, the skin peeling away until only the skeletal structure remained. A red mesh displayed and wrapped the bones, the proposed pattern. Above the graphic, the words WEAVE BEGINNING floated next to a countdown timer that displayed thirty minutes.

"Nanobots are starting the Weave," Dr. Elliot said. "You can watch as the red mesh turns green. We can't actually see it happening, of course, but this screen will give you an idea of their status."

The timer started counting down and the mesh slowly turned from red to green. The first ten minutes crept by, the audience sitting on the edge of their seats, fascinated.

Eric saw another twitch in Frist's eyelid.

This time, Smith noticed. He cleared his throat. "Nathan, are you sure the subject is unconscious?"

Nathan nodded. "Of course. You can see his vitals on the screen. He's completely unconscious. Notice the blood pressure, it's one hundred and five over sixty. He's out. If he weren't, he would be in agony and his blood pressure would be through the roof."

Dr. Oshensker stood and walked behind the machine, threading his way through the cables and IV tubes, inspecting them. "Everything looks good," Dr. Oshensker said. "The diagnostic data is correct. Blood flow is continuing as expected."

Eric stood. "Doctor, something isn't right. Please check again."

"Feldman, run a high-level diagnostic," Dr. Oshensker said to a technician on the other side of the room.

Feldman typed quickly, then looked up. "Everything looks good, doctor." He turned his attention back to the computer. "Wait. That's not right."

Dr. Elliot hurried to the workstation. "What's not right?"

Feldman looked up, his face concerned. "See this? It's being fed from an external database. It's not live telemetry."

Dr. Elliot grabbed him by the shoulder. "What? How?"

"I don't know," Feldman stammered. "I don't understand. Let me clear the connections and reset the diagnostics."

Everyone turned their eyes to the monitor. Everyone but Eric. Eric stared at the nurse, Kara, who smiled coldly.

There was a gasp from the crowd.

"My God," a woman shouted, "his blood pressure is off the charts. He's awake! He feels everything. You've got to stop!"

"We can't stop the Weave," Dr. Elliot said. "If we stop now, the program will crash. It will kill him."

Eric stood and pointed. "It was the nurse," he said. "She's the one."

Everyone stared, first at him, then at her.

Her eyes were wide. "He deserves it," she snarled.

An armed guard appeared beside her and firmly grabbed her arm.

"He deserves it," Kara said as the guard hauled her away.

Both of Frist's eyelids were twitching, and his left hand started to tremble.

Smith stood. "Dr. Oshensker. Sedate him. Now."

Oshensker grabbed a syringe. His hands were shaking, but he managed to fill it and plunge it into the IV drip.

Frist's eyelids slowed their twitching, his hand tremor slowing to a stop, his blood pressure falling back to normal. The countdown timer continued its descent.

"Eric," Smith said, "interrogate that woman. Nathan, continue the procedure."

* * *

John woke, his body on fire, burning from the inside. He wanted to scream. A glow filtered through his eyelids and he knew that beyond that glow was life. Someone who could help.

He tried to twist, to move. There was something hard and round in his mouth. A tube or a hose, going down his throat. He wanted to gag, but even that was denied him.

And, through it all, the pain!

People were talking, indecipherable. If only he could block out the pain, even for a moment, maybe he could make sense of it, understand what was happening, why he was forced to suffer.

He heard a voice. Something about … weave?

The word held no meaning. Just when he thought it could not get worse, he found that what came before was just a prelude. In that moment of agony, he felt a million pinpoints of sharp, prickly needles burrowing through him.

He tried to scream, to make them stop, and then he heard a voice, an old man's voice, powerful and confident. The pain lessened and he realized, as the torment finally ended, the voice had called for sedation.

* * *

Eric strode through the room, and people jumped out of his way.

The nurse, Kara, stared at him, blue eyes shining. He stopped to compose himself, then nodded at the guards. They hustled people out of the room and shut the door, leaving them alone.

He glared at her. "You know who I am?"

She nodded. "You're Wise. You're the new base CO."

"I'm only going to ask once. Once, you understand?"

She nodded again, her eyes losing some of their fire.

"Why?"

She swallowed hard. "I don't regret it. Can you imagine the pain he felt? The torture?"

Eric waited, silent.

She turned away from him, biting her lower lip. "My cousin. Her fiancé's son was on a class trip. He died in the blast."

Eric said nothing.

She continued, "I knew when they brought Frist in. A military man, shaggy hair and stubble on his face. They kept him unconscious until the Implant. I had access to his records, so I dug. Why this man? Then I realized. They had found the man responsible for the Red Cross bombing, the man who killed all those people."

"Smart. So you swapped out the telemetrics for prerecorded data? Then swapped out the anesthesia?"

"Yes," she admitted. "I changed the anesthesia. He only got the paralytic. He was conscious, but couldn't move."

One thing bothered him. "You knew you would be caught. What did you hope to accomplish?"

"Nothing. I just wanted him to suffer," she said. "Can you understand that?"

He imagined the anger and the pain, the desire to balance, at least somewhat, the cosmic scales of justice. Yes, he *could* understand it. "You've put me in a difficult position. I can't just reassign you. You know too much. Do you understand what I'm telling you?"

"You'd have me killed. Or buried in a hole. I know how the Office works." She shook her head, resigned. "I knew it was a possibility before I started. I could tell you I would return to my job and do exactly as ordered, but how could you trust me?"

Eric pondered that. "Would you do your job? Could you put aside your feelings?"

"Have you really thought this project through?" she asked. "We're going to take a monster—a killer and murderer—and make him a better killer and murderer. Doesn't it bother you?"

"I have my orders. Just like you." He leaned close to her. "I've been out in the world, fighting for my country. It's not always pretty, but even in my darkest hour, I believe in America. I've done horrible things, things I wonder if I can ever get off my conscience, but, in the end, I do it because I have faith."

Kara's lower lip trembled. "It's funny. That's why I joined the military. I'm not asking you to plead for me. Whatever happens, happens. But I'd do my job. I wouldn't like it, but I'd do my job."

Eric took her hand in his and squeezed it. "Maybe that'll be enough. I can't make any promises, but I'll talk to Smith. You have to promise me, though, that nothing like this will ever happen again."

She nodded. "I promise."

He left the room and snapped his fingers at the two guards outside. "Make sure she doesn't do anything stupid," he said.

* * *

Smith's office was big, with a real oak desk, made when furniture was still built by men with skill. It glowed a rich brown from the reflected light of the flat-panel computer monitors. The chairs were soft leather, the carpet a brown weave. Eric sat stiffly across from Smith and sighed. "Her cousin's fiancé had a son. He was killed, along with his classmates."

Smith shook his head. "Of course, the school bus. Twenty-three children, I believe." He stood and poured a cup of hot coffee, and delicately added cream and sugar. "Coffee?"

He shook his head. "No, thanks. I interrogated the woman. She wanted him to suffer. Nothing else."

"There often isn't," Smith said as he returned to his chair. "You plan and prepare, but there is one variable you can't account for. The human. The human is unpredictable. It's the best of us and the worst of us. Emotion, passion, justice. It can elevate us to great heights, or take us to great depths. The Germans learned this."

"The Germans?" Eric asked.

"I interviewed a member of the SS, once, a guard in one of the death camps. He was living here, in the United States. This particular man had found influence. His exposure would be … undesirable. We captured him and interrogated him before we turned him over to the Israelis. I looked into his eyes and asked how he could do something so wrong. So evil. He didn't have an answer. He made excuses. Justifications. Then, he told of the humiliation, of how the world had treated his country after World War One. How Hitler inspired them, made them feel proud. Gave them purpose. How Hitler would right the wrongs against them. How the Aryan race would triumph."

Eric felt nauseous. It was one thing to read about history in a textbook, but Smith had actually lived it. "That's what motivated him?"

"It turned him into a monster," Smith said. "We must keep that kind of insanity from happening again. People are unpredictable. Mr. Frist, for instance. A young man, by all accounts, a patriot, obsessed with revenge for an imagined slight against him. How much of it was the shock and horror of war? Or the damage to his mind? But now he is here, and the young nurse, Ms. Tulli, is here as well."

"Yes, she is. She says she's willing to continue working with the program and that she would never do anything like that again."

"Do you believe her?"

Eric paused. "I know it sounds crazy, but yeah, I do."

"Listen to your instincts. What are they telling you?"

"They say we can trust her. Besides, what are my alternatives? Have her locked up? Terminated?"

Smith blinked softly. "Eric. I've watched you for years. You're a good man. If you believe she needs to be terminated, it's your decision. If you think we should free her, that's your decision as well."

A dull ache settled in the back of his head. He believed Smith. He could order the death of Kara Tulli. The guards would execute her, a cover story would be crafted. As head of Project StrikeForce and as the base CO, he could order the complete removal of another human being.

He shook his head. "We'll keep her working on the project. She won't cause any more problems."

Smith nodded. "See that she doesn't. Dismissed."

CHAPTER FIVE

Frist slumped in the chair, his arms and legs held by leather restraints, his head strapped to a thick plastic crossbeam. The monitor in front of him displayed a pulsating test pattern.

Eric watched through the observation window as Dr. Barnwell and Dr. Elliot worked the computers. Dr. Barnwell was the base psychologist, a soft, doughy man in his late sixties, but Eric had read his jacket and knew Hobert Barnwell had been with the Office since the Vietnam War.

"How long will this take?" Eric asked.

"Several hours," Dr. Barnwell said. "This is a fairly ambitious Wipe. We've got to find the trigger, the memory of the bombing."

"You'll just erase it?"

"Hardly," Dr. Barnwell said. "We used to think there were hundreds of thousands of neurons associated with the formation of a single memory. It turns out there are fewer than a thousand. The problem is they cross-link with the neurons around them."

Frist groggily opened his eyes. The monitor started playing idyllic scenes of the countryside. Frist stared at the monitor, unable to turn his head.

"The sedative is working. He's conscious, but not fully awake," Dr. Elliot said.

"Good," Dr. Barnwell said. "The procedure is fairly simple. We'll play images from his life, pictures of where he grew up, his grade school, that sort of thing. The fMRI maps the blood flow levels in the brain tied to neural activity. We'll map the neuron clusters associated with various memories to construct a model of his brain. Then, we'll play back images of the Red Cross bombing. When we have those clusters mapped, the cyclotron will send two streams of high-power particles, and where they meet, the resulting energy will destroy those neuron clusters."

Eric shuddered. "Sounds dangerous."

"Not necessarily. The real problem is that one of the neurons might also contain a link to the word bomb, the overall memory of bombs, how to make bombs, or even something completely unrelated. We don't want to destroy his entire memory, just excise certain aspects of it. What good would he be if we turned him into a drooling idiot?"

"How safe is this?"

Dr. Barnwell smiled. "Everything about this project carries a risk. I thought you understood that."

"Sorry, Doc. If you told me a month ago that you had this kind of tech, I would have called you a liar." Eric shook his head. "What about his time in Gitmo?"

Inside the room, a deep and loud thrumming shook the floor. The pictures changed, morphing from image to image, first a small bungalow with a bicycle in front, then pictures of an early-seventies Ford LTD. Dr. Elliot's computer lit up with a three-dimensional map of Frist's brain.

"When we are done with the Wipe, we'll administer a drug called an HDAC2 inhibitor. We can't completely erase his memories of the past year," Dr. Barnwell continued, "especially memories that have a high emotional content, but the HDAC2 inhibitor will help stimulate the formation of new memories, memories that also have high emotional content. We'll blame any lingering problems on his concussion. His mind will fill in the blanks."

"It's funny," Eric mused. "The one person who should never forget what he did, and he won't remember a thing. He completely escapes punishment."

"It's not my job to punish him," Dr. Elliot said. "It's *my* job to make him ready for training. *Your* job is to make him a weapon."

The images slowly shifted—a grade school, a high school, a recruiter's station. The map of Frist's brain continued to build, a blazing display of bright-colored threads. Dr. Elliot glanced over his shoulder. "This is going to take some time. We'll call you when it's done."

Eric stood and walked to the window of the control room. He watched as the images morphed, Frist unable to turn away. "Doc? You're sure he won't remember Guantanamo?"

Barnwell shook his head. "Not after we're finished. Why do you ask?"

Eric shrugged. "No reason. Keep me posted."

* * *

Deion was jet-lagged and more than a little edgy when he entered the room. The hard-boned man with the intense brown eyes waited, a man he had worked with once before in Afghanistan, a man he had almost forgotten until the previous week. "Steeljaw. I should have known."

Eric smiled. "Glad you could make it, Freeman. I thought you might like a change of pace."

He felt a surge of anger. "Great, one hot shithole to another. I'm supposed to thank you? That it?"

Eric grinned. "We spend most of the time inside the mountain. It's quite comfortable in here."

"Uh-huh," he said. "So you sent a hot piece of tail to sweet-talk me into joining this outfit. What is this place?"

Eric sat up straight, his grin vanishing. "First, don't ever say anything like that to her face. And second, her father just might disappear you. Like, off the face of the earth."

"You're kidding, right?"

"I'm *not* kidding," Eric answered solemnly. "Sorry for pulling you into this, but I need your help. Welcome to the Office of Threat Management."

Deion had never heard of the agency. Until yesterday. "What does that mean, exactly? I worked with you five years ago, then you show up on a prisoner transfer. A week later I've got an offer extended. I was told someone vouched for me. But Area 51? Isn't this place full of aliens?" He knew the CIA had many active intelligence programs but had never heard of one this big, and certainly not buried under a mountain at Groom Lake.

"Walk with me," Eric said. "I'll explain everything."

Eric led him through the maze of tunnels. "No aliens here. That was just a cover story cooked up by the CIA while they were testing the Oxcart, the precursor to the SR-71. I'm surprised you're not up on that."

"Sorry, man, they didn't cover ancient history at the Farm. It was a need-to-know basis and I didn't need to know. What's with this place?"

"The Groom Lake facility is still run by the Air Force, but the Office runs the underground installation, and it has a single mission. To find threats that no one else can find, and keep them from escalating. You know what a Black Swan event is?"

"No idea."

"It's an event that has a massive impact and was completely unpredicted but, in hindsight, was glaringly obvious. It's the unknown unknowns. That's why we exist, to prevent these from spiraling out of control."

Deion was pushing to keep up with Eric's long stride. They moved quickly through the base, finally stopping in front of a large door guarded by an armed MP.

Eric pressed his palm to a reader buried in the wall, and the door opened. He showed his badge to the MP, who studied it, then motioned him through the door. They entered a small room with a wall of glass, another MP ensconced behind it. The door shut behind them. They stood there for several moments until the guard behind the glass spoke. "Name?"

"Eric Wise, escorting Deion Freeman."

The guard watched them intently, then keyed a button, and the far door opened.

"This is one hell of a mantrap," Deion said.

"You've *no* idea," Eric said. "If something's not right, we'd be locked in until an armed squad showed up. The glass is bulletproof. Not bullet resistant. Bulletproof. Not even a fifty-cal would penetrate it. The doors and walls could stop a suicide bomber. If the guard thinks I'm being coerced, he can evacuate the air in the chamber, rendering us unconscious. The guards will then shoot first and ask questions later."

"What the hell?"

Eric motioned him through the door. "You'll understand in a minute."

They stepped through the door into a massive room with stepped flooring. The far wall contained row after row of monitors. Dozens of people sat at workstations, hunched over their keyboards. A tall man stood to the side, the officer on duty. He nodded at Eric and barked, "Commander on deck."

Eric nodded back, then turned to Deion and spread his arms. "Welcome to the War Room."

Deion stared. "Holy shit."

"Holy shit," Eric agreed. "More information flows through this room than any other place on earth. The people here monitor every piece of information in the world. Everything the CIA knows, we know. The NSA. The Pentagon. We have network taps in all the big telecoms, and they stream the data to us. But it's more than just the data. We process it all and look for the patterns, the things that can't be seen. When we find them, we act."

Deion was speechless. He looked from one giant monitor to another. One displayed a data stream from a satellite over the Koreas, another a topographical map of Iran, red boxes on the map in constant flux. Phone numbers scrolled by on another, faster than the eye could see.

In fact, everywhere he looked, Deion saw an overwhelming amount of information. He tried to focus on just one screen, a graph of electronic gaming equipment being purchased through phony accounts and shipped to Syria, but trying to keep up with the flickering text made him lightheaded. He gave up and turned back to Eric. "This is what you do here? How could anybody make sense of this?"

Eric grinned. "Beats the hell out of me. But here, in this room, we protect the United States. Here we protect the world."

Later, after Eric had shown him his quarters, they sat at the small table in the kitchenette.

Deion shook his head in disbelief. "Get out. Truman?"

"Scout's honor," Eric said. "They created the OTM back in the fifties. Been doing it ever since."

Deion let it sink in. He would call bullshit on just about anybody, but Eric was one of the squarest shooters he had ever met.

He remembered asking a Delta Operator called IronMan, a wiry little man from Cleveland, about how Eric got the call sign Steeljaw. IronMan just smiled. "When your ass is in the fire, Wise is the guy you want. He's a stone-cold motherfucking killer. I've seen him hold a kid, pat him on the head while we led the kid's old man outside and threw him in a truck. When we got outside the village, he blew the old man's brains out. Then he wrapped the body up in white cloth and dug the hole himself, then buried him. We asked him why, and he said it was his job, his responsibility. No, if you want the job done, he's your guy."

Now he listened as Eric told the story of his own recruitment, how Smith had blacklisted him, then showed up on his doorstep, offering him the job. Then Eric told him about Project StrikeForce, the Wipe, the Weave, and the Implant.

"You have to understand, the Office operates in secret. There's no accountability. If things go right, nobody knows we exist. If things go wrong, people die. We have to do some questionable things to keep that from happening."

Deion took a sip of coffee, a deep roast that danced across his tongue.

You can always tell a first-class operation by the quality of its coffee.

"We're going to create some kind of supersoldier to take care of these kinds of situations?" he asked.

"You could say that. Only he's not super. He's just a man with some enhancements and *really* good equipment."

"Who is this lucky man?"

Eric paused. "John Frist."

Deion jumped from the table, knocking his chair back. "No way. Absolutely not!"

Eric watched calmly. "You're all in now, Deion. Frist is the man. Don't worry, after the work they're doing, he won't be the same man. They'll undo him."

"Undo him? What does that mean?"

"I wish I could explain it, but I barely understand it myself. Let's just say they're messing with his mind. He won't remember his involvement in the Red Cross bombing. When we're done, he'll be perfect. Look, I need your help on this."

He tilted his head. "What if I say no?"

"You can't say no to this," Eric said quietly. "You're part of the team now. You're still CIA, but you belong to the OTM. When Nancy recruited you, she told you the assignment was unusual."

"I hear that all the time. I never expected it to be true."

"You're going to say yes to this, and you know why? You love your country, you love the CIA, and this is the singular most important thing you could ever do for your country. You *want* to be part of this. Besides, I need help." Eric stared down at his hands. "I need help training him. I need you to watch him. I need you to see the things I can't see, and if it goes bad, I need you to help me clean it up."

He sat back down, contemplating Eric's offer. It was all true. He *did* want to be part of it. He *did* want to help his country. He liked it best when the stakes were high. "Well hell, Steeljaw, when you put it like that, how can I say no?"

* * *

Kandahar, Afghanistan

Abdullah taught Koshen how to grind pellets of fertilizer into a powder using a mortar and pestle, burlap sacks piled high around them. The afternoon air was warm in the small warehouse, and sweat dampened his face. His arm ached and his shoulder burned from the repetitive motion, but he would not complain in front of the young man.

Naseer entered the room. "How many more bags will we need?"

"At least another four," Abdullah said. "How goes the separation?"

"I've just removed the last batch from the water and set it out to dry."

"Good. If the Americans hadn't convinced them to add calcium carbonate, we wouldn't have to wash it." He noticed dismay on Naseer's face. "What is the problem?"

"The Taliban asked for more money. Only a few bags are smuggled on each motorbike."

"Why is this a problem? Many motorbikes cross the border every day."

Naseer shook his head. "They don't like you using their fertilizer."

"They have plans for it?" He continued to grind the pellets into a fine powder, then dumped it into a plastic pan.

Naseer averted his gaze. "They would rather use it themselves."

Abdullah stopped his work. "Who taught them to make bombs? Who taught them to make detonators?"

Koshen looked up cautiously. "You did."

Abdullah waved at Koshen. "Even he knows this. No, they will complain, but in the end they will give us what we need. They may not like it, but they will do it. There is a debt, Naseer. They remember that."

"They respect you," Naseer cautioned. "They know how you've helped the Jihad. No one doubts this." He paused, concern on his face. "Your comments upset them."

Abdullah nodded evenly, but his anger grew. "They continue to use children. They put them in harm's way. Asking a child to spy is acceptable. That is no different than talking. But asking a child to carry a bomb? No, I do not agree with them."

"It is more than that," Naseer said. "You told Azim they should allow girls to learn to read the Quran. They do not agree with this!"

Azim was the local Taliban commander, a weak and dishonest man who Abdullah loathed. "Azim may hold his own opinions as I may hold mine. Girls should be taught to read and study the Quran."

"The suspension is only temporary," Naseer reasoned. "If you just stay quiet, it will soothe the harsh talk against you."

Abdullah sighed. "It will not be temporary if Azim has his way. His goals and mine are not the same. I serve Allah. He serves himself."

Naseer glanced around. "Abdullah! You must not say this!"

"Don't worry, the only one here is Koshen, and he won't repeat this, will you, Koshen?"

"I hear nothing," Koshen said quietly.

"You see, he hears nothing. As do you. You are not hearing. Azim is not of Islam. He is nothing more than a thug. He is allowed to lead because his father was a loyal Mujahideen. But Azim? He is not a man like his father. No, the Mullah recognizes the debt the Taliban owes me. He recognizes a true Mujahideen. That is why Azim will not raise a hand against me." He turned his gaze to Naseer, who froze. "Azim is nothing before a true Mujahideen."

Naseer swallowed. "Yes, sir."

Abdullah went back to grinding fertilizer, ignoring the ache in his arm. He had his suspicions about Azim, but he could not prove them. Still, one day, if he could find evidence of Azim's treachery, he would make Azim pay for his crimes.

* * *

Area 51

"Ready for this little piece of melodrama?" Dr. Barnwell asked.

Eric shook his head in disbelief.

The aircraft hangar was divided into many rooms, hastily built out of plywood and drywall. They entered the largest and found a cemetery. Eric shook his head at the photos of headstones plastered around the walls. The ceiling, thirty feet from the ground, was painted bright blue with fluffy white clouds. The floor was covered in green AstroTurf, and headstones made of styrofoam were taped to the floor. A row of chairs sat neatly in line next to a mound of dirt, the casket waiting to be lowered into the ground.

The entire scene was fake, decorated like a movie set. He shook his head again. "I can't believe Frist will fall for this."

"He'll be drugged," Barnwell said. He rapped his knuckles against the fake gravestone, which almost toppled over. It was inscribed with the names Bob and Phyllis Frist, their birth dates and a death date of 2004. "Smell the air?"

Eric sniffed. The air smelled of grass, freshly turned earth, and rain. He nodded.

"Smell is a vital piece of memory. We're pumping artificial odors into each environment. It will help the overlay. In the end, he might remember feeling concern over his parents' funeral, but he won't remember missing it."

Men and women in dark suits and dresses entered, including a man dressed as a priest, who nodded at Barnwell and took his place in front of the headstones. Two men guided Frist, dressed in his Army uniform, into the room.

Frist's eyes were unfocused, and he stumbled over the fake grass. The men steadied him and led him to the front, next to the headstone. Dr. Barnwell waved for Eric to follow him, and they left through a door painted to resemble a tomb. They could hear the priest begin the service through the thin fake walls.

"The drugs should be wearing off," Dr. Barnwell said, "just enough for him to form new memories. He's still in a highly suggestive state. You need to get ready. The next memory will be the interrogation room."

Eric quickly dressed in camos, his breaching tools hanging from his chest harness, then checked the MP5 for ammo.

"Remember the script," Dr. Barnwell said. "They're placing him in the interrogation room now."

"Got it, Doc."

He glanced through the peephole to the interrogation room and watched as several dark-skinned men bent Frist back, placed a cloth over his face, and poured water over the cloth. Frist struggled weakly, but the men did not relent.

Eric felt a hand on his shoulder and turned to find Deion watching the performance.

"They sure make it look real," Deion said with a grin.

Eric smiled. "Well, look at you. I'd almost think you were an Operator."

Deion grinned. "Look, man, I attended jump school. It's standard training for a CIA NOC. I just never actually graduated."

"You lucky spook bastards with your cushy desk jobs."

Deion laughed. "I don't remember it being all that cushy in Afghanistan."

"Well, you weren't out in the field. You got to kick it easy back in Kandahar."

Deion glanced again through the peephole. "How much longer? They really look like they're giving it to him."

"They are. I told them to act just like insurgents. I even made them stop bathing a week ago. Here," he said, handing his MP5 to Deion. "Weapon check."

Deion popped the magazine and counted out the blanks, refilled it, and checked the chamber. "Clear." He handed his MP5 to Eric, who did the same.

Another dozen men dressed as Rangers approached. Eric nodded to them. "Ready?"

"Yes, sir," the lead Ranger said. "On your mark."

"Ready. Mark!" He kicked the door open and they entered the room as one, rushing through the fake warehouse. The first pseudoinsurgent turned and Eric fired directly at him. A blood squib popped, and blood stained the man's front and back. He fell to the ground, twitching, then went still. Freeman did the same to the man waterboarding Frist.

"Sergeant John Frist," Eric shouted. "Are you Sergeant John Frist?"

Frist coughed, a wet, racking sound. "I'm Frist," he managed.

Eric used his knife to slice through the rope holding Frist's hands to the chair. "We're here to rescue you. Freeman, help him up."

Deion grabbed Frist around the waist. "Can you walk?" Deion asked.

"Maybe," Frist mumbled.

"You'll be fine," Deion assured him.

They put their arms around Frist's waist and dragged him to the door.

As they approached, Eric signaled to Barnwell, who activated the Implant. Frist went limp. The Rangers lifted him, carried him through the door, and dumped him on a gurney.

Barnwell patted Eric on the back. "Very good. Go get changed. Sergeant Moswell will help you with hair and makeup."

The 'dead' insurgents stood and exited. Other men filled the room and tore the walls out. Eric and Deion went through to the dressing room, where Sergeant Moswell handed them their dress uniforms and quickly trimmed their hair. They shrugged off their camos and slid on their dress uniforms.

Deion glanced at Eric. "Hah. Makeup."

Eric grinned. "I've done a lot of things since I joined the Army. I've gone to strange and foreign destinations, met lots of interesting people. Killed some of them. But I've never fired blanks and worn makeup."

When they were done, they entered another room, this one dressed like a green army tent. They took seats at the folding table and waited. Fifteen minutes later, the Rangers brought Frist to the room and sat him at the table.

Frist stared, drooling, eyes glassy. Eric watched as Frist's head lolled right to left, his eyes slowly focusing on his surroundings.

"What? Where am I?" he asked.

"Still having trouble, John?" Eric asked.

Frist looked down at the table. "How did I get here?"

Eric nudged a glass of water across the table to Frist, who took it hesitantly. "It's to be expected. The IED really did a number on you. Take a drink and clear your head."

Frist eyed them groggily. "I remember you two. You were there. You saved me. It's like it just happened—"

Eric shook his head. "That was a year ago, John. Don't you remember? I'm Eric and this is Deion. We're Delta. The IED hit your Humvee outside Baghdad and the insurgents got you. They tortured you for weeks. They even waterboarded you. They wanted to smuggle explosives into the green zone. You did well. You didn't tell them anything."

Frist nodded. "Yeah, I remember. They punched me and kicked me. They put a cloth over my mouth and tried to drown me."

Eric turned to Deion. "See, this man has the right stuff. I told you. He didn't give them anything."

Deion nodded. "Yeah, he's got the right stuff. John, we're here to make you an offer. Delta has a new program and we think you'd be a perfect fit."

Frist stared at Deion, the seconds ticking by. Eric watched intently, looking for any signs that John remembered his previous encounters with Deion at Guantanamo.

Frist continued to stare.

Deion patiently said, "John, the doc says the effects of the IED might continue for a bit. We'll take care of you. Plus, your country needs you."

Frist finally nodded. "Of course. I'd do anything for my country."

Eric smiled. "That's what we like to hear. You won't regret this. You'll be out-processing in a month. We'll see you then."

Frist nodded and smiled back, and then his eyes slowly drooped. He swayed for a moment, then slumped in his chair. The Rangers returned with the gurney and hustled Frist away.

Eric and Deion left as the men returned to take away the furniture and collapse the tent. Dr. Barnwell was waiting for them. "Very good, gentlemen. He now has a framework to build on. His mind will fill in the rest."

* * *

John woke, bleary-eyed, the light from the digital clock casting soft shadows across the room. He took in his surroundings. A soft cot. A desk with a laptop. He could see a bathroom through an open doorway. A locker with clothes. He tried to remember where he was, and, for a moment, *who* he was.

Then it came to him. He was John Frist and he was a soldier.

He vaguely remembered corridors and hallways, entering the room, exhausted, and collapsing on the bed.

He struggled for more and then it hit, a road, more dusty street than pavement. He was hot, sweating. His eyes roving.

Then, a pile of garbage on the side of the street, like a million other piles of garbage. Pieces of stone and concrete littered the roadside along with the Iraqis' trash. Nothing different this time. Nothing but the explosion. A whump of noise, deafening, pummeling him.

His heart skipped a beat and he trembled as the memory came on in full force. The muffled ringing in his ears. The smell of the explosives and the dust gagging in his mouth, the smell of burning plastic and metal stinging his nose. He wanted to spit, to gag.

He turned and saw O'Neill and Gutierrez slumped over. Gutierrez turned to him, his eyes vacant. Blood ran in sheets down his face, down the coppery skin of his neck, and Gutierrez went still. John smelled the piss and shit and he knew Gutierrez—the man who talked about his wife and two kids, how he couldn't wait to get out, go home, drive his kids down to the beach, make love to his wife after the kids were asleep and then lick ice cream off her stomach, the man he had come to call friend—was dead. O'Neill didn't move.

O'Neill might be dead, too.

There were screams from the back, the sound barely audible over the ringing in his ears, and he knew Hernandez was still alive.

Please let Hernandez live.

He screamed, and then the pain. White-hot pain, burning everywhere, a million little needles crawling through him, no escape, the bright glow spilling through his eyelids, and a voice calling for sedation.

He hit the cot, his heartbeat in his throat, his limbs cold. He trembled, clawing at his wrist, trying to find his heartbeat to make sure he still had a pulse. His tongue was thick and swollen, dry as the desert in Iraq. He had an overwhelming urge to urinate and he staggered to the bathroom, voiding his bladder into the toilet, the stream splashing wildly around the toilet bowl.

He beat against the wall until he found the light switch and flipped it, the harsh light shocking him back to reality.

There was a knock at the door. He stopped shaking, forcing himself calm. He made it to the door and opened it. John recognized the man standing there, the kind brown eyes, the commanding presence, and the relief settled his stomach. He saluted. "Master Sergeant!"

"You don't have to salute anymore, John," Eric said. "You're in Delta now. We aren't big on salutes." He strode into the room. "What's wrong? You look terrible."

John relaxed. "Sorry, sir. Bad dream." He felt his heart slow and the impending sense of doom lift. He remembered the warehouse, glass windows up high, light streaming through the dusty streaks. The two filthy and sweaty insurgents, their stink heavy in his nose, delighting in his pain as they beat him. Then, light and hope, Wise bursting in, the two men shot, and his hands finally cut free.

"I just—just can't thank you enough for saving me."

Eric smiled. "It's what we do, John. I'm a little concerned that you're still having flashbacks, though. Doc Barnwell said you'd be getting better by now. How's the scar? Feeling okay?" He reached out and lightly touched John's abdomen, to the right of the solar plexus.

John was baffled. "Scar, sir? What scar?"

Eric frowned. "The scar from the Implant. Don't you remember?"

"The Implant?" He felt it then, an ache in his belly. He lifted his shirt and looked down at the inch-long scar on his abdomen, held together with butterfly tape. "How'd that get there?"

"It was the first stage of the project. They put in the Implant three days ago. You don't remember that?" Eric's voice was filled with concern. "What's the last thing you remember?" He sat at the desk and motioned for John to sit on the cot.

John sank down on the cot, confused. "I remember you and Master Sergeant Freeman in Iraq. You said my country needed me. Then I remember out-processing. Coming home. My parents. I was at their funeral.

I remember Washington. I was in DC?" As he said it, that part did not sound right.

"John, your parents died three years ago. Right after you went back to Iraq, your unit was on patrol and you were hit with an IED. You were laid up for a month. We came to you after you recovered. You out-processed months later and we put you up in DC. We picked you up a week ago and brought you here. You've been resting since they put in the Implant and reading your briefing material. Doesn't this sound familiar?"

John thought about it. "Yeah, it sounds familiar," he lied.

Eric nodded. "I'll send Doc Oshensker to see you. I'm concerned about your concussion. Now, how about the Implant. It isn't hurting, is it?"

"Uh, not really, sir. It's just a dull ache. What the hell is it?"

"It's part of the program. To make you a better soldier. We can inject you with painkillers or stimulants to help you on missions. You really don't remember?"

They had implanted a device in his abdomen? He felt ill. "Not really."

"It's okay, John," Eric said. "It'll come back to you. Project StrikeForce, remember? We're going to turn you into the greatest soldier the world has ever known. That's why we put the mesh on your skeleton."

Mesh? "I don't remember that either."

"We coated your skeleton in a nanocarbon mesh. Your bones are stronger now. We'll begin the treatment to enhance your strength and endurance as soon as your abdomen has healed."

John stumbled over the words. "None of this sounds possible." He owed Eric his life, but none of it made sense.

Eric grinned. "Don't worry, son, we'll have the doc look you over. You'll be fine."

* * *

Eric glanced up from his paperwork as Dr. Barnwell entered his office. "How's he doing, Doc?"

Dr. Barnwell took the empty seat across from Eric's desk and paused to accept the coffee Eric poured. "Quite well, actually. The confusion is normal given what he's been through. His body is healing. The Implant is administering small doses of the chemicals into his bloodstream to heal the brain damage. He's still in a suggestible state, but as his brain repairs itself, the new memories will solidify. When you cover explosives, you can casually mention the Red Cross bombing. Make sure to monitor for any signs of agitation."

"Good plan, because after the muscle enhancements, I'd hate to get him agitated."

Barnwell smiled. "Dr. Elliot assures me that it'll be weeks before the drugs start to take effect."

"Doc, he's already gaining muscle mass at an accelerated rate."

"So try not to agitate him."

"You're a world of help."

Dr. Barnwell's smiled grew wider. "Glad to be of assistance. How are you dealing with this?"

"Now you're head-shrinking me?"

"Everyone sees me on a regular basis. Even Nancy, though she hates it."

"What about the Old Man?"

Dr. Barnwell shrugged. "The only confidence *that* man seeks is his own." He took a sip of his coffee. "A month ago you were retired, without a job. Now you're here, in charge of a top-secret organization, working with a mass murderer. How does that make you feel?"

Eric sighed. "I'm just a grunt, doing my job."

"Fulton thinks more highly of you than that," Barnwell said. "He hand-picked you for this assignment. I should know, I've read your after-action reports for the past eight years. I even listened to the audio of your hot washes."

"Hot washes aren't recorded," Eric noted.

"Yours were. Delta has a unique way of doing after-action reviews. You were brutally honest in your assessment of the things that you did well and the things that needed improvement. Even compared to the other Delta Operators, yours stood out."

Eric shook his head. "You listened in? That's kinda creepy."

"Don't worry, I was the only one who heard them. You had a maturity about you. And you were a professional, although I'm a little concerned about your tendency to be manipulated."

Eric glared at him. "What the hell does that mean?"

Dr. Barnwell took a long sip of his coffee. "You have to know, Eric. You find validation in the military. Your father dead, your mother locked up in that home."

"She's not locked up, and it's an assisted care facility."

"What I'm saying is, don't you see the similarity between you and Frist? Both soldiers, both dedicated to their country. Both without parents."

"I didn't go crazy and kill a bunch of people."

"To operate at this level, you have to have a certain sense of self-awareness. You're in charge of a very complicated organization," Barnwell said. "You were an outstanding Operator, but you've got to take it to the next level." He held up his hand as Eric started to interrupt. "I'm not saying you shouldn't have accepted the job. You have to think like a chess player, except the board has an infinite number of chess pieces and any mistake could get people killed."

Eric sat back in his chair and pondered that. "Is that how the Old Man sees the world?"

"He thinks things through," Barnwell said, "layer after layer. He has a contingency plan. For everything. He showed up on your doorstep after you were sidelined and offered you the job. How long did you stew before you said yes? An hour?"

Barnwell was right, he *had* jumped at the offer. He shrugged. "I'm a soldier. It's what I do."

"Working with Frist ... that can't be easy."

Eric struggled to articulate his feelings. "The IED really messed him up and he's got PTSD for sure, but bombing the Red Cross crossed the line. What do you think, Doc? What makes the measure of a man? His words or his actions?"

"His PTSD might have been a misdiagnosis. The amount of brain damage from the IED was more severe than we anticipated. Tell me, with all the combat you've seen, have you ever experienced any symptoms of PTSD?"

Eric grinned. "Nice try. You think I'd be stupid enough to tell you if I did?"

Barnwell sighed. "I'm not trying to catch you in something, and it's completely off the record."

He shook his head. "Doc, if there's one thing I've learned, it's that nothing here is off the record."

"I could make it an order if you'd prefer."

He started to speak, then stopped. Finally, he said, "Honestly? No, I've never had PTSD. I've had some stress, but nothing severe. I've been keyed up after some missions, but nothing out of the ordinary."

Barnwell leaned forward. "Does it make you feel guilty?"

"I used to wonder if it meant there was something wrong with me. I don't know, you're the doctor. What do you think?"

"I think some of it is luck, frankly. Some of it indicates you're remarkably well adjusted. Some of it is probably training," Barnwell said. "Perhaps it's not a bad thing."

"Yeah, I figured that out a while ago. There's a hell of a lot of guys who would gladly switch places with me, including Frist."

Barnwell shook his head. "I'm sure he would," he said softly. "If he still remembered. We've undone him. He's just a soldier now, not a terrorist. As you build that relationship, you will always know what he did, even though he doesn't."

Eric leaned back in his chair and regarded Barnwell thoughtfully. "Your point?"

"You have to put that out of your head. He's a soldier, giving his life to this project. If you focus on who he was before, he'll know. Subconsciously, perhaps, but he will detect it, in your posture, or the tone of your voice. If you want the project to succeed, you have to believe in him."

"What if I can't?"

"Then the project will fail." Barnwell stood and placed his empty cup on the desk. "Thanks for the coffee." He started to leave, then stopped. "A word of advice. When you're not working with him directly, don't *ever* forget what he did. Always think three steps ahead, because that man has the souls of five hundred and twelve innocent people tipping the scales against him."

* * *

John grunted as he lifted the kettlebells, swinging them up and across his body. The workout area was loaded with benches and power cages, but Eric kept pushing free weights.

The aches felt good, the muscles straining and burning as the weights created micro-tears in the muscle fibers. His mind certainly felt better, clear of the confusion from the previous weeks.

Dr. Elliot watched and took notes on a palmtop computer, along with a pretty brunette nurse named Kara. Occasionally they would present the readouts to Eric, who would holler encouragement.

He liked Eric. He was patient but exacting. He reminded him of his sergeant in boot camp, except Eric was more astute, with a boundless amount of information on guns, knives, close combat—everything but explosives.

He wondered if Eric was afraid introducing explosives would trigger his PTSD. He reassured Eric there was nothing to fear. The bad dreams had subsided, and the memory of the IED faded quickly, a little more each day, until he woke up one morning and realized he had slept through the night.

He found Deion less likable. Certainly less approachable. They were both in ridiculously good shape, Eric all muscle and scars, Deion shorter but leaner, more lithe. The difference was in the eyes. When Deion smiled at Eric, he meant it—when he smiled at John, something was missing.

John thought it was something he might have said or done, some careless word that had pissed Deion off. He worked hard to compensate, trying to learn everything they taught, from the hands-on training to the never-ending reading material.

The amount they expected him to read was overwhelming. There was so much information, he felt if even one more drop entered his head, it would explode. Then, the next day, a whole new section of reading material would introduce him to new procedures, new strategies, and new tactics.

"Drop the weights and hit the rope," Eric shouted.

John dropped the kettle bell and picked up the leather speed-rope. He swung, hopping up enough for the brown leather to swish under his feet. He spun the rope faster, the ball-bearings allowing the rope to become a blur. He lost himself in the motion, his body on autopilot, machine-like in its precision.

His mind wandered to the tech in his body. The day before, Eric had turned a heat gun on his arm, hot enough to burn but not enough to blister. They'd activated the pain meds in the Implant and the relief had been instant. It had felt so cool and sweet he'd almost laughed. He'd tried to explain to them how good the meds felt, but Eric had just stared worriedly.

If only his parents could see him, maybe his old man would finally approve. A sudden jolt ran through him and he stumbled on the rope. Eric and Dr. Elliot stopped their discussion, but he smiled at them and forced himself back into the rhythm of the workout.

So weird. He remembered the news about their death. A drunk driver had crossed the median, just an accident, and they had been killed instantly. He had tried to make it to their funeral. No, he corrected himself, he *had* made it to their funeral.

The memory was foggy. He remembered the priest, the people. Nobody he recognized, though. Funny, old man Peterson who lived across the street hadn't been there. Had Peterson died? What about his mom's friend, Pearl? Unless she was dead as well. Had she died while he was on deployment? Surely his mom would have mentioned it.

Eric broke him out of his musing, showing him the readout. "You set a new personal best. Go hit the showers, then the cafeteria. You need simple carbs and protein. Kara," he said, jerking his thumb at the nurse, "will be by after to draw more blood."

John headed to the showers. He soaped up under the steaming hot water and let slide the thought of the missing people at his parents' funeral. It was probably just side effects of the IED.

* * *

John stood in the training room listening to Eric's lecture. Deion watched, his mouth quirked in a barely recognizable smile.

"The thing to remember," Eric said, "is that this isn't like the training you received in the Army. Your goal is to survive and to kill your opponent. You've been in battle. Did you ever freeze?"

He was embarrassed to admit it, but he had. He nodded.

Eric continued. "What did you feel?"

"Fear," John said. "I aimed my rifle, but when I squeezed the trigger nothing happened. I thought it was jammed. I cleared the chamber and tried again, but it was like moving in molasses. Bullets were whizzing by, I could hear them over the gunfire. It felt like I had all the time in the world, but my hands were clumsy and my fingers felt like sausages. Then it was over. My CO came over and slapped me in the back of the head. I'd had the safety on. Why didn't I realize that?"

Eric smiled. "It's a common reaction, John. Millions of years of evolution. You've evolved so that when the shit hits the fan, your brain processes only the information right in front of you. They call it tunnel vision. That happen to you?"

"Yeah, like a small circle right in front of my eyes, everything else just blurry, like a fun house mirror."

"That's the brain focusing on the important parts, the visual stimuli. Thousands of years ago, it would have been a snake or a lion. The brain dismissed everything except the threat in front of you. Same thing for the clumsiness. The body pulls the blood to your core, and your fingers and feet go cold and numb. Audio does weird things. Sometimes you can't hear anything around you, sometimes you hear things far away. It was really useful then, but not so much now. What we have to do is train you to react to the fight-or-flight situation so that you *don't* lose sight of everything around you. A real fight is short and nasty. You want to kill the other person, not maim or wound them. You want to do a shocking amount of violence to them before they can do it to you, and you want to be as quick and efficient as possible. Now, put in your mouthguard and come at me."

John nodded. He half circled Eric, then lunged in, swinging for Eric's solar plexus. Eric sidestepped and brought his palm up against John's throat, making him gasp for air, but before he could draw a breath, Eric kicked his legs out from under him.

He collapsed and Eric was on top, jamming thumbs into his eyes. He screamed as his eyes watered, curling into a fetal position on the blue padded mat. He felt Eric get up and opened his eyes. Through the tears, he saw Eric standing, an impassive look on his face.

Deion smirked next to him.

He wiped at his eyes, trying to clear the tears. Snot ran down the back of his throat and he coughed, trying to swallow. He spat out the mouthguard. "Sorry, Eric. I don't know what happened."

"You reacted like a normal human being. First, don't *ever* swing a closed fist at someone's jaw or nose—you stand a good chance of breaking your knuckles. You'd have a hell of a time firing a gun after that. If you aim for the nose, the natural human reaction is for your opponent to drop his head, then you hit him right in the skull, breaking your knuckles. You did good going for the solar plexus. A good stiff punch there can take your opponent's breath away. You see how I kicked out your legs? The lunge wasn't a mistake, but it wasn't good either. The more aggressive opponent usually wins."

John nodded, his hands trembling. Eric noticed and had John extend them.

"See that? Trembling is the aftereffect of the adrenaline rush. Your nervous system is wired for fight or flight. It'll wear off shortly. You'll feel tired, like you ran a marathon. All completely normal. We'll be integrating the Implant later. It will give you an edge, but for now we want you to learn to fight without it. Notice that I went for the throat? Funny how a blow to the throat, even a weak one, can take the fight out of someone. Then you continue, you don't ever let up. If this fight had been real, I would have continued when you hit the ground, kicking you in the kidneys, the head, then finished you with a knife or gun. Now, how's the adrenaline? Wearing off?"

"Yeah, I don't feel like I have to puke or piss anymore."

Deion laughed. "Don't let Wise get you down. It wasn't half-bad for a beginner."

"Now," Eric said, "we're going to do it again."

John nodded and calmed himself as he put his mouthguard back in. He circled Eric, looking for an opportunity. Eric shifted his weight, then snapped a palm toward John's eyes. John blocked it and brought his knee forward, catching Eric in the stomach. Eric doubled over but turned that movement into a lunge forward with his shoulder, striking him in the chest.

He stumbled back and swung his palm against Eric's nose, but Eric blocked it smoothly, then continued the hand forward to claw John's eyes. John twisted away, and Eric's palm struck his ear. There was an explosion of pain, and he collapsed, stunned, Eric on him again, striking his stomach and groin. Even though Eric was pulling his punches, he still felt the shock of blows across his body. Eric stopped suddenly and stuck out his hand, helping him up.

Deion laughed. "How you feeling now, John?"

"Like I got run over by a truck," John wheezed. His lungs pumped like a steam locomotive as he struggled to catch his breath. He had a stinging pain where Eric had made contact, and he knew he would have purple bruises the next day. "I just can't seem to hold you off."

"Of course not," Eric agreed, "because I've had a ton of practice and I've had to use it. It's a funny thing, though. With all that I've been through, there's still a moment of hesitation before I'm ready to strike. The trick is to make that moment as short as possible. That's what I'm going to teach you."

"Why do I get the feeling that learning is going to be painful?"

"Because you're not stupid," Deion cackled. "And because you're right. It's gonna be painful."

Eric nodded toward Deion. "Now, Freeman here hasn't been in that much combat. He's had all the training, and he's been on a couple of missions, but he spent most of his time on his comfortable ass, back at base, while us ground humpers did all the work."

Deion shrugged. "Work smart, not hard, that's what my paps used to say."

Eric beamed. "Good, then you won't mind showing John how it's done. John, he's got a lot less experience than me, you'll stand a better chance."

"I'd never go one-on-one. I'd rather come up behind him in an alley and put a bullet through the back of his head."

John shivered. He believed Deion.

Deion put in his mouthguard and approached. He outweighed Deion by thirty pounds and was a few inches taller. He hoped that was enough. He tried a feint to Deion's throat, but Deion blocked it and grabbed his arm, pulling him forward. John tried to strike Deion in the stomach, but Deion grabbed John's shirt and hip tossed him to the mat. He landed hard, and before he could recover, Deion had him face-first on the mat, his arm in a joint lock, and was elbowing him in the kidneys. He yelped, and Deion let up.

Deion grinned. "Now that's how I'd do it. If I had to."

John groaned. "The fun is quickly fading."

"Get used to it," Eric said. "It's only going to get worse."

* * *

Eric circled John warily, his boots shuffling against the padded blue mats. He watched the young man, waiting for the opportunity to attack.

"Why do I have to learn to fight with a knife?" John asked.

"Sometimes you have to get up close and personal," he answered. "Plus, a knife doesn't jam or run out of ammo. Now, come at me again."

John held the rubber knife in his right hand, his fingers wrapped around the hilt, the knife blade sticking out like he was holding a hatchet. "This just seems uncomfortable."

Eric grinned. "That's because you've seen too much television. Remember, don't swing with the knife. If you lead with it, I can knock it away or take it from you. Strike with your left hand. When I move to block it, stab with your right."

He watched John, not focusing on any specific body part, and saw the flicker of motion as John feinted with his fist. He drew back and John never came close, but his frustration grew. "Damn it, John, I told you, that's a good way to break your knuckles. The *side* of your first, and don't aim for the jaw, aim for the ear. I know, it's hard, but you've got bad habits to unlearn."

Deion laughed. "Kick his ass, John!"

John nodded. He feinted again, coming fast against Eric's neck, then swung up and clipped Eric in the ear. Eric winced, then felt John's rubber knife stab into his armpit. He dropped to his knees, but John was waiting. He smashed the heel of his hand against Eric's nose, then stabbed again with the rubber knife, jamming it into Eric's neck.

He hit the floor, John on top, stabbing his neck through the tangle of his hands and arms. He collapsed, and John slashed the rubber knife hard across Eric's neck, which would have severed the artery if the blade had been steel.

"Good, that's good," Eric managed. John stuck out his hand and hauled him to his feet. He shook off the ringing in his ear. "Again."

They repeated the exercise. This time, John's palm struck Eric in the nose hard enough to draw tears, then the knife strike to the throat. Eric stabbed his knife against John's right arm, but it wasn't enough. When Eric collapsed, John switched the knife to his left hand and used his right palm to strike Eric in the nose and eyes, stabbing at his throat, belly, and groin when Eric fell.

"Now you're getting the hang of it," Eric said. "Remember, if you get stabbed or slashed, you *will* bleed. There's not much you can do to stop it. The thing is to continue the fight. You might lose movement in an arm or hand, but you'll survive. The other guy won't. Once he's been stabbed, he won't be able to do much to protect himself. Trust me, I've been stabbed before. It's hard to think straight. Against an untrained opponent, a strike to the throat won't kill them immediately, but they'll bleed out soon enough. Now, again."

Deion watched without comment, shifting from their session to his palmtop computer.

They continued for an hour until they were both covered in sweat, deep circles under the armpits of their shirts, both huffing for air.

"Stop," Deion said. "John, how you feeling? Tired?"

John nodded. "I'm beat."

"Good," Deion said. "It's time to try the Implant. It's probably gonna feel weird at first, but it's just adrenaline and a few other things."

"It'll be okay, John," Eric said. "Just relax this first time."

"Okay, activating it … now," Deion said.

John's eyes widened. "My heart sped up." He nodded, bent down at the knees, and came back up. "Yeah, definitely the heart's pounding. And I'm hot. Really hot."

"Hang in there," Deion said. "Now again, this time, really kick his ass. Wise, you better be sharp, man."

Eric had been waiting to see the Implant in action. The young man was stronger every day and his reflexes were vastly improved. God help them if the Implant juiced him too much.

John circled him again, his eyes bright and his motions faster, more precise.

Eric was exhausted, and it was all he could do to keep John's palm from driving into his nose. He tried to land a blow on the young man's neck, but John spun sideways and stabbed the knife deep into his bicep, making him yelp in pain.

John's foot caught him in the knee, dropping him to the ground, and then John was on him. He felt the rubber knife stab him in the neck, then John's fist in his solar plexus, and the rake of the knife against his throat. He stopped and looked up, John standing over him, his hand extended. He took it and John easily yanked him up.

"Yeah, that's how it's done," Eric gasped. "How do you feel now?"

Deion laughed. "He feels like he just kicked your ass, man. Kicked it."

"Pretty good," John said ruefully. "Everything is bright and clear. I feel like I could take on ten men."

Eric rubbed the spot on his tricep where John had tagged him. *He's quick.* "Yeah, well, don't get cocky. The drugs can make you feel invincible, but you're still human. Lactic acid still builds up in your muscles."

John stuck out his arm and flexed his bicep. "Yeah, but I've got more muscles now."

Eric grinned. It was true. The cocktail of muscle-enhancement drugs, steroids, and human growth hormones was working miracles. John's strict diet helped, the protein, fat, and carbs timed throughout the day to match the cardio and workouts, running and weightlifting, rope climbing and burpees.

John's strength was increasing at a dramatic rate, but Dr. Elliot assured them it would soon level off. For now, he was approaching the top percentile for strength and endurance, and Eric had the bruises to prove it. The simple truth was the young man was strong, and the training was making him more dangerous each day.

"Just remember," Eric said. "The Weave will protect your arms and legs, your ribs and skull, but a jump from two stories onto concrete could break your foot or ankle, or worse, you could suffer an aortic dissection. You can't ignore basic physics. All this tech does is make you tough. It doesn't make you impossible to kill."

"Got it." John turned to Deion. "You hear that! I'm not impossible to kill!"

Deion nodded, smirking.

CHAPTER SIX

John stared at the solid black helmet, a clamshell that hinged on the top, and shivered at the sinister piece of gear.

They were in one of the labs, Eric holding the helmet in front of him while Deion stood behind, his hand on John's shoulder.

"Just relax," Eric said. "When it's in place, we'll close it. When it seals, you should feel a slight breeze as the environmental systems come online."

He eyed it skeptically. "How am I supposed to see out of this thing? It's solid plastic."

Dr. Elliot looked up from his workstation. "Trust us, John. This is the Visual Improvement System for Optical Recognition, or VISOR. It's much more than just a helmet. It might even save your life one day."

Eric and Deion struggled to slide it around John's head. They managed to work it around his scalp, then lowered the clamshell and snapped it in place.

He heard a metallic click and jerked, but Deion's steady hand reassured him. He felt a moment of claustrophobia, the dark interior unnaturally close to his skin, and he took a deep breath. "It smells funny," he said.

"That's just new car smell," Dr. Elliot said, laughing. "Wait for it, the environment system is coming up now."

A faint hiss emanated from the base of the helmet, and he felt instant relief. "That's better, there's a cool breeze and the smell is fading. I still can't see anything, though."

"I'm initiating the display," Dr. Elliot said.

"I see it." A faint glow pulsed in front of his eyes, then the world sprung into view, as clear as a window. "Oh, wow."

"What do you think?" Dr. Elliot asked.

He shook his head and took note of the extra weight from the helmet. "It's amazing. Everything is bright and defined. It's better than real life."

"The sensors embedded in the front of the helmet detect a range of data, including visual and infrared, then merge it and present it to the LCD screens located in front of each eye. Now, let's turn on the thermal overlay."

The world became a rich-hued display of reds and blues, unlike the gray shades he expected. "Hey, this looks like the movie *Predator.*"

Eric and Deion both laughed at the reference, but Dr. Elliot was unamused. "The VISOR cost us a small fortune. It's not a toy. Let me dial the contrast down a bit. How's that?"

"Better, Doc." The thermal colors receded, no longer overpowering the video. When he turned, he saw the red in Eric's cheeks, and the cooler blue in his arms.

"Wait until dark," Eric said. "You won't ever need NVGs again."

Dr. Elliot continued, "It has air filters to scrub smoke and gas. There's a three-minute air supply, and it's rated for fifty meters underwater. Audio microphones on each side of the VISOR work like eardrums, only more sensitive. The gain can be increased until you hear even the faintest sounds, and they have automatic gain reduction so loud blasts won't deafen you. Most importantly, the ceramic plates and carbon fiber weave will keep your head safe from anything short of a large-caliber bullet."

"When can I try it out?" he asked.

"Slow down, man," Deion said. "It's got a learning curve. First you have to train it."

"Train it?"

"There's a band of neural sensors around the skull," Dr. Elliot said. "It works by thought. We'll have you think about the commands and the VISOR will learn to read your brain patterns. You'll be able to switch views on the fly."

He spent the next several hours in the lab, practicing the commands until the VISOR responded to his every thought.

When the VISOR training was complete, they led him to a darkened hangar, where he navigated an obstacle course as if in full daylight.

"The best is yet to come," Eric said.

"Yeah," Deion said, "we have a surprise for you."

They led him from the underground base, his first time outside in over a month.

Eric drove the beat-up pickup through gullies and dusty trails until they passed into a larger valley among the mountains, the stillness of the inky-black night was broken only by the throaty growl of the truck.

He looked up. The VISOR showed him twinkling stars filling the sky, the Milky Way a blazing ribbon of light stretched across the horizon.

They came to a fork in the dirt road, and Eric stopped the truck. John got out, mindful of the extra mass from the VISOR. He was trying to take in the stars all at once, amazed at the VISOR's clarity.

Eric keyed his walkie-talkie. "John, can you hear me?"

The audio was crystal clear. "Yes," he answered.

"The radio in the VISOR is good for about ten clicks. We want you to head out west, through the bomb craters."

"What bomb craters?"

"Activate the night vision," Eric said, "and you'll see."

He concentrated and the valley floor opened in front of him. He saw the pockmarks in the distance, some large enough to swallow a car, some big enough to swallow a house. "Oh, those craters."

"Yeah," Eric said, "this used to be a bomb range during World War Two. The desert floor looks like the surface of the moon."

Dr. Elliot's voice came through the VISOR. "John, we're getting excellent readings back in the command center. We've got a drone overhead, relaying the telemetry. The HUD will combine this with the terrain info and you'll get a sense of what the VISOR can really do."

He was already impressed by the VISOR, but now he was amazed. The screen shifted and the world appeared in hyperdetail. Ghostly blue outlines appeared in the HUD, suspended in front of him. Numbers showed the ambient air temperature and humidity, GPS coordinates, and compass.

A split screen appeared on the right side of the HUD, an overhead display showing him as a small speck standing next to a truck, Eric and Deion lounging against it.

He looked to a large crater off in the distance, and a number appeared on the display. Six hundred and twenty-seven meters. He stepped toward the crater and the number decreased by one meter. He stepped back and the number increased by one meter. He turned his head back to Eric and Deion, and the compass spun to the east. "Whoa."

"Take it easy," Eric said. "You might suffer from sensory overload. If it's too much, just close your eyes and take a deep breath. Now, get hiking." He pointed to the west.

John moved, his boots stepping lightly over the rock. He found himself picking up speed, until soon he was running. For the first time, he felt the effects of the enhancement drugs, the resistance training, and the cardio workouts. His feet floated over the hardscrabble dirt and rock, his body surging effortlessly through the night.

He was halfway to the distant crater when Dr. Elliot called for him to stop. "John, turn back and see if you can spot the truck."

He turned and saw the vehicle in the distance. "Yeah, I see it."

"Good. Now concentrate. Think of increased magnification."

He did and the display zoomed in. He concentrated harder and the display zoomed in closer, until the truck appeared just yards away, Deion and Eric still leaning against it. He focused and the image zoomed back out.

"Good," Dr. Elliot said. "Very good. I'm impressed. You've got it. Eric, give him a show."

He watched as Eric pulled a large rifle from the back of the pickup, loaded it, then turned at an angle and shot off into the distance. The rifle's laser range finder blazed as a visible thread of light projected upward. The path of the bullet glowed, trailing off into the distance, its paths diverging from the laser as gravity inevitably pulled the round back to earth. "Is that a tracer?"

"No," Dr. Elliot responded. "That's a standard round. What you're seeing is the heat signature overlaid with the night vision."

"This thing is incredible."

Dr. Elliot laughed. "Thanks, but remember, this isn't for your enjoyment. This technology is designed to help you accomplish your mission."

He spent several hours tromping across the desert, practicing with the VISOR. At times, he became overloaded with data, but he gradually learned to manage the VISOR's output until the night held no surprises. He was both exhilarated and exhausted as dawn approached and Eric finally drove them back to the tunnel entrance.

* * *

John met Eric and Deion the next morning in the training room and found them standing around a dummy wearing a suit of black fabric and plastic panels. He was still giddy from the night before, but he quickly sobered at the site of the flat-black gear.

"Are you ready for the Battlesuit?" Eric asked.

He paced around the plastic dummy, inspecting it. "Is this like the body armor I wore in Iraq? Because I hated that. It was hot as hell. I always felt like I was smothering."

Eric shook his head. "Nothing like that. The fabric has been treated with chemicals that will help regulate your body temperature. It'll keep you warm when you're cold and cool when you're warm. Don't ask me how it works because I don't know. It's soft and breathable and will stretch to fit your body. The panels are liquid body armor. When a bullet strikes the gel, it instantly crystallizes and spreads the kinetic energy across the entire surface area. It'll stop a 7.62 round at ten yards. It'll stop .45 handgun ammo at point-blank range. Each panel can take several hits before you lose structural integrity."

Deion laughed. "Try not to get hit more than once, man. Otherwise, you've fucked up."

"Good point," Eric agreed. "This isn't a get-out-of-jail-free card. This might mean the difference between living and dying, but whatever is shooting at you, you better shoot back."

He pointed at the webbing that crossed at the chest. "What's with the straps?"

"That's your gear harness. You strap your rifle to it when you HALO jump, it'll keep your weapon from ripping away from your body." Eric pointed to a plastic bump on the back. "This is your backpack. Notice the small size. It's designed to keep your body profile to a minimum. There's room for a basic ration pack and a water pouch with integrated nipple. You don't even have to stop for a drink when you're on the move. There's an emergency medical kit and a survival pack." He pointed to the plastic bumps on each side of the hips. "These are your holsters, one for each hand. When they lock in place, you can run full speed."

"And the ankle sheath?"

Eric smiled. "There's always room for a Ka-Bar knife. What do you think?"

He eyed the sleek and menacing Battlesuit. "I can't wait to try it on."

* * *

Eric was filling out electronic forms when Smith entered. He glanced up and then back down at his monitor. "You'd think a top-secret organization would generate less paperwork."

"A good organization *runs* on paperwork," Smith said. "I thought you'd been in the regular Army." He took a seat across from Eric's desk, lowering himself gently into the padded seat. "These old bones bother me now and then, something I'm sure a young man like yourself hasn't encountered yet."

He smiled ruefully. "I'm beginning to understand. After training with Frist all day and reviewing paperwork all night, I feel ten years older."

There was a soft knock at the door and Nancy entered. She patted her father on the shoulder, and he took her wrist and held it to his cheek. She pulled away slowly, then took the seat beside him.

Eric tried not to notice how well the blue skirt and white shirt accentuated her lithe body.

She squinted at him, then turned to her father. "Did I interrupt?"

Smith smiled at her. "No, dear. Eric was just informing me that he was feeling his age."

Nancy turned back to Eric. "Heh. You don't say?"

"Frist is a handful," he said. That was an understatement. His combat tours had left fewer bruises than he now sported. "I'm introducing him to weapons tomorrow."

"Excellent," Smith said. "Dr. Elliot is quite pleased with the progress, as is Dr. Oshensker. The Implant functions well?"

"It's remarkable. Freeman and I put him through the wringer, a twenty-mile jog with a weighted pack. He was totally spent. We activated the Implant and he went another twenty. Doc Barnwell wasn't too pleased about it, though."

Smith frowned. "For all the enhancements, he's still just human."

"We have to know his limits," Eric said.

"I'm aware of the testing protocols. It's not out of concern for Frist's feelings. He's our only candidate."

"What about his memory?" Nancy asked.

"There've been no signs that he remembers anything," Eric said. "He was confused, at first, but that's gone. We're monitoring for mood disturbances. We've tapered him off the drugs, except for the strength cocktail. Barnwell says the false memories are fully integrated."

Nancy's pale blue eyes were cold and hard. "At the first sign of problems, blow his brains out."

"I'll keep that under advisement," he said dryly.

"How are things on deck?" Smith asked.

Eric paused. "It's overwhelming. There's so much raw intel. The analysts do an incredible job, but I'm still having trouble determining which are actionable and which can be ignored."

"Don't be hard on yourself," Smith said. "Your primary duty is training Frist. You will soon be fully capable of running the command deck, and I'm sure Nancy will show you some of the finer aspects of the intelligence reports."

Nancy arched her eyebrow. "I will?"

Smith patted her hand. "Of course. Shall I make that an order?"

Nancy shook her head. "Hard to give orders when I'm not technically in any command structure."

"Humor your father, will you? Please help bring Mr. Wise and Mr. Freeman up to speed."

"Of course," Nancy said. "Always willing to take one for the team. Blah blah, blah."

Smith silenced her with a look. "You'll do as I ask."

Eric almost missed her grimace.

"Yes, sir. Excuse me, I've got things to do." She stood and glared at Eric. "I'll see you tomorrow morning, before your training sessions with Frist." She left, and although she did not sullenly slam the door, it was close.

Smith eyed the door. "Sorry for that. She doesn't like taking orders, even from me. My fault, really. She didn't have a normal childhood, although I tried to make sure there were a few gentle years."

Curious, he asked, "What's her deal, anyway? What role does she fill?"

Smith adjusted his tie. "She is one of the deck commanding officers. She handles special assignments. She's performed several targeted assassinations." Noticing the look on Eric's face, Smith continued, "Try not to look so shocked. She received combat and firearm training before she could drive. She had just turned eighteen when she joined the Office. She was eager to please her father." His voice trailed off.

Eric waited as the man fumbled with his tie.

"Less so when she found out what we do," Smith continued. "Her first assignment went poorly and she killed a man we needed alive. The operation was a failure. I won't bore you with the details, but many innocent men and women died because of that failure. She took it very personally."

"Everyone makes mistakes," Eric offered.

"Surely they do, and I told her as much. She changed after that, became more aggressive, more stubborn, more violent. The harder she tried, the less effective she became. I finally gave her a choice—either modify her behavior or be removed from the Office. Do you know how hard that was?"

Eric shook his head. "Of course I don't."

Smith's eyes bored into his. "She's my only child. It would be worse to lose her. If she died because of me, I believe I might lose all sense of perspective. Do you understand what that means?"

Eric thought about what Fulton Smith could do with the power and the resources of the Office and felt a cold pit in his stomach.

"Yes," Smith said. "I can see that you do. I've been the Director for over fifty years. I've always done the right thing, you understand? Even Nancy's birth was an accident. I didn't want a child, someone who would suffer through having me as a father. What life could I give her? She wanted to join the Office, but one wrong mission and she could be caught, tortured, or even killed." Smith stopped fiddling with his tie. "No one on this earth would be safe if that happened. I would make the world burn."

Eric shuddered. Smith's life was a lonely place, full of power and responsibility, and his daughter suffered for it. He tucked the sudden insight away and nodded.

"I'm sorry, I didn't mean to burden you with this, but you'll be working with her and I need to know you'll protect her. From those who might hurt her. From herself. You're a man of your word. Promise me that?"

"Yes, sir." Eric rose as Smith stood and shook Smith's hand. "Was there anything else?"

"I'm returning to Washington tomorrow. Continue with Frist. Nancy will be in charge of your training on deck, but remember, you answer only to me. No matter what she may say."

Eric nodded. "I'll remember."

* * *

There was a knock on Eric's door at 0600. He opened it and found Nancy waiting, Deion in tow. "You ready," she asked, "or would you like a hot shower and a donut?"

"I've been waiting for the past hour," Eric said with a grin. "Already went over the duty roster. Even had time for my donut."

Deion smirked but stopped when Nancy glared at him.

She talked as she led them to the War Room. "The first thing you need to understand is that the AIs comb the data, but they're only as good as the analyst who programmed them. Each analyst can change their AI's search criteria. If they tag something, it gets saved and rolled over to the next shift."

They entered through the War Room's mantrap, and the sergeant manning the deck saluted. "Commander on deck!"

Nancy nodded as control was passed to her. "What have we got today, Sergeant Clark?"

Clark sighed. "There's a North Korean trawler that's not where it's supposed to be. We've got something happening in the financial markets in Greece. Al-Sadr's men are causing problems in Iraq, but the surge seems to be holding. There's chatter about a white supremacist group in Colorado. Afghanistan is still Afghanistan."

"Thank you, Sergeant, you're relieved." Nancy turned to question Deion and Eric. "So, which of these requires attention?"

Eric glanced at Deion, but Deion waved for Eric to go first.

"The Greek markets could be serious," he said, "but there's not much we can do about that. Al-Sadr is a pain in the ass, but the surge will hold, based upon evidence, so we pass the concern along to JSOC. The trawler is a problem, though."

"Why so? Freeman, you're up."

Deion nodded. "Ever since Japan captured that trawler a few years ago, tensions have been high. If it's another spy boat fitted out like a trawler, it could destabilize the entire region. We can't just blow it out of the water. That would make it an international incident. Our best option is to pass it along to JSOC as well, let them deal with it."

Nancy turned to Eric. "Do you agree?"

He nodded. "The SEALs could handle it discreetly."

Nancy nodded. "Good call." She turned to Sergeant Clark. "Sergeant, make it happen."

Clark nodded. "I'll pass it along to our people in JSOC."

Nancy turned back to Eric. "Now, what about the white supremacists?"

He shrugged. "It depends on the intel. Sergeant, what's the scoop?"

Clark tapped out commands on his keyboard and one of the analysts, a thick brunette woman, hurried to the control deck, a coffee cup in hand. "This is Karen Kryzowski."

Karen smiled and then explained, "A group we've been tracking for years is acting up. The APR, American Patriot Revolution. There's chatter, but no specifics. It could be drugs, but more likely guns. The part that concerns me is that they're speaking in codes."

"What do you know about this group?" Eric asked.

"Mostly petty criminals until about two years ago. It was guns and meth, but they graduated to armed robbery. They have strong views about an upcoming race war."

Nancy pursed her lips. "Are they on the feebs' radar?"

Karen laughed. "The FBI has a file on them that goes back decades, but they don't know about the robberies and murders of the past two years. They liked them for an anthrax scare six months ago, envelopes sent to a congressman's office. They could never make it stick, but the Office has an email trail. They're good for it."

He felt a knot twist in his stomach. "Great, a white supremacist group with anthrax."

"No, sir," Karen said, shaking her head, "they didn't have anthrax. Turned out to be flour."

"I'd suggest we turn it over to the FBI," Eric said, "maybe send the gun-running info to the ATF."

"Good plan," Nancy agreed. "We funnel the info to them, let them clean up the mess. Dismissed, Kryzowski. Now, what about Afghanistan?"

Eric turned back to Clark. "What's the status?"

"Same as usual. Insurgents all over the place, Taliban mostly. The high-value targets are on the run. They've dug in deep in the mountains or blended into the urban areas. We have picked up some signals, back-channel stuff. We're surveilling their cell phones and what few landlines they have, Internet activity is being logged and filtered, but they've gotten smart. They do everything via courier and paper. HUMINT remains weak. You were stationed in Afghanistan for some time, if I'm not mistaken."

"I'd say that was top secret, but I have a feeling you already know that."

Clark grinned. "Yes, sir. We keep a pretty good eye on the Delta Operators, and your name came up often."

"I'll take it as a compliment. So, what is the nature of the threat, if we don't have hard intelligence?"

"An Internet posting. There was a photo with stego'd information, no details, no names—"

"Is there anything scheduled?" Deion interrupted. "Any major activity planned?"

"No," Clark said. "It's one photo. It could be nothing. JSOC isn't aware of it, and if you pass it to them without hard data, there's not much they can do."

Eric turned to Nancy. "What do you recommend?"

"You'd think with all this information flowing through here we would have more hard intel," Nancy said, "but this is usually all we get. Without actionable intelligence, we have to let it pass. Or we could ping JSOC and have them shake the trees, but each action has a reaction. What do you think might occur?"

Eric recalled his past experiences. "You make the rounds from corrupt politician to corrupt tribal leader, but nobody ever knows anything. What intelligence you get is useless, or worse, deliberate misinformation. Or they shake you down for money. It's a waste of time."

"Exactly. For now, we'll continue to watch. Sergeant, have them follow up with that photo. Find out who owns it and flag it for review."

Clark saluted, but Nancy had already turned her attention to the main monitor. "When will Frist be ready?"

"Hard to say," Deion replied. "Even with the training, his first time out will be rough. It's different in the field."

She turned to Eric, lips pursed. "You think he'll perform?"

"He'll perform," Eric said. "He's shaping up to be a competent soldier."

"He should have been shot."

"You don't like him much, do you?"

"I have no use for him," she said. "The project was my father's idea. Frist is a murderer and a traitor and I'd just as soon see him dead. When you're done with his training today, I want both of you in my office at twenty hundred."

* * *

John took one look and turned back to Eric. "What is this place?"

They were in a small hangar, looking at a construction of drywall and paneling held together by two-by-four walls. There were windows with lights and cables strung everywhere, and inside he could barely discern the furniture-filled room.

"The shooting house," Eric said. "This is where you learn to shoot."

"I thought I *was* learning to shoot," he protested. "I'm at the range every day."

Eric laughed. "We've created the first floor of an apartment building. There are pop-up targets, stationary targets, and movable targets. Don't worry about ricochets, the bullet traps will catch them. Now, it's time to pick your weapon." He led John to a table near the front.

Eric picked up one of the many handguns on the table. "This is your standard Colt M1911. Nothing fancy. It's been cleaned up and fine-tuned, and we swapped out the hammer for an upgrade so you won't get pinched in the webbing between your thumb and index finger. It's a perfectly serviceable weapon."

He picked it up, inspected it, then handed it back to Eric. "Why a forty-five?"

"You lose round capacity over a nine millimeter, but it has more stopping power." Eric picked up another and handed it to John. "This is a standard Sig Sauer M11, but chambered in forty instead of nine mil." He handed it to John, who inspected it as well.

"This one," Eric said, picking up another, "trades stopping power for magazine capacity. It's a Browning Hi-Power, nine millimeter. You get almost double the rounds, and it's accurate. It's the pistol that shoots like a rifle."

John exchanged the Sig Sauer for the Browning, sighted, then looked up at Eric. "What am I supposed to do?"

"Pick one. Your weapon is a personal choice; it has to feel good to you."

The Browning felt good in his hands. He pulled back the slide, checked the chamber, then picked up a full magazine from the table and inserted it.

"Concentrate on the weight of it. The feel of it. Don't sight down it, just let it become one with your arm. Do you feel it?"

John nodded. "Yeah, it feels good, just not quite right." He swapped the Browning for the Colt, and even though he had more experience with it, it held no appeal. "Something is off with this one. It's almost there, but let me try the M11 again."

Eric took the Colt and handed him the M11.

He extended his arm and closed his eyes, letting his hand move with the weight, and he knew he had found it. "I don't know why, but it just feels right. That's the one."

Eric shook his head, clearly disappointed. "I was hoping you'd go for the Colt, but it's your choice. I'm going to teach you to become more than a good shot. Anyone can learn that. You'll become magic. You'll be able to go through the shooting house and put bullet after bullet in the same place. When we're done with that, you'll do it all over again with the Battlesuit. And again with the VISOR. Then with the Implant activated. It gets fun after that, because we'll start with submachine guns like the MP5. I hope you like this place. You're going to be living here."

He groaned.

* * *

Kandahar, Afghanistan

Abdullah and Naseer worked on Fahad's ancient white Toyota Hilux. A dusty lightbulb cast a faint glow across the room, a chill settling in the air as the sun set.

Abdullah pointed. "We place the charges around the engine, along here and here." They struggled to lift the scratched and dented hood from the truck, then set it along the far wall. "Bring me the satchel."

"Others could do this," Naseer protested.

"You must learn patience. If I were to ask another man to do this, I would place my trust in that man. I would take his word that he had done the job correctly. What if he were to make a mistake? Would he take the utmost care? No, if I do the job myself, I know it is done correctly. This is something you must learn, Naseer. You cannot depend on others to help you."

"I don't see why we have to do everything," Naseer grumbled.

"Quit complaining. It is good to work with your hands. You will learn this, in time." He took the discarded American ammo box—prepared with explosives—from the stack against the wall. "This is the mixture of ammonium nitrate and diesel fuel. Here, help me place it."

They worked with the charge, using thin wire to fasten it inside the engine bay.

Naseer eyed it skeptically. "Won't the heat cause it to explode?"

"No, it is stable. We will wire the detonators on top when we are done. Now, bring another."

As they hung more charges around the engine, he questioned Naseer on the timing.

"Fahad is prepared," Naseer said. "When he approaches the checkpoint, he knows what he must do."

"He understands what will happen?"

"Yes."

He nodded. "That is good. He must not turn away from the checkpoint."

"May I ask a question?"

"Never be afraid to ask me a question."

Naseer paused. "Do you hate the Americans because of what they did to your wife?"

Abdullah stared thoughtfully at Naseer. "Did I tell you that I spent time in America?"

"Yes, but you never say more."

"The Americans helped us with the war."

Naseer nodded for him to continue.

"There were many Mujahideen who thought that war was over. I traveled home, to Saudi Arabia, but I found there was no place for me. My brothers had inherited the family business, and they didn't want to hear stories of my days with the Mujahideen. I had done this great thing, fought and sacrificed, but they cared only for money. Then a man contacted me, an American who had helped during the war, the man who taught me to make bombs. He helped me go to America, to New York City."

He stopped and stared off into space. "You can't imagine how large it is. You think the city might go on forever." He resumed tying off the wire holding the charge. "The people were … not unfriendly. I studied at university."

He paused, holding the device inside the engine bay. "I met my wife. She was a student as well. From a good family. A very good Muslim. We mingled there, the men and women. I told her I was an Arab, but she knew, somehow. She called me a proud Afghan and I told her that my people had fled Afghanistan a long time ago but that my father had sent me back at my grandfather's behest. That I had helped fight the Soviets. That I'd committed myself to Jihad. She told me that I'd fallen in love with Afghanistan."

He continued fastening the wire to the charge, tying it to the sidewall. "Have you thought about marriage, Naseer?"

Naseer coughed. "I am committed to Jihad."

He smiled. "Spoken as a youth." He patted Naseer on the hand. "It is a fine thing, to marry. To have children. And so we did. We loved and we married. But we were unable to have children."

"It must have been very hard for you," Naseer said. "Did you think of taking another wife?"

"No. Never. She completed her studies and came back to Afghanistan. I followed the next year. I'd had enough of war. I wanted to marry and live in peace."

"And they begged you to lead?"

"Hardly," Abdullah said. "Her family saw only a hardened man, a killer. The village leaders saw only an Arab, not an Afghan. They wanted nothing to do with us. But this pleased me. I wanted nothing to do with *them*. We found a place to live on the edge of her village. It was quiet, until the Americans invaded. The Taliban came, asking for help. I didn't want to. I was content to live in peace. They persisted. I showed them how to make bombs. They came from far away, and the more I taught, the more came. I didn't mind. I like to teach, and it was nice to have students. I was no longer a fighter, just a tired man who wanted to spend time with his wife. Until they killed her."

Naseer winced. "You don't have to continue."

He frowned. "My life was always for Jihad. I was a fool to think otherwise. Now I will kill the Americans, here and abroad."

He finished hanging the last charge in the engine bay, then with Naseer's help they put the hood back on the truck. "It's time to start on the inside. Help me remove the seat." He waved to the stack of remaining charges. "The night is long and we have much to do."

CHAPTER SEVEN

Area 51

John tossed the flash-bang grenade through the door, the explosion of light and noise illuminating the darkened room. The VISOR displayed a ghostly green image, the sound muted. He rushed through the door and put two shots in the enemy's chest.

His aim had gotten better, as proved by the last hundred shots Eric and Deion had pulled from the dummies. They were now mere fractions of an inch apart.

He continued on, the VISOR displaying simulated thermal imaging from an overhead drone, his own heat signature blazing bright.

As he entered the second room, a dummy popped from behind a couch, spraying his position with Simunition rounds, paint cartridge bullets designed to leave vivid color markings. They hit like a paintball and stung like a bastard.

He sidestepped and put another pair of rounds in the dummy's chest. His HUD lit up, the red outline of a person in the room ahead. He ran through the door, fast and hard, and the dummies on each side fired. He dropped and spun, firing his Sig Sauer, but the bullet jammed.

Damn it!

The heat signature was a blonde in a short blue dress. His amped-up nervous system twitched. Unlike the Simunition rounds, his were real. One wrong move and he could kill her.

Damn it. Damn it!

His mind raced as the dummies tracked him, time slowing. He dropped the magazine, cleared the misfire, and slammed in a new one, cycling the receiver. He spun sideways and put three bullets into the dummy on his left, then tracked to the right, preparing to fire. In the VISOR, he saw the blonde jump up and knew he had only seconds to save her.

He swept his leg out, tripping her, to keep her safe while he took out the remaining dummy.

Suddenly, the woman was upright, a knife in hand. She was behind him, but he caught the movement in his VISOR as the knife arced down. He spun and tried to knock it away with the M11, and in that second, time froze.

He tried to figure out what to do but drew a blank. He had assumed she was a hostage.

Big mistake.

He'd screwed the pooch. If he hit her, he might genuinely hurt her, and she was probably a PFC roped into the shooting house. If he didn't strike back, Eric would give him hell.

Time started to flow again and he kicked her hard in the shin. She grunted and collapsed down on him, the plastic knife finding its way below the VISOR and hitting him in the throat.

It was hard plastic, not the rubber training knives he was used to, and he choked on his own tongue. She kneed him in his groin and he came completely off the floor, choking back vomit.

When the overhead lights blazed on, the blonde sat on top of him, a small pistol in her left hand, jammed into his stomach.

"What was that?" Eric's voice thundered.

He gasped, then popped the catch on the VISOR and flipped open the faceplate. He took raggedy breaths, and the taste of vomit was still heavy in the back of his throat. He looked up at the pretty woman. "You win?"

She stared at him, incredulous. "I win? I gut shot you, and would have cut your helmet off and put the blade through your eye. Of *course* I win."

"Sorry, ma'am?"

Eric and Deion joined them in the shooting house. Deion shook his head, smiling, but Eric didn't let it go. "What happened, John?"

"Sorry, sir. I wasn't ready for a civilian."

"A civilian? You think she was a civilian? After she tried to kill you? I told you the house was live, and I gave you permission to engage the targets."

Heat rushed to his face. "What was I supposed to do? Shoot her? There's never been anybody in the house before, except you and Deion. It's always been training dummies. How was I supposed to know there was a woman in here?"

Eric glared at him. "You weren't supposed to think, you were supposed to react. Besides, I traded out the ammo in your second clip. You didn't even notice."

John craned his head. Sure enough, the dummies sported bright blue splotches from the Simunition rounds. "How about that."

Eric stuck his hand out to the woman. "Nancy? You can get off him now."

The woman stood, still eyeballing him. He struggled to sit, his balls aching, and he finally managed to swallow.

Deion grabbed his outstretched hand and hauled him to his feet. "This is Nancy Smith," Deion said. "She's one of the head honchos."

John took a deep breath while sizing her up. She was a looker, but there was something in her face. He felt it in the back of his head, in the primitive lizard part of the brain dedicated to the primal urges. She was dangerous. He decided to salute, and he held the salute while she glared, until she finally looked away.

He grinned. *Score one for the guy with the aching balls.*

"Nancy will observe your training," Eric said. "She's also going to work with Deion to teach you spy craft. Now, do it again. Go swap out for the MP5 and we'll reset the house."

"Any more surprises?" he asked.

Deion snorted. "Always expect it, man, 'cause in the real world, that's all you'll get."

* * *

Washington, DC

Smith entered his office, carefully shutting the door behind him. His office was located just blocks from the White House, but no one would ever suspect that its occupant was one of the most powerful men in the world. The bare gray walls were empty, no awards or commendations, not even a window. In fact, except for the large desk, steel briefcase, and computer, the room was barren. He sat and plugged in the video camera, connected the network cable, then initiated the video call.

He smiled when his old friend answered. "How is he, Hob?"

"As well as can be expected," Hobert Barnwell said, shaking his head. "You're taking one hell of a risk."

"We need him. *I* need him. What if he discovers the truth before we're ready?"

"It's just a matter of time."

He knew Hobert was correct. "We'll deal with it when the time comes."

"Speaking of, how's your memory?"

"I don't know, how's your drinking?"

Barnwell's smile hardened. "No worse than usual. Keeping tabs on me?"

"Of course. Victoria worries about you."

"She shouldn't. It's under control. Quit avoiding the question."

He can sense it. "I'm not a young man, Hob. I'm reminded of that daily. This *must* work."

"I know. I'll be watching."

"Good. How is Nancy?"

"You can't wish her well, Fulton."

He wanted to yell at his old friend. "There is *nothing* wrong with her. It's her upbringing."

Barnwell leaned closer to the camera. "Biological or environmental, at this point it doesn't matter. I'm not saying she *can* change, but if she does, it must be self-initiated. I'm speaking as a friend, not as a doctor."

He felt the guilt pressing in. "It's my fault, of course."

"Yes," Hobert agreed. "I thought we were beyond that. If you want to *protect* her, let her choose her own path."

He glared at his old friend. "I've done exactly as you suggested."

"That's the best any father can do."

* * *

Kandahar Province, Kandahar

Abdullah scribbled in his journal when Naseer entered with Fahad. He glanced up and was taken aback by Fahad's deathly pallor, his clammy skin, and his sweat-stained pato.

"Peace be upon you," Fahad struggled.

"And upon you be peace," he replied. "You are unwell," he said softly.

Fahad nodded. "I am weak."

"Will you be able to carry out your task?"

"Yes."

He nodded. "Naseer told me you understand your instructions. You are ready?"

"Yes, I am ready." Fahad coughed, the phlegmy rattle deep in his lungs. "I have not taken opium. I am ready for Jihad."

"Remember what Naseer has taught you," he said. "You must perform your task with great care. Allah will be with you in this. We have arranged to send money to your wife. She will not want for food or shelter and your children will receive an education."

Fahad's eyes filled with tears. "Thank you, sir."

There were soft footsteps as Koshen joined them.

Abdullah nodded and motioned him to sit. "Were you able to complete the preparations?"

"The men in Germany will be waiting," Koshen said. "They are preparing for your arrival."

"Very good. Please, stay." He turned back to Fahad. "Will you pray with us?"

Fahad nodded weakly.

"Naseer, bring the mats. We will honor Allah and we will pray for his guidance."

Naseer brought the prayer mats and placed them on the dirt floor. They performed Isha, the nightly prayer, Fahad barely able to prostrate himself. Koshen and Naseer helped him up.

He tenderly grasped Fahad's hand. "Brother, I have faith in you and I have been honored to know you." He smelled Fahad, the sickness and death that clung to him, and knew Fahad had a short time before the cancer claimed him. He held the dying man's hand and gave silent thanks to Allah for sending Fahad to him.

Fahad bowed as deep as his fading strength allowed. "I won't fail you."

* * *

Area 51

John sighed as Eric held up another type of explosives from the table and shook it at him. "C4," John mumbled.

The days were now a blur, and the explosives training was just one more hour in an already full day of strength and weapons training.

Deion stood next to Eric, holding another block, yellow this time. "And this?"

"Semtex."

Eric nodded. "Good. And both are a type of?"

He concentrated, but exhaustion made it hard to think. "RDX?"

"Correct," Eric said. "And how might you find Semtex?"

"I probably wouldn't. They don't make it anymore. Any Semtex I find would be left over from the nineties."

Eric picked up a container of white crystals. "How about this?"

He examined it. "Urea nitrate?"

Eric glanced sideways at Deion.

"He got you," Deion said. "I didn't help him."

Eric picked up another container and handed it to John. "Okay, how about this?"

John took the container full of finely powdered light blue balls. He struggled to place them. They looked like laundry soap, but he instinctively knew that was wrong. He turned the container in his hand, but could not place it. "Uhm. I don't know."

Eric tilted his head. "You sure? You were on a hot streak."

He struggled to remember everything they'd taught him. "I'm stumped."

Deion watched closely. "You really don't remember this one? Come on, man. You got to have an *idea.*"

He closed his eyes. Names tumbled through his mind, and just when he seemed on the edge of finally placing it, the name slipped through his grasp.

Eric nodded patiently. "It's a common explosive, John. It was used here in the US a couple of times."

Eric's words did not register. *Explosives in the US?* He opened his eyes. "Sorry."

"Oklahoma," Eric prompted. "Does that help?"

Oklahoma? That sounded right, somehow, but the details eluded him. "Guys, I don't remember. What happened in Oklahoma?"

"The bombing," Deion said. "You don't remember Oklahoma? McVeigh? The Murrah building?"

"Sure, I remember now. A bombing."

A cool spring day. Had he seen it on television? *Yes.* He remembered his classroom in Pasadena and how Mr. Henry had wheeled a metal cart with a television into the classroom and soberly explained that a federal building had been bombed. "I was in school. We watched it on the news."

"Right," Eric said. "That was ammonium nitrate. Just like this. Ring a bell?"

"Vaguely."

"It was probably the same thing they used in the IED that hit your convoy in Iraq. They also used it in the Red Cross bombing."

The IED had happened so fast. A pile of debris on the side of a dusty road, so familiar, they had passed a million just like it, the heat beating on them, making it hard to concentrate, the fear and the sweat and the dust covering them. The smell of garbage was everywhere and they just wanted to finish their patrol, head back to base, get some chow in the mess, and get back to their air-conditioned tent.

"John?" Eric asked, breaking his reverie. "The Red Cross bombing?"

The memory faded and he stared at Eric blankly. "The Red Cross bombing?" he asked softly. "I don't know."

"Virginia. Someone blew up the Red Cross building? How do you forget that?" Deion asked.

Eric shot a dark glance at Deion. "Are you sure you're not having any side effects from the concussion?"

"No," he said. "I mean, I don't have nightmares anymore, if that's what you're asking."

"No side effects at all?"

"Sometimes I get a little foggy," he admitted.

"Maybe we'll have Doc Barnwell check you one more time," Eric said. "Just to be sure."

"I'm fine," he protested. "Have I done anything to let you down?"

Deion smiled. "You're good, man. You know how Eric is, he's nervous in the service."

"This isn't a joke," Eric said. He turned his glare on John. "We've put a lot into you, John. Another checkup won't kill you."

John nodded. "Whatever you say, Eric."

* * *

Nancy leaned back in Eric's chair. "What does he remember?" she asked.

Eric gave Deion a sidelong glance. "He doesn't remember anything."

"The memory overlay is holding," Deion agreed. "Frankly, I'm surprised."

Eric shook his head. "You still don't like him, do you?"

"Hell, no, man. I try to put it out of my mind, but it's a hard thing to forget. How can *I* trust him? How can *you* trust him?"

"Good question," Nancy said. "How *can* you trust him?"

"I put it out of my mind," Eric said. "I treat him like a recruit. He performs his job. I encourage him. I haven't forgotten what he did but I don't have the luxury of doubt. He can't second-guess himself. Or us. For this to work, he has to believe in the mission. I have to believe in him. To be honest, I kind of like the man he is now."

Nancy's face went blank. "How so?"

Eric sighed to himself. He had planned to broach this subject with her in a more private conversation, but it was too late for that. "If he hadn't been in that Humvee, if he'd finished his tour, he would have come back, and yeah, maybe he would have struggled. But sooner or later he would have found some job, maybe a girl—"

"That's a lot of shit," Deion interrupted. "He grew up without friends, and when he finally did make them, it was with the guys that died in that Humvee. No, he was off, even before the IED. If he hadn't gotten hit, he would have come back to the States and worked a dead-end job until he snapped."

Eric shrugged. "Sorry, but I can't think that. I have to believe in him. If he goes sideways, *then* I'll deal with it."

Nancy took a hard swig of her coffee, watching him over the top of her mug. "You can put him down?"

He leaned back in his chair. "That's the job."

She eyed him warily. "You always do the job, don't you?"

He shrugged.

"He ever tell you how he got the call sign Steeljaw?" Deion asked.

"No," Nancy said. "I don't believe I've heard that one."

The last thing he needed was Deion telling *that* story. "Let it go, Deion."

Deion grinned. "Whatever you say, man."

"Look," Nancy said, "your little experiment is on track, but keep your eyes open. If anything seems off, let the docs know. The last thing we need is Frist going bat-shit crazy. *Again.*"

* * *

Eric stood in the War Room with Deion and Nancy, watching the monitor as Clark and Kryzowski walked them through the day's threats.

"The North Koreans are at it again," Clark said. "They fired on a Japanese fishing boat."

Eric sighed. He finally felt he was getting a handle on the influx of threats, but there were always surprises.

"Dear Leader wants more concessions during the next round of negotiations," Nancy said.

"The SEALs are in place," Deion said. "They could take the ship. The North Koreans would claim sabotage, but they wouldn't have proof."

"That's true," Clark agreed. "It could also harden the Chinese position. We're counting on them to rein in the North Koreans. I'd say we hold off until the negotiations are over. Speaking of the Chinese, we're seeing a coordinated cyberattack against US companies. The People's Liberation Army recruited a branch of hackers to probe the nation's cyberdefenses."

That was news to Eric. "How do we know this?"

"We have an asset," Clark said. "He's confirmed they get their funding and orders from the PLA. Unfortunately, there's not much we can do. We've provided details to the NSA; they're working on a plan to publicly disclose the attacks."

"It's a tough call," Deion said. "China could pressure the US on monetary policy. Or, they refuse to pressure Kim Jong-il. But, if we do nothing, the PLA will think it's open season on the US."

"Exactly," Nancy agreed. "We recognize the threat, even before the rest of the intelligence community, so how do we respond?"

"We will have to see if our asset can get deeper," Clark said. "We have limited access to him. He's in a dormitory. We've been communicating through his trips to a local noodle shop."

"If they figure out he's turned, they'll kill him," Eric said.

"Which is why we have an extraction plan," Karen said. "The asset *has* to be Chinese. They won't trust an outsider."

"Get him deeper," Nancy said. "What else?"

"The white power group in Colorado, the APR," Karen said. "We think they have acquired a supply of cesium-137."

He jerked upright. "What? How the hell did that happen?"

"I *thought* you had an eye on them," Nancy said. "I *thought* they were mostly talk."

"We did," Clark said. "We thought it was just bluster." He moved the mouse and the overhead monitor zoomed in on a facility twenty-five miles south of Denver. "This is Landfrey Medical Waste. They have a contract to decommission and scrap medical devices, including those used for cancer treatment."

"Let me guess," Nancy snapped. "These devices contained cesium-137."

"Correct. The company was slow to dispose of them, and the cesium piled up. Now a truckful is missing."

Eric took a deep breath and let it out slowly. "How much are we talking?"

"Enough to irradiate a large city." Clark paused to let that sink in. "We've got a team on their way to Colorado. We're putting surveillance on the entire group."

"How long before you have them locked down?" Deion asked.

"Three days, tops," Karen said. "We planted malware on their computers over the past several weeks, but we found nothing. The phone calls are all in code, and they switch codes after each call. They've had training."

"Have you informed DHS?" Nancy asked.

"We need more intel." Clark turned to Nancy. "You're going to have to brief the Old Man."

Nancy shifted in her seat. "I hate that."

Clark turned to Karen. "And there's one other thing. Tell them."

"There's been an uptick in chatter from Al-Qaeda, but no details," Karen said. "There's been another picture, and they've used steganography to bury text in the picture. I've managed to decrypt and extract it, and it talks about an upcoming event. Once again, no hard intelligence, but everything is couched in apocalyptic imagery. JSOC isn't taking it seriously."

He thought back to his time in Afghanistan. "Can you pass your analysis to the DIA?"

"I can. There's no indication they'll do anything with it. DIA doesn't want to cause a fuss in Afghanistan. They've been waging a holding war for the past year."

"How about the CIA?" Deion asked.

Eric shook his head. "The DIA doesn't trust the CIA. No offense."

"None taken," Deion said. "We've done a piss-poor job of sharing intelligence."

"I'll send it on. I've got a friend in the DIA who's stationed in Afghanistan. I can strongly encourage him to take another look," Eric said.

"Has there been any other activity in Afghanistan?" Nancy asked.

"No more than usual," Karen said. "A steady stream of IEDs. The usual back and forth between coalition forces and the Taliban. AQ stirs up trouble, and the Pakistani ISI coaches them along."

Deion shrugged. "It's Afghanistan. What can you do?"

Nancy nodded her head. "Send it on, Karen. Keep digging, and if you gather any SIGINT that can help, notify us immediately. Let's hope the DIA takes it seriously and puts resources into HUMINT."

Karen nodded and returned to her station.

Clark flipped the big screen to the data feed from JSOC. "It never ends."

"Neither does our training with Frist," he said. "Come on, Deion, we've got to check on him."

Nancy followed them out. "I'll brief my father."

Eric laughed. "I'd rather get pummeled by Frist."

* * *

Kandahar, Afghanistan

Abdullah stretched back on his stool and worked the kinks from his back and neck. The wind blew through the open window of the warehouse, a warm breeze that tickled his nose with the scent of the desert. He would miss it. As a young man, he had been mesmerized by Afghanistan's stark beauty. The years since had done nothing to diminish his feelings.

There was a soft knock. He turned and beckoned Koshen in. "What did you find?"

Koshen entered and took a seat on the dirt floor. "Naseer is with Fahad. They are practicing one last time."

He studied Koshen. "What do you think?"

Koshen smiled. "I think that Fahad will do as he was told."

"Why is that?"

Koshen paused. "I think it is because of the money."

"Of course it is. The cancer makes him desperate. It is that reason he will do as he's told. Now, how are you?"

"I am well, sir," Koshen said. "I am thankful that you asked."

He took Koshen's hands in his. "You are prepared?"

Koshen nodded. "Yes. I will head south out of the city, along the trail. General Azim's man will take me to Gulistan. There I will be safe. Sir, can I trust General Azim's man?" He looked doubtfully at Abdullah.

"Yes. Azim will not harm you. I've asked an old friend to look for you. If you are not there a week from tomorrow, I will finally have proof of Azim's treachery, and then I will kill him."

Koshen's eyes widened.

He nodded his head. "You've been a good student. You learned quickly." He turned to stare out the window. The sun blazed, unrelenting, and the wind swirled the red dust across the horizon. He sighed. "You will be safe in Gulistan. Find a good wife, Koshen. Teach those who come looking. Teach them to make the bombs the way I taught you."

He took his leather-bound journal and handed it to the young man. "Take this. If you ever need guidance, read what I have written. It talks about bombs, but also my own observations, advice that I think will help you."

Koshen stared at it, then reached out hesitantly and took the book, pulling it close to his chest, his eyes big. "Sir, will I see you again?"

"Perhaps. Naseer and I will go to Kabul to find transport out of the country. We will continue Jihad."

Koshen sat quietly for a moment. "May God protect you."

He laughed. "You as well, young Koshen. Don't worry about me. Naseer will protect me."

Koshen smiled shyly. "I think it is you who will be protecting him."

* * *

FOB Wildcat, Kandahar Province

Specialist Donnie Lucas shot the shit with Specialist Kelvin Davidson as they guarded the side entrance to FOB Wildcat.

Kelvin argued for the hundredth time, "Look, man, I'm just saying. If I had to call it, I'd call it for Johnny's old lady. Those pictures she emailed were fine."

Donnie snickered. "No way. She's got nice tits, but my old lady's got a better ass."

"I do like your wife's ass. I'll have to take it for a ride. Don't worry, though, I'll let you watch. For old time's sake."

Kelvin always made Donnie laugh. "Mighty big of you, but I'll be too busy with your sister."

This amused Wahid, their local interpreter, a short young man with olive skin and a soft black beard. He laughed, an infectious little braying that never failed to amuse them. Kelvin smiled and wiped the sweat from his brow.

The cool early morning air was long gone and Donnie was roasting. It was a quiet detail. The locals barely paid any attention to the base except to come begging for jobs. They were too far from Kandahar to attract attention from the Taliban, and AQ was overwhelmed trying to replace their top commanders lost to drone strikes. Mortars were launched during the night the month before, dutiful attacks by local Taliban trying to prove they were still fighting the foreign invaders, but nothing after.

He had no clue what the spooks were doing under the tents at Wildcat. It was above his pay grade, but he saw the communications gear and the Special Forces guys skulking around and whispering about their tests.

He wished for the thousandth time he was back in Bagram. At least there he could find something to pass the time. Instead, he spent much of his free time with Kelvin, and as much as he liked the man, he was sick of Kelvin's company.

In the distance, a small cloud of dust tracked steadily closer with the daily arrival of the locals and the few who were willing to make the trek from Kandahar to clean the latrines and mess.

He laughed to himself. Some days the distinction between latrines and mess was not as big as it used to be. He sure missed the Burger King at Bagram.

The convoy approached and the lead truck stopped for their inspection. Kelvin caught the driver's eye, the man named Fahad. Donnie and Kelvin liked him, and both had noticed that he looked worse each week. "Fahad, you don't look so good. You okay?"

Wahid translated as the sweat rolled from Fahad's brow. Trembling, Fahad answered in broken English. "Okay. I okay."

As Kelvin inspected the other men, Donnie leaned closer. *He looks like he's got one foot in the grave.* "You need to see a doctor."

Wahid translated again and Fahad responded. They spoke for a short time and Wahid turned back to Donnie. "He says he's feeling better. He says he just needs to work to feed his children."

Fahad nodded, gasping for air. He struggled with the wheel, then grabbed at his chest. The Toyota lurched forward.

"Fahad, stop the truck."

Kelvin turned. "What the fuck, Donnie?"

Wahid was yelling in Pashto, but Fahad did not respond. Donnie tried to reach inside, but the truck rolled forward just fast enough to keep him from grabbing the wheel. "I think he's having a heart attack!" He beat on the side of the cab. "Fahad, stop the truck!"

Fahad slumped down. Donnie was concerned now, for Fahad's well-being, but also for his own. There would be hell to pay if the CO saw them chasing a truck with a dying man in it.

"Kelvin, get your ass over here!" He turned to point at the men riding in the back of Fahad's truck. "Wahid, tell them to get on the ground!"

Wahid shouted at the men and they bailed from the truck bed and scrambled to the ground with their hands over their heads.

"Shit, shit, shit!" The truck was now only thirty yards from the main group of tents.

His PRC-148 squawked to life. "Delta two, this is Delta one, over."

He keyed his radio. "This is Delta two. We've got a local who's not responding. I think he's having a heart attack, over."

"Say again, Delta two, over."

"It's one of the locals. I think he's dying. Can we get a medic out here?"

His radio squawked, and a pair of PFCs came running from the mess hall along with the base doctor and nurse.

They were barely out of the tent when Fahad sat up and gunned the engine, the truck lurching forward.

"What the hell?" Donnie grabbed his rifle and struggled to bring it to a firing position. "Stop the truck!"

He saw Fahad holding a device, turning to mouth something.

Kelvin saw it too and screamed, "Bomb!"

The truck leaped forward and hit the tent at twenty miles per hour, then exploded. The mess hall blew apart, the tent shredded, and the truck became a pile of shrapnel as the shock wave expanded.

Donnie knew he had made a fatal mistake. He had a fraction of a second where time slowed and he saw the shock wave race across the dusty ground, and before he could blink, the shrapnel hit him, moving at twenty times the speed of sound, and then he knew nothing.

CHAPTER EIGHT

Area 51

E ric woke, bleary-eyed, to a furious rapping on his door that roused him from a deep sleep. He staggered out of bed and made his way to the door, stubbing his toe against his desk. He yelped and fumbled around the wall until he found the light switch.

He wanted to kick the desk that held his computer, the endless paperwork now the bane of his existence, but worried he might break a toe. He opened the door and found a young PFC waiting.

"Sir, you're needed on deck."

Eric nodded wearily and turned to put on his uniform, but the PFC stopped him. "Now, sir."

He cast a baleful eye toward the PFC and struggled with the urge to strangle him, then nodded. The PFC was just following orders. Eric checked himself quickly in the mirror. There were deep bags under his eyes and his t-shirt was wrinkled, but it would have to do.

He followed the young man through the labyrinth of tunnels as the PFC explained the situation. "There's been a bombing in Afghanistan. Twenty-six confirmed dead."

"Where?"

"Near Kandahar. There are teams en route from Kandahar and Bagram. The site is secure, but they need to evac the wounded."

The PFC stopped at the security entrance. "Ms. Smith and Mr. Freeman are waiting."

Eric dismissed the young man, navigated his way through the security entrance, and joined Nancy, Deion and Clark inside the War Room.

Nancy gave him a once-over, her eyes lingering on his sweatpants and t-shirt. "You got briefed on the way?"

"Yes. Do we know who's responsible?"

Deion offered, "Too sophisticated for the Taliban. It's AQ, gotta be."

Sergeant Clark displayed a map of Afghanistan on the big screen. The noise and buzz in the room receded as the analysts stopped to watch.

"This is Kandahar." The mouse hovered over the city, and Clark moved it to the northeast. "This is Forward Operating Base Wildcat, twenty-six miles away. The purpose of the FOB was to test the deployment of a new drone, the RQ-170, code-named the Sentinel."

A picture of a gray-painted drone snapped into place on the upper-right quadrant of the screen. "It's a Lockheed Martin flying wing design. It was launching from Kandahar, but controlled by a team at FOB Wildcat. This was a shakeout session, with DIA, CIA and JSOC forces. If the drone had been successful, the operation would have moved to Creech."

"Did AQ know that a new drone was being tested?" Nancy asked.

"There's no indication that anyone knew of the testing," Clark said. "The FOB was built in a hurry."

A live feed played on the overhead, showing the wreckage of FOB Wildcat. Clark continued, "Locals were employed to work in the kitchen and clean the latrines. A man named Fahad drove the truck. He'd recently been diagnosed with terminal stomach cancer. At zero eight hundred local time, he approached the FOB in his truck. During routine inspection, he faked a massive heart attack, drove the truck full of explosives into the mess hall, and detonated the bomb."

On screen, the devastation was evident. The shredded remains of the tent flapped in the wind, plastic and wood debris spreading outward from the point of detonation. The truck frame was a barely recognizable pile of charred and twisted metal.

"Twenty-six are confirmed dead," Clark said, "another six critically wounded. Fifteen more are bad enough to require medical care. They'll be evac'd to Bagram, triaged, and sent on to Ramstein."

Eric's stomach sank as he watched the wounded being loaded into helicopters, body bags full of dead soldiers still lying in the dirt. "Do we have identification on the twenty-six?"

Clark nodded, his face grim. "I'm afraid six members of Delta were killed." He turned to Deion. "And two CIA officers. Also, two Lockheed contractors, the base doctor and nurse, and the rest were DIA or Army."

Eric's stomach twisted. "Do you have the names of the Operators?"

Clark nodded and displayed a list of names on the screen. Eric barely recognized the first name, Joel Wood. His heart thudded at the next three. Joshua Goodman, Cedric Carpenter, and Dwight Spears.

He knew them. *Had* known them. They had been good men. Joshua had been a star quarterback in his Texas high school and used to talk about Texas high school football like it was a religion.

Cedric and Dwight had been good Operators, Cedric a big black man from Philadelphia, and Dwight a skinny little guy from Seattle. They had been best friends, quick to laugh, and quicker to kill. They'd made one hell of a team as he'd found out on a mission with them in 2004.

He drew a blank on the next two names, Tanner and Lott. They must have gone through selection after him. He felt a stab of anger at the senseless loss of life, and anger that he was far removed from the action.

"You have the names of the CIA officers?" Deion asked.

Clark displayed two names, Jack Trevino and Gene Wiggins.

Deion sighed. "I don't know Trevino, but Gene Wiggins was a good officer. I worked with him back in 2005."

Eric glanced at him, surprised. "Was Wiggins the one who tried to push for the operations against the Pakistani ISI?"

"That's the man," Deion said. "Couldn't get it approved, but his heart was in the right place."

"What do we know about the explosives?" Nance asked.

"Ammonium nitrate and diesel fuel, a fairly large yield. This wasn't locals throwing an IED over the fence."

The door to the Operations room opened and Fulton Smith entered, his suit fresh and recently pressed. "Gentlemen. Nancy. You have questions?"

Eric was surprised to see him. "Do you know who did this?"

Smith took a seat at the end of the table. "Intel suggests it is the work of Abdullah the Bomber."

"Never heard of him," he said.

"Not many have," Smith said. "He is a contemporary of bin Laden. We believe he was recruited as a young man in Saudi Arabia. He was trained as a soldier by the Mujahideen and received explosives training by a young CIA agent, Jack Trevino."

Realization dawned. "The man killed at FOB Wildcat."

Smith nodded. "Whether intentional or unintentional, it is quite ironic. Trevino spent much of 1985 training young men to fire stinger missiles and construct IEDs. It was this training that helped the Mujahideen wear away at the Soviet occupying forces, forcing them to abandon Afghanistan."

"What do we know about him?" Nancy asked.

Smith nodded at Sergeant Clark, who displayed the file on the overhead.

"We believe his family is originally from Afghanistan but fled to Saudi Arabia in the forties," Clark said. "The case reports are thin. He's highly intelligent, and a master of improvised munitions. It's possible he spent time in the West. We have no SIGINT on him. Based upon HUMINT gained after the invasion of Afghanistan, we believe he spent the last few years training others. The sophistication of IEDs coming from both Afghanistan and Iraq increased dramatically after 9/11."

"And you think this Abdullah is the one responsible," Eric said.

"Guy sounds like a major player," Deion said.

Eric agreed. "How do we not know anything about this man?"

"Because he's *very* smart and *very* careful," Smith said. "We found a reference to his name in a training document in 1993, after the World Trade Center bombing. We've been trying to learn more ever since. We've spent thousands of hours combing through the records of immigrants after the Soviet withdrawal from Afghanistan. We suspect he entered the US without record. He's gone to great pains to conceal his existence." Smith turned to glance at each one of them. "This man is not a foot soldier. This man was a valuable member of the Mujahideen and most probably a very powerful member of Al-Qaeda. He's declared war on the United States."

"Kryzowski believed she found a website associated with AQ," Nancy said.

Clark nodded. "Yes. Based on the encoded text that Karen found, we believe this was merely a warm-up. Make no mistake, this is a smart and dedicated enemy. There's no telling where he will strike next."

"To that end," Smith said, "I'd like Mr. Freeman to go to Afghanistan and start investigating. This is exactly the kind of threat the OTM needs to stop." He turned to Deion. "Mr. Freeman, your investigation will be in addition to the JSOC operation. Find intel on this man."

Deion grinned. "I've still got contacts. I'll find more in a day than they'll find in a week."

"I'm sure you will," Smith said. "Your knack for languages and interrogation will be most beneficial. Your CIA cover is still valid. Nancy will accompany you."

Nancy grimaced, and Deion squirmed uncomfortably in his chair. "Sir, with all due respect, and to Nancy as well, a woman won't be welcome where I'll be going."

"I assure you, she will not hinder your investigation," Smith said.

Eric was itching to go to Afghanistan, to help his former teammates. "Sir, what about me?"

Smith turned to Eric. "Your place is with Frist. Sergeant, isn't there still missing cesium?"

"Yes," Clark agreed reluctantly. "It's still a concern, but wouldn't it make sense to deploy Frist to Afghanistan?"

Smith ignored the question and addressed Eric. "Take Frist to Colorado and find the missing cesium. Report on Frist's stability and watch for any signs of unpredictable behavior. You have no higher priority."

Eric wanted to go with Deion to Afghanistan, but he was a professional. He bit his lip. "I understand my orders," he muttered.

Smith stood. "I have the utmost confidence in you. All of you. Sergeant Clark, the deck is yours." He nodded at Nancy, Deion, and Eric. "Good hunting."

* * *

Washington, DC

The light in the bunker cast dark shadows under the President's eyes as he glared at Smith. "I *want* him in Afghanistan."

Smith was tired from the flight to Washington. The frequent trips were wearing on him, more so every year, but when the President requested an audience, he knew he must appear. "He's not ready."

The President sat his porcelain coffee cup on the table, the Presidential Seal outlined in delicate gold filigree. "After the money we've spent, I want him in Afghanistan."

"He's months away from being fully operational. Sending him to Afghanistan would be a disaster."

The President leaned back in his chair, glaring. "We've got twenty-seven dead now. One died on the way to Germany."

He understood the President's anger. "I'm sorry, but sending Frist won't change that."

The President slumped in his chair. "We can't get any traction in Afghanistan. This drone was supposed to bail our asses out of the fire. The Joint Chiefs are all over it. We need it operational. The insurgency is increasing."

Smith nodded, more to himself than the President. "I know, sir. The data shows we are at significant risk of Afghanistan becoming a failed state. The risk to the region is severe."

"I sold this to the public as a chance to end Al-Qaeda. They don't understand what will happen if Afghanistan fails. It could be a breeding ground for terrorists for the next hundred years."

"Some understand," he said softly, "but people are tired of war. They want peace and comfort. They don't want to know their safety is hanging by a thread, ready to plunge into chaos."

The President eyed him sourly. "You're damned depressing today."

"I'm paid to be a pessimist."

"What are we going to do?"

"I've got a team on the way to Afghanistan," Smith said. "They'll find out who bombed the base and why. In the meantime, we've got another issue."

The President's eyes widened. "Christ. It never ends."

"A small amount of radioactive material has been—misplaced, shall we say."

"Ours?" the President asked.

"Yes, sir. Medical devices. We've got a team on the way. They will find it and secure it."

"Fulton? Did I ever tell you this job isn't worth the headache?"

He knew how the President felt. "All the time, sir."

* * *

Bagram AFB, Afghanistan

Deion stepped off the plane and the smell of jet fuel hit him like a hammer. While it was suffocating, it wasn't as bad as the wind blowing over the latrine pit, a smell he thought he'd left behind the year before. He sighed and led Nancy through the checkpoints to the CIA and DIA shared office.

He saw Valerie Simon approaching, still looking fit in her camo pants and black t-shirt. She had a few strands of gray in the peak of her short ebony hair but otherwise could have been mistaken for early thirties instead of midforties. Their romantic fling had ended after his transfer to Guantanamo, effectively ending their relationship before their age difference became an issue. Still, he'd kept in touch.

They had ended as friends, but he still had feelings for her. He stuck out his hand, but she grabbed him in a fierce hug. "I thought you hated Afghanistan," she said, laughing.

He grinned. It really *was* good to see her again and he realized just how much he'd missed her. "Valerie, this is Nancy Smith. We're here to investigate FOB Wildcat."

Nancy stuck out her hand. "So, you worked with Deion."

Valerie shook her hand and smiled. "We spent three years trying to track the Taliban's movements through eastern Afghanistan and into Pakistan. I'm glad you're back," she said, the grin fading. "This Wildcat thing is FUBAR'd. The DIA is trying to shut out the CIA, and the CIA is complaining about the DIA to JSOC." She shook her head, the smile gone. "It's fucked up."

Deion nodded, noticing the dark lines under her hazel eyes. "When does the next helicopter leave for Kandahar? I'm looking to dig up an old contact, see if he knows anything."

Her eyes widened. "Another lone-wolf mission? Isn't that what got you into trouble the last time?"

The memory of that operation angered him, but her assessment was fair. "You never know, Val, maybe I'll win them over with my charming personality and complete disregard for regulations."

Valerie shook her head sadly. "The next helicopter leaves in two hours. Nancy, can I steal him for a moment?"

"Absolutely," Nancy said. "He's all yours."

They stepped away, out of earshot. Valerie turned to glance at Nancy, then back to Deion. "Nice-looking girl. Seems a little cold, though."

He laughed. Jealousy was the *last* thing he expected. "She's just a coworker, Val. Trust me, there's nothing there. Besides, I still haven't gotten over you."

"Funny, I almost believe that." She smiled, and it made her look ten years younger. "It's good, Deion. *We're* good. It was just ... something to occupy our time, right?"

He tried to smile, but it faltered. "You know it was more than that." He reached for her hand and took it in his, gently squeezing her fingers. "You know what kind of problems our relationship meant for our careers. Not to mention the CIA paperwork."

She nodded, still grinning. "It was worth it to see you naked."

"Back at you." He wanted to hold her, to hug her, but the people streaming through the tents made that impossible. He caught her eyes and held her gaze. "I missed you."

She bit her lower lip. "Back at you. But it's history. You've got a job to do. Let's get your weapons checked out."

They rejoined Nancy, and Valerie led them to the armory, where he selected M11 pistols and MP4 rifles for himself and Nancy. Nancy leaned over and pulled an old Ka-Bar knife and sheath from the armory. Deion raised his eyebrow, but she just shrugged.

Valerie signed for their weapons and ammo while they changed into local clothes. When done, Deion grabbed a backpack, filled it with handfuls of extra magazines, and slung it over his shoulder.

Valerie gave him an appreciative glance, then gave Nancy a quick once-over, pausing at the bulge under her pant leg where she'd strapped the Ka-Bar knife. "The helicopter leaves soon. You guys hungry? By the time we finish, they'll be ready to spin up."

She led them to a small tent with plastic tables where several agents ate boxed sandwiches from the chain restaurant on base. She grabbed extras and passed them out.

He took a bite and shook his head. "Nothing like fast food in Bagram."

"Hey, the soldiers like it. The least the Army can do is offer them a taste of home."

She filled him in on the status of former coworkers while they ate. Nancy maintained a polite smile, but he could tell she was bored.

They finished their meal and prepared to board the helicopter when Deion saw his former special-agent-in-charge, Jim Rumple. The man stuck out like a sore thumb among the other agents, his clothes grubby and creased, his hair thin and graying, seemingly detached from the urgency and professionalism around him. "Freeman. You're back."

He smiled and contemplated decking the man. "Jim. Still in charge?"

Rumple turned to Nancy. "And you are?"

"Just leaving," Deion said, sticking his arm out to brush the man away.

Rumple frowned, then placed his hand on Deion's chest. "I'm afraid I'm going to need more than that."

Nancy frowned. "You've received a copy of our mission orders?"

"I have," he said.

"Then you have our security clearances. That's all you need to know."

Rumple glared at her. "A little cooperation goes a long way. We're in the middle of an all-hands-on-deck situation."

Nancy glared back. "We're not going to hinder your investigation, but we have our own."

"Then you won't mind me contacting your superiors. I want to be briefed on your mission."

Nancy smiled grimly. "You already tried that. Your friend, Grant, back in Langley told you to drop it."

Rumple blanched. "How did you know that?"

Deion started to interrupt, but Nancy silenced him with a look. "Drop it now," she said, "or you'll be sitting in your apartment back in Maryland wondering why your buddies at Langley couldn't stop your discharge." Nancy turned to Deion and Valerie, her voice hard as steel. "Come on, we're going. If this idiot keeps it up, I won't just have his job, I'll have his retirement. He'll be cleaning the fry bin at McDonald's for the rest of his life."

They hustled out of the room, Rumple watching them, his face a mask of anger and disgust. They found their way to the Chinook and took seats halfway in the back.

He leaned in close to Nancy. He wanted to ask her about Rumple, then thought better of it. Instead, he said, "You don't look happy."

"I don't like it when I'm not the one flying."

"Don't trust the pilot?"

"Not especially. It's a control issue."

Valerie turned to them. "That was good. I've never seen Jim called out like that." She smiled at Nancy. "You've got balls, lady, bluffing him like that."

"Who said I was bluffing?" Nancy said.

Valerie's smile faded as the engines whined and the rotors began thump-thumping.

* * *

Kandahar, Afghanistan

Neil Burch greeted them when they exited the Chinook at Kandahar. Neil was a short man in his late forties who Deion liked and respected. He was glad to see Neil still in the field and not riding a desk in Washington. "Neil, looking good, man." He tousled Neil's curly blond hair.

"Good to see you, too. I thought for sure they wouldn't allow your ass back in country."

Deion laughed, then introduced Nancy and Valerie.

Neil shook Valerie's hand. "Glad to finally meet you, Ms. Simon. Your reputation precedes you."

Valerie returned the handshake and grinned. "Yours, too, and call me Val."

Nancy shook Neil's hand. "Mr. Burch, your record speaks for itself."

"Keep it up," Neil said, winking. "Flattery will get you everywhere." He directed them to a waiting Humvee and they sped northeast to a small hangar, exited the truck, and showed their identification to the MPs guarding the entrance. After a thorough inspection, the MPs saluted and handed them their IDs, and Neil led them inside.

A large wedge-shaped aircraft sat on the floor of the hangar, painted in subtle shades of gray and black. "This is the Sentinel," Neil said. "We were testing it with Delta, near the mountains. The plan was to shake out the bugs and start deploying them along the Pakistan border. This really wrecks our schedule. Not to mention the loss of life. It's just tragic."

"Yeah," Deion said. "We've heard. What do you know so far?"

"Not much. We think it's AQ."

"The local Taliban are trying to distance themselves," Valerie confirmed.

Deion whistled as they walked around the drone. It was bigger than he had expected. "What's so special about this drone?" he asked.

"It can intercept thousands of cell phone calls," Neil said. "You know there's not a lot of landlines here; everyone uses cheap cell phones. Instead of tapping cell towers, this scans all cell phones within a thirty-kilometer range. It can also pull data from the phones, including text and pictures."

Deion's eyes widened. The drone would be a game changer for SIGINT and would allow JSOC unprecedented flexibility in tracking high-value targets. He shook his head. Of course AQ would be terrified of the Sentinel.

Neil led them out of the building, and they got back in the Humvee and headed southwest to the DIA headquarters.

As Neil drove, Deion watched off-duty soldiers playing soccer, no field in sight, just a bunch of men, black and white and brown, stirring up dust and kicking the ball. He sighed. Nothing had changed since he had left. The rest of Afghanistan was a powder keg of hostility and resentment, thousands of years in the making. They were still no closer to achieving a stable and democratic Afghanistan. "Did you make those calls I emailed you about?"

Neil nodded as they drove past a no-parking fire-lane sign. "I did. The local Taliban commander is named Azim. He's more concerned about maintaining power than repelling the infidel horde. He fights just hard enough to keep AQ off his back. His man will talk to us, but we have to go to him. His man said you'd know the location."

Valerie cleared her throat. "Is that safe? I mean, how could that *possibly* be safe?"

"Hell no, it's not safe," Deion said. "We have to go to the middle of Kandahar. If we go in heavy, Azim's man will be in the wind."

They entered the brown tent, the feeble air conditioning barely making a dent in the heat. Nancy tapped Deion on the shoulder. "Is this the same cowboy shit that got you sent to Gitmo?"

"Yeah."

She stared at him quizzically. "You sure about this?"

He nodded.

She shrugged. "It's your show."

They greeted the officer on duty and set up temporary desk space on a wooden table near the back. The tent was a beehive of activity, with countless missions in progress, but no one paid them any attention as Neil produced a map of Kandahar and circled a residential section. "Here's where we need to go, about two blocks from a market. Deion knows the area. The ladies will have to wait in the truck."

"No way," Nancy said. "We're going in with you."

"That might be a problem," Deion countered. "You know how the Taliban are about women."

She glared at him. "It's not open for discussion."

He started to argue, then realized it was pointless. "Val, what about you?" He hated to put her in danger, but it wasn't her first time on an operation deep in enemy territory.

She frowned, then slowly nodded. "I'm in."

"How do we do this?" Neil asked.

Deion pointed to the surrounding buildings. "We'll have guys here, here, and here. I want choppers spun up and ready, and drone support if we can get it. Once we enter the building, it's just the four of us."

Valerie pursed her lips. "When does this happen?"

"At dusk," Neil answered.

Deion glanced at the digital clock at the front of the tent. "That's not a lot of time."

Neil smiled. "Don't worry, I've got Delta there and waiting. The site is as clear as it's going to get."

Deion snapped his fingers. "Let's make it happen."

CHAPTER NINE

Denver, Colorado

E ric's teeth rattled as the C-17 touched down on the Buckley AFB runway. He missed the Gulfstream, but it lacked the capacity to carry the two black Ford Econoline vans that were strapped down in the cargo bay. The plane taxied to the hangar and the crew got busy unloading the vans.

He shivered in the morning chill, his light windbreaker providing little comfort. He took John aside. "We've got a few minutes. You ready for this?"

John nodded. "This is what I've been training for, right?"

"This isn't like missions in the Army. We'll be mingling with citizens. We don't want any screw-ups. We just need to get to the storage unit and find the cesium."

"Got it," John said.

Eric introduced him to the other former Operators he had recruited with Nancy's help. Taylor Martin, a black man with massive hands, had worked with Eric years before in Afghanistan and was second-in-command. Martin had an easy sense of humor, with intelligent, deep-set eyes. He trusted Martin and knew the man would rather die than fail his commanding officer.

Roger Johnson, a thin young man with a receding hairline and jutting chin, would be their third, followed by Mark Kelly, a bland-looking man with sad brown eyes.

They were all dressed in civilian clothes, and none would look out of place on the street unless you noticed their eyes. They all had the thousand-yard stare.

"Martin, John, and I will be in the first unit. Johnson, you and Kelly will follow in the second. Any questions?"

"We have a location?" Kelly asked.

"What we have," Eric replied, "is the location for a storage unit, rented to Jeff Fletcher. He's a known associate of the APR, and a drone overfly detected unusual amounts of radiation."

Martin spoke up. "We're ready, Steeljaw."

"Remember, we don't have any firm intel, so be careful."

The crew chief of the C-17 approached and saluted. "Your vehicles are unloaded and ready to go."

Eric saluted back. "This is it, gentlemen. Once more unto the breach."

They loaded into the vans and Martin headed west on US-30 toward downtown, John in the passenger seat, Eric in the back.

"Why does it have to be a white power group?" Martin grumbled. "I hate white power groups."

Eric smiled. "Don't be full of the black hate."

Martin looked up in the rearview mirror, a wide smile on his face. "Smart-ass."

Eric laughed, then turned serious. "Remember, there's enough cesium to light up Denver."

All three men looked at each other, the laughter gone. They followed the GPS coordinates to a storage complex on the southern edge of downtown Denver, the landscape dotted with pawnshops, nail salons, and check-cashing services.

"This is it," Martin said. He pulled the van over a block from the storage shed and Kelly wheeled in behind them.

John opened a black plastic case and removed the FGRD, a Fast-Cooling Germanium Radiation Detector.

Eric interrupted his fiddling. "Didn't you check that thing before we left Groom Lake?"

"Yeah," John said, "but it's finicky. Never can be too careful."

"Good point," Eric agreed. He pulled his M11 from his shoulder holster, checked it, then put it back, covering it with his windbreaker. John did the same.

They checked their earpieces, and after ensuring the MBITR radios worked correctly, Eric exited the van. John followed, clutching the FGRD case. Traffic was light and no one noticed as they headed to the front of the storage property.

They stopped in front of the gate and Eric peered at the numeric keypad that controlled the front gate. "It's an SSW—iLW unit," he said over the radio.

"Hang on, Steeljaw," Martin replied over the earpiece. "We'll have the override code momentarily." There was a pause. "The override code is one two pound four five asterisk. That should unlock the gate."

He gave a silent prayer to modernity, keyed in the code, and was rewarded when the green light blipped and the gate opened.

They headed for the second row of concrete storage sheds, and John removed the FGRD and computer from the case and started the FGRD's cooling cycle. After several minutes, the display turned blue.

"Well?" Eric asked. "Anything?"

"Analyzing data," John replied. He stood still for several moments, staring at the small screen.

"Nothing?"

"It's not as easy as I'm making it look," John said.

Eric grinned. "Just trying to light a fire."

"Okay, it's complete. There's definitely abnormal amounts of radiation. Which unit belongs to Fletcher?"

"Two seventeen, that's three rows back. Let's get moving."

They headed deeper into the storage yard, moving quickly. As they rounded a corner, John raised his hand, staring at the computer screen. "We're getting closer."

"Glad it's you two in there," Martin's voice crackled. "Remember that ten years from now when you're both sterile."

John frowned and Eric slapped him on the shoulder. "He's just messing with you, John. There's nothing to be worried about." *I hope.*

As they walked through the gravel lot, John said, "Getting stronger. It's definitely coming from this row."

Eric's earpiece crackled. "Heads up," Martin said. "You've got incoming. Brown Ford station wagon, four males."

"It's this unit," John said, pointing to 217.

"How much time?" Eric asked.

"They're at the keypad," Martin answered. "Thirty seconds."

"That's not enough," John said.

"Is Fletcher with them?" Eric asked.

"Cannot confirm, repeat, cannot confirm," Martin said.

John's eyes widened. "What do we do?"

Eric thought quickly, dismissing scenarios, then grinned. "We improvise. Make yourself scarce."

"Gate is opening," Martin said.

"Okay," Eric said. "We're going to play this by ear."

"Roger that," Martin said. "Vehicle is through the gate."

John hurried around the row of storage units, while Eric pulled at his jacket, ruffling it to hide the shoulder holster, then moved down two units. As the station wagon came around the corner, he backed up and pantomimed placing keys in his pocket, as if he had just finished closing the storage unit door.

The men in the car eyed him suspiciously as they shut off the engine and piled out. They were dressed in blue jeans and dirty t-shirts, and Eric recognized the driver, Jeff Fletcher, from his rap sheet.

"Oh, hello," Eric said. "Weird, huh?"

Fletcher regarded him coolly. "What's weird?"

"You almost never see anybody in these storage faculties," Eric replied, walking closer. "I mean, I drive past places like this all the time, but I never actually see anybody." The men stepped forward, giving each other sidelong glances, as he continued. "I've been here a couple of times and this place is always deserted, then you guys showed up. Isn't that weird?"

Fletcher glared at him. "It's a mini warehouse, dumbass, someone has to actually put stuff in and take stuff out."

The three other men smirked but eased back.

Eric watched them, the thousand-yard stare allowing him to keep track of all four men with his peripheral vision. He stepped forward again. "I know, but it's still weird."

He was now close enough to have raised their guard, if not for his nonsensical speech. "Seriously, when was the last time you saw someone else here? It just doesn't happen. Never, wouldn't you say?"

He was close enough that Fletcher finally took notice. He had invaded the personal space a stranger should never occupy and was within a step of striking distance. The man to Fletcher's right was tall, six foot, stocky build, a Harley-Davidson shirt stretched across his muscular frame. The men to Fletcher's left were shorter, but not by much. They were all well-muscled. All wore tattoos of different shapes and colors, all indicating time served in prison. Fletcher was the only one without ink.

Eric grinned. "Hey, do you guys belong to a biker club? Those tattoos are cool."

"What are you, Walter fucking Cronkite?" Fletcher asked. "You writing a book? Get outta here and mind your own business."

"Didn't mean to bother you," Eric answered. He took the last step forward. "I'm not looking for trouble."

He finally triggered some kind of internal alarm, the distance too close for a crazy person on the street, and Fletcher's eyes widened. Before he could move, Eric slammed his palm under Fletcher's chin. The man's jaws slammed together and he went down hard in the loose rock.

Fletcher's friend, the big man with the Harley shirt, lunged forward. Eric sidestepped, and a quick chop with his left hand collapsed the man's windpipe.

Then the two shorter men were on him, one throwing wild punches at his head, the other bolting forward but being knocked senseless from the other man's flailing fists.

He saw John come from behind and strike the wild puncher in the kidneys. The man screamed as he went down.

The other man scrambled up and dove toward Eric, catching his legs, taking him to the ground. He grunted from the pain as his head slammed into the rock. Fletcher rose, dazed, but managed to kick him in the groin before John stepped up from behind and clapped his hands on the sides of Fletcher's head.

Fletcher screamed as his eardrums ruptured, and John spun and drove his fist deep into the solar plexus of the other man, who collapsed, white-faced and motionless.

Eric was rising when Fletcher pulled the gun, a stubby nickel-plated revolver. He struggled to pull his M11, watching in slow motion as the barrel of Fletcher's revolver inched higher, when then there was a double wham.

Two holes appeared in Fletcher's chest. Fletcher dropped his revolver and collapsed on the ground, eyes glassy. John stood behind him, his M11 drawn, a wisp of smoke wafting from the chamber.

John's gaze flickered from Fletcher to Eric and back again. "Holy shit," he managed, his face tinted green.

Eric stood and surveyed the damage. "Are they all dead?"

John quickly checked the bodies. "Yeah."

Eric sighed. "I was trying not to kill them."

"The training took over," John said. "I didn't have time to think." His hands started to tremble, then he doubled over and threw up, long heaves that emptied his stomach onto the white rock.

"Steeljaw? What's the sitrep?" Martin asked. "We heard shots fired. Do you have Fletcher?"

Eric stooped and searched Fletcher's pockets. He found Fletcher's keys and tried several until he found the one that opened the lock on the sliding door. The storage unit was filled with dozens of brown ammo boxes and a crate of M16s, but most of the space was full of empty barrels emblazoned with the Landfrey logo.

He turned to John, who was still on his knees, wiping spittle from the back of his mouth. The four dead men lay where they had fallen. He looked back to the warehouse, which contained no cesium, and screamed in rage. "Fuck!"

* * *

119

John watched as Martin, Johnson and Kelly loaded the men into body bags. He turned as Eric clapped him on the shoulder. "Thanks, John. Fletcher was going to shoot."

"I didn't mean to kill them," he said. "It was reflex."

"You didn't kill them all," Eric said. "The guy with the collapsed trachea was mine."

Eric's words didn't make him feel better. He watched as Martin and Johnson picked up the body bags, one by one, and flopped them into the back of the van. "It's not the same."

"What?" Eric asked.

"Killing a man up close. It's not like Iraq. They were always shooting at us."

"I won't lie to you. Killing a man up close *is* different. You see their eyes, you feel it when you hit them. You see the bodies jerk, smell it when their bowels release. There's nothing glamorous about death. Taking a life isn't pleasant, but it's part of the job. It was us or them. I don't like killing, never have, never will."

He shrugged. "I feel horrible."

Eric smiled. "Good. It means you're not a monster."

They finished loading the last body in the van, then Martin handed a cell phone to Eric. "We found this burner in Fletcher's car. The rest of the men were clean."

Eric pulled his cell phone from the pocket of his jacket and held it next to Fletcher's until Fletcher's phone beeped. "Clark, did you get that?"

Clark replied over the earpiece. "We got it. Karen's running the backtrack. There was nothing else in the storage unit?"

"It's a dead end," Eric said, "but if we track where that phone's been, we know where Fletcher's been."

John was listening over his earpiece, but it suddenly went quiet. He tapped it, thinking perhaps it had been dislodged, but Eric shook his head.

"That's right," Eric said. "It was just like that." He paused, then continued, "That is correct. Everything is under control. We'll continue with the mission."

John wondered what Clark was saying and why he had been cut from the conversation. Was it about him mistakenly killing Fletcher? He replayed the events in his mind, how Eric had struck Fletcher, how he had come to help defend Eric, the blur of the fight.

It had happened so fast, his body on autopilot. He had punched the first man in the kidneys because he knew that a blow to the kidneys—if hard enough—would incapacitate most men.

When he had struck, he had known something was wrong. His arm was a piece of iron, driven by the power of a freight train. The man had collapsed like a puppet with its strings cut. Then, the sickening crunch traveling up his arm as he'd hit the second man in the solar plexus, and the split second when he knew he had collapsed the guy's sternum.

He was so strong, so fast. He had known as he'd struck that it was a killing blow, the heart destroyed as the bone shards lanced through it, only seconds before it would start spasming, blood leaking into the body cavities, blood pressure dropping.

It was the eyes that haunted him. They went wide, the pupils dilating, but he had no time to waste as he saw Fletcher struggling to pull a gun. Eric was still on the ground, dazed. Everything had slowed and he had known that Fletcher was going to kill Eric.

He couldn't allow that.

He had pulled his M11 and fired, two quick shots that left his ears ringing as he had hit Fletcher center mass, just like in the shooting house.

Time had sped up and he'd realized his mistake. He had killed Fletcher, their target, the man with the cesium.

Oh no.

He'd turned and seen the man Eric had killed, a wet spot spreading across his pants as his bladder loosened.

He'd turned back to the first man, the one he'd kidney punched, dead on the dusty white rock. The second man he'd killed lay there as well, glassy eyes staring emptily. Eric scrambled up, grabbing Fletcher, searching his jacket and his pockets.

He couldn't take it. He'd lurched forward and heaved, his body convulsing as he emptied his stomach of breakfast, the bitter taste of coffee and bile burning his throat. He'd watched Eric open the door to the storage unit, enter, then storm out, yelling in frustration. The rock had crunched as Martin, Kelly and Johnson had roared up in the second van.

The mission had come up empty. There was no cesium in the unit, and he just killed the man who could have told them where it was.

His earpiece crackled to life, jolting him back to the present, and he heard Clark's voice. "It's a burner, all right, purchased two days ago at Walmart. The backtrack is triangulating his position from the cell phone towers. We also have his incoming and outgoing phone calls. There's only one number, and it tracks back to another burner cell, purchased at the same Walmart. We're running a backtrack on that phone, too."

Mark Kelly picked up the spent shell casings from John's M11 and handed them to him. He shook his head and Kelly shrugged, pocketing the brass. Roger Johnson handed him two new bullets and said quietly, "Don't forget to reload."

Numb, John thumbed the decocking lever and removed the magazine from his M11, added the two bullets, and reinserted it. His hands moved of their own accord, muscle memory ingrained from countless hours on the gun range.

"We've got something," Clark finally said. "The other phone has gone off-air, but we have a day's worth of data and a physical convergence at a bar named the Rusty Bucket not far from your current location."

"Roger that," Eric said. "The cesium has been moved. We've probably only got a few hours before they notice these four missing and everyone bolts. Can you ping the cell phones in the bar and start a backtrack on each of them?"

"Already in progress."

Eric addressed John and the men. "We're going in. If the cesium is on the move, it could be out of town or out of state before we can stop it. We've got a limited window. Someone in the APR knows where it is. We'll level that place if we have to, but we *will* find that cesium."

* * *

Kandahar, Afghanistan

The market buzzed with activity as people hurried to finish their shopping before evening prayers. As Deion and the others threaded their Toyota down the dirt road, the Afghan men looked askew at the Americans before quickly glancing away.

Another truck pulled up behind them and four men in camos exited, each holding an HK416. They took up defensive positions while managing to look casually bored. Their leader, a big, raw-boned man named Joshua Morse, gave Deion a nod.

The blistering heat was finally lifting, but Deion still felt the trickle of sweat worming down his back. The air was full of smells, from trash piles near the edge of the market to the lingering smoke from outside cooking. The market was lined with stalls selling bicycle parts, sandals, and vegetables. Although he had been gone for over a year, it felt like he had never left. He sighed as his radio crackled to life.

"We have eyes on you, Freeman. It's clear." The voice belonged to Bill Burton, a Delta Operator everyone called Redman for the constant wad of chew in his mouth. His men were staked out in positions on the rooftops, waiting for Deion's team to arrive.

Deion keyed the PRC-148. "Keep an eye out, Redman. We can trust this guy for the meet, but that's it."

"Roger that, Freeman."

Neil led them to a room in the back of a building to meet General Azim's representative. The room was dingy white, with a tattered and threadbare rug on the floor. The man waiting for them couldn't have been more than seventeen, with the barest trace of a black beard, but he was old enough to carry an AK-47 over his shoulder.

Deion noted his robe, the sandals, and the dead eyes. Physically he was a kid, but his dead eyes suggested a lost innocence. Outside, the sky was darkening, and the room was meagerly lit by a single bulb on the ceiling.

"What's your name?" Deion asked in fluent Pashto.

The young man registered shock and answered back in Pashto. "You speak well for an infidel."

"Thank you. I'm Deion."

"I am Jaabir. General Azim would like you to know the Taliban had nothing to do with the attack on your base."

Deion raised an eyebrow. "Really? Why should I believe General Azim?"

"The Taliban would not attack a small outpost in the desert. We would only attack the foreign occupiers who were brandishing their weapons against the brave and honorable Afghans who wished only to repel the invading army."

Nancy tapped him on the shoulder. "What's he saying?"

Jaabir drew back, glaring at her, but spoke in broken English. "I do not speak to women. Their presence here is an affront to Allah."

"Settle down, Jaabir." He turned to Nancy. "Relax. Take Val and Neil and go outside. I want to talk to him alone."

Nancy's eyes narrowed, but she motioned Neil and Valerie to the hallway, leaving him alone with Jaabir.

Once they had left the room, he continued, "My man in Kandahar told you to pass along the message to Azim—"

"General Azim!"

"Sorry," Deion corrected, "*General* Azim. The Army will find out who did this. A lot of Taliban could get killed. A lot of innocents, too. General Azim wants what's best for Afghanistan. He's a proud man who knows that sometimes you have to work together for a common goal."

Jaabir frowned, considering that. "You are not like I expected."

"How's that?"

"I have seen television shows of America," Jaabir admitted. "I saw how black men are treated by the Christians who run the country." His eyes darted to the hallway, then back to Deion.

Deion smiled. The kid was earnest. "It's entertainment, Jaabir. It's not a bad place. Someday Afghanistan will be like that. You'll lay down your weapons and your kids will go to school, get an education, maybe get an opportunity like I did."

Jaabir nodded. "I think I will probably die fighting before that happens. I am committed to Jihad."

"Of course," Deion agreed. *That's the problem with this place.* "You never know, though. Look at us right now."

The boy nodded wisely. "General Azim said you would be very kind to me so that I would turn to your cause."

Deion frowned. "I'm just trying to find out who attacked our men. I don't want a full-blown assault on Kandahar. That wouldn't be good for your people. I'm betting that General Azim doesn't want that, either. I'm betting he gave you instructions."

Jaabir nodded. "He did. The attack was planned by an Arab named Abdullah. He was considered to be a great Mujahideen, but General Azim was always suspicious of this man. Abdullah planned the attack and carried it out without consulting General Azim. General Azim would like you to know that this man is no longer welcome in Kandahar."

"What else can you tell me about this man, Abdullah?"

The boy considered his words carefully, then spoke. "He is known as Abdullah the Bomber. He disappeared for many years after the war. Some said he went home and some said he went on Hajj. He came back with a wife, but your drones killed her. He has committed himself to Jihad."

Deion thought quickly. As far as he could tell, the boy was telling the truth. "Jaabir, was there anything else General Azim told you?"

Jaabir nodded. "We have one of Abdullah's men. General Azim will provide this man to you, as a show of respect."

"Really? And what does General Azim ask in return? A gift must be answered with a gift."

Jaabir nodded. "A gift is freely given, but if answered with a gift it shows respect and honor."

"And where might this man be kept?"

Jaabir smiled. "Not far from here."

"Of course," he said. "I must talk with my people."

Jaabir nodded. "I will return in one hour."

He led the boy through the hallway to the front of the building, then keyed his radio. "Status?"

"Clear," Redman answered. "Freeman, sorry to tell you, but we got a call while you were in the building. We have new orders to return to base."

"What? In the middle of the operation?"

"Sorry, Freeman. We've got our orders. Watch your six."

"Thanks, Redman. Much appreciated."

He turned to Neil and nodded. Neil placed a brown leather satchel on the floor and took a step back. Jaabir picked it up, nodded to Deion, then exited the building without looking back. By the time they entered the street, Jaabir was long gone, lost in the twilit maze of buildings and alleys. They got back in the Toyota.

"What was that all about?" Valerie asked.

"Azim's quite the businessman," Deion said. "Sometimes he plays on the American side, sometimes on the Taliban's. He knows that sooner or later we'll pull out and he's jockeying for position. He'll fight us if he can, but he prefers to let the other Taliban do the fighting. If he appears weak, Al-Qaeda will replace him in a heartbeat. He confirmed the attacker was Abdullah the Bomber, and he's got one of Abdullah's men. We just paid him one hundred grand in cash for Jaabir to lead us to him."

Nancy shook her head, amazed. "I can't believe your cowboy routine *actually* worked."

"Yeah, but we have a problem." He paused, considering his words. "I think you really pissed off my old boss, Rumple. If I had to guess, he's the one who got Delta recalled. We're on our own."

Nancy's eyes widened and her face reddened. "I'll have his ass for this," she spat out.

The Delta Operator from the second truck, Morse, came forward to shake Deion's hand. "We're out. Redman says sorry and good luck."

"No problem," Deion said. "Thanks for the assist."

He watched as the Operators got in their truck and left. The market had cleared out while they were in the building, the bustling throng of people dwindling, many of the carts now missing. A few remaining Afghans watched them with curious eyes, but most were busy tearing down their stalls in the twilight.

"I'm a little worried," Neil said.

"Me, too," Valerie agreed. "We've got one drone overhead and no support. I know you like to play cowboy, but this is insane."

"I can take care of Rumple," Nancy said, "but it'll take time. How long do we have?"

"Jaabir will be back in an hour," Deion said.

Her eyes narrowed. "That's a long time for us to sit with our dicks in the wind."

He started to speak but she interrupted. "It's your call, Deion. You know this area and you know the people."

"Neil? How about you?" he asked.

Neil nodded but his eyes were wary. "I'll back your play but it's a hell of a risk."

"You're all crazy," Valerie said, "but if you're in, so am I."

CHAPTER TEN

Denver, Colorado

J ohn shook his head. The Rusty Bucket was in a seedy part of town, the bar's name sloppily painted in faded black letters on the dingy white exterior. The sidewalk was cracked and broken, and cigarettes and beer cans littered the front.

They were parked a block away, discreetly watching the entrance, the second van parked behind them. No one had entered or left the building in the thirty minutes they had been watching. "Not a happening spot," he muttered.

Martin laughed. "I'm glad you white boys are going in. There's Klan in there for sure."

"Don't worry," Eric said. "We won't send you in there. You'd stand out like a big black sore thumb."

"Your lack of empathy for my racial concerns is disappointing," Martin said, sadly shaking his head.

John liked Martin's sly wit, his easy disposition, and his quiet confidence. Kelly and Johnson were both excellent soldiers, but Martin was much like Eric—mature, responsible, and capable.

Eric fiddled with the radio, which was playing an old Hank Williams song, then sighed. "Clark, have you got anything?"

John's earpiece crackled. "The Rusty Bucket is their known hangout," Clark said. "Everett Dyer, the APR founder, is the co-owner. We've tracked his cell phone. It's there now."

"Are you sure?" Eric asked. "The place looks dead."

"We've backtracked other members of the APR. When they reach that bar, their cell phones go off-network. We tried to remotely activate them and use them as bugs, but they are unresponsive. They must be shielding them, probably in a foil-lined bag or box."

Kelly sighed through his earpiece. "I hate it when douchebags become technically competent."

"I don't like this," Eric said. "Doesn't this seem too sophisticated for them?"

"Karen has a theory," Clark said. "She thinks they might try and sell the cesium to another white power group, or maybe neo-Nazis."

It was Eric's turn to sigh. "How good is that theory?"

"She's given it a very low-fidelity score, but it remains a possibility."

"Just great." Eric turned to John. "You ready?"

He nodded, trying to quiet the butterflies in his stomach.

"Good. Martin, stay here. Kelly, Johnson, I need one of you, your choice."

"I'll go," Kelly volunteered. "Nothing like overt racism mixed with a side of jingoism to get the blood pumping."

The butterflies had been replaced with belly flops. "Eric," John interrupted, "can I talk to you for a minute?"

Eric eyed him. "Guys, hold here." He motioned for John to get out of the van. They exited and stepped behind the vehicle. "What's up?"

John stood, silent, then took out his earpiece and deactivated it with the edge of his thumbnail.

Eric looked puzzled but did the same.

"I'm sorry about earlier," he managed.

Eric smiled. "I told you, it wasn't your fault."

"I screwed up. If I'd left one of them alive, we wouldn't be blindly walking in there."

Eric gazed at him thoughtfully. "It's the killing, isn't it?"

He could not meet Eric's gaze. "I've had this dream for the past several weeks. I'm angry, very angry. There's a crowd of people and I want to hurt them. Then I wake up and I'm covered in sweat and my heart is beating a million miles an hour. Now I'm feeling the same way, my heart is beating like crazy and I'm scared that if we go into that bar, I might have to hurt someone."

"You're a good soldier," Eric reassured. "The dreams might be from the PTSD. I don't know, I'm not a shrink. Did you tell Doc Barnwell about any of this?"

"I know what happens if I speak to Barnwell. I could be deemed unfit for duty. I don't want people thinking I'm a basket case."

Eric spoke softly. "I'm sorry, but you have to come to terms with it. You *will* have to kill. I've seen men who enjoy killing, enjoy making people hurt and suffer. What we do in the OTM, we do for the good of the country. You have to accept that. The people we kill, they're *not* good people, John. Of all the human beings on this earth, they are the ones who dirty up the gene pool."

"We don't know that," John said. "We don't know what these guys have done."

"They've stolen enough cesium to make a city uninhabitable. Think of the children and the elderly. There's no way to evacuate them all. The elderly could die immediately, the kids lost to leukemia or lung cancer—they're the bad guys, John. That makes us the good guys."

The feeling in his gut still gnawed at him. "I don't feel like the good guy. I feel like a killer."

Eric clasped him by the shoulders. "Sometimes we gotta do what we gotta do. Tell me right now. Can you do this?"

John thought about the men he had killed, about weaponized cesium, about the potential dead who would weigh on his conscience. "I can do it."

Eric smiled. "Good. Get Kelly and let's make this happen."

* * *

Eric entered first and squinted as his eyes adjusted to the dim light, his boots squeaking against the dirty wood floor, John and Kelly close behind.

He tried to put John's words out of his mind but kept going back to the nightmares. If John were starting to remember his past, it could be a real problem for the project. Not to mention that he counted on John to have his back.

In part, he agreed with him. He did not enjoy killing, either, but to save a life, he might have to take a life. God have mercy on his soul, but he wouldn't hesitate to kill one to save a thousand.

He knew it was unfair to resent John's newfound sense of morality. John no longer remembered the Red Cross bombing. In fact, John was eager to please, constantly trying to impress with hard work and determination. What galled him was that John was now *his* responsibility. He was to befriend him, instill him with confidence, all the while knowing that he might have to put a bullet in the back of his head.

He gritted his teeth. John *had* to perform. The project depended on it.

He pushed the concerns out of his mind. He couldn't let his distraction get them all killed.

The few overhead lights cast dim spots on the floor, but he made out the long bar top that took up the length of one wall. A dozen square wooden tables filled the rest. The floor was stained, and stale beer and urine gave the bar a toilet smell.

The bartender glanced at them, a big man with a red spider tattoo plastered around his bald head, a crooked nose from too many breaks, and beady black eyes.

Two heavyset men wearing leather jackets with the APR patches sat at one of the tables. He knew their type, shaggy hair and beards, the start of potbellies from too much time on motorcycles and too little exercise. Two younger men in blue jeans and denim work shirts nursed their beers in quiet conversation at another table.

The bikers glanced their way, then pretended to ignore them. The younger men tracked his movement as he approached the bar.

He took a seat, resting his arms on the sticky bar top. John and Kelly joined him. The bartender approached and there was an awkward pause until Kelly spoke up softly. "Coors draft?"

The bartender squinted at him and nodded.

"Make it three," Eric said.

The bartender poured the drafts and slid them across the bar top. He tossed a filthy bar towel over his shoulder and walked to the other end of the bar, leaned heavily against it, and lit a cigarette.

"Stellar customer service," John said quietly.

"What did you expect? It's not even noon," Eric replied. "I recognize the two bikers by their rap sheets. No sign of Dyer." He caught the bartender's eye and motioned. The surly man nodded and approached. Eric noticed the lightness to his step.

A boxer, maybe.

"Need something else?"

Eric nodded. "Yeah, I'm looking for a man named Dyer."

"Don't know him." The man started to turn.

"I think you do," Eric said.

The bartender stopped, his glare still hostile. "Lots of men come in here."

Eric smiled. "This man preaches."

The bartender laughed. "I don't ask no questions and they don't tell no lies. If they want a drink, that's their God-given right, preacher or not."

"This man preaches a certain type of message. We like that message."

"I said, I don't *know* any Dyer." The big man leaned forward. "Whatever you're looking for, you won't find it here."

Eric decided to push the issue. "I've heard the American Patriot Revolution gathers here. You sure you don't know anything about that? We like what they stand for."

The bartender's eyes narrowed. "You'd like to join the APR? Do you believe in racial purity?" His eyes darted between Eric, John, and Kelly. "You say you like the APR. What's the first rule of the APR?"

Luckily, Eric had glanced over their website. "Do not mix with the races. We don't. I'm of German descent, myself, and my friends can trace their families back to England. Like I said, we want to meet Mr. Dyer."

The bartender nodded. "What's the second rule of the APR?"

"To take all means necessary to keep the races separate but equal."

"And the third?"

"To use whatever means necessary to restore this country to its former greatness and to adhere to the Constitution as originally written," Eric responded quickly.

The bartender smiled. "Funny, most cops can get that off the Internet. It doesn't mean shit that you know it. You come in here with your cop haircuts and your cop eyes and spout something you memorized."

Eric laughed. "I can promise you that we are *not* cops."

"If you're not cops, you're something worse. Federals, maybe. Either way, you need to move along. You're done here."

He heard the scraping of chairs behind them. John and Kelly turned, and he knew the four men had stood and were coming their way.

The bartender lunged forward, his hand scrabbling for something under the bar. Eric drove his arm forward, the palm of his hand not stopping until there was a popping crunch in the man's nose. He turned to see John hit the two young men like an offensive lineman, driving them back.

Kelly jumped from his bar stool and tried to tackle the two bikers, but one of them struck Eric a glancing blow to his head, knocking him to the floor.

He shook his head and caught the other biker along the neck with the heel of his hand. The man sank to his knees, stunned. Eric turned to see the other biker kick Kelly in the ribs with his boot. Kelly grunted in pain and doubled over.

John was rolling on the floor with the two young men, then he jerked up and came down with his knee into the chest of one of them. There was a sickening crack as the sternum broke and the man went limp.

The second man tried to punch John in the crotch. John jerked backward and the man staggered up and tried to kick him, but John smoothly pulled his M11 and put two bullets through the man's chest and another in the middle of his face, blood spraying from the back of the man's head.

Kelly was still struggling with the other biker until he caught the man's foot and twisted, knocking him to the floor. Before the man could react, Kelly was on him, gouging his eyes, then twisted the screaming man around and put him in a choke hold, squeezing against his neck to stop the blood flow to the man's brain.

Eric turned to the other biker, the one he'd thought stunned, but apparently he wasn't stunned well enough. The man flipped open a serrated knife and took a lunging stab at him. He kicked the biker's hand and felt the wrist break as the man gasped. The biker went for his revolver but Eric knocked it away, then grabbed him by his leather jacket and jerked him upright. "Where's Dyer?"

The man winced in pain and shook his head. "I'm not telling you anything!"

John screamed, "Eric!"

Eric turned as the bartender came up from behind the bar with a sawed-off shotgun. He jumped back, spinning as he went, and the roar of the shotgun deafened him. Hot fire raked across his right arm, and he knew he was hit, but then he heard the double wham of John's M11.

The bartender slumped onto the bar, his dead weight pinning him to the bar top. The biker that Eric had fought lay dead on the floor, caught by the brunt of two barrels of double-ought buckshot, the side of his head and shoulder bloody hamburger. He turned as Kelly continued squeezing the other biker's neck, his eyes red and bloody from ruptured blood vessels, then heard a crunch as Kelly dropped the dead man to the floor.

He grasped his arm, cradling it. The pain burned up and into his shoulder, but he knew it was a flesh wound. He shook his head, trying to clear the dizziness. "John, check the bathrooms. Kelly, check in the back. Dyer's got to be here somewhere."

Kelly nodded and left through the back.

John kicked in the door to the men's bathroom, looking for Dyer.

He removed his jacket, gingerly pulling it over his right arm, then took the first-aid kit from his jacket. He tore open the small packet and sprinkled the powder on the bloody wound. It burned like fire, but the clotting agent kicked in, staunching the blood flow, the painkiller reducing the burning fire to a dull throb.

"Steeljaw? You need help?" Martin asked.

"Negative. Hold your position. Anyone tries coming in, shoot them."

"Roger that. Any wounded?"

"Just me. Hurts, but I'm fine."

John came out shaking his head, then did the same sweep of the women's bathroom. "Clear," he hollered.

Kelly reentered the bar. "There's no one in the back," he said. "Just a door to the alley."

Eric's earpiece crackled. "Johnson was watching the back. No one came out. Dyer's got to be inside," Martin insisted.

It didn't make any sense. "I don't know where the hell he could be."

"We need to check the back," Kelly said. "Sometimes they have stairs to basement storage."

John crept around the bar and checked the bartender for a pulse. "He's gone."

"So are these four," Kelly said.

John lifted a rug from the floor and threw it over the dead bartender. "Yep, there's a trapdoor." He motioned for Kelly to follow him.

Eric struggled to his feet. "I'm going, too," he said.

"You're injured," Kelly said. "We got this."

Eric gritted his teeth. "I'm going." He stepped around the bar and saw the trapdoor, heavy wood planks nailed together with an iron ring in the corner.

John lifted the door and Eric peered down the stairwell. "It's dark down there."

John flicked a switch that turned on the light below, and they carefully lowered themselves down the steeply pitched stairs to the dirty cement floor.

The basement was brimming with beer cases stacked to the ceiling. Eric pointed to a steel-plated door, the only other thing in the basement. "A reinforced door? He's in there."

"How are we going to get in?" Kelly asked. "The breaching charges are in the van." He inspected the wall, looking for hinges.

John put his hand on Eric's arm. "I can open it. Activate the pump."

Eric looked from the door to John, then nodded. "Clark, we need an enhancement."

"Roger that," Clark replied. There was a long pause. "Pump activated."

John shuddered and his eyes widened. "Oh yeah," he breathed. "That's the stuff."

"You sure you can open it?" Eric asked. "It's damned big."

John clenched his fists. "Stay back." He stepped to the far wall and then sprang across the room, a rolling wave of energy. He hit the door with his shoulder, a moving blur.

There was a crash and a pinging noise as the hinge pins sheared off. The door exploded inward, thrown completely into the room and against the far wall with a mighty crash. Eric followed John, Kelly right behind him, their pistols drawn. A long table with twelve chairs filled most of the room, but it was the chair at the far end that caught his attention.

Everett Dyer, the head of the APR, sat at the head of the table. He was a tall man in his late sixties, his face a mass of wrinkles and liver spots, his hair a badly dyed comb-over.

Dyer had preached for years in favor of strict racial separation, and the FBI had investigated him for a string of bombings at universities across the country, targeting professors of ethnic studies, but somehow Dyer always got off.

Eric knew what made Dyer dangerous. He was a true believer. He structured the APR as both a political party and a religious group. He invoked the Federalist Papers while preaching from the pulpit. His message about racial separation played well with the bigots.

No, Dyer was dangerous, and now he sat, impassive, his left hand on the table, his right hand holding a device in his skeletal grip.

"Good morning, gentlemen. I'm assuming you're here to arrest me or kill me," Dyer said in a voice barely a whisper.

"We're not here to do either. We just need some information," Eric said.

Dyer tilted his head and laughed softly. "You killed the men above, yet you are not here to kill me?"

"They drew first," Eric said. "We just defended ourselves. It didn't have to go that way."

"Do you know what this device is?" Dyer asked.

Eric's stomach dropped. "That's a dead man's switch."

John and Kelly took a halting step backward.

"That is correct. If I take my thumb off this trigger, it will be a bad day for you, indeed. Now, are you with the police? Or the FBI?"

Eric shook his head. "None of those. We don't care about your white power group. We just need information. We can all leave here today."

"White power, is that what you think we are? I founded the APR in hopes that we could stop the mixing of races in this great country. I'm not a racist. I'm a *patriot*. As any true patriot, I am willing to spill my blood to refresh the tree of liberty. The men above, however, were innocent."

Eric saw John flinch. "I told you," he repeated, "it didn't have to go that way."

"You killed without mercy, or due process under the law. You killed my men and now you wave your guns at me. Tell me, young man, do you love this country?"

"As a matter of fact, I do." He wanted to put a bullet in the man, but he couldn't risk killing the one man who might know the location of the cesium. "That's why I serve it now."

"Ah, spoken like a military man. Tell me, do you know what the single greatest threat to this country is, young man?" Before Eric could answer, Dyer continued, "The mixing of the races. Negroes mixing with whites. Mexicans mixing with the Negroes. When they befriend each other and share their cultures, it dilutes them. Look at the Japanese. They don't encourage it. They have retained a racial and cultural purity that keeps them strong, yet we encourage everyone to come here. The great melting pot, we call it. What will become of the Negro culture? What will become of the white culture? I'm thinking of the children, you see."

Eric nodded. "Mr. Dyer, I know who you are, and I have a good idea of what you've done."

Dyer nodded his head. "I regret that I've done some *distasteful* things, but like all true patriots, I'm forced to do what is necessary."

He was through humoring the old man. "We know the APR stole the cesium. Where is it?"

Dyer smiled. "An angel lifted his voice and cried, 'Will you prove your love for the Lord?'"

"Tell me what you did with the cesium," Eric said. "You don't have to die here."

Dyer smiled sadly. "Did you kill Fletcher?"

Eric glanced at John, who nodded.

"A shame. He was a good man. He knew the risk when he acquired the cesium, yet he did it without complaint."

"Is it still here?" Eric asked.

"The coming tide will lift up the white race. The chorus of angels will sing from the heavens and the end shall become the beginning." Dyer nodded his head to an unseen choir. "You will never find it in time, I promise you. The angels have spoken, and it is for *no* man to undo the word of God."

Dyer is never going to tell us anything. "I don't want to shoot you, but I will if I have to."

"I'm wearing a vest of C4 wired to this switch," Dyer said calmly. "If I lift my thumb, it will kill us all. I'm prepared to die for my cause. I ask you, are you prepared to die for yours?"

Eric slowly shook his head. "No, I don't think so. I think you're a smart man, and a smart man wouldn't hold a dead man's switch without some kind of safety."

Dyer shook his weathered old head. "It is wired to the explosives, I promise you."

"That I believe, but a smart man would build in a delay, say, half a second." He turned and winked at John. "With a half-second delay, you'd have time to put your thumb back on the trigger, just in case it slipped off."

Dyer nodded. "Perhaps you are correct. What could you possibly do in that time?"

"Me? Nothing. *John!*"

Dyer lifted his thumb and smiled to the heavens, a crazy glint in his eye, then Eric's breath woofed out as John hit him, practically folding Eric in half, driving him into Kelly. The three men went flying sideways out of the room and back into the basement as the C4 detonated, the blast filling the room with a bloody, smoke-filled haze.

Eric hit the cement floor, the impact slamming through his body and knocking his teeth together. He lay for a moment, ears ringing, then struggled to his feet.

John and Kelly rose as well. Kelly appeared woozy and John rubbed at his ears, eyes wide, looking into the remains of the room.

Martin and Clark were yelling in Eric's earpiece, but he couldn't understand. He grabbed John by his arm and yelled, "Good job!"

John gaped at him. "What?"

"I said, *good job!*"

Kelly gave him a hound-dog stare and pointed at the devastation. "What do we do now?" he yelled.

Eric felt as if he had cotton in his ears, but he could finally understand Martin's voice over the earpiece. The news wasn't good. "First responders are on their way," Eric told Kelly and John. "*Now* we talk to the police."

* * *

Kandahar, Afghanistan

Nancy hung up her phone and turned to Deion. "Okay, they've got eyes on the drone feed and they've tapped the cell phone towers in the area. Clark is working on overriding Rumple's commands. As soon as the orders come in, Delta will be back on-site, but it's going to take time."

"What's the drone's capabilities?" Deion asked.

"Video and night vision. It's enough to let us know if we're in trouble, but it's not armed."

Deion didn't like it, but Jaabir offered their only lead. "If we want this guy, it's all we're going to get."

She nodded. "I agree. He's too valuable. We need him."

He could tell she was pissed about Rumple, but at least she was focusing on the mission. "Let's tell Val and Neil."

He found them at the truck, checking their M4s. "We're on. Jaabir should be back anytime. We've got drone coverage and we're getting the Delta callback orders rescinded, but they probably won't make it back before the meeting time."

"We understand," Valerie said, concerned. "It's just that this is a little more cowboy than we're used to."

Deion grabbed her hand and gave it a quick squeeze. "It'll be fine, Val. I wouldn't let anything happen to you."

Neil squinted at him, uncertain. "What about Nancy?" he asked, motioning to the house. "Can we count on her?"

Deion laughed. "She's the most dangerous one here."

Neil nodded, but the skepticism on his face suggested he did not share Deion's opinion. The sun was almost below the horizon, and it cast long red shadows down the street. They finished their weapons check and entered the house to wait for Jaabir.

Deion removed an earpiece from a pouch on his belt, plugged it into his PRC-148 and keyed the mic. "Clark? Do you read me?"

"Loud and clear, Deion," came Clark's voice seconds later. "We're patched into the MBITR network. Karen has your position on screen. We're combing the area for signs of suspicious activity."

"Roger that. Keep us informed."

Nancy pulled the heavy curtains over the front window aside to watch the front of the building. She motioned to him right before there was a soft knock on the door. He opened it and found Jaabir waiting, his AK slung low.

"We take your truck," Jaabir said.

They piled in the Toyota, with Neil driving, Jaabir in the passenger seat, and Valerie, Nancy and Deion in the back, guns ready. Deion left his seat belt unfastened, just in case someone threw a bomb into the truck. It was easier to bail out that way, a lesson learned during his previous time in Afghanistan.

Jaabir guided them through back alleys and side streets, headlights off, navigating by the faint light cast from open windows. It took less than ten minutes before they came to a small house, a green bulb glowing in the front window.

"Here," Jaabir directed.

They exited the Toyota, weapons lowered but alert. It looked like any other street in Kandahar, the dirt road nearly empty as the people heeded the call for evening prayers blaring from a mosque in the distance. Jaabir knocked on the door and an old man opened, nodded to Jaabir, and swung the door wide. They entered the room and the old man motioned for them to move back, pulling aside a dusty red rug to expose a trapdoor, opening it with Jaabir's help.

"You sure about this?" Deion asked.

"Yes. He is down there." Jaabir whispered something to the old man, who smiled crookedly and exited through the front door. "Wazir will keep watch for us."

Deion shook his head. "I don't find that reassuring."

Jaabir smiled and motioned them down the steps. Everyone followed Deion down and into a small room where a young man sat tied to a chair.

"His name is Koshen," Jaabir said, kicking the young man in the leg. "He helped Abdullah prepare the bomb."

Deion gave Koshen a once-over, and the young man stared back, his face blank. Koshen's face was covered in bloody red scabs and heavy purple bruises. Flakes of dried blood caked his nostrils and the young man coughed heavily.

"Looks like you already questioned him," Deion said.

"We asked about his involvement in the bombing. General Azim was eager to find information that might stop this misunderstanding between our people."

Deion nodded. He was familiar with the shifting allegiances in Afghanistan and knew that Azim was only looking out for himself.

"We found this," Jaabir said. He pulled out the remains of an old book from a backpack under his pato, the leather-bound cover charred and covered in soot. "He burned it before we captured him." He passed it to Deion. "Will this help?"

Deion opened the cover, only to find the pages charred beyond recognition. Whatever secrets the journal had contained had been destroyed. He sighed. *Of course it wouldn't be that easy.* He turned to the young man and spoke in Pashto. "Your name is Koshen?"

Koshen blinked, his eyes focusing on Deion, then looked down to the remains of the journal.

Jaabir smacked him across the face, the crack of skin on skin echoing against the cement walls. "Answer his question!"

Koshen turned his gaze to Jaabir but did not answer. Jaabir drew back and smacked him in the face, hard enough to send a trail of spit flying from the young man's mouth.

"You will answer," Jaabir demanded, "or I will *make* you answer."

Deion motioned for Jaabir to step back. "There's no reason for that. He wants to talk, don't you?"

The young man said nothing, watching Deion with wide brown eyes.

"We just want to ask you some questions. We won't hurt you, we just want to talk."

Jaabir raised his hand but Deion grabbed it. Koshen glanced from Jaabir to Deion, then spoke. "Yes, I am Koshen."

Deion smiled and nodded. He tossed the remains of the leather journal in the corner, then stepped to the side of the room and took an empty chair, dragging it across the floor, setting it down across from the young man. He sat, facing Koshen. "That's good, really good. It's nice to meet you, Koshen. We know you were involved in the bombing."

Koshen nodded, swallowing hard.

"That's good," Deion said. *Just keep working him.* "You helped rig explosives in the truck, didn't you? You can tell me. I'm not going to hurt you. It's in the past. Can you answer a few questions, Koshen?"

His earpiece crackled to life. "Deion, we're picking up an increase in cell phone traffic within a mile of your position."

He turned. From the scowl on Nancy's face, he knew she had also heard Clark's message. "Jaabir, did anyone know you were bringing us here?"

Jaabir shook his head. "Just General Azim and his closest men."

He keyed his mic. "Anything from Big Bird?" he asked Clark.

"No visual. Karen is running down the SIGINT."

He turned back to the young man. "Koshen, was the man you helped named Abdullah? Was he the man who planned the bombing?"

Koshen glanced down until his chin touched his chest, then shook his head.

"You can tell us the truth. The man's name was Abdullah. You helped him with explosives, right? It was a fertilizer bomb, wasn't it? Koshen, look at me, you can tell me."

Koshen raised his head and looked from Jaabir to Deion, then slowly nodded. "Yes, I helped Abdullah."

"See, it's okay." He smiled. "What we don't know is why Abdullah picked that base." He paused, trying to figure out how to ask without putting more pressure on the young man. Koshen was loyal, but not stupid. If Deion could give him an out—a way to give them the information they needed without betraying Al-Qaeda—he knew he could get the young man talking. "Do you know what they were doing at that base?"

Koshen shook his head.

"They were testing new equipment. That's all." *Time to spin it.* "They were just men and women doing a job. Then Abdullah sent a man with a bomb. There were a doctor and a nurse. They weren't enemy soldiers. The doctor provided health care to some of the locals."

Koshen said nothing.

Deion looked around and found a dirty water bottle on a table against the wall. "Jaabir, can we get Koshen some water? He looks thirsty."

Jaabir frowned, but he grabbed the water bottle and roughly poured some in Koshen's mouth. "I do not think you should be so kind," Jaabir grumbled. "Ask him your questions and I will beat him until he answers."

"That's not the way we do things. We're the good guys."

In the back, Nancy rolled her eyes while Valerie and Neil watched in silence.

"There, you've had some water. Do you feel better? I bet you were thirsty, weren't you?"

Koshen tried to avert his eyes, then finally caught Deion's gaze and nodded.

"Do you think Abdullah made a mistake? Anyone can make a mistake. You think maybe he just picked the wrong place?"

Koshen opened his mouth and closed it. "No, he did not make a mistake."

"Why did he pick this base?" Jaabir asked, swinging his hand back.

Deion caught Jaabir's hand again. "No. We don't hit someone who is cooperating. We thank them. Koshen, why did Abdullah pick that base? Was it because he knew about the testing? Was it the drone?"

His earpiece crackled again. "We're picking up movement," Clark said. "The area is getting hot."

He whirled around. "Jaabir, did you set us up?"

Jaabir backed away, but Deion jumped from his chair and grabbed Jaabir's pato, wrapping it around his fingers, tightening the rough fabric against Jaabir's throat. "Was that the plan? Get us here and kill us?"

Jaabir trembled as Neil grabbed Deion's hands. "Whoa, look at him, he's terrified. Jaabir, what's going on?"

Jaabir's eyes darted around the room. "We must all leave. Now!"

"We can't leave without getting our info," Nancy said. She raised her pant leg and pulled the Ka-Bar knife, then pointed at Koshen. "Either he tells us what we need to know, or I start cutting off fingers." She took a menacing step towards the young man. "You understand that? Tell me what I want to know or you'll have two bloody stumps."

Valerie jumped in and grabbed Nancy's shoulder. "Jesus, Nancy, we don't do that kind of thing!"

"The fuck we don't," Nancy growled. She turned back to Koshen, who cringed from her gaze. "Why did Abdullah want to attack that base? Where is he now? Who helped him?" She advanced, knife in hand.

"Calm down," Deion said. The situation was escalating out of control, but their lives depended on remaining calm. "Jaabir, what happened to your man, Wazir?"

Jaabir struggled to pull free of Deion's grasp. "He's outside. Watching."

"Watching for what? Is it the Taliban?" Realization dawned on him. "It's not Azim's men. It's Al-Qaeda."

Jaabir nodded his head. "Yes. We must not let them find us. They will kill us all."

"Why?" Valerie asked.

"Because," Koshen said in heavily accented English, "Azim was to deliver me to a safe house in Pakistan. Abdullah promised that if General Azim did not keep me safe, Abdullah would have him killed. Now they will kill you and parade your body through the streets as proof of Azim's treachery."

Deion let that sink in. Neil and Valerie were concerned, Nancy was angry, and Jaabir scared, but Koshen showed no emotion. "Koshen, can you stop this?"

Koshen shook his head. "Why would I?"

"We've got to get out of here," Valerie said.

Valerie's words struck a nerve. He'd *promised* her she would be safe. "Clark, can you get us an exit?"

"No go," Clark said. "There's no pathway out. You're in a defensible position. The enemy will be there in five. They'll have AK-47s and RPGs. You're going to have to hold your own until the cavalry arrives."

"How long?" Nancy asked.

"Twenty minutes," Clark responded. "Delta has their new deployment orders and they're bringing Rangers with them."

Nancy rushed up the stairs and they heard her footsteps pounding across the floor, streams of dust falling through the floorboards and catching the light from the bare bulb. She came back soon after with the duffel bag full of ammo and equipment. "Wazir is gone," she said.

"He is old," Jaabir said with a shrug, "but not very brave."

Nancy snorted. "Smartest man I've met today." She opened the duffel bag and passed out ammo magazines and grenades.

Deion grabbed an extra handful for his MP4. "Jaabir, you can run, but they'll probably catch you. You're better off with us. Your choice."

Jaabir shook his head. "I do not have a choice. If they catch me, they will kill me."

"Val, you and Nancy take the first floor, Neil and I will take the roof. Jaabir, guard the rear."

Nancy pointed to Koshen. "What about him?"

"Koshen," Deion said, "if you have anything else to tell us, now is the time. Why did Abdullah target that base?"

Koshen licked his lips. "He blamed a man there for killing his wife. That is why he targeted the base."

"He wasn't after the drone?" Nancy asked.

"No," Koshen answered. "Abdullah wanted the man to pay for his crimes."

"Where is he?" Deion asked. "*Where* is Abdullah?"

Koshen smiled sadly. "You will never find him."

* * *

Area 51

Eric was finishing the after-action report when Hobert Barnwell knocked on his door.

"Got a minute?" Barnwell asked.

The words on his computer screen swam in and out of focus. He shoved the keyboard away. "I could use a break."

Barnwell took the chair across from him and placed a metal lunch box on the desk. "Writing up the Denver affair?"

Eric shrugged. "This place runs on paperwork."

Barnwell laughed. "Don't I know it." He opened the lunch box and withdrew a bottle and two plastic cups, pouring three fingers of golden liquid in each. "I love what you've done with the place."

Eric glanced around. There were Colt M1911 parts strewn about the coffee table in front of the couch. Except for that and the boots in the corner, the room looked as it had when he arrived. He shrugged. "No sense in it."

Barnwell grinned. "Fair enough. Now, drink up," he said, passing one of the cups to Eric.

"This part of the after-mission therapy?" Eric asked.

"Think of it as two men shooting the breeze. Sorry for the scotch, I know you're a beer man."

Eric raised the cup and took a long sip. The smell reminded him of peat moss, but the liquor burned his mouth, then warmed everything on the way down, settling as a fire in his belly. "Normally I'd pass on the scotch, but in this case…"

Barnwell smiled and took a drink from his own cup. "How's the arm?"

Eric gingerly flexed his right arm. "It's good. They stitched me up and gave me a pain patch."

"That's more than a pain patch," Barnwell said. "In twenty years, they'll be in every pharmacy in America. It dramatically speeds up the healing time and cuts down on the scar tissue."

"The muscle is still sore," he said.

Barnwell laughed. "What do you expect? Miracles? Tell me about Denver."

"You want me to lay down?" he asked, pointing to the gray fabric couch against the wall. When Barnwell did not respond, he shook his head. "It didn't go well."

"I know. I was with Clark, listening. And this isn't therapy. Do you know what I do here?"

He knew Barnwell was the base shrink, but the man's fatigues were devoid of insignias or rank. "You work directly for Smith. I've seen enough paperwork with your name on it to know that you unofficially run the place. What's your story?"

Barnwell smiled and took another drink. "I was a soldier once, a long time ago, during Vietnam." He paused. "I was something of a promising student, a doctorate in psychology at twenty-one. I was going to attend medical school and eventually get my license in psychiatry. My whole life was mapped out." Barnwell paused to take another drink, this one a long pull from the cup.

"Didn't work out that way?" Eric asked.

"No," Barnwell said, laughing. "Instead of my attending medical school, my deferment was denied. I attended basic training, like everybody else, but instead of continuing to Advanced Individual Training, I was deployed to Vietnam. I was put in charge of a psychological operations unit, reporting to both Army Intelligence and the CIA. My doctorate research had caught Fulton's attention. He recruited me into the Office, and I spent the rest of the war waging psy-ops. When the war was over, I became his right-hand man."

"That's why you don't wear rank?"

"Very perceptive," Barnwell said, toasting him with his plastic cup. "You have a knack for reading people. Yes, I could still claim rank if I wanted, but there's no need, and it's my petulant way of poking my finger in Fulton's eye." He shook his head. "When Fulton isn't here, I'm his proxy." He trailed off, then realized his drink was almost empty. He leaned forward, poured himself another, and settled back. "So, now that you're done stalling, how was Denver?"

"A cluster. The thing with Fletcher—"

"Yes?"

He paused. "Things went sideways and we're no closer to the cesium."

"And John?" Barnwell prompted.

"He saved my life," Eric admitted. "Fletcher had the draw on me. I was so busy trying not to kill him that it almost cost me my life."

"Is that why you're upset?"

It was his turn to laugh. "I'm not upset, Doc."

"Then why are you about to break that cup?"

He looked down and noticed the plastic cup between his fingers, squeezed almost to the breaking point. "Huh."

Barnwell smiled. "Not so unusual. You were in a highly stressful situation. It's not the same, is it?"

"What?"

"I think you know."

"It *is* different," Eric admitted. "It's easy in Afghanistan or Iraq to distance yourself. Everything looks different, smells different. The people? They don't look like you. But Denver? It's home…"

"I understand. Completely. We've put you in a very unique position. Tell me about John. How did he perform?"

"He did exactly as he was trained."

Barnwell raised an eyebrow. "He killed those men."

"Yes, he did. He was perfect, Doc. He's a hell of a lot stronger than before, though. I guess we didn't plan for that."

"Yes," Barnwell agreed. "For all of our technology and planning, we still make mistakes. What about Fletcher?"

"It happened so fast," Eric said. "Maybe he would have missed, I don't know. I was trying for my weapon when John shot him."

"John saved your life but you lost Fletcher."

Eric shrugged. "Fletcher could have known the location. Or, maybe not. Dyer was paranoid. Fletcher might have been another dead end."

"Perhaps. John cost you that intel."

"He saved my life, Doc. Can't blame him for that." He tipped up the plastic cup and drained the last of the scotch. He passed it to Barnwell, who poured more and carefully handed it back. "He's nothing like you expect. He killed those men, but he was tore up about it—"

"How so?"

"He's been in firefights, but not like this. Not up close and personal. He was like"—Eric paused—"like a lost puppy dog. A cliché, but true."

Barnwell nodded. "How does that make you feel?"

Eric squinted at him. "So this *is* a therapy session?"

"Call it what you like. I'm just trying to assess his performance. Yours, too. So, how *do* you feel?"

Eric thought about it. "Angry. He's a killer, Doc. A psychopath. And an asshole. But he's not, anymore. He's completely different, and I have to hold his hand—"

"You think he deserves something else?"

Eric pondered that. "I don't know. What's been done to him, it turned him inside out. Where does his responsibility end? The man he was, or the man he is?"

Barnwell smiled. "A very astute question. Can I offer an observation? John is just about the right age to be someone's younger brother. Your younger brother?"

Eric laughed in spite of himself. "I feel responsible for him, like an older brother?"

"It's not so crazy, is it? You've killed men, but you didn't know them, not the way you know John. You didn't train them and mentor them and watch as they tried to impress you. You didn't get to know them as people. John is different. You *know* him."

Barnwell made a lot of sense. He sighed. "I guess I do."

"Let's continue. How about the bar? And Dyer?"

Eric took another swig from the cup. "Another sideways situation."

"And once again, John saved your life."

"Without hesitation. He saved Kelly, too. Then we found Dyer."

"What's your opinion of Dyer?"

Eric snorted. "A lunatic. He'd been spewing the same hateful bullshit so long, he convinced himself he was a patriot."

Barnwell leaned forward. "He was wearing a suicide vest. You're lucky to be alive."

"Lucky? It was John. He's impressive as hell. If he hadn't knocked us completely out of the room, we'd be dead right now."

"Yes, I heard. The Weave. The Implant. The drugs. It's almost miraculous, isn't it? He's operating at the peak of human capacity, but he's not unbreakable. He can be hurt and he can be killed, just like you."

"There's no way I could have broken down the door, or knocked us out of that room. I'm in decent shape for a man my age, but I'm not young anymore."

"No, you're not. An Operator has a relatively short shelf life, before the stress on the body starts wearing away at them. You've been shot, hit with shrapnel. Your last MRI shows stress and strains on the ligaments in your knees. You've got mild hearing loss. No, you're not a young man anymore. You're going to be thirty-seven. About the time an Operator starts to transition out of day-to-day ops."

Barnwell's assessment was disturbingly close to his own. During John's training, Eric had noticed his own body aching and knew it was only going to get worse. "Uplifting speech, Doc."

Barnwell chuckled. "I'm just saying that you've got some miles on you. The body is not what makes an Operator. It's their spirit, their mental determination. In some ways, they're the opposite of a regular soldier. They're rugged individualists. You know what motivates an Operator? Telling him he can't do something. That's what John needs. You have to teach him."

He sighed. "I'm doing my damnedest."

"I know." Barnwell eased back in his chair. "Dyer killed himself rather than be taken alive."

"Yeah. The police and FBI were *not* happy."

"Fulton wasn't pleased, but he understands. It's not the first time we've had an operation involve the local authorities."

"We played the DHS card, but they were mad as hell about DHS operating in their city without their knowledge."

"They'll suffer through," Barnwell said.

"Doc, I've been thinking about Dyer. All that stuff about angels. Could he mean Los Angeles?"

Barnwell sat back, his fingers forming a steeple, thoughtful. "Why Los Angeles?"

"He wants a race war. What better way to start one than set off a dirty bomb in Los Angeles, then blame it on a black militant group?"

Barnwell nodded slowly. "An interesting theory, but there's no indication that he was working with anybody else, and there are very few members of his organization left to interrogate."

"What about the codes they used? The cell phone shielding?"

Barnwell shrugged. "You make a good point. Perhaps you're right."

Eric nodded. "I asked Karen to dig deeper, try to find the remaining members who've gone to ground. In the meantime, what about drones over Los Angeles?"

"Too risky," Barnwell said. "Every time we do a drone overfly, we risk alerting the civilians. It creates ... complications. We have a stealth blimp, but it would take weeks to re-outfit it with radiation sensors."

Eric considered their options. "What about DHS?"

"Pass it along," Barnwell said, "and they can send a VIPR team, but it's a needle in a haystack. You need actionable intelligence."

Eric grunted. "I'll work on it."

"And, if you don't mind me asking, when was the last time you had sex?"

The question surprised Eric. "Kind of personal, isn't it?"

Barnwell grinned. "I'm not one for casual relationships, myself. I've been married to the same woman for almost forty years. I make it a point to fly out every night, if I can, to our home in Vegas. You younger folks are a different matter. We have a high single rate in the Office. That's why we allow the dating culture. It's well established, and there are rules that one must follow. It allows human contact and keeps everyone from going stir-crazy."

"It's been a year, maybe."

Barnwell raised an eyebrow. "Really? Hasn't it been closer to two?"

"Keeping tabs on me?" Eric asked, annoyed. "I didn't work for the Office then."

Barnwell laughed. "We weren't keeping track of you if that's what you're thinking, but it's plain as day. It was your last relationship."

"Yeah, I guess. I didn't realize it had been that long."

"Perfectly all right. Just consider sex a healthy form of stress relief. One of the rules is that no rank or position can be used. Take Karen Kryzowski. She's married, but they have an arrangement."

"Karen? Really? She's attractive, I guess, but not the first woman who comes to mind."

"She's reasonably fit," Barnwell said, "and moreover, quite enthusiastic. My advice would be to get the pipes cleaned, so to speak."

Eric coughed. "I'll take that under advisement."

"Just a piece of advice, though," Barnwell said. "Don't even consider Nancy."

The thought hadn't occurred to him, but once stated, he had to ask. "Out of curiosity, why?"

"Suffice it to say the last relationship ended poorly for the young man." Barnwell shook his head and stood to leave, placing his empty plastic cup back in the lunch-box and snapping it shut. He was almost out the door when he turned back to Eric. "He's stationed in Israel now and considers it much safer than here with her."

* * *

John woke, his eyes darting around the room, his heart thudding in his chest. He tried swallowing, but his tongue was as dry as the desert outside the base. He lurched out of bed, caught his foot in the blanket, and slammed to the floor. He threw the blanket across the room, cursing, then staggered to the bathroom.

He scooped water from the sink in the palm of his hand and swallowed, spilling most of it down his chest.

Christ, what a nightmare!

He turned to the toilet and pulled down his briefs. His bladder felt near bursting, but no matter how hard he tried, he could only manage a few starts and stops of a stream. He slumped to his knees and wondered if he was going crazy.

The memories of the dream came back. He was in Denver, shooting the men. They were all there; the bartender, Fletcher, and the rest. He saw blood spray in thick gouts, a fire-hose of red.

It wasn't like that.

The men came for him, grinning, and suddenly a pink mist exploded from the bartender's head, then the man's body opened as blood and organs splattered to the ground. The bartender slipped in the gore, sprawling in his own entrails.

Fletcher stumbled over the fallen man, then turned back to John, a leer on his face. John stumbled backward and shot, bullets tearing chunks of flesh from Fletcher's face, but still he advanced.

His heart was racing, his lungs on fire.

I'm dreaming.

Still Fletcher kept coming.

One of the young men from the bar leaped on John, bearing him to the ground, and the coppery scent of blood was thick in his nose, until the man released his bowels.

John heaved and tried to roll away, but Fletcher knelt and pinned him to the ground.

Please let me wake up!

Fletcher laughed as the rest of the men approached, smearing their blood in wide swaths across his face, rubbing it in his eyes and nose, then sticking their bloody fingers in his mouth. He gagged on the taste, all copper and salt, and felt his gorge rise.

Please wake up!

A thump, like a clap of thunder, shook the ground. Then another. The men parted and Dyer stood before him with milky eyes. He smiled and opened his mouth, his tongue waggling. "Look, boy."

A hand gripped his head. He resisted, but the hand twisted his head until he saw a building in ruin. There were people, some sitting on chunks of concrete and some sprawled across the pavement, soaked in blood. A girl in a tattered dress stared at him, holding the remains of her left arm. A cacophony of screams filled the air.

Then, glorious silence. The building was whole again.

He felt the relief as a physical thing.

Please wake up!

Too late. The building shook and a school bus parked in front turned to shrapnel, the front of the building collapsing, bodies tossed through the air. A man frantically tried to push his intestines back in his abdomen. The man turned to him, empty eye-sockets leaking blood.

A woman lay in the rubble, her body jerking in agony, a stalk of metal protruding from her chest, the blood scarlet against her white silk blouse. She gurgled bloody spittle from her mouth.

Please!

And, like that, he was fully awake, still kneeling in front of the toilet, the cold tile floor sapping the heat from his knees.

He stumbled to the kitchenette and grabbed a bottle of water from the refrigerator, draining it in choking gulps. The cold water was an icy spike in his stomach, but it calmed him.

He went back to the bathroom and snapped on the light, looking in the mirror. The harsh glow cast shadows on his pale skin, his pupils dilated. His hands shook as he traced his fingertips over his face.

He would ask Eric if this was an aftereffect of the adrenaline.

No, he couldn't ask Eric. He couldn't ask Doctor Barnwell, either. It would be recorded and placed in his file. Better to keep it to himself.

He left the light on and retrieved his blanket, damp from sweat, returning to bed.

What the hell was that about?

The light peeked from the gap under his door. He took comfort from that, as well as the light streaming from his bathroom. He shivered, pulling the soft blanket tightly against him as he prayed in vain for sleep.

CHAPTER ELEVEN

Kandahar, Afghanistan

Deion crouched on the dark rooftop, his MP4 propped up against the parapet that ringed the roof. All they had to do was hold their position without getting killed. He glanced over to Neil, clutching his rifle on the east side of the roof.

Neil was nervous. They all were. He grimaced. They had to pull together as a team or none of them would make it out alive.

I wish Steeljaw were here.

The building was nestled in a long line of single-story houses, with little space to the east and west. The back opened to a narrow alley littered with trash and rubble. It was the safest area, which was why he asked Jaabir to guard it.

Truthfully, he didn't trust Jaabir, but the young man's life was on the line, just like theirs.

Valerie and Nancy were holed up on the first floor. He had forgotten how much he enjoyed Valerie's company, her smile, how good she smelled, even in a dirty place like Kandahar. It angered him that she was in danger.

She was right; his cowboy shit got results, but at a high price. First his posting in Afghanistan, then Valerie as they drifted apart.

No time for that now.

He focused on the mission, craning his neck to assess the street layout. The fighters would come from the north, he was sure of it. It offered the clearest path back to the main thoroughfare.

He shifted the MP4 and sighted through the ghostly light of the night vision scope, looking to the west. There was a northbound street two houses over, and the fighters coming around the corner would enter his kill zone. Neil would do the same on the right. Nancy and Val would have to cover the same area from their windows on the first floor.

He'd parked the Toyota Hilux as close as possible to the front door, blocking it to provide Valerie and Nancy a modicum of protection. He just hoped it was enough.

"Freeman? You there?" came the voice through his earpiece.

"Wise? That you?"

"I'm here. Delta is inbound, just hold tight."

Eric's voice was calm, but Deion knew better. During Frist's training, he had learned to read Eric, and he could detect the concern in Eric's voice. "Go skiing in Colorado? Next time, you can have Afghanistan and *I'll* take Denver."

There was a pause before Eric replied. "Denver didn't go as hoped."

Uh oh. "You find the cesium?"

"Still working on it," Eric said. "Sorry I'm not there with you."

"We need to have a serious discussion when I get back," he said.

"Can the chatter," Nancy's voice cut through the earpiece. "We don't have time for it."

"Nice to hear from you, too," Eric said. "Can you guys do one thing? Try to not get killed."

Deion sighed. "We'll do our best."

"We've got drone data on the screen. I see your position. You've got fighters coming from the north."

"I'm on the roof, west side," Deion said. "Neil Burch is on the east. Nancy and Valerie Simon are on the first floor. A local kid is watching the back."

"Taliban?"

"Affirmative. If AQ gets him, they'll kill him. Or worse."

"He better fight, then."

Deion nodded to himself. "He better."

"Mr. Burch? Ms. Simon? My name is Eric. I'll be your Overlook, along with Sergeant Clark. Can you hear me?"

Neil and Valerie confirmed they could.

"Very good. We're going to get through this together. Deion, how much ammo do you have?"

"Four mags each for the M4s, and a couple of grenades. Plus our sidearms."

"Remember," Eric said, "conserve your ammo. Slow and steady, maximize your kill shots. Deion, it's just like training, and you've become a fair shot."

It was true. During John's weapons training, Deion had learned just how good Eric was, and after Eric's gentle coaching, Deion found himself on a level he had never thought achievable. *I hope it's enough.*

There was a long pause. "You've got enemy on the southbound road, ten o'clock, two hundred meters away," Eric said. "Two men on a motorbike with AKs. They'll come around the corner in ten seconds."

"Roger that." He turned his head. "Neil, get set. Anything that comes from the east, you kill. Single shots only."

Neil glanced back across the shadowy rooftop and shook his head. "I want you to know I *hate* this."

Deion gave him a quick thumbs-up, then went back to his scope. He heard the motorbike's engine, a soft buzz growing louder, and the men emerged on the motorbike.

He sighted and pulled the trigger. The rifle bucked against his shoulder and the driver slumped over in the intersection, dead. The motorcycle's front fork twisted, spilling the passenger in the dirt. The passenger came up shouting, struggling to raise his AK, when a crack rang out and Nancy's bullet took the man in the stomach.

"Nice shooting," Eric said. "That'll give them pause, but when they come, they'll come in a group. Mr. Burch, there's four coming from the east. Deion, you've got more coming from the north, at least a dozen behind them. They've found the two in the street."

Below, the motorcycle passenger Nancy had shot tried crawling away, kicking uselessly in the dirt. Deion considered putting him out of his misery, but it was a waste of ammo. The man would be dead in minutes.

The shouting grew louder, and the approaching fighters cast long shadows down the street. He sighted down the scope as a man peeked out and then ducked behind the edge of the house on the corner.

"They've got trucks," Eric informed them. "It's about to get hot. Remember, folks, conserve ammo. Concentrate on holding them off."

Deion waited for the fighter to peer around the corner. The seconds ticked by, and when the man leaned out, Deion snapped off a clean shot to the head. The fighter spun backward and dropped to the ground in the bloody dirt.

Then all hell broke loose.

Fighters ran around the corner, too many to count. They cut loose with their AKs, peppering the side of the building. Deion ducked and came up, squeezing the trigger and dropping one man, but the fighters continued their forward assault until he heard a *crack-crack* as Nancy shot two more. The dead fighters sprawled in the dirt and the remaining men screamed, spraying the building with gunfire.

The bullets zinged around him, chips of stone and mortar stinging Deion's face. He dropped and covered, then came back up and squeezed off another round. The bullet caught a pudgy, bearded insurgent in the leg, and the man collapsed, the AK spilling from his hands into the dirt. The man behind him picked it up and pulled the trigger, but the AK was empty, causing the young man to scream in frustration.

Deion heard the yelling, then, "Allahu Akbar!"

"Mr. Burch," Eric said, "prepare yourself."

Deion heard the *crack, crack, crack* of Neil's rifle, then Eric's calm voice. "Keep at it, Mr. Burch. There's two left."

Bullets tore up the east side of the building, but there was nothing Deion could do about it. "Val, help him out!"

Another rifle joined in, matching Neil's *crack, cracking.*

Meanwhile, it was all Deion could do to hold off the fighters from the west. The first group of men had retreated but were now joined by a horde. They would run out, spray the building, then take shelter. He managed to pick off one more, then heard Eric's voice. "Here come the trucks. Deion, use those grenades."

"I've got the first one," he said.

"I'll take the second," Nancy joined in.

Two trucks barreled around the corner and men jumped out, firing their rifles. Deion hugged the rooftop, then pulled the pin from his grenade, stood, and lobbed it toward the first truck. He felt a hot stinging pain in his left arm, bullets singing in the air around him, and then heard screams as the grenade detonated with a loud *whump-whump.*

He fell back and grabbed his arm where a bullet had penetrated. He winced, picking up his M4, fire screaming down his bicep. He managed a quick glance over the edge of the building and saw bodies scattered like rag dolls, in various stages of dying. The remains of the devastated trucks blocked the street, providing cover for the remaining enemy to hide behind, randomly standing and squeezing off rounds.

"I'm hit, but not bad," Deion said between gritted teeth.

"Where?" Eric asked.

"Left arm, through and through."

"Suck it up," Nancy yelled from below.

Deion had an urge to scream. The whole thing was her fault. Her interaction with Rumple *caused* their loss of Delta support. "I'm okay. How's it look from above?"

"Men are entering the building across from you," Eric said.

Deion gritted his teeth tighter. The road between buildings wasn't that wide. He popped up just as the sound of muffled gunfire erupted in the house. He saw flashes of light through the windows across the street. "There go the civilians," he said.

"Hang in there," Eric said. "There's a CIA Predator in the area and I'm working on rerouting it, but I have to override the CIA's control."

This is officially a cluster. "How long before we get backup?"

"Nightstalkers are spinning up the Little Birds and a Black Hawk full of Operators. They're leaving now."

Deion struggled to remain calm. "We *need* extraction," he said.

"Just a little longer," Eric responded.

Across the street, the gunfire stopped.

"Oh, shit," he breathed. The fighters had killed the last of the Afghan civilians. "The house across the street, everyone. Light it up!"

He fired at the windows across the street and the enemy returned fire, glass panes shattering. The rest of his team joined in and it became a raging gun battle as the fighters on the street unleashed everything they had.

There was a flash of light across the street, a trail of smoke, and a deafening explosion as the enemy RPG impacted the side of his building. He looked toward Neil but found a chasm had opened in the roof. He could see down to the first floor. Valerie was covered in debris, her head caught against the wall, her legs quivering.

"Nancy? Are you injured? Can you get to Val?"

"Christ, that was close. No, I can't get to her," Nancy said over the gunfire. "The front of the house is gone. They've got me pinned down."

"What about Jaabir?"

"No idea. I don't hear anything from the back."

Deion cursed as the battle raged, the bullets pinging around him. Another RPG from the house across the street whumped into their Hilux and blew it apart in a cloud of shrapnel, leaving a smoking husk that belched smoke and flames to the sky.

Neil paused long enough to holler, "They'll take that out of my pay!" He went back to firing, swapping magazines as his gun went empty.

"You've got more enemy coming," Eric said, voice strained.

"We can't hold them," Deion shouted as a group of AQ fighters rounded the corner and took cover behind the trucks in the intersection, their AKs joining the din.

They were still taking fire from the house across the street. He heard a scream as Nancy killed a man. The flashes of light from the fighters' guns lit the rooms like strobe lights. He saw a squat man struggle to the broken windows with an RPG launcher.

"RPG, across the street," Deion screamed. "Another RPG!"

He heard Eric's voice, calm and determined. "Take cover. Hellfire is inbound."

He pressed against the rooftop as a whisper of sound, like a bottle rocket, grew louder and then the explosion thumped through his chest, his bones shaking in sympathetic vibration. He put his hands over his ears, but the sound was still deafening.

He peaked over the rooftop and saw a mushroom cloud of smoke and fire rising, the fire from the burning Hilux illuminating it from below. He turned his head, waiting for the rock and gravel, but the missile had been so fierce that the debris had blown far past their rooftop and was raining down on the houses behind them.

The house across the street was gone. The Hellfire had blown the building apart and collapsed what was left. The AQ fighters stopped firing and looked in awe at the rubble. Deion took the opportunity to calmly shoot the biggest man through the chest. The man dropped, breaking the spell, and the AQ fighters screamed and started shooting again. He saw another man fall and knew that Nancy hadn't run out of ammo.

Yet.

"Neil, how you doing?" he hollered.

"Still alive," Neil shouted, "but I'm down to my last magazine."

"Me too," he said. "Eric, got any other miracles?"

"No more Hellfires," Eric said, "but I do have some good news. Little Birds are almost there. Just one more minute."

The fighters behind the truck stepped out and started to advance.

"We don't *have* a minute," Nancy yelled.

The men came in a deadly wave. The street was a kill zone, barely passable from debris, and the flashes from their weapons sparked in the night.

Deion shot another fighter. The bullet struck the man in the side of the face, but as he fell, another took his place.

Deion's M4 ran dry. He pitched it aside and pulled his M11 pistol. He saw Neil do likewise.

"Sorry, Eric," Deion said. "We just can't hold them."

Below, he heard Nancy's pistol firing again and again.

In the midst of all the gunfire he heard the whine of turbines, and in the distance he saw black helicopters silhouetted against the moonlit sky.

As the AQ fighters approached, the pair of MH-6 helicopters unleashed their missiles. The remains of the two trucks in the intersection erupted in flames. The AQ fighters turned to run, but there was no shelter. The pilots unleashed their M134 miniguns and the street became a deathtrap, the high-pitched whine of the miniguns piercing the night sky in a continuous scream, the men in the street desperately trying to run away.

They found no refuge. The chain guns tore into them and left a pile of useless meat in their wake.

Four Delta Operators were positioned in the doors of each helicopter, two per side, their feet resting on metal platforms. When the chain guns stopped, the men spooled ropes from the helicopters and dropped to the street. The eight heavily armed Operators took up positions as the MH-6s returned to base. Within seconds of their departure, a Black Hawk swooped over the intersection long enough for eight Rangers to rappel to the ground.

His radio squawked. "Things get a little hairy?"

He smiled at the familiar voice. "You just saved our ass, Redman."

The lead Operator approached the building, entering carefully, two others following. "God almighty, what a mess," Redman said. "Steeljaw, your people are secure. You owe me one, brother."

"Add it to my tab, brother," Eric said. "Thanks for the assist."

Deion and Neil shoved aside the debris on the stairs and exchanged positions with the pair of Delta snipers that relieved them. They joined Nancy, who was checking on Valerie.

"She's alive," Nancy said. She tossed aside the bricks covering Valerie's leg. An Operator with a shaggy red beard lifted Valerie up and carried her outside.

Deion watched, numb, then looked around. The house was in shambles, the front room exposed to the street, the walls pocked with bullet holes. The wall that separated the front room from the kitchen was nearly destroyed and Deion gave silent thanks that the house hadn't collapsed.

Jaabir lay dead in the corner. Shrapnel had taken his right arm off at the shoulder, and his ribs and chest were split wide, blood and organs spilled on the dirty floor. Deion knelt and took a moment to pray for the kid in whatever afterlife he would find.

"He stayed with the fight," Neil said behind him.

"Yeah," Deion said. He looked for a rug or blanket to cover Jaabir's body, but the room was empty.

"We need to check on Koshen," Nancy said.

The trap door in the floor was covered in rubble, but Redman helped him clear the biggest pieces until they could open the door. Redman handed him a flashlight and followed him down into the cellar.

The room was quiet. Koshen dangled from the back of the wooden chair Deion had sat in only a short time before. His pato was wrapped around his neck, his sightless eyes staring off, the charred leather journal resting in his lap. The other chair lay in splinters.

Nancy joined them. "Valerie's going to be okay." She saw Koshen's body and her face fell. "Shit."

"He tipped himself over, broke the chair, then hanged himself," Deion said. "That's a hell of a lot of determination." He turned to Nancy. "I want to talk to you."

Her eyes narrowed. "Don't bother."

He gaped at her. "Don't bother?"

"I know," she growled, starting back up the stairs.

"We've lost our only asset that knew anything about Abdullah. What next?"

She shrugged. "We go home."

"This isn't the end of this conversation," he said. "We're going to talk about this."

"No, we're not," Nancy replied as she left the basement.

* * *

Area 51

Karen was getting lunch in the cafeteria when she saw Eric sitting alone, head down. She had watched as Eric's team had struck out in Denver and then as he'd worked to save Deion and Nancy in Afghanistan. She approached and cleared her throat. "Is this seat taken?"

He glanced up. "Help yourself," he said, shoving the chair out with his foot.

She took the offered seat. "How's the CO doing?"

"Just fine," he said. "How's the hunt?"

She paused, her fork loaded with broccoli. "Nothing so far. There's so much data to process, it's—"

"Like finding a needle in a haystack?"

She laughed. "That's a dumb cliché. Every piece of data we gather is available and searchable, but there's just so much of it..."

He leaned forward. "How do you do it, exactly? I mean, I know the basics, but how did you learn to analyze it?"

She noticed his eyes, a mottled bronze, and felt a warmth in her cheeks. She loved her husband. Brad was a good man and a good soldier, but Eric was intriguing as hell. *God, he's handsome.* "I took the ASVAB in high school and scored a perfect one hundred. I didn't think much of it until the recruiter called. It was right after 9/11. I joined up, went to basic, then I was asked to take a new test. It was weird—random paragraphs and contextual analysis. I thought I'd bombed. Then I got sent to Fort Meade and wound up working with some NSA crypto geeks. That's how I was recruited into the Office."

She took another bite of her broccoli and regarded him. She could see in his eyes that the failed missions weighed heavily on him.

His smile widened and his face softened. "That's how you got here, but how do you do what you do?"

"It's hard to explain, really." She stabbed at her blueberries. "I call it the Pattern. When you look at the data, it's a stream. You see pieces of it here and there, but you can't stop and take a drop from the stream. Someone dies and it triggers emails, phone calls, a ripple in the stream. Or, a blockbuster movie comes out and everybody's talking about it. They call their friends, who call their friends, and so on. Another ripple. Those ripples don't amount to much."

He leaned forward. "Then what does?"

She searched for the correct words. "Say IBM buys a company in Taiwan. Taiwan and China are not on the best of terms. What kind of tech does the company make? Is it commercial? Does it have a military use? Could it impact the US, now or in the future? The people that work there, are they loyal to the company? What kinds of friends do they have? Are they dissidents? Where does the money flow? That's a big ripple. Even then it's just a ripple. You can't get caught up watching the ripples and lose sight of the stream. Our job is to keep an eye on the stream, looking for the Pattern."

He nodded as she spoke, but the look on his face was puzzled. "Tell me about the Pattern."

"It's not something I can teach. Trust me, I've tried. Once the event happens, anyone can see it. The trick is to see the ripples coming together. If we see the ripples starting to merge, we can see the Pattern before it's fully formed. That's when the Office can take action. Take 9/11. All the ripples, all the threads of data, split across so many different agencies. The Office didn't have a full-blown data center like we do now, just case officers sorting through reports, trying to find the Pattern. Obviously they failed. It's easy to look back now and see the Pattern, but why didn't we see it then? Because there's a whole stream. When it's just one small eddy, it's hard to see before it becomes a full-blown Pattern."

She paused and licked the juice from the pineapple on her fork. "My coworker, Cassie, has been analyzing commodities manipulation for the past several months. She specializes in economic threats that endanger the world economies. She sees some ripples. She's trying to figure out what they mean. Is it insider trading? You'd be surprised how few wealthy individuals control the world economy. She's got a computer model of a couple hundred people who are in control, directly or indirectly, of sixty percent of the world's wealth."

Eric started to speak, but she shushed him. "I'm not saying that's good or bad, but what's the impact of having so few people control that sum of money? Wars have been fought over less. Look at the world today. OPEC is an ally, sometimes, and sometimes a danger. Putin seems to have an economic plan for Russia, and that includes the energy sector, but the Russian presidential election is only a few years away. Who knows what happens then? They don't have as much wealth, but Russia can still poke us in the eye. There's so many ripples and the consequences of not acting to prevent another Pattern from emerging—"

"Another 9/11," he said, grimacing. He shook his head and ran his hands through his short brown hair.

She looked down at her empty plate. She knew that every officer felt the same, since 9/11, but she voiced it anyway. "If I could stop something like that and didn't…"

Eric reached across the table and cupped her hand in his. "I learned a long time ago not to worry about things I can't control. Second-guessing yourself robs you of energy."

She grinned. "Isn't that what you were doing when I came in?"

Eric shrugged. "Nancy and Deion were lucky. It almost ended differently."

"But it didn't. Don't second-guess your decisions, right?"

He tilted his head, frowning. "I should have been there," he said.

Karen squeezed his hand. "You see your own Pattern. I get that. At least you can do something about it."

He gently pulled his hand back and stood to leave. "Thanks, Karen. I needed a pick-me-up."

"No problem, boss."

She watched as he left, his stride powerful and focused. Brad would understand if she slept with him, hell, he would encourage her, but it would be better if she waited. With the OTM on alert, there was too much at stake. The last thing she wanted was to distract her CO. But, once things settled down…

She smiled to herself. *Eric Wise, you're going to be one hell of a lay.*

* * *

Landstuhl, Germany

Abdullah stood on shaky legs, smiling at the blond-haired man who opened the cargo container. "Peace be upon you," he said.

The young soldier returned the smile, but his eyes darted around the dimly lit aircraft hangar. "We have to go, sir. I'm sorry for the rush, but you're not safe here."

He led Abdullah and Naseer from the green cargo container to a waiting Humvee. Abdullah and Naseer climbed gingerly in the back, their muscles and joints still knotted from ten hours spent hiding in the metal container.

The soldier threw an oil-stained tarp over them. "Stay still and don't make a sound."

They huddled under the tarp while the Humvee rumbled off, eventually coming to a long stop. They heard voices questioning the young man and the man answered, then the truck accelerated.

"Can we trust this American?" Naseer whispered.

"Yes. He is committed to Jihad." When Naseer snorted softly, he added, "These people are vital to our plans."

He bristled at Naseer's casual dismissal of the Americans' good intent. These precious few Americans had risked everything transporting them out of Afghanistan, hiding them in the cargo plane from Bagram. He marveled at their ingenuity, sneaking them on the base in Bagram and then out again at Ramstein Air Force Base.

The Humvee finally stopped, and they heard the young man open his door and slam it shut. Then their door opened and the tarp came off. Abdullah strained his eyes to see in the dark hangar as the young man led them to a small white car.

"In the trunk," the soldier directed.

They struggled to fit themselves into the trunk of the compact car, pushing and shoving to squeeze in place.

"There's air holes under the seat. You'll be okay, we tested it ourselves. We've got one more checkpoint to go through and then we'll be safe."

They struggled to breathe in the trunk as the car accelerated, the whine of the tires making further conversation impossible. The car stopped and started as their driver navigated them through the base, until he finally yelled, "We made it!"

When the car finally stopped, Abdullah breathed a sigh of relief. The trunk opened and they staggered out. The car was parked in an alley, packed between the two apartment buildings, and situated to block the view from the street. They followed the young man into an apartment where two young Americans waited.

The first, a thin black man with chocolate-brown eyes, shook his hand. "We're so glad you made it. Peace be upon you."

Their driver turned toward the door. "I've got to get back." He nodded to the two young soldiers, who smiled nervously. "They'll take good care of you." He shook Abdullah's hand and left.

Abdullah turned to the young black man. "You are Shahid?"

The man nodded. "I'm Terrill, but now I go by Shahid."

Abdullah smiled. "There is nothing to be ashamed of, Shahid. You have chosen to commit yourself to Allah. It is a great honor to meet you." He turned to the squat, coppery-skinned man next to him. "And you are Mahbeer? Your family is from Mexico?"

Mahbeer smiled. "Mexican by way of Los Angeles. Name's Hector. You speak very good English. You got almost no accent."

"I studied in America," Abdullah said. "I was forced to learn English. Naseer is not so lucky."

Naseer nodded politely as if following the conversation.

Shahid stuck out his hand. "You're safe here."

Naseer shook it and Abdullah did the same.

"Excellent," Abdullah said. "Do you have tea? We are very thirsty."

Mahbeer nodded and went to fix tea. Abdullah and Naseer sat back on the soft brown couch as Shahid explained the preparations.

Abdullah's heart lightened, and he nodded as the plan unfolded. "You have the truck?"

"Yes," said Shahid. "Just like you requested. I've got the C4, too. I've been covering the paperwork."

Mahbeer returned with tea and Abdullah drank, then turned his attention back to Shahid. "Tell me, what made you choose to follow Allah? You were not born a Muslim, I take it?"

Shahid laughed. "No. I grew up in Cabrini Green, Chicago. Joined the Army after 9/11, then got sent to Iraq. Nobody cared about them people. They just wanted some payback. There were these kids. Some of our guys were mean, laughing at them." He paused. "We were on patrol and I saw this kid. He just wanted a bottle of water. A guy chucked a bottle of water, hit him in the head, the other guys laughing like it was the funniest shit in the world. It wasn't right. They had some stuff on the base, learn the culture kind of thing, and there was a copy of the Quran. I started reading it. Found something in it. It was like—"

"Like you were touched by Allah," Abdullah said softly.

"Yeah, like that. I started to see how we treated the world. How we treated Muslims. Look, I'm not saying everybody in America is bad, but we kiss up to Israel. And why are we even in Iraq? For the people? We don't care about the people."

Abdullah nodded, then quickly translated the conversation for Naseer, and for the first time in a long time Naseer smiled. Abdullah turned to Mahbeer. "You have a similar story?"

Mahbeer nodded. "Just a dirty Mexican, that's all I was. There was this kid from Yemen. Not a lot of kids from Yemen in South Central. He got the shit beat out of him. Me and my cousin, we started hanging out with him and I found out he was Muslim. I asked him about what being a Muslim was like. My mom was pissed when she found out I was interested in Islam. She's old-school Catholic, man, you can't even imagine. I found out she wanted to send me back to live with my grandma in Mexico City.

Why the hell would I want to go to Mexico? So I ran away and hung out with my cousin, Manny, playing video games until I turned eighteen. I joined the Army and got sent to Iraq. Shahid got me a copy of the Quran. Helped me understand it."

"What about the driver?" Abdullah asked.

"That's Greg," Mahbeer said. "He's a good Muslim. He's the one who arranged to have his friend in Bagram sneak you on the plane."

Abdullah considered that. "And you had to ship heroin?"

Shahid shrugged. "His friend in Bagram needed the money, and we needed to get you on the plane."

Abdullah smiled and patted Shahid on the hand. "It was a good thing. But, please, the heroin should not be used by Muslims."

Shahid nodded. "We'll make sure of it."

Abdullah let the lie pass. It wasn't Shahid's fault. The heroin business funded Jihad, whether Abdullah liked it or not. "Before we continue, we should pray."

Mahbeer and Naseer pulled the coffee table to the side of the room, and Shahid placed the prayer mats on the floor. They performed wudu, the ritual cleansing, washing their faces and arms, pulling up their sleeves to wash to the elbows, then finished with their feet. When the ablution was complete, they sat on the mats facing Qibla and performed dhurh, the midmorning prayer.

When they were done, Shahid led them to the basement. The makeshift tables were loaded with munitions and wire. "We did it just like the instructions," Shahid said, "but I'd like you to check for yourself."

Abdullah nodded. "Just as I described." He followed the wires from the switch to the circuit board, through the spaghetti-like loops of wire, to the detonators. "Very good. You have the truck?"

Mahbeer had joined them. "It's not far from here. You want to see it?"

"Yes."

"It's not safe now, too risky," Mahbeer said.

"Better wait until after dark," Shahid agreed. He stuffed the improvised trigger and detonators in a green canvas bag and led them upstairs. Mahbeer and Shahid left while Naseer kept watch through the front windows.

Abdullah took a seat on the couch and read from Mahbeer's copy of the Quran while they waited. His mind was spinning with excitement, but he used the time to calm himself.

The soldiers returned near dark and Shahid fixed them a light supper, then Naseer and Shahid argued about whether evening prayers were necessary. Naseer was convinced that since they were traveling they were not, and Shahid was convinced they were.

The argument brought a smile to Abdullah's face. "We may skip maghrib prayers," Abdullah said. "I would very much like to see this truck."

They all squeezed into the white car and Mahbeer drove them through the darkened streets of Landstuhl. Abdullah watched the German town pass by, the streets so neat and orderly, so unlike Afghanistan.

Within minutes, they were on the outskirts of the city and creeping down a narrow lane. Mahbeer parked the car beside an old wooden barn.

"We rented this from a local man," Mahbeer said. "His family doesn't farm anymore. Nobody comes around; there's no prying eyes." He led them inside, where the overhead light spilled a soft glow over the ambulance.

Greg, the young man who had smuggled them off the American base, was there to greet them. "Sorry I couldn't stay earlier. I was still on duty. Anyway, here's the ambulance. It's all fixed up, just like you wanted."

Abdullah nodded. The ambulance appeared factory-original. The soldiers had done an excellent job restoring it. He turned to Mahbeer and smiled. "Very good, my dear friends. *Very* good."

Shahid grinned at the compliment. "We had to hollow out some stuff to get it all in. Greg will drive, and trigger it when he's reached the front."

Abdullah watched as Shahid took the canvas bag and dumped the wires and detonators on the workbench. Soon, Shahid and Mahbeer were working diligently, inserting detonators in each brick of C4.

Abdullah turned to Greg and gently took his hand. "This is a great thing you do for Allah. Are you prepared for this martyrdom operation?"

"Yes," Greg replied softly. "Allahu Akbar. God is great."

Abdullah patted Greg's hand. "Allahu Akbar."

* * *

When they returned to the apartment, Mahbeer showed them the bathroom. "Here are the items you asked for," Mahbeer said, passing them a plastic bag. "The clothes are in there," he said, pointing to others on the floor, "and in there." He motioned to the two travel bags hanging from the back of the bathroom door.

Abdullah nodded and Mahbeer left. He opened the plastic container with the grooming scissors and handed them to Naseer. "First we trim our beards."

"Must we do this?" Naseer asked, opening and closing the scissors. "It is every man's duty to grow a beard."

Abdullah smiled and spoke slowly, as if to a child. "We are not doing it from choice, but from necessity. We must change our identity. If we shaved our beards from personal choice, it would be a minor sin, but we do what we must for Jihad."

Naseer took the scissors and started trimming his beard, the wispy black hairs drifting lazily into the sink. Abdullah dug through the bag until he found the safety razors and shaving cream. Naseer kept trimming away until only short hairs adorned his face. He glanced at Abdullah for approval.

"Now you must shave," Abdullah said. Naseer reached for the razor but Abdullah stopped him. "No, wash your face with soap and water." Naseer started to argue, but Abdullah stopped him. "I *know* these things. Wash your face with hot water and soap. It will soften the hair and make the shaving easier."

Naseer washed his face with hot water and the bar of hand soap next to the sink. When he finished, Abdullah instructed him to use the shaving cream to lather his face. With Abdullah's help, his face was soon smooth and bare.

Abdullah eyed him critically. "Take the scissors and trim your eyebrows."

"My eyebrows?" Naseer asked, incredulous.

Abdullah couldn't help but laugh. "We must not look like Mujahideen. We are Indian businessmen from Mumbai. *That* is our new identity. The Americans accept Indians."

"How am I to trim them?"

"Cut them short. You must look well kempt, as if you lived in a city."

Naseer grumbled but trimmed his eyebrows, twisting the scissors back and forth to cut the fine hairs. When Abdullah opened a black plastic container and removed electric shears for haircutting, Naseer shook his head sadly. "I only do this because it is for Jihad."

Abdullah smiled at Naseer's discomfort, then proceeded to cut away most of Naseer's hair. After much fussing, he had Naseer well groomed.

"Now bathe," Abdullah said. "When you are done, put on the clothes. Make sure you put on undergarments. That includes the white undershirt. Then the socks, pants and dress shirt."

Naseer had never spent much time in cities, let alone a Western-style city, and Abdullah remembered how it had felt when he'd first gone to New York. He had been completely lost, with no idea how to act, dress, or speak. He sighed. "Naseer, I wouldn't ask you to do this if it wasn't important."

Naseer smiled reluctantly and Abdullah left him to bathe and dress. When Naseer finally opened the door, Abdullah nodded his praise. "You look like a different man."

Now it was his turn. He ushered Naseer out and went to work cleaning the remains of his Afghanistan life from his body. When he was done, he inspected himself in the mirror. His beard was gone, his face soft and supple. His hair was trimmed and the streaks of gray dyed black. He looked ten years younger than his forty-six years. He dressed in the Western clothes and paused for effect.

Yes.

He looked the part of a successful businessman, from the fashionable suit to the shiny leather shoes. He stood, lost in thought, and wondered about what might have been, if only he had convinced his wife to stay in New York instead of moving back to Afghanistan.

The memories of his destroyed house came, unbidden, his ears ringing, his screams muffled as the others in the village emerged from their houses, looking on in shock.

He ran to the remains of his house and saw his wife, eyes empty, her body stained with blood. He held her in his arms and begged her to come back. He begged until his voice was ragged, her blood cool and stiff against his clothes, but he knew she was gone. He screamed, howling like a maddened animal as the villagers stared, their faces bearing silent witness.

The realization finally broke through his grief, and he knew they had *never* accepted him.

His wife may have been born there, but he was a foreigner, a Saudi. Someone had passed information to the Americans. The local Taliban leader, Azim, had just been promoted, but he was a vain and shallow man and disliked Abdullah.

He had been betrayed, either by Azim or the locals. They had fed information to the CIA, perhaps even to his old friend Jack.

Jack, the man who had come to see him shortly after the towers fell in 2001.

Jack had asked for his help in tracking bin Laden, in helping overthrow the Taliban. As much as he had wanted to help his old friend, the man who had taught him to build bombs, the man who had smuggled him out of Afghanistan and gained him entry into the United States, he'd wanted nothing to do with the madness.

He'd begged Jack to leave him in peace. And, for a time, it had been peaceful, until the Mujahideen had come. He'd wanted nothing to do with them, but they begged.

And, after all, they were brave and loyal Muslims and it was my duty to help with Jihad.

Someone had betrayed him. Even now it brought forth such rage he found he could no longer see his image in the mirror. The world went black, only a pinpoint of light in the middle of his vision. He focused on that spot and took deep breaths, his hands grasping the cold porcelain sink for balance.

That man, Azim, that man who pretended to be a good Muslim, that man would pay. Abdullah had seen to that. The Mujahideen owed him many favors, and after Koshen was safe, they would execute the traitor.

As for his old and dear friend Jack, it took months before he found Jack's location, but when he learned of the Army base to the northeast of Kandahar, he knew that Allah was guiding him and that Jack must pay for what he had done. That bomb was the beginning of his war against the Americans, those who had taken so much from him. The American military would pay the price.

Or perhaps the civilians.

No. He shook his head. Those were Naseer's words. He would not think of it. They were innocent; he knew that from living in New York City. They lived blissfully unaware of what the military did in their name, of the lives they destroyed.

Oh, how he missed his wife. If only he could talk to her, ask for her opinion, beg her for help; but to do so would be to commit shirk. Only the living could answer pleas for help. The dead were beyond such things.

His hands trembled on the cold porcelain. *Nothing will stop me.* He prayed to Allah for strength. Slowly, ever so slowly, his hands stopped shaking, and he felt his rage and grief and pain slip away until there was only the plan. He would strike back in the name of Allah, and his enemies would finally know justice.

* * *

Washington, DC

Hobert Barnwell answered the video call with a grin. "Miss me?"

Smith glared at the video monitor. "Your humor is lost on me. Was she hurt?"

"She's fine."

He breathed a deep sigh of relief. "Did they find anything?"

Hobert shook his head. "Nothing."

"I hate sending her into danger."

"You can't protect her forever. Besides, it's one place where she might have an advantage."

"I could remove her from the OTM," he said. "It would ensure her safety."

Hobert sighed. "She would never forgive you. Could you live with that?"

Smith slammed his hand on the desk. "How could it have come to this? I *never* should have agreed to let her join the Office."

"You didn't have a choice," Hobert answered. "Once she entered your world, there was no turning back."

Smith sat back in his chair. "It's hard to let her go, Hob. Much harder than I expected. I worry endlessly."

Hobert nodded, his face softening. "You've done everything you can."

He wanted to remove his daughter from the OTM, lock her up in a padded room where nothing bad could ever hurt her, but he knew that like all good parents he must let his daughter find her own path. He laughed mirthlessly. "It's killing me."

"I know," Hobert said.

He switched gears. "How did he perform?"

"Well above expectations," Hob said. "He's the one."

"Why so surprised?" he asked.

"I'm not surprised," Hobert said, raising an eyebrow, "but I prefer skepticism. That way I'm rarely disappointed. And, occasionally, pleasantly surprised."

CHAPTER TWELVE

Area 51

Eric waited for Deion in the infirmary. "How's the arm?" he asked when Deion entered.

Deion grunted as Doctor Elliot and Nurse Tulli inspected the wound on his arm while Deion kept pulling away. "They stitched me up in Kandahar," Deion protested.

Doctor Elliot smiled. "We're going to inject something to kick off the healing process."

Nurse Tulli pulled a large syringe from a drawer, then a bottle of clear liquid from a refrigerated container.

Deion watched the needle, his eyes wide, and said, "That's big enough for an elephant."

Nurse Tulli chuckled. "Just relax. You'll feel a little pinch." Deion gritted his teeth as she stuck the needle in his arm and plunged the contents into the muscle. "The wound looks clean. I can get you something for the pain if you'd like."

Deion smiled. "I'm man enough to accept it. Tough guys like Wise, they'd probably just fight through it."

Elliot left, and Nurse Tulli brought Deion a paper cup with some pills and a glass of water. "Take these. Come back in twelve hours and we'll change the dressing." She left Eric and Deion alone in the infirmary.

"Look at this, matching scars," Eric said. He lifted his right arm to show the bandaged pad across his bicep.

"That happen in Denver?"

"Double-ought buckshot, right through the fatty part."

"Hurt?"

Damned if I'll tell him how much. "Not bad. You should see the other guy. Took the rest of it in his face and shoulder."

Deion winced. "Messy way to go."

"Yeah. By the way, I'm not that tough. This bandage has some kind of painkiller in it," Eric said, grinning.

Deion laughed, then grimaced in pain. "Tell me about Denver."

Eric broke it down—the empty storage unit, the Rusty Bucket, the final encounter with Dyer and the police encounter that followed.

"The cops fell for that?" Deion asked. "Homeland Security?"

Eric shrugged. "Why not? We actually have DHS people on the payroll. It gets messy, though. Every encounter like that means more potential exposure. Smith doesn't like it."

Deion shook his head. "I can imagine. What have you found since?"

Eric sighed in frustration. "Nothing. Karen's been searching, but we've come up with a big fat goose egg."

Deion rolled his eyes. "How can a truck full of cesium disappear?"

He was wondering the same thing. "No idea. We did another drone overfly of Denver. It's gone."

Deion considered it for a moment. "You think Los Angeles?"

"That's the million-dollar question," Eric said. "You think that's what Dyer was hinting at?"

Deion rolled his eyes. "Or he was just nuts."

"That crossed my mind," Eric said, "but we have to do *something*. I've got drones flying a search path between Denver and Los Angeles, plus a couple of DHS VIPR teams on the ground."

"Not a lot to go on," Deion said. "How did John handle himself?"

"Good. He hesitated after the storage yard. I wasn't sure, for a minute, but he did really well at the bar. Saved my ass. And with Dyer?" He gave Deion a hard look. "He's scary as hell. Think about it. The guy's body is like a machine. He hammered that door in. When Dyer took his thumb off the button, John hit us like a runaway truck. I've never seen anything like it. The process worked, Deion. He's a human weapon."

Deion grunted, his face skeptical.

"You still don't trust him?" Eric asked.

"I didn't say that," Deion countered. "Think about it. How do we know what all those drugs did to him? What about the brainwashing?"

"It wasn't brainwashing, it was memory replacement."

Deion rolled his eyes again. "Call it what you want, but we messed with his mind. If he ever remembers, we have to put him down. I know you're excited that your pet psychopath is up to snuff, but he's still a murderer."

"I haven't forgotten," he said quietly. "How could I? I'm just saying, the project worked. StrikeForce is a success."

"It was *one* mission," Deion said. "You ready to send him out on his own?"

"No," Eric admitted.

"Yeah, well, I'll be happier once he's got a few more under his belt."

"We have to give it time. He's hitting his mark." Then it dawned on him. "But that's not what you want to talk about, is it? You're avoiding something."

"You read the reports from Kandahar?" Deion asked.

"I did."

"Yeah, well, thanks. For everything. You saved our lives. No joke." Deion scowled. "We were *screwed.*"

"I'm just glad you made it."

Watching the drone feed as the fighters approached, Eric had wanted nothing more than to be there with them. He'd worked frantically to take control of the CIA drone, earning the ire of the CIA's Director of Clandestine Services as well as JSOC. The OTM didn't usually have such direct involvement, but Eric wasn't about to let Deion and Nancy die, especially if there was a way he could save them.

"Yeah," Deion said, "thanks to *you.*" He bit his lip, then spat out the words. "It wouldn't have happened if Nancy hadn't pissed all over Rumple."

Eric nodded. "*That's* it."

"Yeah," Deion said. "I know she's Smith's daughter, and I like the Old Man. I respect him. Nancy is ... she provoked Rumple. She's a ball buster. You want to know something else? She scares me. Sometimes it's like there's nobody home. At least John had a reason for being a psychotic nutjob. She's just—"

Eric cleared his throat. "That's a little strong, don't you think?"

"She was good in the fight, that's for sure, but I don't trust her. She's unstable. She could have got Neil and Val killed."

"What can I do?" Eric asked. "She's the Old Man's daughter."

Deion nodded. "You're stuck, man. I don't envy you one bit."

* * *

Eric led Deion through the base until they joined Nancy, Karen, and Sergeant Clark in the briefing room. Karen had a line of empty paper coffee cups in front of her and Sergeant Clark lectured her about potential caffeine addiction.

"It's not like I drink a lot," she protested, tapping her fingers against the tabletop. "Maybe six cups a day. Or eight."

"Those are twenty-ounce cups," Clark retorted. "That's a lot of coffee."

"I've built up a tolerance," Karen muttered under her breath.

Nancy watched the exchange, stone-faced, turning to greet Deion and Eric with a nod.

"Let's get started," Eric said. "We've all had a chance to read the reports. What do we know?"

Deion nodded to Nancy. "You first."

"The contact hanged himself," Nancy said. "Abdullah inspires loyalty, we know that. He's smart. AQ respects the hell out of him. The local Taliban, not so much. His target was someone in FOB Wildcat, not the drone program. I think there's an obvious answer. Abdullah was a CIA asset. Any disagreement?"

"I've been digging through the records on the CIA agents, Trevino and Wiggins," Clark said. "It was definitely Trevino. He spent time there in the eighties. I've requested the paper files be sent here. They're still gathering them."

"Paper files," Karen said with disgust. "It's like the stone age."

Clark sighed. "Case reports were filed on paper because that's all they had access to in the mountains. Plus, Trevino ran a lot of missions off-book. I'd be surprised if we found anything. You have to remember, not everyone thought arming the Mujahideen was a good idea. Trevino funneled a lot of weapons and supplies, most of them untraceable. Let's say he taught those men to make IEDs. Let's say he found a very motivated student, maybe he develops a friendship. Maybe he gets this guy into the US after the war. No idea what happens then, until 2002. Suddenly, there's a surge in high-quality bombs in Iraq and Afghanistan. Remote triggers, cell phone activated, instructions and schematics popping up all over. Someone very gifted is writing it all down and distributing it."

"That's a stretch," Deion said, "but it fits."

"I agree," Eric said. "It's a working theory. So, FOB Wildcat was personal, something with Trevino. Koshen claimed Trevino killed Abdullah's wife. Revenge is a good motivator."

Nancy turned to him. "Who cares about his motivations? I just want to find him and kill him."

Deion shrugged. "She's got a point."

"Maybe so," Clark agreed. "What indication do we have that he's not in Pakistan?"

"There's been no chatter," Karen said. "No intercepts. They're talking about the bombing, and there's chatter about this kid, Koshen, but nothing about Abdullah."

Eric sighed. They lacked info. They had no idea whether he was still in Afghanistan, or what his next move might be. Drone overflights near the Pakistan-Afghanistan border showed how porous it really was. If Abdullah was traveling light, or even alone, he would be impossible to track.

A quick motorcycle trip and Abdullah would be across the border in Pakistan, where the ISI and AQ would shelter him. Or, he could still be in Afghanistan, in a hidey-hole carved into the mountains. Eric had seen the caves firsthand, some dating back to the Soviet occupation, some dating back to the English occupation one hundred years earlier. No, if Abdullah went to ground in the mountains, there would be no finding him.

"Without any more to go on," he said, "we have to assume he's holed up. How's security right now?"

Deion grunted. "Safety there is an illusion, man. You know that. The Army is stretched thin. There's a joint op between the CIA and Delta looking for the bomber. Are we going to give up the intel? They're working blind without it."

"Give them the intel," Nancy said. "We know the attack wasn't targeted at the drone." She glared at everyone around the table. "This is a JSOC problem, not an Office problem."

"I disagree," Eric said. "There's no direct threat to the drone program, but what if he strikes again?"

Nancy frowned. "The purpose of the Office is to protect the country from threats that require action that no *other* agency can provide or has jurisdiction for. We can't be everywhere. It's not within our purview."

Clark jumped in. "We all know the mission, Nancy, but what if he's the next bin Laden? What if we could stop him now? I'd say that falls within our purview. We should run it up the ladder."

"Look," Eric said, "I'm the CO, so it's my responsibility to take it to the Old Man. Thanks for your input. I'd like the room. Nancy, if you could stay?"

They left, single file, Deion giving him a long glance on the way out.

He was alone with Nancy, who sat facing him, not quite meeting his eye.

"You're angry," he said, "and I don't know why."

"Keeping me after school? You don't agree with my assessment, so you'll go to my father?" she spat out.

"That *wasn't* why I kept you, but let's start there. I don't think it's a good idea to drop Abdullah into JSOC's hands. You do. That's okay, we can disagree. The Old Man makes the decision. I'm taking it to him because while I may be the CO, he's the Director. If you have a problem with your father, take it up with him."

She leaned forward, her face red. "Wait, if it wasn't that, then what do you want to talk to me about?"

"What happened at Bagram?" he asked.

"Bagram? We were attacked in Kandahar."

"You did well in Kandahar. Do you know what the odds are of a few soldiers holding off an AQ attack like that? Even trained Special Forces? Burch and Simon weren't prepared for anything like that, and certainly not Deion. They're spies, not soldiers. It should never have come to that."

She glared at him. "So, that's it? Deion told you?"

"He didn't have to tell me. Why else would Rumple have pulled Delta? What did you say to him?"

"Nothing to justify that. He's an asshole!"

"He may be," Eric admitted, "but you pushed him."

Nancy kicked back in her chair, face flushed. "Maybe I did."

"You did or you didn't. Which is it?"

She shrugged. Tears rolled from her eyes, and she rubbed at them. "You want me to say it? I pushed him. I shouldn't have, but I couldn't stop myself."

He watched her lip tremble, but he had no idea what to do. He had never been good at dealing with female emotions. "You made a mistake. It's okay."

She sat up straight. "Do you think I'm crying because I'm sad? It's a normal reaction to anger and stress. Do you know what I'm feeling? I'm pissed. Sometimes I do things and I don't know why. I've got anger problems. I try and keep it under control, but sometimes it gets away from me. I don't know why I let Rumple push my buttons. I wanted to put a bullet in his head. And then, after the combat, I was so horny I almost jumped Deion on the trip home. If his arm hadn't been bandaged up, I would have fucked him silly in the back of the plane."

That was more information than Eric had expected. "I don't even know how to respond to that."

She leaned forward, grimacing. "Look, I know that's a normal reaction, too. I mean, Deion's not even my type. The anger and the sexual frustration, it's all just aftereffects from the firefight." She continued rubbing at her eyes. "Since I'm baring my soul, might as well go all the way. Do you even know why you're here?"

"What do you mean?"

"I mean, of all the Operators, why did my father pick you? You weren't the best. Why you?"

Eric hated to admit it, but the thought *had* crossed his mind. "You know why?"

"I have my suspicions," she said. "You think outside the box, sometimes. You don't get personally involved in your missions. You're committed and focused, but you're also completely alone."

"My mother is still alive."

"I don't mean anything by this, but your mom is gone. She's a shell of the woman you knew."

It was hard to hear, but she was right. "So, what, I'm here to take *care* of you?"

"Think about it. They needed an Operator, not necessarily the best, but someone who wouldn't be tempted to use or abuse their power. They needed someone to watch over Frist. He *idolizes* you. How effective would his training be without that? And you're my type, Eric. You're the kind of guy I'm attracted to. My father *knows* that. You don't think he'd have killed two birds with one stone? Come on, he practically gift wrapped you and left you outside my door."

"Stop right there," he sputtered. "We work together, nothing more."

She stood and walked around the table, sitting down in front of him, close enough that her leg rubbed his. He tried not to notice her scent, not of perfume, but of soap and skin, the fragrance intoxicating.

"You're a man," she said, matter-of-factly. "I could snap my fingers and you'd be servicing me before you had time to think."

He considered that. "You're wrong," he lied.

"You've been here for months and you haven't taken part in the hookup culture. I'd have heard about it."

"Doc Barnwell just filled me in about that."

"He give you the speech? No feelings? No catches? And you haven't slept with anyone?"

"No." He paused, then continued. "I think Karen is interested."

Nancy laughed. "You should take her up on it. I hear she's good in the sack."

"Doesn't matter," he said. "I'm not some high school kid looking to get laid in the back of his old man's car. I have self-control."

"It would be best if I had some, too—is that what you're implying?" She tilted her head. "I'm messed up and I know it. All I have left is the Office. What do you have? Why are you even here?"

"It's what I do," he said simply. He wanted to reach out, hold her hand, but was afraid anything he might do would only aggravate the situation. "The world is complicated and crazy, and the only thing holding it together is people like me. I *can't* be distracted. I *have* to do the job."

"Quite a hero complex, Captain America." She stood and glared at him. "If you really want to know why you're here, talk to my father. Ask him about the family business. *Mine* and *yours*."

She slammed the door on her way out.

* * *

Eric scanned through the images of his father's military records. He knew his father had served in Vietnam. When Eric was a kid, he'd begged his dad to tell stories, but his dad had always refused. He would say the past was the past and there was no need to fill his head with nonsense, then send him outside to play. Reading through the records, he realized his dad might have had other reasons for not talking about his time in the service.

The records painted a different story than he'd expected. His dad had been Special Forces, and the paper trail was blank from his entry into Vietnam in August of 1963 until he'd out-processed in 1968.

He had stayed in country for five years. Nothing noted in his records about missions, either. *What did he do for those five years?* Even in the world of Special Forces, there were records. His father's record was empty. Expunged.

Eric stood and stretched his legs. Why hadn't his father told him? He checked the clock. It was late, but he made a brief stop in the cafeteria for coffee before heading to Smith's office. Light peeked from under Smith's door. He knew Smith had flown in just hours before, but Eric had not yet been summoned for a briefing. He knocked politely and entered.

Smith sat at his desk, phone pushed to the corner, shuffling a well-worn set of cards. He smiled at Eric. "An indulgence from my youth. It allows my mind to wander freely. What may I do for you?"

"I hope I didn't cause any problems with the override of the CIA drone."

"They were not happy," Smith said, "but the issue is resolved. Mr. Rumple has also been summoned to Washington. I thought it best that he have no further contact with our people. The CIA Director agreed."

"Nancy wants to pass the info back to JSOC and be done with it."

Smith paused his game, glancing up. "What do you think?"

"I think that Abdullah could be the next bin Laden. I think we should keep it."

"The Office has a limited amount of resources. This might hamper your investigation into the missing cesium. How goes that?"

"We've come up blank, sir. Karen is working on it, but nothing so far."

"You're the commanding officer," Smith said. "There's no need to bring this to me."

"Nancy seems to think there is," he said.

"She's not the CO, Eric. Go with your gut."

"Yes, sir." He turned to leave, then stopped. "Sir?" He hesitated. "Did you know my dad?"

Smith stared at the cards on the table. "You've been looking through his service records," he said without looking up. "Yes, I knew your father quite well."

It was the admission Eric had been waiting for. "In what capacity?"

Smith swept up the cards, then placed them in his desk drawer. "He worked for the Office, which you suspected."

Eric nodded.

"He was also my friend," Smith said. "As was your grandfather, Joseph."

"Grandpa Joe? How did you know Grandpa Joe?" He hadn't expected that, and his head was spinning. "Is that why you picked me?"

"You spoke to Nancy," Smith said, shaking his head. "When Truman tasked me with creating the Office, I was nothing more than a child. I needed someone with experience, someone with a military background. Your grandfather was an exceptional man. He had been in the Airborne during World War Two. He'd suffered through the Ardennes during the Battle of the Bulge. He was my boot camp instructor, and he left quite an impression. Not for his training methods, but because of his mental and moral strength.

Smith continued. "He was ready to retire. I offered him a job. Just a year. He stayed for three. He was my right-hand man and eventually my friend. Your grandmother as well. A sweet woman, dedicated to her husband and her young son, William. I kept in touch with Joseph as his son became a man. Then William joined the Army. It was a chaotic time, and my advice to the President about Vietnam fell upon deaf ears. I had recruited a young man, Hobert, to run a psychological warfare division."

"Doc Barnwell?"

"Yes. Hobert was brilliant, but not all of his ideas were without consequences. We needed someone who could clean up our mistakes. Your father was a good man, rugged, like his father. You are like him in so many ways. You are a good man, like your father and your father's father."

Smith paused. "I'm old, Eric. I can feel it, more so every day. My bones ache. I forget things. I need someone to run the Office after I'm gone. Someone young and full of life. Someone who can hold the line."

Eric considered the bombshell. "Why didn't my dad tell me? He never talked about it. Grandpa Joe, either."

"Your father had had his fill of the Army. He wanted a clean break. I visited your parents in the hospital. I watched as your mother held you. Your father took me aside and told me that his son would not be a military man. I visited again, when you were a young boy, on your eighth birthday."

He visited my house? "I don't remember."

"Of course not. You were young. William's position had hardened. No, the Wise family had paid their debt in blood. It was time for them to move on. He was quite chagrined to learn that you had joined the Army. He called me and made me promise to keep you safe. I told him it was a promise I could not keep. He told me in no uncertain terms that as long as he was alive, his son would not follow in his footsteps. I agreed."

"He died."

"Yes," Smith said softly, "he died, and my promise died with him. I *need* you. The Office *needs* you. You were born for this job."

"What about Doc Barnwell?"

Smith took a deep breath. "Hobert is my dear friend, but his time is almost past."

"And what about Nancy? She thinks you brought me here to watch over her."

"Not entirely untrue," Smith acknowledged. He gazed at Eric with hooded eyes. "She's damaged. Fragile. And dangerous. I know what happened in Afghanistan. She needs someone to care for her. I want you to help her if you can, but your primary duty will always be to the Office. I would like to name you my successor."

Eric rocked back in his chair. "Sir, I don't know what to say. A few days ago I'd have jumped at the chance, but it's hard to wrap my mind around all this."

"I understand," Smith said. "I'm ... sorry for withholding the truth."

Eric's mind raced. He'd thought he knew everything about his family, about why he had chosen his career. "I'd like to think about it."

Smith nodded. A smile played across his lips. "Of course. Do not make this decision lightly. You have a week."

* * *

Landstuhl, Germany

Abdullah was fast asleep when Naseer gently shook him awake. Abdullah was momentarily confused before remembering where he was. The bedroom was small, but Mahbeer had given it to them as a sign of respect. "What time is it?" he asked, wiping at the crust in his eyes. It was still dark outside, the room illuminated by Naseer's laptop.

"Almost morning." Naseer scowled. "The Americans have killed Koshen."

"What?" He bolted upright. "How did this happen?"

Naseer shrank back, pointing at the laptop. "It says that Azim gave Koshen to the Americans. The Mujahideen attacked. There was a great battle and many were killed. The Americans got away, but Koshen was killed, along with one of Azim's men."

Abdullah sagged against the bed in shock. "He was just a young boy."

Naseer paused. "He died a martyr."

"He was just a boy," Abdullah repeated. *So young!*

"I am sorry. What should I do?"

He stared at Naseer's laptop resting on the floor. "Send this message. 'We will avenge the boy's death. He was martyred by this false Muslim, Azim. He will be executed for his actions.' Send that message."

Naseer typed the message and clicked the button to encrypt the data, then uploaded the picture to the website. "It has been sent."

He placed his hands gently on Naseer's shoulders and noticed his damp eyes. *Naseer had liked Koshen, too.* He shook his head, but he had to ask Naseer. "I must continue Jihad. I must go to America, but Azim must pay. Will you go back?"

Naseer's eyes widened. "To Kandahar?"

"Yes," Abdullah said. "*You* must lead the Mujahideen. You *must* execute Azim. His treachery *must* be punished. Koshen *must* be avenged. Will you do this for me?"

Naseer smiled proudly. "I will do this. For Koshen and for you."

He managed a weak smile, even though his heart was broken over Koshen's death. "You have been a faithful student. I know you will make Azim pay for his betrayal."

"I will pray for you, Abdullah, that you may strike the Americans down and make them suffer for their affront to Allah."

"The preparations are underway?"

"Yes. Mahbeer's cousin will be waiting. I wish I could be with you when you strike the Americans."

"It is Allah's will," Abdullah said. "Strike the false believer in Kandahar while I strike the Americans." He grasped Naseer's hand, clutching it tight. "For my wife. For Koshen."

* * *

Area 51

Eric was returning from Smith's quarters when his cell phone buzzed, paging him to the War Room. He pounded through the brightly lit tunnels, making it in record time. The War Room was alive with activity. "What's the situation?"

Clark greeted him and pointed to Karen. "Karen's got a hit. She's working it now."

Karen ran a hand through her short black hair. "It's the website again. Do you understand steganography?"

"Yeah," Eric said. "It's hiding a message in another message."

Karen nodded. "Exactly. It could be anything, like the hand signs you were taught to give if caught and taped by the enemy. I mean, there's a whole history behind this stuff."

She paused as Deion and Nancy entered the War Room. "We've been tracking Al-Qaeda for years via steganography. Basically, when you encode an image in a jpeg, you wind up with a bunch of ones and zeroes. You can swap out thousands of them in an image, and the effects are unnoticeable to the human eye. But if the receiver knows the pattern, they can take those values and extract the message. Google's web bots crawl the Internet cataloging websites for their search engine, and we get a copy of that data and run scrapes against it, looking for patterns. There are thousands of Jihadists' websites. The active ones have provided useful SIGINT, but the dormant ones are the ones I find interesting."

She took another drink of coffee, then continued. "After the FOB Wildcat bombing, I saw a stego'd message on what used to be a dormant site. Just a brief message indicating they had performed a successful operation, but after your mission," she pointed at Nancy and Deion, "there was another message filled with details about that Koshen boy's death. Well, now there is a new post talking about avenging the boy's death. Here, let me pull it up."

The screen displayed the message, and Eric's stomach sank. "You think this is Abdullah?"

"Could be him," Karen said., "or it could be his proxies."

"Can you track the image?" Clark asked.

"Working on it. I've tracked the previous posts back to Kandahar. They're routing the traffic through web anonymizers. But, after FOB Wildcat, I rooted a bunch of their anonymizers and now I've got my own back door. From there I can track the IP back, hop to hop, until I find the source. I should know something in a few minutes."

Deion turned to Eric with a raised eyebrow. "I'm glad she's on our side."

Eric grinned. "Better watch your porn surfing."

"No porn surfing on base," Karen said over her shoulder, her fingers typing furiously.

Eric watched as Karen did her magic, the map of IP addresses a foreign language to him. Soon, she banged on her keyboard.

"We've got a winner!" Karen exclaimed. "It's Europe. Registered to a German carrier. The range is blocked off for home use, in Landstuhl, Germany. Why does that sound familiar?"

"Ramstein Air Force Base," Eric said. "That's where the hospital is."

"Oh, yeah. Landstuhl Regional Medical Center. Isn't that where the Iraq and Afghanistan wounded go?" Karen asked.

Eric turned to Deion. "Get John. I want us wheels up in thirty."

Deion nodded. "You got it, boss." Deion tore out of the room, pushing aside analysts as he went.

"I'll have the jet loaded and ready," Nancy said, her voice determined. "We'll be there before lunch."

CHAPTER THIRTEEN

Landstuhl, Germany

The squeal of the Gulfstream's wheels woke John from his sleep, like the cries of the men and women in his dreams. He wiped the sweat from his brow with trembling hands, trying to put the dream behind him.

Eric, Deion, Nancy, Taylor Martin, and Roger Johnson sat at the table in the front section of the plane, deep in planning for the upcoming mission.

"Look," Eric said, "I know we've been over this already, but I want it clear. No mistakes." He pointed to an aerial photo of an apartment complex in the Landstuhl area. "John and Roger will go through the alley, then breach the door. Taylor, you and Nancy come from the west, and Deion and I come from the east. I want no more than thirty seconds between breach and lockdown. Do we have the layout?"

John shook off the effect of the nap and joined the planning. "The front and side doors open to a living area and kitchen," he said, pointing. "Bedroom and kitchen are on the first floor. Stairs are here"—he moved his finger—"and lead to the upstairs bedrooms here and here, bathroom here. Also, stairs to the basement, no windows."

"Right," Deion agreed. "No egress in the back. Just the windows there and there." He pointed. "We go in standard close-quarter formation. Clear the first floor, then the upstairs, basement last."

"Remember," Eric said, "We need them alive."

John noticed surreptitious glances from the rest of the team and felt his face flush. "That's not fair."

"Just a gentle reminder," Eric said with a grin.

"We've had surveillance on the building for the past couple hours," Deion said. "Nobody's gone in or out. It's thin."

Eric shrugged. "It's all we have."

The plane taxied off the runway, stopped, and the engine's whine faded as they powered down. Greg Clayberg, their pilot, opened the cockpit door. "Your contact is waiting. I'll get the plane turned and refueled."

John liked Greg, the man with the salt-and-pepper beard and hair. There was a twinkle in Greg's eyes and he delighted in needling Nancy at every turn. John was surprised that Nancy allowed it. She didn't seem to take shit from anyone, but somehow Greg came away unscathed.

They grabbed their duffel bags, checked that everything was in place, then proceeded to where the young PFC was waiting for them.

The PFC, Klein, handed them the paperwork they needed for free rein of the base, and keys to two unmarked Volkswagens. They split up, three to a vehicle, and made their way off the base and through the picturesque streets of Landstuhl.

John rode with Roger and Deion. Roger drove the unmarked car around the neighborhood, circling the block twice before stopping fifty meters from their destination. John watched in the side-view mirror as the other vehicle did the same.

John checked his M11, nodding as Roger did the same. "You ready?" he asked.

Roger grinned. "I'd say I was born ready, but then I'd sound like an asshole."

"That's the *only* thing that makes you sound like an asshole?" Deion said.

John laughed. He barely knew Roger, but their shared experience in Denver lent them a familiar camaraderie. Through their earpieces, they heard Eric question the surveillance team. "Any updates?"

"No movement," the man helming the surveillance team responded.

"Let's do it," Eric said.

Here we go. John got out of the car and strolled down the street with Roger, chatting about the scenery. They came to the alleyway next to the apartment building, turned quickly, and headed for the side door. They paused for a moment to allow the others to reach the front door and waited for Eric to make the call.

"On three," Eric said.

Roger pulled a flash-bang from his jacket pocket and on three, John kicked the door as hard as he could, right above the doorknob. Whether it was from the drugs or the exercise, the door splintered around the lock and swung, hitting the wall and ricocheting back.

Roger caught it with his shoulder and threw in the flash-bang. They entered the room with drawn pistols as the grenade exploded, followed by another from Eric in front. They each took a predetermined quadrant, pistols moving with practiced precision, looking for targets.

Eric yelled, "Clear," and they rushed forward in a tight group, Deion kicking in the door to the bathroom.

"Clear!" Deion yelled.

They took the stairs two at a time and entered the bedrooms and then the shared bathroom. "Clear!" Nancy yelled.

They swept back down the stairs and hit the basement, Eric flicking on the light. When they reached the bottom, Eric stopped them with a raised hand. "Oh no," Eric said, pointing to the multicolored wiring that splayed across the squat wooden table like spaghetti.

The materials filled John with dread. "Oh no," he breathed.

* * *

"Clark," Eric said, "Abdullah was here. We think he's made another bomb."

"I'll alert the base," Clark said. "Any intel in the apartment?"

Eric kicked at the living room table. "Wiring in the basement. Prayer mats. Looks like grooming supplies in the bathroom."

"Any ID?" Clark asked.

"It's clean. Did you have any luck with the apartment manager?"

"He works for a Berlin firm," Clark said. "He claims he rented it to three American soldiers. A white guy, a black guy, and a Latino."

Martin rolled his eyes. "Sounds like a bad joke."

"I don't think these guys are joking," Clark responded. "What's their target? What at Ramstein is worth hitting?"

"Delta has an office here," Eric said, "to keep tabs on their wounded."

Deion joined in. "CIA has offices, same thing. Could be supply planes?"

John listened intently. He knew the base ran a constant string of supply planes to military bases across the world, including Iraq and Afghanistan, but hitting the supply planes would only disrupt the military's logistics, not stop them.

"Call it in," Eric ordered. "Put the base on alert. THREATCON Delta. Lock it down."

"Karen's on it," Clark said. "Nobody will be allowed in or out."

John glanced around the apartment. "No computers anywhere. No notes."

"This site's blown," Nancy agreed. "We can have forensics sweep it later. Do we have satellite imagery?"

There was a pause. "The latest overfly is days old," Clark said. "Karen is backtracking now."

"No sense staying here," Eric said.

They piled into the Volkswagens and headed back to Ramstein. They were within eyesight of the entrance, a long line of cars backed up as people waited for the inspections to occur and the THREATCON to lift, when they heard the explosion off in the distance, a crack and a deep whoomp.

There was a moment of silence and then klaxons blared to life. John turned to Roger, who stared off into the distance, his knuckles white on the steering wheel. Roger nudged him and pointed toward the mushroom cloud blossoming into the sky.

"Fuck me," Deion said in a hushed tone.

John's stomach churned and he tasted bile in the back of his throat. They had failed.

"Clark, you getting this?" Eric asked.

"It's the Regional Medical Center," Clark said. "We're getting video online." There was a pause before Clark sucked in his breath. "Oh God."

Ahead, Eric's car gunned the engine and executed a sharp U-turn, Roger following suit. They raced down the winding narrow streets of Landstuhl, tires squealing as they cornered hard, screaming west until they came in view of the hospital's north entrance.

John surveyed the damage. The front of the building was devastated, open to the world, smoke and fires everywhere. Bodies were strewn throughout the rubble, a head here, an exposed leg there. Soldiers ran, screaming.

"What. The. Hell?" Roger breathed.

John stared, uncomprehending. "Why would someone do this?"

Humvees roared up behind them, blocking the narrow road. Airmen jumped out and started yelling at them, surrounding their cars.

"Clark," Eric said. "We've got a problem. People, don't make any sudden moves."

"I've got the Installation Commander on the phone," Clark said over their earpieces. "It's going to take a few minutes before it filters down to the Chief of Security Forces. Just do as the nice Airmen ask and sit tight until we get it sorted."

They got out, their hands raised, as the soldiers approached. John watched as Eric spoke softly to their commanding officer, and, after much communications back to their base, the Airmen released them.

They milled about. "Clark," Eric said. "We need something to go on."

"They let you go?" Clark asked.

"Yeah. You pulled the right strings."

"Good, because Karen has something. The last overfly shows a car in the alley at the apartment. She's matched that against another photoset. The same car was at a barn not far from there, in the countryside. I'm sending you the coordinates."

Eric glanced down at his cell phone, then lifted it to show the rest of them. "Okay, people. We've got something to go on. Let's get the bastard who did this."

* * *

Eric approached the barn slowly. It sat nestled among the trees, its red paint long since faded from time and weather, the white car parked alongside. He pulled the Volkswagen over and watched in the rearview mirror as Roger did the same behind him.

Martin tapped him on the shoulder, turning off his radio and motioning for Eric to do the same. "I hate to point it out, but we don't have any gear," Martin said quietly.

"We've got the MP5s and our handguns," Eric said. "That's enough."

"No body armor. We're out of flash-bangs. I'm just saying, maybe we should bring in the locals."

"We bring in the locals and we lose control," Eric said. "Then they start asking questions."

Martin sighed. "They just blew up a hospital. This'll hit the news, big. If you really want to keep the OTM on the down low, we need to split."

"We have to find Abdullah. If he makes it out of this, he's the next boogeyman. We can't let that happen. We can't let him slip away like bin Laden in Tora Bora. We had him cornered, remember?"

"I was *there*," Martin reminded him.

Eric nodded. The memory of their failure still haunted him. "I'm not letting Abdullah get away. Not again."

Taylor shrugged. "I'm with you."

They turned their earpieces back on.

"We're going in," Eric said. "We're going to take him down."

There was a chorus of agreements. Eric got out and the rest followed, approaching the barn. They had it surrounded when a young black man with a high-and-tight haircut opened the door, saw them, and dove for the car.

Eric opened fire with his MP5, joining the others who strafed the side of the vehicle. There was yelling inside the barn and then an automatic weapon opened fire on their position. Eric recognized the sound, an M16 on full-auto.

Eric dropped to his knee and turned sideways, minimizing his profile, the tree line too far behind him for cover. He fired on the barn, and the others shifted from the man behind the car to the half-open barn door.

The black man opened the car door and crawled inside, started the car, and floored it. Rooster tails of rock and grass sprayed from the front wheels, then the rocketed forward, aiming for the weakest point in their perimeter, right in front of John.

John froze.

"Get back!" Eric shouted.

John stood, dumbly, as the car headed toward him.

Deion and Nancy turned their fire on the car, bullets tearing up the side, but the car did not stop.

Deion took off in a run and tackled John. Time slowed for Eric as he aimed carefully and fired. The bullet caught the driver in the side of the face. There was a spray of blood from the back of the driver's head and the car veered to one side, barely missing John and Deion. They watched helplessly as the car accelerated down the road until it sideswiped a tree and smashed into another, the engine sputtering to a stop.

The man in the barn screamed in anger and his M16 stopped firing. While the man reloaded, Eric turned to Martin and motioned for him to go around the back.

Roger and Nancy reloaded and Eric took off at a run, dropping his own magazine and slamming in a new one. He cycled the bolt and saw the Airman, young with dark olive skin and wearing camos, drawing down on him from the doorway. Eric shot first, stitching bullets across the man's abdomen.

The man dropped his M16 and collapsed.

Eric hit the edge of the barn and plastered himself against it, waiting for more gunfire, his senses amped, his ears ringing. He approached the young man and kicked the M16 away.

"Clear," Martin yelled from inside the barn.

The others rushed forward, all aiming at the downed man.

Eric grabbed him by his camos and lifted his head up. "Where's Abdullah?" he asked.

The man looked up, face ashen, his eyes glazing over. "Allahu—"

Eric knelt. The man's name, Guardado, was stitched across his camos. Eric checked the man's pulse. It was fast and erratic. "*Where is Abdullah?*" he repeated.

Guardado's eyes focused momentarily and he dribbled bloody spittle.

Eric grabbed Guardado's camos and shook him in frustration. "Why the hospital? Where is he?"

Guardado's lips parted and foamy blood poured from his mouth as his body convulsed.

Eric watched the man die. He had seen similar injuries. There was no saving him. Guardado's legs kicked slower, then stopped. Eric shook his head. The man was gone. He turned to Nancy. "Check the guy in the car."

Nancy nodded and left with Roger in tow.

Martin joined him. "Nobody else here. Looks like it was just these two."

Eric helped Martin survey the site. There were tools and an air compressor, and the place smelled of paint. Parts for emergency vehicles lay half-disassembled on the dirt floor. A pair of sawhorses held a door, fashioned into a makeshift workbench, and a half-empty box of detonators sat next to spools of wire.

John joined them. He picked up the spool of wire and shook his head.

Nancy and Roger returned. "We found his military ID," she said. "His name was Terrill Johnson. There were suitcases with clothes and cash in the trunk."

"Looks like they were going to disappear," Roger said.

"Well, they're gone now," Martin said.

Eric nodded grimly. "Yes, they are."

* * *

Atlantic Ocean

The water stretched as far as John could see. Far below, the occasional ship spread a long white arrow of foam in its wake. Nancy was in the cockpit with Greg, and the rest of the team slumped in the cabin seats.

John watched Taylor Martin's chest rise and fall. Martin's eyes were partially shut and he appeared to be asleep, but John had met soldiers who slept like that, never quite awake but not quite asleep. Roger was at the front of the plane typing away on his laptop, writing up the after-action report.

He turned and found Eric staring back at him. John nodded and Eric dipped his head in acknowledgment, then got up and walked down the plane, taking the seat across from him.

John knew it was coming and wilted under Eric's gaze.

"What happened?" Eric finally asked.

John shrugged. "I froze."

Eric's eyes bored into his. "What really happened?"

John glanced down at the table between them. "It was the hospital. Why would someone do that?"

"Some people are evil."

John squirmed in his seat as he tried to explain his lack of action. "He was clearly working with Abdullah and he was a traitor, but I couldn't kill him. I saw enough death at the hospital."

"It hurts to take a life," Eric said. "It steals something from you. I think everyone who has a conscience and has killed knows that feeling."

That surprised him. "You feel this way, too?"

Eric smiled. "Of course. I'm not some inhuman killing machine. Is that what you think Delta Operators are? Killing machines? I joined Delta to serve my country, to keep war at bay, not to become a common killer. It's all about intent. If you kill to protect, you can find a way to live with yourself. If you kill because you take pleasure in it? That's what makes you a monster. I told you in Denver, you're not a monster."

Relief washed over him. "You've been good to me, Eric. I know it sounds dopey, but I want to make you proud."

Eric patted him lightly on the shoulder. "Don't worry, kid. You're doing fine."

CHAPTER FOURTEEN

Mexico City, Mexico

The airplane dipped lower and Abdullah glanced nervously through the window as the plane approached the runway. In the distance, Mexico City stretched out through a cloud of smog, a jumble of buildings and streets as far as he could see, sharp-toothed mountains in the distance. The plane landed and taxied to the terminal where he disembarked.

He half-expected jackbooted thugs to scream at him and tackle him to the floor, but the flight from Homburg ended peacefully and he was allowed through customs. He smiled and answered all the questions, just a successful businessman from India. They waved him through and he offered a polite smile to the two masked federal officers who guarded the customs exit, then headed to the food court, where he met the young man, Emmanuel, who eyed him suspiciously.

He nodded at the young man and offered his hand. "Peace be upon you."

The young man rolled his eyes. "I'm Manny. My cousin told me to get you over the border. I don't wanna know your shit, understand?."

Abdullah nodded and leaned closer. "We need to leave the airport as soon as possible," he said quietly.

Manny shrugged and led him through the parking lot to a beat-up silver Nissan Sentra. The walk to the car was pleasant and Abdullah was surprised at the climate. The thin air reminded him of the mountains of Afghanistan. When they got in the car, he asked, "Would you mind if we listened to the radio?"

Manny shrugged. "Whatever, man."

Abdullah dug through the channels until he found an English-speaking newscaster. He listened intently as they drove through the heavy traffic of Mexico City, the crisp air thick with pollution. "How long to the border?"

"You kidding? A long time, man."

Abdullah resisted the urge to smack the young man. Manny might not be a Muslim, but he was a cousin of Mahbeer, and Mahbeer promised that Manny would smuggle him over the border.

The man on the radio spoke about two American soldiers tortured in Iraq, beheaded, their bodies desecrated. Abdullah grimaced. Killing for Jihad was one thing but desecrating the dead? That was unacceptable.

The newscaster was interrupted by a bulletin about a bombing in Germany, devastation at the scene, many dead, and the manhunt to find the culprits. Manny gave him a sidelong glance, then turned his attention back to the packed streets of Mexico City.

* * *

Area 51

Eric sat with the rest of the team in the briefing room. The flight back from Germany had sapped their energy, leaving them drained, but it was important to continue the investigation. He dreaded the answer, but he asked anyway. "How many dead?"

Clark turned to him with weary eyes. "Two hundred and thirty-six."

"Why?" John asked. "Why target a hospital?"

"Who knows?" Deion said. "Could be a target of opportunity. Could be to spread fear."

Eric nodded. It felt right. First the attack on FOB Wildcat. Then the Landstuhl Regional Medical Center. "Does it occur to anyone else that he's primarily targeting military installations? What do we know about the collaborators?"

Karen displayed their bios on the screen at the front of the room. "Terrill Johnson, twenty-six, by all accounts a mediocre Airman, converted to Islam three years ago. Hector Guardado, twenty-five, converted to Islam about the same time. Their service records were undistinguished. Guardado's the most probable source of the C4; they've found discrepancies in the base inventory going back years. Greg Johansen, twenty-five. He was a quiet one, no known Islamic ties. Recovered footage shows that he drove the ambulance. He was vaporized in the blast. We've tracked their movements as best we could. There were no red flags, no reason to think they would do something like this."

"But they did," Nancy said, her face a stony mask. "What about Abdullah?"

"No sign of him. DNA samples taken from the wastebasket in the bathroom of the apartment shows two other men were there. Best guess, they left before you arrived. I've flagged all flights from Europe to the US, but I don't have to tell you how many people were in the air. We've got agents tracking down those loose ends, but I doubt we'll find anything."

"What about other destinations?" Eric asked.

Clark shrugged. "Working on it. Canada had quite a few flights that day. Mexico's not helpful. The narco-gangsters have too much influence and you can't get good intel. It goes downhill after that. We get nothing from Venezuela, of course."

Eric nodded. "Focus on Canada."

"What if he's headed back to Afghanistan?" Martin asked.

"There's always a chance," Eric said, turning to Karen. "What else?"

"I've got an intelligent agent watching the militant websites. It'll flag any new posts."

"Keep at it," Eric said. "We've *got* to find this guy."

* * *

John sat on his neatly made bed, moaning softly. He was on the edge of remembering something important but had no idea what. He remembered the IED in Iraq as if it just happened, but everything after was a blur.

There was a hole where certain things should be. He remembered his parent's funeral, bits and pieces, but the service itself was hazy.

He remembered a man holding him down, beating him, drowning him. He remembered other men, their hot breath in his face, asking about bombs. No, *a* bomb. *The* bomb.

What bomb?

He shrugged off his clothes and lay on top of the covers. It was the hospital in Germany that haunted him. He could still smell it, burning rubber, dust, and everywhere the smell of death. Then, the two Airmen, the machine gun fire.

Every dead body was tearing away at him.

He wanted out.

The more he thought about the bodies, the more nauseous he became until he ran to the bathroom, retching, emptying his stomach into the toilet. He spat and swished water from the sink in his mouth to remove the taste.

The bombing.

There was more than just PTSD or a concussion like the Docs claimed.

Something about Eric and Deion. The recruitment. It was so fuzzy. His body was stronger than ever, but his mind was a blur of half-formed images, and none made sense.

I'm going crazy. Do they still lock crazy people away?

He stretched out on the bed, hoping for sleep, but repeatedly jerked awake to check the clock until a fitful sleep claimed him.

His sleep was disturbed by the dream. He watched as the building and school bus were consumed in an explosion, so sudden, not like TV or a movie, just a bone-shaking whump. The shockwave knocked him down into the loose rock on the rooftop. He remembered being surprised. He struggled upright, looking down at the devastation.

The Red Cross. The children. The dead.

He came awake as his memories returned, like a puzzle coming together. The Red Cross.

It was me! Oh god, it was me!

He remembered the anger and hate, to tear flesh from bone with his teeth. He wanted to lash out, to make them suffer!

And Deion. Deion was *not* his friend. Deion had tortured him.

He'd made it home, just as planned. It was all over the news, but he was too excited to watch. He spent the night in bed, listening to his police scanner, as the emergency crews responded to the bombing. He was leaving his apartment the next day and opening his truck door when he heard the noise behind him. He turned but strong hands smashed his face into his truck door, then slipped a bag over his head. They threw him into a vehicle—a van, maybe. He hit the floor so hard he thought his ribs cracked.

He struggled up and the men punched him in the stomach, then bent him over and hog-tied him. He cursed and kicked his legs, but there was a sharp pinprick in his neck and that was all he remembered until he woke, hot and sweaty, the air chokingly humid. He was tied to a chair in a concrete room, men glaring at him.

Americans.

Deion was there, asking him questions. Why did he bomb the Red Cross? Who helped? How did he do it?

How did they find me? He asked and someone beat his legs with a stick, and the questions started again. Why did he bomb the Red Cross? Who helped?

Oh, how he wanted to kill them. He fantasized about breaking free, tearing them apart with his bare hands.

They lifted him from the chair and left him hanging from chains in the ceiling until his shoulders burned and he howled in pain until his voice cracked.

They beat him, sometimes with sticks and sometimes with boots. They slapped him across the face. They put him in a little box and he felt like his heart would burst, his body crushed in the tiny space.

They removed him from the box and held him down, covering his face with a cloth and pouring water over it. He choked, frantic, and when he started to black out, they pulled the wet cloth off his face and rolled him to his side so he could retch out the water.

He broke. He told them about his request for emergency leave. He told them about the Red Cross. He told them about how the country was falling apart.

They beat him. Sometimes it was Deion, sometimes another man.

He smelled shit and he knew it was his. He screamed and cried and didn't care. They were going to kill him. He prayed they would do it and end the torture.

They stopped.

It was dark. Someone brought him water and a bowl of rice. He tried to eat but found he couldn't swallow. He choked on the water and it came right back up.

His balls ached from their kicks. He gagged at his own smell.

They came back the next day and took off his clothes, smacking his head with their palms, then they chained him up again and sprayed him with freezing cold water. He could not answer their questions through chattering teeth.

The day continued as before, then the next, and then the one after that. The questions, the beatings. Sometimes they would turn on a siren, his head splitting from the noise.

Time slipped away. He forgot who he was and why he was there. He thought the men were aliens come to eat him, to harvest his organs. Then he thought they might be demons and screamed in fear when they entered.

Why did you bomb the Red Cross? Who helped you?

Their questions made no sense. Something inside him had broken.

He slept on the floor, the rough concrete cold against his bare skin. The beatings had stopped. He was given water and broth. He watched himself from a distance, an out-of-body experience, and knew he had gone crazy.

Deion was there. "Nothing else to say? You got nothing?"

He choked out a sob. "I don't know."

Deion left and the room went dark. Time passed but he could not track the days. He tried to track the feedings but he lost count.

The food got better. Water and bread at first, then water and a sandwich. Other men came but they all looked the same, all wire rim glasses and beefy necks.

They took the plywood from the window of his cell and he could suddenly track the passage of the time. At first it was important to him, then he realized how little it mattered.

He knew where he was. The heat. The humidity. The bright light. There was only one place he *could* be.

Guantanamo.

They came and chained him to the floor and a new man appeared. Eric. He tried to explain to the man why he blew up the Red Cross, then braced for the torture to start.

Eric stuck him with a needle.

Blurring. He was somewhere else.

Oh God the pain!

His body was on fire, a million pinpricks moving under his skin. He prayed to die, and then he heard voices, yelling and shouting. He tried to scream.

He came awake from the dream, wide-eyed. He was in his bunk at Area 51, the covers kicked to the floor.

He remembered his recruitment, his parent's funeral. How could he have made his parent's funeral?

Because it was all a lie. He was not recruited into a secret Delta operation. He was a guinea pig. They put things inside his body. They altered his memory.

Eric was *not* his friend. Neither was Deion. They were using him, testing him.

He remembered the Red Cross bombing and he loathed himself for it. What kind of human being was he? How could he have done something so heinous?

He was trapped inside the mountain. If he left, he wouldn't make it ten miles before they would find him and kill him.

He deserved it. If only he had died in Guantanamo.

Eric is wrong. I am a monster.

* * *

Nogales, Mexico

Abdullah dreamed of his wife, the way she smiled when she cooked. Oh, how he missed watching her cook. It made her so happy. So content.

Manny nudged him awake.

He rubbed his eyes and looked out at the darkening streets of Nogales, Mexico. No matter where in the world he went, he was always surrounded by squalor. Nogales was no exception. They pulled up to the house on Independencia Street, not far from the border, and Manny pulled binoculars from the glove compartment, opened the door, and scanned the sky.

Abdullah was confused. "What are you looking for?"

"Drones," Manny replied. "Cops are always watching us. Got to be careful."

"Have you ever seen a drone?" he asked.

"No," Manny admitted, "but everybody knows about them. Don't you watch TV?" He put the binoculars back and led him inside, where five men greeted them. The biggest pulled a semiautomatic pistol from his waistband and pointed it at them. "What you got us into, Manny?"

Manny held up his hands and took a step back, almost bumping into Abdullah. "Whoa, chill. This is the guy."

"Fuck this guy. You heard the news? That shit in Germany? Your cousin was in on it. He's *dead.*"

Abdullah's heart sank. *No!* Shahid and Mahbeer were supposed to escape and join him!

Manny turned to him and grabbed his shirt. "You got Hector killed? Why would you do that?"

Abdullah calmly placed his hands on Manny's shoulders. "I am sorry, Emmanuel. Your cousin was a good man and a good Muslim. He was martyred." He turned to the men. "What of the others?"

The big man said nothing, but a smaller man with a goatee spoke up. "Yeah, some other dude was killed, too. They hunted them down and killed 'em all. That's what they been saying on the news!"

Abdullah stepped back. He had lost both young men, Shahid and Mahbeer. He felt their loss, like a physical blow, but he knew the precarious situation could quickly spiral out of control. "They were both martyrs. They died as heroes."

Manny shook him by fistfuls of cloth. "You crazy pendejo. We should shoot you right now."

Abdullah sympathized with Manny but tried to reason with him. "If you kill me, my people would send their heroin elsewhere. I thought you liked the steady supply, that it was safer than dealing with the cartels."

The big man nodded slowly and lowered his gun. "He's got a point, Manny. I know Hector was your cousin, but we got business with his people. We *can't* kill him."

Manny held him tight, squeezing the fabric of his shirt, then sagged forward and relaxed his grip. "You're right, we can't kill him." He glared at Abdullah. "The only reason you live is because we need those drugs."

"Of course," Abdullah said gently. "May I go? I'd like to get changed before we cross."

The goateed man led him to the bathroom, where he changed into denim jeans and a heavy black t-shirt. When he returned to the living room, most of the men were busy playing video games. Abdullah watched silently, but he did not understand the point of the game, other than that it involved shooting large monsters with different kinds of weapons.

The big man, Carlos, approached. "C'mon, we got to get you across."

Carlos led him to the basement, a featureless concrete box, with a metal filing cabinet in the corner. Carlos pulled on the metal cabinet and it opened on a hinge, revealing a hole in the concrete wall that led to a shaft with a makeshift elevator.

It was nothing more, Abdullah noted, than a welded-together metal box with a winch on it, but Carlos opened one side and motioned for Abdullah to get in. He followed, closed the door, then activated the winch, which made distressing grinding noises while dropping them slowly to the tunnel floor below.

Abdullah was amazed. They had carved the tunnel out of the ground, an opening large enough for a man to walk through, with metal beams evenly spaced and plywood holding up the ceiling. There was a big pipe leading down the tunnel for ventilation and a string of lights. Metal rails led off into the distance, and an electric cart approached on the track, piloted by a bald little man.

The cart came to a stop, and the man smiled and pointed to the flat bed and said something in Spanish. "Rafael says get in," Carlos said. "It's six hundred feet to the other side. We don't usually ship people, but for you, we make an exception. Manny'll be right behind you."

Abdullah smiled. "His cousin was very brave to do what he did."

Carlos glared at him. "Where we from, cousins means something. You understand?"

Abdullah nodded. "I do." He got on the cart, and the little man flipped the lever. The electric motors hummed as the cart sped down the track, leaving Nogales, Mexico, and entering Nogales, Arizona.

The other end of the tunnel emptied into a small cinder-block room. The little man grinned at him and pointed up, then pointed back down the tunnel. Abdullah waited as the little man hummed off into the distance and soon returned with Manny.

Manny grunted and Abdullah followed him up an aluminum stepladder and into a darkened warehouse. A fat man greeted them and Manny smiled. "Sup, Julio?"

"Sorry about your cuz," Julio said. "This him?"

"Yeah. Is it ready?"

Julio pointed to the dark blue Ford Taurus in the first bay. "Got a full tank of gas." He handed Manny a set of keys.

They got in the car and Julio opened the rolling metal door. Manny slowly pulled out, glancing in both directions, then turned the corner and headed for I-82, out of Nogales toward Dallas.

* * *

Area 51

"We've got something," Karen said. "Chatter on the Jihadist websites."

Everyone but John was in the briefing room. Karen, between chugging vast quantities of coffee, was excitedly showing how she had found the images that might lead them to Abdullah. Nancy, Deion, and Clark watched the explanation, Clark without comment and Deion with the occasional eye roll and blank expression. Nancy sat ramrod straight, her face hard.

Eric's pulse sped up as he pointed to the wall display. "Show me."

Karen clicked over the decrypted images. "These are instructions to the Mujahideen. It looks like they're providing an escort across the Pak border into Afghanistan. The US has stepped up patrols in the south, so it's probably going to be near Jalalabad."

Eric turned to Deion. "The ISI?"

"Yeah," Deion said. "That's no man's land. Real rugged area. The tribes go back thousands of years. They don't trust outsiders. The only way the ISI operates is because the tribes allow it. They've either got sympathizers or tribesmen in positions to stop any kind of reform."

"Yeah, I've had operations in the area. We couldn't prove they were helping the Taliban, but we strongly suspected. The CIA have any contacts we can exploit?"

Deion shook his head. "Nah. The government doesn't know and they don't *want* to know. Plausible deniability."

"Can you get a team in?" Clark asked.

"Not likely," Eric said. "What about on the Afghan side?"

"Not without involving the CIA," Deion said. "What about you? You said you did some operations there. You still have any of those contacts?"

Eric thought about that. Yeah, there were a few that might talk to him. *Maybe.* "This is the first solid lead we've had. I'll head to Afghanistan with John and see what we can dig up."

They filed out of the room, but Nancy held him back.

"I want to go," she said, her arms crossed.

"No. I need you and Deion here. We still have the missing cesium, remember? We can't spread ourselves too thin."

Her face was red, but she avoided his gaze. "You can trust me."

He sighed. "It's not a matter of trust. You're a woman. That would be a problem where I'm going. Don't read anything into it."

She grabbed him, her hand clenching his shoulder. "I said you can *trust* me."

He spoke slowly. "It's nothing personal, Nancy. I *mean* that. If I thought you couldn't handle it, I'd tell you. Do you believe me?"

She took a deep breath. "Yes. I'm sorry about what happened in Afghanistan. I want you to trust me, to count on me."

He took her hand from his shoulder and clasped it tightly in his. "Help Deion. Find that cesium. That's all I ask."

* * *

Bagram AFB, Afghanistan

They made the flight in record time. Greg Clayberg had pushed the Gulfstream to its limit, and they left him on the tarmac to turn the plane while they prepared for the chopper flight outbound to the mountains.

Eric heard the booming voice behind him. "Is that Wise I see?"

He turned and smiled. "Good to see you, Redman." He embraced the dark-haired Operator in a fierce bear hug.

Bill 'Redman' Barton was a solidly built Georgian and Eric liked and respected the man. Redman was one of the best Operators he had ever worked with, and he knew he could count on him no matter what the mission.

Redman glanced over at John, awkwardly watching their reunion. "Who's this?"

John stuck out his hand. "John Frist. I'm with him."

Redman glared at him. "Is that so?" He broke into a big grin. "I hope you do better than your other friend."

Eric laughed. "Thanks. You really came through for Deion."

Redman joined in Eric's hearty laughter. "Anything for you, brother." He leaned in closer. "Look, I don't know what happened after you got burned, but you're up to something. I can *smell* it. You need help?"

Eric considered his offer, then nodded. "Actually, yeah. I could use some backup, somebody I can count on."

John gave him an odd look, then walked away.

"What's his problem?" Redman asked.

I'm wondering the same thing. "No idea. I'll talk to him before we leave. Look, the thing I'm doing now, it's beyond classified. You choose to go, it never happened, understand?"

Redman's eyes widened. "What have you gotten yourself into, Steeljaw?"

Eric grabbed his hand. "You wouldn't believe me if I told you, brother." He gave Redman a quick breakdown of the mission, and Redman left to requisition the needed gear. Eric went searching for John and found him standing near an aircraft hangar door, watching flights take off.

Eric stood with him, roasting in the heat, the stench of JP-8 heavy in the air. "Nervous?"

John shrugged. "No."

"Then what's the problem?"

"I'm sick of this," John said. "I don't want to do this anymore."

What the hell? "What are you talking about? Is it about what happened in Denver? The men you killed?"

"It's not Denver," John said, shaking his head.

"Germany? Everyone hesitates. Even me. You can't blame yourself."

"It's not that, either," John said. "It's … everything. It's too much."

I don't have time for this. "Pull yourself together. We've got a mission. We've got to find Abdullah and make him pay."

"Pay? How are we going to do that? Throw him in a hole somewhere? Torture him? Or are we just going to put a bullet in his head? We are not above the law."

"*Sometimes* we *are*. We're the good guys, remember?"

John watched him with hollow eyes. "We are?"

Eric's temper flared. "We're flying out soon. Get your head straight. If Abdullah escapes, if he kills any more people, those deaths are on us. You get that? They're on *us*."

John nodded slowly. "Yeah, I got it. It's on us." He turned and headed for their chopper.

CHAPTER FIFTEEN

The Black Hawk banked hard and John leaned into the turn as they rounded the mountainside, navigating through the terrain toward the Pakistan border, on their way to Tora Bora.

He watched as Eric and Redman checked their gear, noticing the easy way they worked together. He could tell Eric worried about him, but he wondered what Eric would do if he knew the truth. A bullet to the head, perhaps. Or maybe Eric would just open the door of the Black Hawk and throw him out.

He had deliberated since his memories had returned. The Office clearly had no use for the man he was. They would probably try and brainwash him again.

They might just kill me.

He could not escape. They would follow him anywhere in the world. No, he was stuck. Eric's words gnawed at him. If he could catch Abdullah, wasn't it his responsibility to do so? Would Abdullah's victims weigh on his conscience?

He was so tired. He thought for a moment about opening the door of the helicopter and stepping out. A few seconds of blissful peace and his suffering would end.

Eric's words haunted him, like the victims of the Red Cross bombing who haunted his dreams.

No, Eric was right. They had to stop Abdullah.

The Black Hawk finally came down low and hovered, the downdraft blasting dust and dirt in a hazy circle. Eric signaled to a waiting man, a young Afghan. The helicopter touched down and they jumped out with their gear, the chopper kicking up another cloud of dust as it took off, heading back to Bagram.

Eric smiled broadly at the man. "Ali. It's been a while." Eric turned and introduced them. "Ali and I worked together in 2001 You've grown since then. How's your father?"

Ali grabbed Eric and hugged him, smiling. "He is good, Mr. Eric. He complains a lot, but he eats well."

Eric laughed. "I remember. It will be good to see him."

Ali led them through the hills to the largest stone building in the small village.

Once inside, Eric was glad to see Ali's father, Wahid, sitting at the table waiting for them. He pulled his gloves off and shook the man's hand. "Peace be upon you."

Wahid was the leader of the local tribe and a former Mujahideen. His family was well respected, and while Wahid was a good Muslim, he disdained those who justified murder in the name of Allah. Wahid smiled and shook his hand, then put his hand over his heart. "Mr. Eric. It's been too long. I thought you forgot us."

"Wahid, these are my friends." Eric introduced him to John and Redman, both of whom removed their gloves to shake his hand. "I brought you something." He pulled out a small stash of chocolates wrapped in silver foil and handed it to Wahid, whose smile grew bigger. "A little something for that belly of yours."

Wahid laughed and slapped his stomach. The man had grown larger, his hair shot through with white, but he still appeared healthy and strong. "Please, sit. Ali, bring us tea."

They sat in the rickety wooden chairs, drinking, and Eric found the tea exactly as he remembered, sweetened with raw sugar and having a savory aftertaste. The rest followed suit, and Wahid nodded approvingly. Eric and Wahid exchanged pleasantries until Eric judged that he had satisfied the Afghan requirements for honor. "Wahid, I need your help."

"Is it to hunt bin Laden again? It did not work so well last time."

"No, it is not about bin Laden. It is another man. They call him Abdullah the Bomber."

Wahid's eyes widened. "I know this man … from a long time ago. He fought with the Mujahideen when he was young, younger than Ali when we hunted bin Laden. He had a gift. What has he done?"

"He attacked our men, here and in Germany. What can you tell me about him?"

Wahid shrugged. "He left after the war. He might have gone back to his country—"

"*His* country?" John asked.

Wahid laughed. "His grandfather was a very important man in Afghanistan, but after the King was assassinated, he found himself at odds with the new king, so he fled with his family to Saudi Arabia. When the Mujahideen needed fighters, his grandfather sent Abdullah. Abdullah walade Muhammad Younis." Wahid bowed his head, lost in thought. "A smart boy and a devout Muslim. Like his grandfather."

Finally, a name. Eric smiled. "We need to find him. He's going to kill a Taliban leader named Azim."

Wahid's eyes narrowed. "I've heard of *General* Azim. Why do you want to help him?"

"We don't want to help *him*," Eric said. "We want Abdullah. We think some of the Mujahideen might help him cross the border."

Wahid glanced around. "Here? No, he would cross in the south."

"I don't think so. Perhaps you could find out?"

Wahid paused. "Mr. Eric, this is no business of mine. Things are quiet now. Why go looking for trouble?"

"Abdullah is a bad man. He bombed our wounded in Germany, men and women receiving medical care. Hundreds died."

"Mr. Eric, this pains me greatly. It is against Islam to hurt the wounded. Still, I do not know these people." Wahid shrugged but stroked his beard slowly.

"Some of the dead weren't soldiers. Some were local Germans. Women. Children. They were there for free medical care. Just kids."

Wahid stopped stroking his beard. "I'm sorry, Mr. Eric. I cannot be seen helping you."

Eric understood. Wahid was a good and just man, well respected and well liked, but he also had a village to feed and protect. His involvement could invite the wrath of the Taliban or Al-Qaeda, the same groups that Wahid and his family had fought against just a few years before.

No, it was not Wahid's fault. The man had gone into battle with his own sixteen-year-old son to hunt bin Laden, and now Ali was twenty-one, probably ready to marry, and Wahid himself looked to be approaching fifty.

"I understand. I'm sorry to have troubled you."

"It is no trouble to host a friend, Mr. Eric. You know that. Please, stay and eat. I would be most honored."

John caught his eye and glanced to the door, but Eric shook his head. "It would be our pleasure."

They exchanged pleasantries, whiling away the time, and when they did eat, the food was remarkable. The skewers of grilled lamb were exceptionally good, and Eric noticed that John and Redman both helped themselves to plenty, wrapping the lamb in pieces of thin bread. He joined in some banter between Wahid and Ali, and it felt good to spend time with them. He remembered the hours they had spent hiking through the western edge of the mountains during the battle of Tora Bora. It was good to see Ali growing into manhood.

"We have to leave soon," Eric finally said. "It's an hour back to our pickup site."

Wahid clasped him by the shoulders. "I hope that you will come back. It is good to see you, Mr. Eric."

Ali led them back down the mountain to the extraction site. They could hear the beating of the approaching chopper's blades when Ali handed Eric a slip of paper. He read the note from Wahid and smiled, then turned to John and Redman. "Ali is going with us."

Ali nodded. "I'll show you the way."

* * *

John opened the two large plastic cases in the fading light. The VISOR gazed back, its soulless face watching. He stripped quickly to his socks and briefs, shivering in the cold. He was in the mountains, not far from where Ali had led them. Eric and Redman were already on their way to their sniper positions, leaving John to suit up.

He pulled on the pants and fastened them at the waist. They were tight, but the advanced composition fabric quickly warmed to his skin. He took some deep knee bends and stretched his legs to get the pants fitted, then pulled on the undershirt and jacket. The modified harness system came next, snapping and clicking into place, providing extra protection to his crotch as well as his chest. He strapped the pistol holsters to both legs and checked the pistols themselves, the modified M11s lighter than normal, then holstered them. He put on his combat boots, one of the few stock items, then loaded the hard points of his Battlesuit with his medical kit, extra magazines for his pistols and rifle, and an old-fashioned Ka-Bar knife that slid into a molded sheath on his right calf.

He took the HK from the other case and checked it. It was so new they had yet to give it a name. It fired 7.62mm NATO rounds, had a thirty-round magazine, and featured a laser and optic sight that integrated with the VISOR.

It made him a one-man killing machine.

Lastly, he picked up the VISOR and activated the clamshell. He took a deep breath and put it on, closing it, and for a brief moment felt a suffocating panic until the display came to life. A cool wash of air caressed his face as the environmental system came online, the smell of plastic and charcoal fading swiftly. The screens blazed on, the desert illuminated in full and vibrant color. The HUD showed his stats, the link between the Implant and the VISOR, and the thirty rounds in the HK, and then the communications package came online.

"Eric?" he asked.

"I'm here."

The VISOR displayed Eric's position on a topographical map.

"Redman, too."

Redman's position popped on the map. Both men were on the move.

"Clark?" he asked.

"I'm here, John," Clark said, from half a world away. "We've got a drone over the area and we're capturing video from the VISOR."

John concentrated and the map shrank, replaced with a live feed from the drone. He concentrated again and the video zoomed in until he saw himself standing in front of the two cases. He waved up at it, and the man in the video waved up as well.

He concentrated and the screen changed again. He saw Eric, a ghostly white figure, moving at a fast pace as he neared a ridge. The screen changed again and he saw Redman doing the same. He zoomed out and saw their objective, a natural depression on the desert floor, hundreds of feet across, surrounded by piles of stone and the remnants of several bombed-out trucks. In the center of the depression stood a stone bunker, built by the Mujahideen during the war with the Soviets. It had been bombed and rebuilt over the years, and Ali had assured them it was still in use.

He started hiking and the VISOR plotted his course, the GPS guiding him to his destination. The pace was quick and his body moved smoothly, the months of training helping him eat through the miles of hard rock scrabble.

While his body was engaged in moving through the desert, his mind was restless. He kept replaying the Red Cross bombing, his terrible actions, and the actions of the Office. Eric had been so helpful during his training, always willing to answer every question. Eric had been his friend, he had thought, but it was all a lie. Eric's job was to turn him into a killer.

Is that me? A killer?

He arrived at his destination, not far from the rock stronghold. Twilight had faded and the sky was black. The fortification appeared deserted, but he knew better. Surveillance had shown different men, four at last count, entering and leaving over the day. He checked Eric and Redman's positions and found they had reached their positions.

"We've got a truck on visual," Clark said. "We've tracked it as it crossed the Pak border. We believe it contains the target."

"How far out?" John asked.

"Five kilometers," Clark said. "Moving slowly, should be there in twenty minutes."

"Should we hit them when they arrive?" John asked.

"Negative," Eric said. "We don't know who's in that truck."

"If it's just AQ," Redman said, "my vote is for a missile strike."

Eric laughed. "Copy that, but our mission is to find Abdullah."

They waited in silence. John watched the drone data, the video of the truck bouncing over the rough foot trail now used as a road. When it was within eyesight, he turned off the drone data and turned on the VISOR's night vision mode, the world coming alive in ghostly greens and whites. He activated the thermal overlay at ten percent and saw a heat bloom from a rodent hiding quietly near his feet. He tossed a small pebble and the heat bloom scurried off into the distance.

Smart mouse.

The truck finally reached the fortress.

"Look alive," Eric said.

John was crouched just a few hundred meters from the building. He kicked up the amplification of the VISOR and saw the truck come to a stop.

There were three men in the truck and two in the back. The men in the back were heavily bearded, with thick wool caps and patos over their shoulders, AK-47s hanging from their necks. They jumped from the bed of the truck and looked around, scanning the desert.

He crouched lower but knew that his black Battlesuit was invisible in the night. The passenger opened the door and got out, but the driver's body obscured his face. All John could see was his cap.

"You got an ID?" Eric asked.

"No," John said. "Driver's in the way. Hang on." He rose and moved quickly for a better view as the driver came around the truck, the men in back joining him. He had gone twenty meters when he got a glimpse of the passenger. The details were blurry through the VISOR but John could see the man was clean-shaven.

They entered the stone building and the door shut, opening again soon after as the two men from the truck bed exited the building and started patrolling the area.

"Eric," he said. "That man didn't have a beard."

"That's not a lot to go on," Eric replied. "Did you get any audio?"

"Nothing I could understand. Clark? You get anything?"

"Karen is cleaning up the audio." There was a pause. "Unable to make an ID."

"It's *him,*" John said. "These guys have beards, it's their religious duty. Remember the razors and hair samples in Germany? It's only been a few days, not enough time for him to grow anything but stubble. It's him."

"There were *two* sets of DNA," Clark said.

"Fine, then it's the other guy. He'll know where Abdullah is."

There was a long pause.

"John has a point," Eric said. "Mission is a go."

John nodded to himself. *One way or the other, it will soon be over.* He grabbed his HK and started to approach.

"I'll take the left guard," Eric said. "Redman, you take the right. Then, hit the truck engine. John, are you ready?"

"I'm activating the Implant," Clark said.

John felt the rush of adrenaline, like electric fire, coursing through his veins. His blood sang and his doubts and fears fell away. He wanted to shout to the heavens. It leveled out momentarily, but he still felt sharper, stronger, and quicker. He ran, his legs propelling him across the loose rock and dirt like a marathon sprinter.

He was coming up on the building, the guards on opposite sides. He thumbed off the safety on the HK. "I'm going in." He covered the distance at breakneck speed, his feet practically flying over the sand and loose rock. He saw the men fall, then heard the faint double report of Eric and Redman's sniper rifles.

"Both targets down," Eric confirmed.

The truck in front of him shook and holes appeared in the hood, then another double report. The .50-caliber bullets had blown completely through the engine block, rendering the truck useless. He was running toward the door when it opened and an older man with a scrabbly beard appeared, his AK-47 rising. John pulled the trigger at a dead run and put three bullets through the man's chest. The man registered surprise before collapsing as John ran past, practically exploding into the main room of the building, tossing a flash-bang as he cleared the door frame.

Three men sat at a low wooden table, the beardless man with the cap at the head. Two young men sat on wooden stools on the far side of the room and an older man stood in front of a small tin stove, warming his hands. They looked shocked, then blinked and yelled as the flash-bang went off.

The VISOR attenuated the sound and light, which gave John time to stitch fire across the two men on stools, dropping them where they sat. The old man at the fire grabbed at his AK-47 and started firing wildly as the three men at the table stood. He ducked and came up shooting, catching the old man in his chest. The old man fell, dead before he hit the floor.

John wheeled around and saw the three men at the table turn it over and cower behind it, the beardless man in the middle. He turned the HK to the right of the table and cut loose. The bullets punched holes through the wooden top, and he heard screams from the other side.

The fighter on the far left of the table stood and fired, catching John high in the chest. He stumbled back, but the liquid body armor did its job, spreading the kinetic energy of the 7.62mm rounds across the large meaty part of his chest. He emptied the rest of the magazine and the man collapsed, his eyes already sightless.

He dropped the magazine from his HK and put in a fresh one, cycling the bolt. He heard the beardless man gasping for air and knew that he had one chance to get him to surrender.

"Drop the weapon and stand up," he commanded.

There was no response.

"I said, drop the weapon!"

The man came up with his AK-47, smiled, and shouted, "Allahu Akbar." The man did not fire but glanced down. John realized he was buying time and turned to run from the room, the beardless man cutting loose with his AK, screaming.

He had just cleared the doorway when there was an explosion, and he felt the impact in his back like a giant pillow slamming into him. He crashed into the dirt and rolled up, turning back to the room.

The stillness was absolute. The VISOR struggled to filter the stench of cordite from the air as he entered the room. The beardless man's legs had been blown completely off and pieces of shrapnel had shredded his arms and chest. His face, though, remained untouched, the empty eyes staring at him.

He's too young. It's not him.

Eric's voice came through the VISOR. "What's the sitrep? Do you have him? Is he secure?"

John sighed and left the room, motioning for Eric and Redman to approach. The bodies of the two guards that Eric and Redman had shot lay no more than five meters from him, their bodies blown completely in half by the .50-caliber rounds.

"He's dead," John said. "Blew himself up. And it wasn't Abdullah. This guy's my age. *Was* my age."

Eric cursed, and John knew their mission had failed.

* * *

Bagram AFB, Afghanistan

John turned away in disgust at the remains of the man, his trunk in one bag and the rest of him in another. "What do we do now?"

The smell from the corpse was thick in the stifling heat of the tent. "I don't know," Eric said. He stood quietly next to John, waiting for the results of the DNA analysis. "You killed the one man who could give us Abdullah's location."

"That *wasn't* my fault," John protested. "What was I supposed to do, shoot him and hope he didn't set off the IED?"

Eric started to speak, then stopped. "You did your best. It's just bad luck."

John left the tent and headed for the Gulfstream. Greg was performing his preflight checklist, and John watched the soldiers give the plane a final once-over. The morning sun baked down, well on the way to another hundred-plus-degree day, and the sweat stained his shirt as he loaded the Battlesuit cases into the Gulfstream.

Eric approached. "They matched the DNA from the corpse to hair samples from Germany. He was the other man with Abdullah."

John grunted.

"What's your problem?" Eric asked. "You haven't been right since Germany."

"It's this," John said, pointing at the runway. "What did we accomplish? We killed some Mujahideen. We saved General Azim and we don't even care about him. How did this help anyone?" He kicked the VISOR case in frustration, knocking it over.

"Not true," Eric said calmly. "We stopped whatever this man had planned, but it wasn't to help Azim. We did it to find Abdullah."

John shrugged. "We didn't find *anything.*" Then, before he could stop himself, he rushed ahead. "I know."

Eric blinked. "You know what?"

"Who I am and what I did. I remember everything."

"I don't know what you're talking about—"

"Stop lying! It's probably the drugs they gave me. I remember Iraq, the IED. I remember coming home and the Red Cross." Tears streamed down his face. *One way or another, it's over.* "I'm responsible for all those people. And Deion? I remember what he did to me in Guantanamo. They should have shot me. It would have been better for everybody!"

Eric faced him, expressionless. "You're not thinking clearly."

John shook his head. "You can't lie to me anymore. If you're going to shoot me, just do it. I won't resist." He sat down on the hot tarmac and stared at Eric.

Without warning, Eric grabbed him by his shirt and hauled him to his feet. "You know what you're going to do? You're going to go back, and you're going to help me catch Abdullah. What you did can't be forgiven. All you can do is try and make it right. You're going back and you're not going to say a fucking word about this to anyone, because if you tell anyone about this, they'll kill you."

John nodded. The weight had lifted, and he was flooded with relief. He understood the risk that Eric was taking for him. Eric was giving him a second chance.

He wasn't sure he deserved it.

* * *

Eric shook Redman's hand. "Thanks for the backup."

Redman pulled a wad of stringy chaw from a pouch and put it in his mouth, chewed a few times, then stuck his hand out. "Anytime, brother. I know I'm not supposed to say anything, but that boy was *damned* impressive. Whatever you been feeding him, it sure as hell worked."

Eric smiled, but it faded quickly. "Yeah, he's something else."

Redman nodded. "You need any help, you know where to find me." He turned to spit out a mouth of juice, then strolled away.

For a moment, Eric envied him.

The fight in Afghanistan was easy. He knew the players, he understood the politics. The OTM was different. He headed back to the Gulfstream, where John waited.

He was taking a big risk. His first instinct had been to put a bullet in John's head. Smith would understand, and Nancy had wanted to do it from the start.

He couldn't. Doc Barnwell was right. Eric was more than just John's mentor. He was John's friend. It was hard to separate the feelings he had for John the terrorist from those he had for John the man who desperately begged for his approval.

They needed him. That was the simple truth. They needed the project to succeed, and John had proved that it did. Sure, back in his Delta days, Eric could have taken that stone building with his own team and air support, but John had blown through the place like an avenging fury.

He boarded the plane and took the seat across from John. John was different than the broken man he met in Guantanamo. John was a real human being, who felt pain and sorrow. John felt remorse.

No, John would live. *For now.*

* * *

Europe

The Gulfstream was fifty-two thousand feet above Europe when Eric answered the secured video conference call. Nancy, Karen, Clark, and

Deion sat in the briefing room in Area 51, and he could tell by their excited faces that they had finally caught a break.

"We've got a lead," Deion said.

Karen joined in. "I had a trace on cell phones associated with the American Patriot Revolution. We got a hit. His name is Jimmie Jakobs, a longtime member of the APR, and he just turned on his cell phone and called his wife. Nothing important, just that he was set to finish his trip and be home soon. We've tracked him to a Motel 6 on the outskirts of Dallas. Jakobs is a dim bulb. He can't possibly be planning anything on his own. He's probably passing the cesium off to someone else, someone smart enough to know how to use it."

"We've got a surveillance team on the way," Deion said, "but if the deal is about to go down, we need someone there." He leaned towards the video camera, the anticipation evident. "I'll take Nancy, Martin, and Johnson and we'll wrap this up before you get back."

Eric turned to John, asleep in his reclining chair, oblivious to the conference call. "Can it wait? I want to be on that mission."

Deion shook his head, his grin bigger. "Not enough time. You're ten hours out. We can be there in two. Authorize it. The plane is already loaded, we'll be wheels up in twenty."

"It makes sense," Clark said, nodding. "Surely they can handle one man?"

"It's not one man I'm worried about," Eric said. "You've no idea who he's meeting."

"You won't make it in time," Nancy said. "We *have* this."

He hated to admit it, but she was right. Deion was a fine operative, and Nancy could hold her own in a firefight. Plus, he trusted Taylor Martin and Roger Johnson. They were good Operators. They could handle themselves. "Fine, but keep me looped in. Get Jakobs and get that cesium."

CHAPTER SIXTEEN

Fort Worth, Texas

They touched down at Carswell AFB, on the outskirts of Fort Worth. Deion rubbed the bullet wound on his arm. It didn't make him unfit for duty, but he took another pain patch from his pocket, peeled the old one off, then pressed the new one in its place. The lingering pain had eased by the time they taxied to the hangar and unloaded the vans.

Nancy, Martin, and Johnson waited, eager to go.

"Look, we all know what this is about," Deion said. "Don't make any mistakes. It's one racist redneck from Colorado. The important thing is to keep that cesium out of the wrong hands, which is anybody's but *ours*."

He paired up with Nancy in the first van while Martin and Johnson followed them east through the city. They eventually found the restaurant parking lot, across from the Motel 6, and met up with their surveillance team, Brad and Nikki.

Deion gave them the once-over as they entered the van. Nobody would mistake them for agents. Brad wore jean shorts and a faded Iron Maiden t-shirt, and his wife, Nikki, was dressed in white denim shorts and a stained pink halter top. They looked no older than twenty, but Deion knew they had worked deep undercover for the Dallas PD before the Office had recruited them, and dozens more like them, in each major city.

"The target left, went to Denny's behind the motel, then returned to his room," Brad said.

"No phone calls since the last one?" Deion asked.

"No," Nikki said. "He's kept the curtain shut. We can't get eyes inside." She pointed across the street to the Motel 6 parking lot. "See the brown F-150 with the dirty topper? He's got cardboard over the back windows. Whatever's in the back, he doesn't want anybody to see."

"Did you put a tracker on him?" Nancy asked.

"Yeah, we tagged his truck while he ate," Nikki said.

"What'd you use?" Deion asked.

"An XB-10," Brad said.

Deion was familiar with the unit. It was no bigger than a silver dollar and had a day of battery life. He dismissed the couple, who quickly left.

"Here's the play," he said to Nancy. "We follow him wherever he goes, wait to see who shows up, then take them down."

Nancy shook her head. "I disagree. We go in now, take him, and get the cesium."

"Relax," Deion said. "We can take them all at once." He settled back in his seat, watching the dumpy blue motel. "We'll take Jakobs and be home before the sun goes down."

Nancy grunted.

"How long before he leaves?" Martin asked through the earpiece. "This bar and grill across the street smells good."

"Quit your bitching," Deion said. "You've got a thermos full of coffee, I saw Roger load it. That'll have to do."

Martin snickered and Deion grinned. He watched Nancy out of the corner of his eye. She was staring at the motel room, her body tense. He reached up and turned off the mic on his earpiece, then pointed for her to do the same. "What's up with you?" he asked.

She frowned. "What do you mean?"

Deion could tell she had no interest in pursuing the conversation, but he had to try. "We haven't spoken about Afghanistan, and now you're wound tighter than a clock spring. What's up?"

"I'm not..." She turned to him. "Look, I'm kind of messed up, emotionally. Maybe it was my childhood. That's always the easy answer. Maybe it's because I'm not even thirty but I feel like an old woman. Maybe I just need to get laid. Who knows." She turned back to the motel. "I'll do the job."

He considered his words, then went for it. "You scare me. You're not like any woman I've ever met. You're a trained killer, like John, but at least Eric watches out for John. You don't have anybody to protect you, except your dad. It couldn't have been easy. I mean, he probably LoJacked you at birth."

Nancy's icy blue eyes softened. "You have no idea. There's something else, though. I think my father asked Eric to keep an eye on me."

Not surprising. "The Old Man thinks you need protecting?"

"He won't say it. Actually, I think he wants me to fall for Eric."

Deion considered it. Eric was a straight shooter, a good-looking guy if Deion had to admit, and maybe the Old Man thought he would be a stabilizing influence. "Sounds cold. You gonna let that happen?"

"There's no *letting* it happen," Nancy said. "It's like being set up on a date. I *resent* it. I told Eric what my father intended. There's no way he would have anything to do with me now."

Deion shrugged. "You both got your heads on straight. It could be trouble if you two were involved, given what we do. Might make things … complicated."

Nancy looked wistfully off in the distance. "That's one thing I'm not. I don't have a life. Just the job." She flicked on her earpiece and focused her attention back on Jakobs's motel room.

Deion nodded. He understood. The same focus cost him his relationship with Val. He turned on his earpiece and sank back in the van's seat, waiting for Jakobs to leave.

* * *

Dallas, Texas

Abdullah directed Manny through the McDonald's parking lot. Manny circled the building, and Abdullah saw Ahmed waiting patiently in a Toyota Camry. "There," he motioned.

Manny eased the Taurus next to the Camry. Abdullah turned to him. "I would like to thank you for your help. I am sorry for your loss."

Manny turned away, face flushed. "I promised to get you here. There's your ride. We're done."

Abdullah wanted to comfort Manny, but nothing he could say would ease the pain. He knew that better than anyone.

He gathered his bag and watched the young man speed off, then got in the Camry and shook hands with Ahmed. He had last seen Ahmed as a young boy, no older than thirteen, the wisps of hair just appearing on his chin, but the boy had finally filled out, lean and wiry, now sporting a dense black beard. "It is good to see you again."

"I am glad to see you, too, sir, but I have bad news. We received word this morning. Naseer is dead."

His heart sank. *Dead?* He had said goodbye to his student just two days before, sending him back to Kandahar to lead the Mujahideen in a battle against Azim. "How?"

Ahmed started the car and pulled out of the parking lot, heading east. "No one knows. Just that he was killed by Americans."

Abdullah felt the anger rise. He took a deep breath which caught in the back of his throat. Naseer was the closest thing he'd had to a son. He had known that he was risking his life, but Naseer's? "We must fight on," he said. "We must kill the Americans."

Ahmed nodded. "The Brotherhood have been waiting for such an opportunity. Muhammad has grown soft. This cesium will be our weapon. With your leadership, we will strike them down."

Abdullah nodded his agreement. "What about the meeting?"

"We will meet him in a junkyard. He believes he is selling it to a street gang from Los Angeles."

"Does he know what we actually plan?"

"Of course not. We will have to kill him once we have the cesium."

Abdullah nodded. "The man would betray his own people. Allah will find no fault with us."

He stewed as Ahmed drove. The cost of revenge inched higher, taking the lives of good young Muslims. The Americans were to blame. He thought about what Naseer had said, about there being no innocents in America, and he thought about his one-time home in New York City.

It is madness.

He did not believe in killing innocents. *How innocent are they, really? Any of them?* And Allah did say that innocents killed during battle would know the mercy of Allah—they would become martyrs.

It had been unthinkable the week before, but now?

They had just reached Hutchins when Ahmed spoke up. "We will be there soon." He pointed in the back. "There are guns under that blanket."

Abdullah stretched back and lifted the corner of the plaid blanket. "Do you expect trouble?"

Ahmed shrugged. "This is America. There is *always* trouble."

* * *

Deion kept pace with Jakobs's Ford F-150, maintaining a hundred-yard distance through Hutchins. He glanced back in his mirror to make sure Johnson and Martin were still following.

"He's slowing down, looks like he's turning," Nancy said, monitoring the GPS tracker on her laptop.

"You got a location?"

"A junkyard," Nancy said. "Pull over." She pointed to a stand of trees.

He pulled the van to the side of the road, Taylor following suit. To the south he saw a rusty chain-link fence that marked the property line. Beyond lay a maze of rusted automobile frames of every make and model, waiting to be crushed.

"Roger, get the quadrocopter airborne and get us eyes on Jakobs."

"You got it, boss," Roger said.

He scanned the site through his binoculars, but the trees and stacks of cars obstructed his view. He joined Nancy in the second van as Roger took out the quadrocopter, a device three foot square and painted light blue. Roger checked the battery pack, then set it on the ground and activated the powerpack. The four sets of blades whirred to life and the quadrocopter shot up and was soon out of site, the whir of the electric-powered blades fading to a quiet whisper.

Deion looked up, squinting, but there was no sign of the quadrocopter. He turned to Roger. "Nice."

Roger grinned. "Can you imagine what I would have done with this in college? The mind boggles. Anyway, video is up."

They gathered around the laptop and saw the bird's-eye view from the drone. The junkyard appeared deserted, except for Jakobs's F-150 slowly moving through the aisles of junk, stopping roughly in the middle.

"Must be the meeting point," Martin said.

"I don't see anybody else," Deion said.

Roger activated the thermal imaging, but the summer heat made the entire junkyard a wash of red. "That's no help. Can't tell if he's alone in there. What's the plan, boss?"

Deion put on his combat vest, opened the weapons locker, and withdrew an MP5SD. "Stay with the drone and get Wise on comms. Nancy, you and Martin are with me." The others put on their combat vests, grabbed their weapons, and headed south. They hopped the chain-link fence and started threading their way through the piles of junked cars.

Eric's voice came through comms. "What's the sitrep?"

Deion was explaining when Eric interrupted him. "Why are you going in? You don't even know who he's meeting."

"We got this, Eric. Roger, how we doing?"

"You're within thirty yards of the truck," Roger said. "There's a car entering to the east."

"Occupants?"

"Can't tell from this angle."

He motioned for Martin to take the entrance. The big man nodded and headed to the entrance, his MP5SD at the ready.

"Nancy," Deion said quietly, "Be ready. I'm going to flank him."

Nancy gave him a thumbs-up and he worked west until he could see the F-150 through a crack in the wall of cars.

"Car is in the lot," Martin said over comms. "Crown Vic. Two black males."

"Let them pass," Deion said.

They waited until the Crown Vic eased into the narrow clearing. Two black men got out, one short and wiry and one with a shaved head. The driver, the short man, approached Jakobs, who climbed out of his truck. Deion was close enough to hear their conversation.

"Darrell?" Jakobs asked.

The bald man nodded. "You got the stuff?"

Jakobs hitched his thumb to the F-150's tailgate. "In there. You got the money?"

Darrell pointed to the Crown Vic. "Blue bag in the backseat."

"People, we got a problem," Roger said over comms. "There's another car pulling in. Silver Camry."

Shit. "Martin, do you have eyes on the car?"

There was a pause. "Two men. Middle Eastern."

"Deion, you need to call for backup," Eric said over comms. "Call in the locals."

"We got this. Roger, we need you."

"On my way," Roger answered.

Jakobs opened the door to the back of the Crown Vic, grabbed the black duffel bag, then spun at the sound of the approaching car. "Who is that?"

"Just some friends," Darrell said, arms outstretched, palms up.

The car slowed, its tires crunching on the loose rock, then stopped. Both men got out.

Jakobs drew back, his face red. "Nobody said anything about any towel-heads. Bad enough I got to deal with you two."

The passenger, an Arabic man with a clean-shaven face, stepped forward and spoke in lightly accented English. "There is no reason for concern. You have your money."

Jakobs backed away. "No way." He turned to Darrell. "I was told to sell it to you. Dyer didn't say nothing about their kind," he said, pointing at the Arabic man.

"No problem, man," Darrell reassured. "It's cool. You got your money."

Jakobs shook his head. "Forget it," he said, pulling a chrome revolver from the back of his pants.

The black man produced his own gun and the two stared each other down.

Time to introduce ourselves. Deion stepped through the cramped space between the cars and yelled, "Federal agents, lay down your weapons!"

All five men turned to face him. On the other side of the clearing, Nancy burst through a crack in the junk piles. "Federal agents!"

Jakobs fired his pistol wildly and the bullet zinged off the car next to Deion. Deion ducked and fired at the same time as Nancy, the muted bark of the MP5SDs echoing among the cars. He caught Jakobs across the chest. Jakobs crumpled forward, and Deion saw Nancy's weapon catch the bald man in the stomach. The man pitched forward, a look of shock on his face. The wiry black man jumped into the car and came up with an AK-47, cutting loose, forcing Deion to take shelter behind a crumpled SUV.

"Deion? Are you hit?" Nancy yelled.

He peeked around the car, bullets pinging and ricocheting, as the man in the car peppered his location. He saw the backs of the two Arabic men running down an aisle of cars before they turned the corner and were gone. He hated to admit it, but Eric was right—things had spiraled out of control. "Roger, meet up with Martin. Block the exit."

"We've got another car," Martin breathed. "And another one."

In the distance, Deion heard gunfire, a mix of different weapons, and knew the operation had gone sideways.

The wiry man stopped firing. Deion glanced around the corner and saw the man get back in the Crown Vic, rev the engine, then throw it into gear and plow diagonally into the pile of cars where Nancy hid. He jumped out and sprayed the car with gunfire, but it was too late. The stack collapsed backward.

"Nancy!" He rushed forward and yanked open the door to the Crown Vic, only to find the wiry man a bloody mess, shredded by his MP5SD. The smell of death stuck in the back of his throat, and he choked on the smell.

"Deion?" Nancy yelled from the stack of cars. "I'm stuck. I'm in the floorboards of a car on the bottom. I can't get out!"

Thank Christ. "Hang on," he hollered. "You're safe for now. I've got to help Roger and Taylor."

"Don't you dare leave me, you asshole!"

I'm going to catch hell for this. "Just sit tight, I'll be back in a minute." He pictured the junkyard from overhead, the way he remembered it from the drone video, then ran toward the front.

He heard more gunfire.

"Man down," Martin gasped.

Man down?

"Deion," Eric said. "Fall back and regroup. You can't stop them if you're dead."

"Martin, get your ass to the southeast, near the entrance." He waited, but there was no acknowledgment. "Martin?" He threw caution to the wind, racing down the empty row of cars and turning the corner, almost stumbling over Roger's body.

He was too late. Roger's head was slick with blood, a clump of hair dangling from the back, and when he turned him over, he saw the small hole in his cheek. The bullet had gone slightly to the left of Roger's nose, under the eye, and exited through the back of the head.

He didn't have time to mourn. As he stood, he heard a noise behind him. He turned as the older Arabic man fired at him with an AK-47, the younger Arabic man joining in. In a flash of insight, Deion wondered whether the older man was Abdullah.

The bullets slammed into his chest, like a sledgehammer, and his world erupted in pain before everything went black.

* * *

Abdullah wasn't surprised by the man's unwillingness to sell them the cesium. The two federal agents were another matter. He watched as Jakobs was cut down in a bloody hail of gunfire, and then the woman opened fire on the bald man, killing him instantly.

Ahmed grabbed the AK-47s from the Camry and yelled at Abdullah to run.

He was stunned, but Ahmed's voice broke the spell, and he tore off through the junkyard, leaving the gunfire behind. If they were captured, his plans would be for naught. He heard yelling behind him and he stopped to let Ahmed catch up and hand him one of the AK-47s.

They ran through the stacks of cars until they came to the entrance. The scene was chaos. Several Latino men lay on the ground, their bodies riddled with bullet holes. Two cars had entered and were now abandoned as a group of Latino men fired at a lanky black man with a bulletproof vest like the other federal agents. The agent ran between the junk, bullets pinging madly around him, but was hit by the combined gunfire and fell to the ground.

Abdullah recognized the dark blue Taurus and saw Manny standing next to it, eyes wide, raising a semiautomatic pistol. Abdullah beat him to it, pulling the trigger on his AK-47, the gun barking in his hands. Manny screamed and dove to the side, barely escaping as the bullets chewed up the ground where he had stood.

Before he could aim, Ahmed shoved him out of the way and dropped to his knee, firing at Manny. Ahmed missed but caught several of the men in the chest. They fell, and Ahmed took the opportunity to yank Abdullah up by his shirt. They headed back through the junkyard, seeking shelter.

As they rounded a corner, a white man with thin black hair and a bulletproof vest burst through. Abdullah pulled the trigger on his AK-47, and the man's eyes widened, one of the bullets catching him in the face. The man's head snapped back and he dropped like a stone, lifeless.

Ahmed grabbed his arm. "Hide," he hissed. Abdullah saw a rusted metal fuel tank, cut in half, and he ran to it, pulling Ahmed with him. They took shelter behind the tank just in time as the first federal agent rounded the corner and stumbled over his teammate's body.

Abdullah pressed against the tank, then carefully eased around the side, his denim shirt catching against the rusted steel. The federal agent was hunched over, checking his teammate, and Abdullah aimed, slowly and with great care. The man stood and turned as Abdullah emptied his gun into the man.

The agent staggered forward, then sprawled over his dead friend.

He turned to Ahmed, who stood wide-eyed. "We have to get the cesium."

Ahmed shook his head. "We must leave."

"Allah is protecting us." He saw the fear in Ahmed's face and smiled. "We have not come this far to give up."

Ahmed nodded and they headed back to the middle of the junkyard. As they approached the pickup truck, they heard the roar of an engine. The Taurus tore around the corner and he registered Manny in the driver's seat, his face contorted in rage, as the car blew past. The driver spun around the next corner, moving too fast to stop, then they heard the car's tires sliding through the loose rock and the squealing impact of metal on metal.

Abdullah spied a stack of oxygen tanks not far away and pointed to them. "Help me!"

Ahmed nodded and they ran to the tanks. Abdullah grabbed the top of the first brown cylinder. "Lift on the bottom," he commanded.

With Ahmed's help, he set the oxygen tank on a car frame and then searched wildly until he found a sledgehammer with a broken handle.

There was a squealing of metal and the engine roared as the Taurus backed around the corner, front tires spraying rock. Abdullah motioned for Ahmed to duck. When the car was next to them, Abdullah stood and swung the hammer, knocking the valve assembly off. With a mighty whoosh, the tank shot forward, striking the car in the driver's side, smashing the door like a tin can, then bouncing off. It spun wildly, bouncing around the aisle, knocking into car frames, finally coming to rest in the dirt.

Ahmed emptied his AK-47 into the car. Manny screamed as the bullets struck, and his screams turning to wet gurgles. Ahmed's gun ran empty and he stopped, panting from adrenaline and exhaustion.

Abdullah aimed his AK-47 at the passenger, Rafael, the short Latino man who had helped ferry him through the underground tunnel in Nogales, and calmly shot him. The little man jerked to the rhythm of the gunfire, then slumped forward, blood staining his white undershirt.

Abdullah turned at the sound of approaching footsteps. His gun was empty, so he held it by the barrel, like a club. When Darrell came around the corner, Abdullah took a deep breath and smiled.

"We have to go," Darrell shouted. "It's a war zone in here. The cops will be here any minute."

They hurried back to the F-150. They heard a woman's screams from the stack of collapsed cars.

"What about her?" Darrell asked.

Abdullah shook his head. "She's trapped. Leave her."

Darrell nodded and searched Jakobs's pants for the keys, then started for the driver's side of the truck.

"No," Abdullah said, grabbing Darrell's arm. "They already know about the truck." He took the keys from Darrell and opened the truck's topper. "Get those," he directed.

Ahmed and Darrell struggled to unload the two blue barrels from the truck while Abdullah opened the trunk of the Toyota Camry. When they had both barrels unloaded, Abdullah opened the tops and withdrew one of the stainless steel cylinders, like the metal thermos he had used for coffee when he'd lived in New York City. "Take these canisters and load them in the trunk. Put whatever remains in the backseat."

He found a blanket in the back of the F-150, and within minutes they were pulling out of the junkyard and heading south, Darrell and Ahmed in the front and Abdullah in the backseat, the rough brown blanket covering the stacks of stainless steel containers next to him, the rest safely stored in the trunk.

As they took the on-ramp to the Lyndon Johnson Freeway, he heard sirens in the distance and breathed easy. Allah truly was with them.

CHAPTER SEVENTEEN

Area 51

E ric knocked before entering Smith's office. Smith sat at his desk, shuffling the worn playing cards.

"My daughter is safe," Smith remarked without looking up.

"Fire and Rescue finally cut her out. She was more angry than upset."

Smith continued his game, his fingers surprisingly delicate as he shuffled through the cards. Eric noticed the many fine white scars, faded almost to invisibility, covering the old man's knuckles. Smith glanced up, his pale blue eyes fixing intently on Eric. "Mr. Johnson's death was unfortunate. How are the others?"

"Deion's in rough shape," Eric said, "but they stabilized him in Dallas. His vest took the brunt of it, but a round got inside, bounced around, and chewed up his liver and pancreas. Doc Elliot is consulting with the doctors in Dallas. He wants to move him here as soon as he's safe to travel. Martin's got multiple bullet wounds to his arms and legs, nothing serious, but one creased his skull. They think he'll pull through if they can relieve the pressure."

Smith nodded. "Don't blame yourself. You weren't there."

"No, but I should have been. They should have waited."

"Mr. Freeman took a risk," Smith said. "What about the cesium?"

Eric's stomach knotted. "Gone. It was Abdullah, I'm sure of it. Now he's in the US and we have no idea where he went."

"Then find him," Smith replied. "Have you given any further consideration to my offer?"

During the mission to Afghanistan, he had hardly thought of anything else. Until the conversation with John. "I'm not sure I'm cut out for the position."

Smith picked up the cards, shuffled them, and placed them in a neat stack on the desktop. "I was hoping you'd accept the position willingly."

Willingly? "And if I don't?"

"It's who you are," Smith said, eyes glinting in the reflected light. "I won't insult your intelligence by calling on your patriotism or your sense of duty. The truth is, the world is a scary place and it's getting scarier. The technology that Doctor Oshensker used to reprogram Mr. Frist's brain has far-reaching implications. We are twenty years ahead of the best research, but make no mistake, that technology will become available. Can you imagine the implications? What if every soldier could be Implanted? What kind of power would an army of such men wield? The VISOR? The Weave? Imagine an army of nanobots programmed to strip the flesh from bone, dropped in the heart of an enemy country. Or worse, a shopping mall. Things are spiraling out of control. I need someone who will never betray their country or the Office." Smith shook his head wearily. "Truman once told me I was a man of high moral character. I've been tempted over the years. I am human, but I never crossed that line. I need the same in my successor. I need *you*."

Eric digested that. "What aren't you telling me?"

Smith bowed his head. "How is Mr. Frist?"

"Well above expectations," Eric lied.

"This project is vital to national security. We need to get ahead of our enemies, Eric. We need an advantage. Mr. Frist served his purpose but we won't have that advantage for long."

That gave him pause. "Why is that?"

Smith sagged back in his chair. "Did you really think we could do those things to him without consequences? There've been no long-term human trials studying the effects of nanoparticles. The nanobots that performed the Weave? It's never been tried in a human being. The process is killing him. Do you know what cancer is? Unregulated cell growth. The very drugs we used to heal him will eventually fill him with tumors."

Eric felt sick. "You knew this from the start."

"Oshensker's frequent MRIs aren't evaluations, they're diagnostics," Smith said, eyes narrowing. "We can't keep him alive forever."

"I've been his mentor. His friend. You should have told me."

"What would that have changed?" Smith asked. "His life ended when he bombed the Red Cross."

"I've lied to him! I've looked him straight in the eye and told him that we would be there for him."

"We will. He's of no value to us dead. If the project fails, however, then all this must be shut down. Loose ends cleaned up."

"You mean the people."

"Yes," Smith said. "The circle of trust must remain small. Too many know too much."

Surely he had misunderstood. "What about Nancy?"

Smith leaned forward, his palms on the table. "She will be looked after. The low-clearance employees will be shuffled back into the defense department. The rest? Oshensker and Elliot? Mr. Freeman? Or yourself?" He paused, watching Eric with hooded eyes. "You're a bright man, Eric. I *need* you. They *need* you."

His stomach sank. "I can't—"

"You have forty-eight hours."

* * *

New York City, New York

Abdullah followed Ahmed into the coffee shop and spotted Muhammad al-Hamid waiting for them. Abdullah smiled at the man's neatly trimmed beard, black slacks and long-sleeved white dress shirt. Muhammad appeared as sophisticated and respectable as Abdullah remembered. He glanced around at the other patrons, men of varying ages with dark skin, black hair, and well-trimmed beards. The coffee shop was popular with the Islamic Brotherhood, but they maintained a respectful distance from Muhammad.

Muhammad returned the warm smile. "I am glad to see you, dear friend."

Abdullah hugged the man. "I have missed you, my friend." They sat, and Ahmed left to get them coffee. "You know my plans?"

"Yes, I know your plans," Muhammad said, shaking his head. "I am sorry, Abdullah, but I cannot agree to this."

Abdullah nodded. It was as he feared. Muhammad had grown soft. "I am sorry you feel that way, but it is the will of Allah."

Muhammad frowned. "I know that losing your wife was a great blow, but the Islamic Brotherhood is moving in a different direction. We want to find a political solution to the problems facing Muslims around the world. Jihad still continues, but the fight will be political." He shook his head sadly. "I remember when you first arrived in the city. You were so eager to learn. You loved it here. Then you met Diwi. You were so happy. You should not have left."

Abdullah bristled. "She wanted to return home. What was I to do?"

Muhammad took Abdullah's hand and squeezed it tightly. "I know you wanted to make her happy. What you've faced is terrible, but you place all the blame on the Americans. Who betrayed you? It was not them."

Muhammad's voice filled him with cold anger. "Someone betrayed me, but it wasn't the Taliban that bombed my house. It was the Americans. A man I trusted. Do you know why? Because the Americans are evil." He pointed to the window. "This shop? This city? It is against Allah. *That* is why these terrible things happen."

Ahmed returned and sat two coffee cups carefully on the table, glancing between the two men.

Muhammad eyed them sadly. "I'm afraid your grief has turned you mad, my friend. These people have done nothing against you."

He wanted to scream at Muhammad. "These people will pay for their affront to Allah." He wanted to make his old mentor see the truth, but realized the man's cowardice ran deeper than expected.

"Is this what you intend?" Muhammad asked quietly. "To strike them down? I thought you were going to attack their military."

"I have seen too many young men die," Abdullah said. "Too many have martyred themselves. This is the only way. Allah *demands* it."

"Please do not do this," Muhammad implored, clutching Abdullah's hand. "Attacking the Pentagon would be bad enough, not only for yourself but for Muslims everywhere. If you attack this city, they will strike us down. Legitimate reforms are coming. Don't let your wife's death harden your heart. Think of the young, of what it means to them."

Abdullah yanked his hand away. "I'm doing this *for* them," he insisted. "Allah demands justice."

Muhammad shook his head. "No, my friend. Allah would not condone killing innocents. I cannot agree to this."

Abdullah took a deep gulp of the hot coffee. It scalded his lips, his tongue, burning all the way to his stomach. "The Islamic Brotherhood is split. The young want to fight."

Ahmed turned to Muhammad and bowed his head. "Sir, with respect, Abdullah is right. We must strike now."

Muhammad drew back, his eyes narrowed. "Do you really believe this? Do you even remember growing up in your village, Ahmed? You complain of how America treats Muslims, but you have benefited from this city. It sheltered you, educated you." Ahmed started to speak, but Muhammad raised his hand. "Would you so willingly throw away your life for this man?" he asked, pointing to Abdullah. "He is overcome with grief. Do not do this, I beg you. This is not the will of Allah. This is the will of Abdullah."

Abdullah rose and shoved the half-empty coffee cup across the table. At least he had tried to reach Muhammad. He loved the man, but Muhammad had grown soft living in the decadent city. "Goodbye, my friend. I hoped you would bless this operation. I hoped that you still believed in Jihad."

Muhammad rose and grabbed Abdullah's arm. "Allah will not bless this operation, and the Islamic Brotherhood will not help."

Ahmed spun on his heel, his face filled with disgust. "Some *will.*"

* * *

Newark, New Jersey

Abdullah glanced around the inside of the rundown brick building near downtown Newark, not far from a massive construction project Ahmed assured him would mask their comings and goings. The warehouse was a beehive of activity as Ahmed showed him the final preparations.

"We stole the truck a week ago," Ahmed said proudly.

Abdullah nodded. The truck *did* look passable. Inside, two black men finished wiring the detonation cord around the last of the stainless steel containers bolted to the bottom of the roof. The young men looked up from their work and smiled, nodding at him. He smiled back and motioned for them to return to their work. "How much longer?"

"Only a few minutes," Ahmed said. "Then they will load the rest." He pointed to metal drums of improvised explosives made from fertilizer and diesel fuel, much like Abdullah had worked with in Afghanistan.

"Excellent," Abdullah said. "The cord will cut through the containers and the explosion below will spread the cesium up and out in a cloud."

"You are sure we should change the target?" Ahmed asked uncertainly.

Abdullah tilted his head and sighed. "I was a fool to think anyone in this city is innocent." He pointed to the young men milling about, including Darrell. "They have been helpful?"

Ahmed nodded. "Without them, we couldn't have acquired the cesium. The APR thought they were selling the cesium to a street gang from Los Angeles."

Abdullah smiled and watched as the men finished with the last of the detonation cord and started placing the loaded barrels in the back of the truck. He turned back to Ahmed. "Did someone check the manhole cover?"

"Yes," Ahmed said. "Naseer checked yesterday. It is still there." Ahmed's phone rang and he answered it, then turned to Abdullah. "It is Muhammad."

Abdullah nodded. "Go. Talk to him. Perhaps he has changed his mind."

Ahmed stepped away, speaking rapidly. His voice rose in frustration, then he keyed off the phone and returned. "He has not changed his position."

"It is of no concern," Abdullah said. He turned back to the truck as they finished loading the last barrel. "I only wish we had time to repaint the truck."

"Do you think it will be a problem?"

Abdullah shrugged. "It would be better if we had time to paint it correctly, but this," he said, waving to the PEPCO label, "will have to do. Are you ready?"

Ahmed nodded.

"Good," Abdullah said. "Let us strike the Americans. For my wife. For Naseer. For Koshen. For all the young men who have died in the name of Allah."

* * *

Area 51

John watched Eric mechanically chew his food. Nancy stared off into space, head down. The catastrophe in Dallas weighed heavily on them all.

He tried to reconcile his current feelings. Deion tortured him and yet he felt the man's failure as his own. He hoped that Deion would soon be stable enough to return to Area 51. He worried about Nancy, her eyes downcast, the light gone from them. Eric appeared deflated.

On the other hand, he half-expected Eric to pull his sidearm and calmly shoot him.

Then he remembered Taylor Martin and Roger Johnson. Martin was in critical condition, but finally stabilized. Roger Johnson had died for the Office. John felt the loss sharply. He had liked Roger. They had only worked together in Denver, but Roger's grin had been infectious.

Nurse Tulli entered the cafeteria, caught his gaze, and scowled as she poured hot water into a cup. She placed a teabag in the steaming water, dipped it, then glanced at him again, utter loathing in her eyes.

She knows.

He could not put his finger on it, but he knew it to be true. She knew what he had done. With all the time he had spent in the infirmary, how had he never noticed?

He turned back to Eric. "Is there going to be anything for Roger?"

"No," Eric said. "No wife, no kids. His parents are still alive, so they'll get a letter. They'll know he died a hero."

"Doesn't seem right," John said. "We ought to do something for him."

Nancy stirred. "He's gone. Get over it."

Eric glanced at her but said nothing.

"What next?" John asked.

"We hope Karen finds something," Eric finally said. "Dyer intended for the cesium to wind up in Los Angeles, but we've identified the bodies from Dallas. They were members of the Thirty-Ninth Street Bloods, an LA street gang turned Muslim militants. Dyer got played. The cesium is with Abdullah. He could be anywhere. The VIPR teams in Dallas and Los Angeles are coming up empty."

"You think they'll attack Dallas?"

Nancy slammed her palm on the cafeteria table, and people in the room turned to stare. "For Christ's sake, John, give it a rest."

Eric's phone beeped and he sat up, read the text message, then pointed to them. "Karen's got something. Let's move."

They dumped their trays at the door on their way to the War Room, their feet pounding against the tunnel floor. Karen greeted them on the inside. "We found something."

"Put it on the screen," Clark prompted.

She typed furiously and the audio file displayed on the overhead screens, next to a phone number with a New York address. "I figured if Abdullah was in New York in the nineties and he was a devout Muslim, he had to have spent time in a mosque. I cross-referenced the list of known Muslim clerics from *that* time with clerics who have ties back to Afghanistan and the Mujahideen, then put taps on their phones. This man, Muhammad al-Hamid, made this call ten minutes ago."

They listened to the voice speaking in Arabic. Karen translated. "Al-Hamid is speaking to a man named Ahmed, pleading with him to abort the operation. Ahmed is saying that it will be a great blow to the city and to the Americans. al-Hamid says he will pray to Allah that Ahmed will come to his senses, that the operation is a mistake. Ahmed says it is no use arguing, their friend has too much influence and the youth are behind him. The attack will happen by noon." Karen turned to them, her face ashen. "Noon? If that's the East Coast, that's only forty minutes from now."

They all sat back, stunned. Clark was the first to speak. "City? Does he mean New York?"

Eric nodded. "Sergeant, pass the info to DHS. They need to issue an imminent threat alert. Nancy, get Kelly and get the jet ready. I want wheels up in fifteen."

"There's not enough time," Nancy said. "We need a contingency plan."

Eric turned to Clark. "We have one. Is the Black Lady still on standby?"

Clark's eyes widened. "You can't be serious."

Eric nodded and grabbed John by the shoulder. "Grab the Battlesuit and meet me at the entrance tunnel in five."

* * *

John grabbed the plastic cases and ran to the tunnel entrance, the wildly swinging cases banging into his legs. Eric was waiting in a Humvee, and when John tossed the cases in the back, Eric gunned the engine and they went screeching out of the tunnel into the hot desert air.

"Put on the suit and VISOR," Eric said.

John opened the cases, strapping on the Battlesuit armor. He struggled to clip on the combat harness as the Humvee bounced across the desert floor, barely managing to click the tabs in place. He put on the VISOR and activated the electronics, the HUD winking into existence before his eyes. "If you keep driving like this, I'm going to puke inside this thing."

"You won't be able to take your HK, just your handguns. There's not enough room."

Not enough room? "Eric? What's the Black Lady?"

Eric floored the Humvee and headed for the main runway at Groom Lake. He pointed his finger, and John's mouth dropped as the plane pulled onto the tarmac. It was a giant black dart, one hundred and forty feet long, with bulges in the middle and gigantic engine nacelles near the rear. Men worked on something underneath the plane's belly, but John could not make out the details.

Eric smiled. "*That* is the Black Lady. Smith dug it out of the black budget. You'll be in New York in no time." Eric hit the runway, the tires squealing as they bit concrete, and brought the Humvee to a screeching halt near the middle of the aircraft.

John struggled to load his M11s, and he shivered when finally got a good look at what the men were working on. "You've *got* to be kidding."

It was a bomb casing, split in half, with a hollow center. Eric thumped him on the shoulder. "The Black Lady is a one-seater bomber, but we've turned it into a delivery vehicle. For one man. You. When you reach your destination, the pilot will drop you. A couple hundred feet above ground, the top will blow off, and the retrorockets will kick in and slow your speed. When you're within five feet of the surface, the harness will blow and you'll have a short drop to the ground."

John's mouth went dry. "That's *insane.*"

"They got the tech from an egghead at NASA. They call it a sky-crane. They're going to use it on some Mars probe." Eric smiled. "Don't worry, either it'll work or you'll be paste. It's a tight fit. I hope you're not claustrophobic."

He wanted to scream at Eric that he was, indeed, claustrophobic. He keyed off the comms on the VISOR so that no one could hear their conversation. "I don't want to go."

Eric turned to him, his gaze unwavering. "I know you're angry at us. I know you probably want to take a swing at me—"

"I don't," John said. "I don't want to hurt anybody. I don't ever want to hurt anybody again."

Eric paused. "Think of what happens if Abdullah succeeds. You want that on your conscience? Think of it as karma. You can't ever make up for what you did, but maybe this can pay some of it back."

John shook his head. "I'm not ready."

"You're ready," Eric reassured. "You'll do this because you're a good man who wants to do the right thing. No matter what else you may think, understand this. I *believe* in you."

John realized he'd been holding his breath, waiting for Eric to shoot him, but Eric's words filled him with hope. He didn't want to let the man down. He keyed his comms back on. "How do I get in that thing?"

* * *

John felt suffocated inside the bomb casing, even though the VISOR was piping fresh air across his face. His HUD showed his elevated vitals and erratic pulse. He blinked rapidly as the aircraft vibrated, preparing for takeoff.

The bomb casing provided its own heating and cooling and two hours of air. When he had asked Eric why two hours, Eric had shrugged and said that within two hours, he would be either where he was supposed to be or dead.

"John, can you hear me?" Eric's voice crackled over comms.

John took slow breaths in an attempt to calm his breathing. "Yes."

"As soon as the Black Lady is airborne, we'll be following in the Gulfstream. You'll be in New York in less than thirty minutes. We're going to drop you on the edge of the city. We have a ground team ready and waiting. They'll pick you up. Just hang in there."

John hesitated. He tried not to think of how little space there was inside the bomb casing, but no matter how he tried, even the tiniest of movements reminded him that he was flat on his back and packed in like a sardine. "Eric? It's *tight* in here. I feel like I can't breathe."

"John? It's Doctor Barnwell. We can trigger the Implant to inject a mild sedative until your deployment."

John sighed. "That would be fantastic."

"Activating the Implant."

Calm washed over him as his vitals dropped to normal, and he suddenly felt sleepy instead of panicked. "Thanks, Doc."

A whine increased in pitch, becoming a dull roar, and the VISOR worked hard to dampen the sound of the engines. The plane shook as it rolled down the runway, then the g-pressure increased.

The sense of motion intensified, and the VISOR could no longer muffle the roar of the engines. He felt his entire body shake like a taut bowstring, and then his stomach dropped out and he knew they were airborne.

CHAPTER EIGHTEEN

Karen slammed down her tenth large coffee. Her bladder was killing her, but she was too caught up in her work to pee.

She shook her head. They really needed to put more coffee machines in the War Room. Or maybe she could requisition one just for her desk. No, Clark would never agree. Everyone thought she had a problem with caffeine. She tried to explain that it kicked her mind into overdrive, but no one listened.

Brad understands.

She stared at her monitor. She missed her husband. The casual sex on base helped, but it wasn't the same. It might be interesting with Eric, though, and if she had her way, he would be next on her list.

Focus, Karen. Somewhere in NYC there is a clue to Abdullah's plans.

She fed video from NYC to all the available analysts, everyone watching in real time for aberrations, for the pattern in the stream. There were thousands of video cameras, though, and the analysts were overwhelmed.

If only we had more time.

She was leading a shared instant message chat session with the analysts when a private IM alerted her that Dewey Green wanted to speak. She had met Dewey at the NSA on one of her first projects. She thought he suffered from Asperger's syndrome, and every time he opened his mouth she was proven right. He was brilliant, in his own way, and she had submitted his name for recruitment.

Dewey had a preternatural ability to process information and had seemed like a perfect fit for the Office until his personality quirks had quickly gotten him banished from the War Room. Now he worked on special projects in his own office, on the lowest level of the base, far from prying eyes. Or people to offend.

It was for the best. His constant stream-of-conscious talk frazzled her nerves.

If I have to listen to another recap of WKRP in Cincinnati, I'll go crazy. God, why can't he at least obsess about something recent?

CAN'T CHAT, DEWEY, she typed.

WORKING ON SOMETHING?

YES.

HAHA, I KNOW, I TAPPED YOUR VID STREAM.

She sighed.

Of course he did.

YOU'RE NOT SUPPOSED TO BE WORKING ON THIS DEWEY. I THOUGHT YOU WERE ON A PROJECT?

I'VE BEEN WORKING ON THE O/R WITH AI/NEURAL NETWORK THING. YOUR VID STREAM WAS THE PERFECT OPPORTUNITY TO TRY IT OUT. IT FLAGGED SOMETHING.

Her heart skipped a beat. Dewey was weird and could come across a little creepy, but he was also the *smartest* person she had ever met.

WHAT?

HERE.

Her IM client collapsed, replaced with video from a single camera. She growled in frustration as he took over her workstation.

Sometime soon, we are going to have a serious talk about boundaries.

The video was clearly from a tunnel entrance, but she didn't recognize it. Vehicles passed through, each outlined in a pixelated white box, each popping a tag with a brief description. Then, a blue-and-white panel truck approached and entered the tunnel. The truck was tagged with a description.

SERVICE TRUCK/FIDELITY 95%/ANOMALY 73%/FLAGGED FOR REVIEW

The video collapsed and her IM client resumed.

THAT WAS THREE MINUTES AGO, AT THE HOLLAND TUNNEL, INBOUND TO NEW YORK CITY.

She almost spat out the last of the coffee as alarm bells started ringing in her head. WHY WAS IT FLAGGED AS AN ANOMALY?

THE PROGRAM NEVER MATCHED A TRUCK LIKE THAT IN NEW JERSEY. SHOULD BE CON ED. PEPCO IS DC. PRETTY COOL, HUH?

ARE YOU TRACKING IT?

OF COURSE. IT'S HEADING FOR MIDTOWN.

A series of videos displayed quickly, showing the progress of the truck, and she knew that it was Abdullah.

THANKS, DEWEY.

NP, K. WANNA COME WATCH SEASON 2 OF WKRP?

IT'S ALL HANDS ON DECK, DEWEY. THINGS ARE CRAZY. I OWE YOU ONE.

* * *

Western United States

They had just left Area 51 when Nancy joined Eric and Mark Kelly at the video monitor in the Gulfstream. Karen and Clark were on the split screen and both appeared worried.

"Show them, Karen," Clark said.

An aerial shot of Manhattan appeared. "Times Square," Karen said. The photo zoomed in until they could see the area in detail. "This is a stock photo. Now, watch this." The stock photo was replaced by a series of grainy video camera images, showing different angles of the famous landmark. "This is from the Bank of America security camera on Forty-Sixth."

Eric sucked air over his teeth as he watched the panel truck with the blue PEPCO logo pull up on the curb. "You think it's him?"

Karen nodded. "It's an anomaly. It should be a Con Ed truck. PEPCO is in DC. What would a DC power truck be doing in Manhattan?"

A cold pit settled into Eric's stomach. "Clark, is there time to call DHS and get a VIPR team?"

Clark shook his head. "We're trying. It will take thirty minutes to get through the proper channels, and besides, the VIPR team in New York is running light. Most of them are deployed to Dallas and Los Angeles."

Eric watched as two men got out and placed rubber cones around the truck. "We don't have thirty minutes. How far out is the Black Lady?"

Clark's eyes widened. "You *can't* be serious."

"Get the Old Man on the phone. I want it authorized."

Clark sighed. "On it." His screen went black.

"Karen? What can you do for us?"

Karen scowled. "What can *I* do?"

"Let's assume he's not a suicide bomber. Let's assume a remote detonator."

Karen squinted, then her face lit up. "He'd probably use a cell phone. I can kill cell phone service in Manhattan, but people are going to freak. Eric? What you're suggesting with Frist? It's crazy. We're supposed to be a *secret* organization."

Eric agreed, but they were simply out of time. "Do it."

Nancy stared at him from across the small table. "I hope you know what you're doing."

Eric noticed her rare display of concern. "Let's hope John can do this," Eric said. "Otherwise, parts of New York will be uninhabitable for years."

* * *

Eastern United States

Jim Blix was piloting the Black Lady through the thin atmosphere at one hundred and twenty thousand feet when the new destination popped in his HUD. At that moment, he knew something had gone terribly wrong.

When the CIA had come knocking on his door, it had been a no-brainer for him to leave the Air Force. The Lockheed X-100 bomber, code-named the Black Lady, was a test bed for experimental scramjet technology. His first experience in the Black Lady had been close to orgasmic, and he had been crushed when the aircraft had been scrapped after 9/11. He had been surprised when a man had shown up on his doorstep the next year, offering him a new job in an organization so secret that even mentioning it could get him locked away for treason.

He triple-checked the new orders as the ship's computer recalculated his flight plan, then called to confirm. "Pleasure Palace, this is the Black Lady. Requesting a confirmation of new deployment."

"Please hold, Black Lady."

There *had* to be a mistake. He knew what was in the weapons bay. The man's vitals were displayed on his HUD. *Someone must have made an error.*

"Black Lady, do you copy?"

He recognized Fulton Smith's voice and gulped. "Roger that, Pleasure Palace."

The Old Man's voice was crystal clear. "Please verify your orders."

He punched in the challenge code and there was a pause, then the orders came back with the correct response.

"Orders are confirmed," the Old Man said. "You have your destination."

He felt the plane roll, making the corrections. The HUD displayed his new trajectory and speed.

He was coming in over Pennsylvania at 7800 miles per hour and was headed for New York City, starting his descent. He could see the curvature of the earth in the distance, and knew he had to slough off the majority of his current speed to deploy the package. Opening the weapons bay doors at his current speed would make the aircraft unstable. The computer couldn't compensate and the aircraft would disintegrate.

His stomach dropped as the plane dove into the heavier atmosphere, the air piling up in front of the ship as it became a glowing hot ball across the sky.

He began to shake as the ship plunged towards the earth and he felt the plane skidding through the air as the computer worked the control surfaces, too fast for any human being, to maintain the configuration that kept the ship aloft. Airspeed dropped dramatically, and the airframe whined as the weapons bay door opened. The ship vibrated wildly, the aerodynamics now compromised.

He considered the talk button, then pushed it and said to the man in the weapons bay, the man he had seen for the first time just minutes before, "God go with you, son."

The skyscrapers of Manhattan approached, the ship's speed finally dropping to subsonic as the scramjets flamed out, slow enough to finally release the package. He imagined the people below, looking up as the roar of the sonic boom finally caught up to the sight of the black aircraft, and wondered what they would think.

The skyline rushed closer, the tall buildings a giant canyon so close he felt he could reach out and drag his fingers across the concrete and steel, and then the ship jumped and he knew the package had been released.

The most powerful jet engines ever developed roared to life, slamming him skyward. He felt his body compress and his flight suit inflate against his skin, desperately trying to counteract the g-force and keep the blood flowing to his brain. The ship headed for the edge of space, where the scramjets could once again come to life. A quick burn over the Atlantic to meet up with the modified KC-135 for refuel, and he would soon be heading home.

* * *

New York City, New York

John was barely conscious of the outside world until the ding of his comms alerted him to Eric's incoming call.

"John, we have a development."

He blinked sleepily. "Where am I?" His body vibrated, shaken by an invisible hand, and then he remembered.

He was a human bomb.

"They're activating the Implant, John."

He felt a surge of adrenaline through his veins and gasped for breath. The previous experiences with the Implant had never felt so intense, his body and mind going into overdrive as his heart hammered in his chest.

"What's happened?"

"We believe a PEPCO truck loaded with the stolen cesium just pulled into Times Square."

The Black Lady shook and he felt grinding through the airframe.

His VISOR displayed a grainy video, and he watched as two men dressed in PEPCO uniforms walked steadily away from the truck, heading west.

"We believe the taller one is Abdullah," Eric said. "The younger one is a member of the Islamic Brotherhood, a kid named Ahmed. They're two blocks west on Forty-Sixth Street, and Karen says they are looking at a manhole cover. They're probably going to try and trigger the bomb remotely, but Karen's locked down the cell towers in Manhattan. Are you ready?"

He wanted to scream. *Of course I'm not ready!* "As ready as I'll ever be."

"Good answer, because you're going to be dropped any second now."

He heard an unfamiliar voice whisper through the VISOR. "God go with you, son." Then the Black Lady shook and his stomach dropped away as the bomb was released.

He watched the altimeter plunge in the VISOR. The HUD showed his trajectory as he came in over Eighth Avenue at six hundred miles per hour, and then there was a thump and a jerk that took his breath away as the sky-crane deployed.

With a mighty bang, the bomb casing split in half and the carbon fiber panels blew apart, the sky now open to him.

The view was incredible.

He rocketed through the air, feet first, clear blue sky above him. As he arced down, the skyscrapers of Manhattan came into view over the tips of his boots, and he knew that he was seeing something no one had ever witnessed—Manhattan in the open air, at six hundred feet. The g-forces added up and the altimeter continued to plunge, and then the sky-crane was blasting away.

He was coming in hot, the people below him turning to look up, their faces shocked. The numbers continued to drop, slower now, and the sky-crane's rockets blasted harder and there was a metallic snap as the wires from his harness released.

He was just meters above the hood of a passing tan Volkswagen, stopped to honk at someone in the crosswalk. He had time to register the driver, a harried silver-haired woman, face frozen in fear, before he slammed into the hood, crumpling it like a beer can, the impact sending a stinging pain through his legs.

He jumped from the hood onto the crosswalk at the corner of Forty-Sixth and Seventh, pedestrians shrinking back in fear and pointing at him.

He had arrived in Times Square.

* * *

Abdullah pulled the truck onto the curb in Times Square as the noonday traffic rushed around them. He absently fingered his coat with the PEPCO label. The New Yorkers went about their business, oblivious, as he got out and Ahmed helped him place orange cones around the truck.

They each took a stack of cones and headed west, down Forty-Sixth Street, against the flow of traffic. Police officers milled to the south, but none had noticed the truck. Ahmed walked faster, but Abdullah pulled him back.

"Do not rush."

They continued past the theater and the New York Church of Scientology headquarters until Abdullah motioned to the manhole cover in front of the Paramount Hotel. "Here."

Ahmed placed a cone on the west side and Abdullah placed a cone on the east, then they withdrew steel rods with rings on one end and hooks on the other from their coats and worked together to lift the manhole cover out of place. The midmorning rush of traffic stopped in that lane, cars honking. Abdullah smiled and waved at them to go around. A turbaned cab driver in front of him saluted him with his middle finger but Abdullah just waved pleasantly.

Across from him, Ahmed looked up. "You are sure?"

"I studied civil engineering. I worked in these tunnels. Now, hush, child. In the name of Allah." He punched in the number, hit the send button, and waited.

Nothing happened.

He felt the first twinge of panic.

That is not right.

He ended the call and dialed again, but the call did not connect.

The cell phone displayed no signal. He held the phone up to the sky, but still no signal. He looked around and noticed that people up and down the street were holding their phones aloft, faces puzzled.

The Americans have jammed the cell phones.

He grabbed Ahmed by the coat. "They have shut down the phones. We will have to trigger the bomb manually," he said through clenched teeth.

Ahmed nodded, face pale. "I will do it."

He turned to leave, but Abdullah grabbed him by the shoulder. "No. I will go."

He turned and started back toward the truck, trying to appear nonchalant. He was almost there when he heard a roar echo throughout the concrete-and-steel walls of Manhattan.

He turned his gaze skyward. An arrow-shaped black aircraft was plunging toward Times Square.

Impossible!

He wanted to run to the truck and trigger the explosives, but he froze in awe. Something hurtled from the plane, and then with a roar that made him clap his hands to his ears, the aircraft rocketed off, windows shattering in its wake, the people below running from the shower of glass raining down.

An object had dropped from the aircraft and arced down, moving fast, and then it blew apart and the top half shot skyward, rockets firing, cables dragging a form below it, a shape he realized was a man.

People around him gasped in awe and terror, and Abdullah joined them. He watched, dumbstruck, as rockets slowed the man's descent and he got his first look at the man's back.

He was tall and dressed in black body armor and matching helmet. With an explosive crack, the man was cut free, falling onto the hood of a stopped car. The man jumped to the street and rushed north to the PEPCO truck.

It was too late to stop the man from disarming the bomb. His only chance lay in escape. He turned and saw Ahmed watching from the distance, still standing in front of the open manhole. He ran back, waving to the manhole. They had only moments before the armored man would come for them.

He reached Ahmed and motioned to the hole. "Down, you fool! Hurry!"

Ahmed scampered down the ladder, deep into the dark, and Abdullah followed, taking the time to put on a headband lamp from his pocket. The walls of the tunnel were shiny and slick as they descended the ladder, heading toward their escape.

* * *

John ran to the back of the PEPCO truck. He bit his lip, then tried to turn the door handle. There was no explosion, but the door was locked.

"Try the front," Eric said.

He came around the truck, but two police officers from the corner had made their way through the crowd.

"Don't move," yelled the first officer, his gun drawn. "Don't you *even* move!"

The other officer, a short man with a mustache, put his hand on the first officer's arm. "I don't think he's a bad guy, Bill. You see what just happened?"

"I'm a federal agent," John said. "This truck is loaded with explosives. You have to evacuate the area."

The first officer lowered his gun slightly. "What agency are you with?"

John read his name badge. "Officer Scarpello, if you don't evacuate this area, you'll be held responsible." He pointed to the second officer. "Help me with the front door."

He ran to the front of the truck while asking the police officer, "What's your name?"

"Joey. Joey Knox," the man said.

"Well, Officer Knox, today is the day you help save New York City."

The passenger door was locked and John glanced down at his gloves, then punched the window, his fist spiderwebbing the glass. He punched again and the glass collapsed. He reached in, unlocked the door, and climbed inside, Knox close behind. He opened the door to the rear and heard Knox gulp.

"Oh, man," Knox said in a hushed tone.

"I need help, Eric." He swung his head back and forth, making sure the VISOR got a clear glimpse of the explosives-packed truck.

"There should be a cell phone wired to blasting caps," Eric said. "Look to the left."

John turned his head and saw the cell phone wired to a circuit board. "Do you think it's safe to pull?"

There was a pause before Eric replied. "Doesn't appear to be any booby traps."

I wish he'd said yes.

He turned to Officer Knox. "You feel lucky?"

Officer Knox gulped. "I don't think this is a good idea."

He nodded his agreement, but took the circuit board in one hand and the cell phone in the other and pulled hard, snapping the wires. He looked around at the now-inert explosives. "Hey, it worked." He pushed a green-faced Knox backward out of the truck. "Get your partner. Call DHS. Tell them to get a VIPR team here as soon as possible."

He turned to go. Scarpello yelled something, but Knox stopped him. "He's one of the good guys," Knox explained. "The truck was wired. He disarmed it."

He gave Knox a thumbs-up. "There's a manhole west of here. That's where they went. I'm going after them. Stay with the truck and make sure it's secure. Send backup when DHS gets here."

Knox nodded, and with Scarpello's help, the officers started yelling at the New Yorkers crowding around the truck, waving them back.

John sprinted west on Forty-Sixth as bystanders scrambled from his path.

"Nice work," Eric said, "but when you go underground, we'll lose contact. The VISOR's signal won't penetrate the ground."

John made it to the open manhole cover, his lungs aching and fire screaming up his legs. People stood in front of the Paramount Hotel, pointing and staring. He looked down at the hole, then climbed inside.

The ladder deposited him into a concrete tunnel twenty feet below the surface of the street. He looked to the left and right. There was no sign of the two Arabic men. He mentally flipped a coin, pulled his M11 from his holster, then headed west down the sloping tunnel.

The darkness pressed in and he activated the night vision's thermal overlay, cranking up the resolution until he could see a dim outline of the tunnel wall.

He came to a tee and looked to the right, but it appeared to dead-end in the distance. He turned left, and as he went deeper, his thermal vision showed clouds of heat from the steam pipes on each side of the tunnel. He continued on, heading under what he believed was the building to the south.

He rounded the turn, and a small crack in the steam pipe to his left sent a billowing cloud that turned his thermal vision red, blinding him. He stepped forward and felt his left shin catch on something, and he knew he had made a mistake.

There was a thunderous explosion that smashed him against the wall and everything went black.

CHAPTER NINETEEN

John floated in a liquid syrup. He knew he should wake, but he preferred to remain bathed in the warmth—until the nagging voice roused him.

"John Frist. Wake up, John Frist."

Don't wanna.

"Wake up, John Frist. You are in danger. Wake up."

He opened his eyes and tried not to puke in the VISOR. He hurt everywhere, but especially his left foot. He tried to move it and white-hot fire shot up his leg. The VISOR hummed as it tried in vain to clear the acrid smoke from inside the helmet.

"John Frist. You must wake up. Your vitals are falling. You are in danger."

Where is that voice coming from? "Who the hell is this?"

The voice rattled inside the VISOR, insistent. "I am the Emergency Medical Adviser. You have been seriously injured. You must assess the situation. Are you alone?"

John took a choking breath. "Yeah, I'm alone." He looked down at his left leg. It was a mass of blood and glowed sickly red in the thermal vision. His foot was barely connected to his ankle by strands of flesh and ligaments, the boot shredded.

"Confirming you are alone," the VISOR said. "Have you been wounded?"

"Yeah," he managed, inching his back up against the wall, dragging his leg, the pain so intense his vision blurred and he thought he might pass out.

"Are you bleeding? Your blood pressure is low. I've activated the Implant. You should feel a reduction in pain."

"It's not working," he groaned.

"You have been receiving pain medication for the past thirty seconds. You must stop the bleeding."

Right. "How am I supposed to do that?"

"You must stop the bleeding."

He wanted to scream. Elliot and Oshensker and their stupid VISOR! The displays in the HUD were a mass of red and he knew the VISOR program was correct. He *had* to stop the bleeding.

He removed his emergency medical kit, a small black Kevlar pouch attached to his harness, and tore open the package of white clotting agent, then screamed as he dumped the powder over what remained of his left foot. The clotting agent worked quickly, but he was still losing blood at an alarming rate.

"I'm still bleeding," he panted.

"Okay, you are still bleeding. You must stop the bleeding."

"I *know* that!" He dumped the contents of the medical kit on the wet concrete, rummaging until he found the black nylon strip. He reached down and pulled his pant leg up from his boot. He placed the nylon strip around his calf, right above the boot line, and threaded it through the end of the device, then pushed the button on the side. It activated, pulling tight, and he screamed again as the emergency tourniquet locked in place, slowing the blood flow to his leg.

He felt his heart thudding in his chest and knew he had lost a lot of blood. There was no way he could go on.

I'm dying.

"Your vitals are stabilizing, but you must seek medical attention."

"Fuck you," he said weakly, "and the Office. And Eric." He took stock of his injuries. The Battlesuit was shredded and he bled from more places than he could count. The VISOR had shielded his head but his brains felt scrambled.

If he could just sleep, for just a few minutes. No one could blame him. He had done his best.

The two men would get away.

No.

He might be a complete screw-up, but this was his chance. He could make things right. He was responsible for all those he had killed at the Red Cross, but he *could* make a difference.

Eric believes in me.

He pulled a roll of black fabric tape from his medical kit and wrapped it around his foot, across the gaping holes in the flesh and bone and the remains of his boot. He covered as much as he could, then sprayed the accelerant over the tape.

It smoked as the quick-set epoxy hardened, tendrils of steam drifting up and mixing with the steam that geysered above his head.

The pain was exquisite. His heart hammered hard in his chest, then stopped.

His eyes went dark, only a pinprick of light in his vision, then a massive jolt thudded into his chest.

"I've activated the defibrillator in the Implant. You must seek medical attention."

"No time for that," he choked out. He grabbed the scalding hot steam pipe, burning his hands through the gloves, and pulled himself up, staggering forward, walking on his good foot and dragging the remains of his left.

* * *

Abdullah led Ahmed through the steam tunnel until they came to the fork. If they continued left, it would lead deeper under the city and he had no confidence that he could find his way out, but the right tunnel led to an access door under the Hirschfeld Theater, where they could easily make their way to the surface.

They had been so close, but the Americans had foiled his plan.

I will make them suffer for the innocents they have killed.

An explosion echoed down the tunnel and he knew that someone had stumbled into his hastily built trap.

Ahmed grinned. "At least you killed that American!"

He smiled and they continued forward, nearing the access hatch, until they came to a gleaming gray wall that blocked their path.

No!

Ahmed grabbed his arm. "What is this?"

"They must have walled off the door after 9/11," Abdullah said. He took the steel bar they had used to lift the manhole cover and started beating at it, small concrete chips whizzing away, the stinging impact buzzing up his arm. "We have to break through. The door is on the other side."

"Can we go back?"

"No, I do not know another way to the surface. We will be stuck here until they find us." He pounded the wall, and Ahmed joined in at a furious pace, but they both quickly tired, gasping for air.

From down the tunnel, they heard a *scrape-scraping*, the sound of something dragging across the tunnel floor.

"It can't be the American," Ahmed said, eyes wide, trembling with exhaustion.

Abdullah feared it was. "We must kill him."

"Stay here," Ahmed said. "You must continue the Jihad."

Abdullah wanted to argue. He thought of brave Naseer, now dead, and of Mahbeer and Shahid, and of poor young Koshen. He nodded. "I will pray for you."

Ahmed hugged him. "You must escape. Allah is with you." He turned and stumbled back down the tunnel.

* * *

John struggled forward, his left foot dragging against the ground.

Scrape-scrape.

He shifted his weight to his right foot, then again dragged his left foot forward. He thought about stopping with each footstep—about the hard tunnel floor and how nice it would be to rest—then took another step forward.

Scrape-scrape.

The young Arabic man, Ahmed, stepped from the tunnel ahead. The man had dropped his PEPCO coat on the tunnel floor and was carrying a steel rod in his hands, a yard long, with a hook on one end and a ring on the other.

John stopped and stared as he realized his M11 was dozens of yards behind him. He reached down as Ahmed surged forward, but before he could pull the M11 from his left hip holster, Ahmed was on him, screaming, the metal rod catching his left hand as it pulled out the M11. The handgun went spinning through the darkened tunnel, and John screamed as the impact shattered his wrist.

Ahmed did not let up. He swung again and again, striking John in the head, the VISOR's HUD flashing with every strike. John tried to throw a blow to the man's neck, but he stumbled and his left leg exploded in pain.

The liquid armor plates absorbed much of the damage, but the blows hurt more and more and he knew the plates were losing their effectiveness, no longer able to distribute the kinetic load.

With his right hand, he pulled the Ka-Bar knife, then grabbed the man by the leg, tripping him. He pulled himself along the struggling man until he could plunge the knife into the side of the man's neck.

The young man went rigid, then kicked wildly as John pulled the knife free and plunged it into Ahmed's neck, again and again, as the blood spurted out in rhythm to the man's frantically beating heart.

The young man slackened his grip, then went still.

John rolled off. It was a struggle to stand, every part of his body crying in protest, and he cursed the young man, barely out of his teens. He cursed at the unfairness of it. He cursed Abdullah. He cursed the Office.

"John," the VISOR said, "You must seek medical attention."

"Yeah," he panted, head spinning. "I heard you."

* * *

Abdullah chipped away uselessly at the concrete wall blocking his escape. There were small pockmarks from his desperate hammering but no sign that he was about to burst through. He heard Ahmed's screams trail off, then silence. He backed against the concrete wall, trying to will himself through it.

The man in black came forward, *scrape-scraping* the floor. His foot was a mess of blood and his armored suit was split and torn, pieces of armor plates broken and hanging loose or missing. He carried a knife in one hand, and the other hung limply at his side.

The man stopped in front of him, an arm's length away, his faceless helmet staring at him, then dropped to his knee and pitched forward.

Abdullah's heart soared. He lunged forward, swinging the steel rod against the man's helmet. It bounced off and he swung at the man's back. The man woofed and Abdullah went wild with fury.

"You will not kill me. Allah will protect me!" Abdullah struck the man again and again, with all his might. "You will die," he screamed, "for all the innocents you have murdered!"

* * *

The VISOR went crazy, alarms buzzing and shrieking. Abdullah beat him and every blow brought him closer to eternal darkness.

In a moment of clarity, between Abdullah's screams, he knew he was going to die. Abdullah would kill him. Abdullah would escape.

He had failed.

Something inside him, the last remnants of the old John Frist, whispered in his ear. *Give up. Death will bring peace.*

No.

Between blows, he licked his lips and tried to speak. "No." He choked on a mouthful of blood and tried again. "No," he managed, louder.

Abdullah screamed with primal fury and hit him in the head so hard the VISOR went black, the onboard computer finally silenced.

Sightless, John reached out and grabbed Abdullah's leg, pulling on it, and he felt the man go down. He heard the air woof from Abdullah and used the opportunity to pop the clamshell open, pull the VISOR off, and smash it into Abdullah's face.

The headband lamp went spinning from Abdullah's head, the light dancing along the slick tunnel walls, and he saw crimson red gush from Abdullah's nose.

249

His eyes locked with Abdullah's as the man frantically tried to shake him off.

"Allah is with me," Abdullah said.

John took the Ka-Bar knife and, using his body for leverage, plunged it into Abdullah's stomach.

Abdullah convulsed and John pulled the knife back and stabbed again, this time aiming for the kidney.

Abdullah stopped struggling. He looked at John with empty eyes. "I miss my wife."

John lay over Abdullah's body, pinning him, as the man died. He reached out and took the dying man's hand and held it tight. He wanted to speak but had no words. The man stopped breathing, his body limp.

John collapsed next to him and looked up at the dark tunnel ceiling.

The damage was catching up. His arms and legs were cold as ice, his body racked with shivers. His vision swam, then the light faded as he had one last thought.

I didn't fail.

CHAPTER TWENTY

Area 51

Nurse Tulli prepared John for surgery, and Eric was reminded of a picture his mom had taped to her refrigerator of his father in the hospital, IVs dripping chemo in his arms. Dr. Elliot and Dr. Oshensker were scrubbing up and preparing to operate while a host of other nurses and technicians monitored John's vitals.

Mark Kelly stood next to him. "*Jesus*," he breathed. "He looks worse than when we snuck him out of Bellevue."

Nancy nodded. "At least they managed to keep his heart beating," she said.

Eric dismissed them and walked next door to the recovery area. Deion lay in a hospital bed, but his eyes were open and he pulled himself up and grinned, giving Eric a thumbs-up. Eric saluted him. Deion tipped his hand to his temple in a mock salute, then settled back in bed, smirking.

Martin Taylor lay in the next bed, his head bandaged from the emergency brain surgery. He did not smile, but he nodded weakly before closing his eyes.

Eric shook his head and went back to the observation room. He watched as the operation started, until Fulton Smith entered, the door closing softly behind him.

Smith stood quietly, watching the surgery. "Excellent work, Mr. Wise. You saved New York City."

Eric shook his head. "John saved New York."

"Did you have problems retrieving him?"

"No, we flashed some paperwork and the locals handed him over. The feds weren't too happy. I'm afraid DHS might be causing some trouble."

Smith smiled icily. "No, they won't. What about the VISOR?"

"Nancy removed the evidence bag from the NYPD, along with the rest of the Battlesuit."

"Very good." There was a pause. "It was a bold move, dropping him in Times Square."

Eric returned the icy smile. "It worked."

Smith raised an eyebrow. "Indeed it did. How is Mr. Frist?"

"He's got severe trauma to pretty much everything. They're going to have to amputate his foot. He's got a broken wrist, multiple fractures to his skull and ribs, several cracked vertebrae. Shards of nanocarbon from the bones in his foot lacerated his other leg. And he has a concussion."

Smith turned back to the operating table. "He will live?"

"The docs think so. Everything will heal, except for the foot. They want to fit him with a prosthetic."

Smith leaned closer to the window. "You sound morose."

"You don't actually care about him," Eric said. "He's just a guinea pig."

Smith glanced sideways. "After what he did? The people he killed? Tell me why I *should* care?"

"Because he's still a person," Eric said. "In the end, he almost killed himself to stop Abdullah. He did the job."

Smith turned, a genuine smile spreading across his face. "You're a good man, Eric, that's why I want you as my successor." He stuck out his hand.

Eric reflexively took it, then paused. His eyes had been opened to what the Office did and how it operated.

Try as he might, he couldn't think of anyone he trusted to do the job.

He shook Smith's hand firmly. "I guess I'm your man."

Smith nodded. "I always knew you were."

* * *

Washington, DC

"Do you know how many problems you've caused?" the President asked. "I've got the Joint Chiefs on my ass wanting to know why the hell a secret space plane was flying through Manhattan."

Smith blinked in the harsh light of the underground bunker. "It's not as bad as it appears. The Pentagon has known for years that work continued on a supersonic stealth aircraft, ever since Project Aurora."

The President frowned. "It's called stealth for a reason, Fulton."

"Mr. President, the world knew we had a stealth plane, just not how advanced it was. But think of this. What good is a weapon if your enemy doesn't know about it? The entire concept of MAD was based upon both parties knowing they had the capability to annihilate their enemy, and furthermore, their enemy knowing the same. Without Russian displays of nuclear force, would we have been so hesitant to attack? I can assure you, Mr. President, I was there for those discussions. It was closer than you realize."

The President shook his head, but his face softened. He picked up his coffee cup and blew on it before taking a long sip. "The military isn't supposed to operate on domestic soil. I could be found guilty of treason. Impeached, at the very least. My own party thinks I'm an incompetent boob, and the Vice President is ready to measure the Oval Office for new drapes."

Smith noticed the President's weary face, the deep bags under his eyes. He understood the weight of such a position and what it cost a man. His relationship with his daughter was a daily testament. "I can handle the Vice President. I'm afraid he's not fit for this office. His heart isn't in it."

"You could keep him from running?"

"Nothing like that. It's his heart. I've seen his medical report. It couldn't handle the strain."

"What about the Joint Chiefs? What am I supposed to tell them?"

Smith handed the President a folder. "Here is the report. DHS stopped a man from attempting to detonate a primitive bomb in Times Square, and through the hard work of the NYPD and DHS, this tragedy was prevented. Unfortunately, the mentally ill man, an Afghan engineer, was killed. He was driven mad with grief over his wife's death from cancer and blamed the entire city of New York for her lack of medical care. The crude explosive device was dismantled and destroyed."

The President leafed through the folder, then closed it, staring at the cover. "Even an idiot wouldn't believe that. You think that'll play in Peoria?"

"The backstory has already been created. They can claim a conspiracy if they want. In fact, that might tamp down a few of these more troublesome groups."

The President opened the folder again and leafed through it. "What was the real reason? Why did this Abdullah fellow want to nuke Times Square?"

Smith shook his head. "He wanted to set off a dirty bomb, to spread fear, to create panic. To strike back."

"Why?"

"We killed his wife. Jack Trevino, one of the CIA officers killed in FOB Wildcat, mistakenly authorized the strike based upon SIGINT from the Sentinel drone. They bombed Abdullah's house, killing his wife. Revenge is a powerful motivator."

The President leaned back. "We make our own problems, don't we?" he mused. "What about Frist? What do we do with him?"

"Project StrikeForce has succeeded beyond our wildest hopes."

"I still don't trust him," the President said. "What if I told you to cancel it?"

"The project would be terminated and all assets erased," Smith said solemnly. "Unfortunately, we need him."

"Doesn't mean I have to like it. I'd like to keep that option open."

"Of course. Mr. President? There's something else. I told you I was looking for a successor? I found him."

"You trust him?" The President took another sip of coffee, watching him over the lip of the mug.

"Yes. I have done my duty, sir, well and above what is required of any man. I need to know someone can take my place."

"At least something good came out of this debacle. He's a good man?"

"Above reproach."

The President nodded and stood. "When that time comes, I'll be glad to work with him. Fulton, I've never told you this, but your guidance has been a comfort." He stuck out his hand.

Smith smiled at the still-young man from Texas and shook the proffered hand. "It's been an honor."

* * *

Washington, DC

Jim Rumple snapped awake, heart pounding as he struggled to sit up. The room was so dark he could barely make out the dresser against the far wall.

He strained his ears but heard nothing except the normal sounds of late-night traffic. He reflexively felt for the soft spot where his wife slept, before remembering she had left years before.

He sighed heavily and scratched his balls, wondering if the urge to pee justified getting out of bed. He decided it didn't, and was almost on the verge of sleep when he heard the noise again. He bolted upright and hit the light with one hand while his other fumbled for the Glock on the nightstand. He blinked, squinting, trying to make out the approaching shape, and then he screamed as something hard smashed into his wrist.

He dropped the Glock and rolled across the bed. He came up on the other side and saw the woman from Afghanistan with a gun in one hand and a collapsible police baton in the other.

He froze. "What are you doing in my bedroom?"

"Calm down, Jim," the woman said. "Sit back. We need to talk."

There was a cold knot in his stomach, his wrist hurt, and he could barely see. "You can't do this. I'm CIA!" The woman said nothing but motioned again to the bed. He scrabbled back until his head bumped the oak headboard. "What is your *problem?*"

The woman took a seat on the edge of the bed. "Where's your wife, Jim?"

"What? She's—I don't know. Somewhere in New York, I guess."

The woman nodded. "Couldn't handle the stress? I'm assuming you read her in. Was it the travel that got to her? Or the lying?"

"Something like that."

"You almost got my team killed. You know that, right?"

"You didn't provide official orders!"

"You were told to stay out of it, but you pulled the Delta team back. You're a good officer. People respect you, even though they don't like you. I can understand that. People don't like me, either. We're two peas in a pod. Why did you pull the team back?"

"I'm not telling you anything!" The sleepy confusion was gone and his heart was pounding. The woman was clearly insane. He tried to reason with her. "How was I supposed to know you'd get caught by Al-Qaeda? As soon as the orders came in, I redeployed the Delta team to your location. I saved your life!"

The woman stood up, the pistol shaking at him with every word. "*You. Saved. My. Life?* My *teammates* saved my life. You don't even know why you did it. You pulled them back because you don't like what you don't understand."

As she talked, he remembered what his superiors had said when he made it back to Washington.

Don't ask more questions. You screwed up. Don't talk about it. Compartmentalized security. Need to know. Take the paid vacation and relax.

He desperately tried to remember what his instructors at The Farm had taught him about establishing a rapport. "That's not—"

"That's not what?" she interrupted. "Not true? You made a mistake. Like I said, I understand. You just had to know who I was and why I was in Afghanistan and how I got your orders countermanded. So you asked around. You really shouldn't have done that." She shook her head.

"Look, I'm sorry. You're right, I couldn't let it go. That's no reason to do whatever it is you're thinking of doing. Just leave. Nobody will know you were here." He trembled as his voice broke.

I won't go out like this. I'll knock the gun away, tie her up, then call the Agency. They'll take her away and I'll finally find out who she is and what agency she works for.

The woman smiled cruelly. "If you think you can escape, you're wrong. You *can't.*"

His surge of hope faded. "This isn't right," he said, deflated. "Someone will hear the gun."

"It's a forty-five with subsonic ammo and an integrated silencer. It's no louder than a sneeze."

"Why are you doing this?"

"I'm messed up in the head," she answered calmly. "I mean, I'm trying to be a better person. There's a man I like, a good man, and I want him to like me, too. But I'm like you. I just can't let things go."

He saw the look in her eyes and knew the conversation was over. He wanted to scream, to run for his life.

All those thoughts ran through his head in the fraction of a second it took for her to pull the trigger. As he saw the flash he wondered if his ex-wife would care when they told her he was dead, a bullet through his brain and his bowels released over the bed they had shared, and that was his last thought as the bullet stopped his thinking forever.

ABOUT THE AUTHOR

Kevin Lee Swaim studied creative writing with David Foster Wallace at Illinois State University.

He is currently the Subject Matter Expert for Intrusion Prevention Systems for a Fortune 50 insurance company located in the Midwest. He holds the CISSP certification from ISC2.

When he's not writing, he's busy repairing guitars for the working bands of Central Illinois.

Made in the USA
Columbia, SC
16 May 2022

60468364R00155